GRIS-G

MW01195038

"GRIS-GRIS GUMBO is a literary grimoire full of skin-crawling incantations. Well after I closed this tome, I still hear its pages whispering. Whatever dark arts Rick Koster is dabbling in here, he certainly cast a spell over me." —Clay McLeod Chapman, author of *Ghost Eaters, Whisper Down the Lane* and *The Remaking*

"GRIS-GRIS GUMBO is a wild, weird trip to the pre-Katrina Big Easy. Koster creates an atmosphere born out of paranoia and fear with a fresh, hip voice that makes him unlike any writer who's taken on one of America's most conflicted cities. GRIS-GRIS GUMBO is a boiling, spicy broth of music and voodoo and insanity. A highly recommended view from a writer who knows and loves this world." —Ace Atkins, NY Times bestselling author of the Quinn Colson series and Robert B. Parker's Spenser novels

"GRIS-GRIS GUMBO is a wild ride through the midnight territory, evoking both the ghosts of New Orleans and the dark side of the supernatural. Rick Koster is an exciting new voice in the field of supernatural thrillers." —Douglas Clegg, NY Times bestselling author of the Vampyricon Trilogy and winner of the Bram Stoker and International Horror Guild awards

"GRIS-GRIS GUMBO is a whirlwind. I'm a sucker for the weird and wild, the local myths and half-renounced religions and nearly forgotten magics. GRIS-GRIS GUMBO scratched that itch. It's sharp and fascinating and filthy in the best kind of way, with a steady pulse of violence and music and threat just beneath the surface." —Dan Franklin, author of *The Eater of Gods*

"Koster's evocative portrait of an unseen side of New Orleans voodoo, through the refreshingly unique perspective of French Quarter slackers, is bold and original. With wit, ratcheting tension and select scenes of supernatural dread that are some of the scariest I have ever read, I'm convinced GRIS-GRIS GUMBO will become a staple of New Orleans horror literature." —Daniel Waters, author of the *Generation Dead* series and *Break My Heart 1,000 Times*

GRIS-GRIS GUMBO

A NOVEL BY RICK KOSTER

JOURNALSTONE
YOUR LINK TO ARTIST TALENT

ISBN: 978-1-68510-102-2 (sc)
ISBN: 978-1-68510-103-9 (ebook)
Library of Congress Catalog Number: 2023940143

First printing edition June 23, 2023
Published by JournalStone Publishing in the United States of America.
Cover Artwork and Design: Maria Reagan
Edited by Sean Leonard
Proofreading and Cover/Interior Layout by Scarlett R. Algee

JournalStone Publishing
3205 Sassafras Trail
Carbondale, Illinois 62901

JournalStone books may be ordered through booksellers or by contacting:
JournalStone | www.journalstone.com

For Eileen—same as it ever will be.

Remembering October 2, 1997, New Orleans.

GRIS-GRIS GUMBO

PROLOGUE

June 23, 1998. St. John's Eve. New Orleans, Louisiana

The old black man standing in Jackson Square swallowed and dabbed his forehead with a sweat-dotted handkerchief. In front of him, butted up against the pike iron fence surrounding the old parade grounds and the defiant statue of Andrew Jackson, was an easel bearing a half-done sketch of a figure drawn in charcoal.

"Screw it," the old man muttered, tearing the drawing off the easel and wadding it into a ball. He looked up at the sky, where a sliver of late afternoon sun crept behind the buildings of the French Quarter. The air seemed to wheeze with humidity, and on the breeze ruffling the banana tree leaves was an electric tension that promised a thunderstorm by midnight.

He put his charcoal away and locked his supply cabinet in a rented space in a parking lot on St. Ann. There were plenty of tourists out, but he was nervous and more than ready for a beer and a shot. He hated St. John's Eve.

Plodding down a section of Chartres Street choked with vintage clothing shops, the old man saw a small parade of twenty-something revelers laughing and dancing down the *banquette*. They were dressed in cheap approximations of voodoo regalia—white muslin outfits and colorful scarves—playing congas, shaking tambourines, and chanting *patois*. Three of the crowd, pretty white girls with shining eyes, held a huge rubber snake—Damballah, the serpent god—overhead in merry supplication.

The fact that anything was an excuse for a party in New Orleans was one of the city's charms. But he wished he could clear out of town on St. John's Eve. He sighed. *They have no idea...*

Later, after downing several drinks in an attempt to induce exhaustion, the old man lay tossing in the darkness of his cottage bedroom as the wild storm had its way with the night. He drew a shallow breath of air into his lungs, wishing he could head back out onto the streets, maybe work his way through a few exorcising tunes on the piano over at Tom's Bar in the Marigny. The old man had occasional gigs there, as well as his regular weeknight at Lafitte's Blacksmith Shop on lower Bourbon. But someone else would be playing tonight. He'd be welcome, but jamming with other cats didn't seem appealing; playing at *all* just didn't feel right on a night like this. It was a desecration.

He supposed he could call Green Hopkins, but what would he say? The white kid had become a perhaps unlikely good friend, but he knew nothing about the significance of St. John's Eve—and now wasn't the time to bring it up.

He closed his eyes against the grumbling of thunder and the pick-ax explosions of lightning illumining his tiny bedroom. He was drawn back to another St. John's Eve long ago, on the banks of the Bayou St. John, where bonfires lit the moist night and a spinning coterie of half-naked dancers capered, possessed with the manic energy of Damballah; where live cats were tossed into steaming cauldrons—and a young woman called Maman Arielle had torn the finger from the corpse of a suicide victim dragged from its tomb. Over the hammering of the drums, she'd shrieked with glee, invoking the *loas* of Power and Darkness—beseeching favors from Baron Samedi, the lord of the cemetery. A few miles away, in a graveyard, another corpse was laid out like a wedding night groom, awaiting her advances...

The old man bolted upright, eyes bulging, as a shotgun blast of thunder shook the windows. He gasped at the noise, realizing that he'd actually been at the gates of sleep, when a quick pop of lightning lit up the bedroom.

He saw a woman sitting in the chair by his window.

The brief instant of illumination was long enough to know it was *her*. Though fear choked his heart and bubbled into his brain, there was also a sensation of relief. The waiting, maybe, was over.

"You...you back," he whispered into the darkness. For a moment, the only sound was the whiplash of rain against the tile on the roof, and he clung to a brief hope that her image had been nothing more than the lingering wisps of nightmare.

Then she spoke. It was soft and musical and achingly young, like a springtime breeze on a lazy island. "I never been away, *cher.*" Another lightning flash, and in that quick revelation, he could see she was as beautiful as always, as forever lost as yesterday.

The old man's heart thudded like a trip hammer. It occurred to him that he might simply hiss into nothingness—a dying fire's last cinder. He strained against the darkness, trying to see her. "You come for me finally?" he managed to say.

After a long moment, the voice said, "No. I just want you to know I still think about you. I remember everyt'ing you done for me, Hipolyte." Her lilting tone was tender, concerned. Then it dropped to a whisper. "I remember *everyt'ing.*"

The room was suddenly choked with a smell of river mud, sour oyster shells, swamp grass, and traces of patchouli and citrus oils. The old man felt tears slide down his cheeks. He was overcome by a suffocating sense of doom. He started to speak—to beg her—but a final, dizzying burst of lightning bathed the room in light.

She was crumpled to one side, clad in a tattered funeral dress dappled in blue-green mold and traced with drying moss—the weathered corpse of someone long dead. Her skull, scaled with shredded chips of flesh, angled limply against the windowpane, plopping fat drops of dirty bayou water on the hardwood floor.

The old man fainted.

PART ONE

CHAPTER ONE

Six weeks later

Crayton Breaux stepped out of his apartment in the St. Ignatius complex in the lower Quarter and took a quick look at the August morning. Instead of his normal tortoise-shell horn-rims, Cray was wearing prescription shades to combat a sun already intense as a welding flame. He wore black jeans, Topsiders with no socks, a dime on a red string around his ankle—the voodoo good luck charm his nutty boss had given him—and a t-shirt designed by his neighbor, Green Hopkins. It depicted a pelican, a crawfish, and an alligator in a high-kick chorus line over the legend WELCOME TO LOUISIANA.

Crayton was six-five but a skeletal hundred and seventy pounds, with near-albino skin, and a nose and Adam's apple that brought out the Ichabod Crane references. He gelled his clump of cornstalk hair skyward in a free-form pompadour. Dyed tomato soup red, it was one of the few affectations Cray had come up with during a painful loner's adolescence that gave him any identity at all. At twenty-six, Cray was long removed from high school cruelty, but he'd hung with the look. It was natural by now.

Cray headed out of the courtyard and cut over to Dauphine, moving from the residential Quarter into the more commercial district. Most tourists never even realized the Vieux Carré was actually a residential community with an elementary school, Mom 'n' Pop groceries, a hardware store, laundries, and a dog park—all to counteract the lunacy of the strip joints, souvenir shops, restaurants, and live music joints clustered on the upper end of Bourbon and running the length of Decatur.

At Toulouse, an old guy with a garden hose, washing down the sidewalk, knelt painfully to lower his hose so a passing hound could have a drink. *Beautiful,* Cray thought. Sure, the Quarter could be ugly in the harsh light of morning: an occasional drunk passed out in a gutter; runaways camped out in Jackson Square or shooting up in the alleyways; and the smell of liquor and urine slow-cooking in the heat. But there was a possibility to the mornings that was just as intoxicating as the sin served up there every night.

Just past Conti, Cray angled across the brick street. Before he reached the Voodoo Shoppe door, Cosima rushed out holding a small, wrapped package.

"Cray, where's your car?" she shrieked. "I need you to deliver this, like, right away! Oh, my, you don't have your car."

Even in everyday conversation, her voice sounded like someone wrenching a nail out of a piece of tin. A bony white woman in her late forties who favored tie-dyed muumuus, Cosima had the attention span of an acidhead. Her long, straight gray hair had bangs clipped at eye level, like Moe Howard.

"Well, no," Cray said. "It's in the apartment garage. But I can leave from there."

She looked relieved. "Then you'll do it?"

"Sure." Cray shrugged, still trying to figure the delivery angle. "Where am I going anyway? Do we even *do* deliveries?"

"Well, this poor woman called twice, totally desperate. She's from out of town and needs something for her father. I finally said okay." Cosima grinned proudly. "So, if you could, take this..."—she checked the label—"...to Mister Joshua Arcenet, at 219 Vivienne Street."

"Glad to do it," Cray said. Then a thought struck him. "What am I delivering?"

The idea that *anything* from Cosima's Voodoo Shoppe's inventory of hokey herbs, spell candles, and secret potions might be utilized in a real voodoo rite was surprising to Cray; it was strictly a tourist joint.

Cosima twisted lengths of hair together. "It's Five Finger Grass. For protection, of course."

Cray almost asked, *Protection from what?* But, though Cosima knew her merchandise in the context of someone who memorized the copy in catalogs, and claimed on some level to follow voodoo ritual, she also believed in UFOs, worshipped moon goddesses, and thought Bobby Kennedy and Elvis were badminton partners in heaven.

Grinning, Cray held his hand out for the box, saying, "Have gris-gris, will travel."

Cosima asked, "Can you find it?" A worried look crossed her face. "It's in the Ninth Ward."

Cray shrugged. "It's voodoo," he joked. "I didn't expect Archie Manning's house. And don't worry. I've got a street map."

Driving out Claiborne past the Saturn Bar and Fats Domino's house, Cray studied street signs until Vivienne materialized across a set of railroad tracks that threatened to take out his suspension. He hooked a left and slowed down, eyeing the addresses till he spied the two hundred block, which was a row of shotgun shacks broken up by a small series of retail stores. There was 207, a fish market, and 213 was a liquor store... Mr. Arcenet's house should be...*a funeral home?*

What the fuck? But there it was, in polished silver *bas-relief* letters on the side of the building: MADDOX & SONS MORTUARY 219 VIVIENNE. Cosima hadn't mentioned that the guy worked in a funeral home. It was a neatly painted, gray, one-story wooden building with white shutters. Even in the heat, the lawn was lush green and cropped.

Cray eased the Camaro around two waxed black hearses and parked in front of the funeral home. He took off his sunglasses and got out of the car with the package. He opened the door to the funeral home. Maddox & Sons was tastefully lit, antiseptically neat, and smelled of flora and air freshener. Classical music was playing in the background. One of those Brahms guys, doing sad. To the left was a reception area. A black woman in a navy suit sat behind a paneled walnut information booth reading a paperback. She peered over half-rimmed gold glasses and smiled kindly at Cray as though inappropriately dressed white guys walked into Maddox & Sons on a regular basis.

"Can I help you?"

"I hope I'm in the right place," said Cray. "I've got a delivery for Mr. Joshua Arcenet."

The woman glanced at a clipboard on her desk. "The memorial service for Mr. Arcenet is scheduled for 11:30 in the Pastoral Vistas room."

Cray rocked back a step. Joshua Arcenet was *dead?*

The receptionist pointed down a corridor. "It'll be the third door on the right," she was saying. "You'll see the floral arrangements off by the casket." She smiled and re-opened her book.

"Thanks," Cray said. She thought he was a delivery dude from a florist. He took a deep breath and set off down the neat, carpeted hallway. He passed the Eternal Peace and Golden Hereafter rooms. Each had small, temporary signs with snap-on letters to identify the deceased within. There were recessed waiting areas outside each room with a few empty chairs.

Next was Pastoral Vistas. The sign read "Joshua Arcenet 11:30 a.m. Memorial Service." Sitting stiffly in a chair by the closed door of the visitation room was a light-skinned black woman. Her straight, cropped hair was brushed to one side. She was wearing a conservative black dress and a small silver pin around her neck. A white handkerchief was crumpled in one hand. She was staring at the floor. She started when Crayton stepped into the waiting area with his package, then stood up.

In a hopeful near-whisper, she asked, "You from the Voodoo Shoppe?"

"Yes, ma'am," Cray smiled with what he hoped was gentle confidence. "Uhm, you're Mr. Arcenet's daughter?"

She nodded wearily. "Right. I'm Janice Arcenet, the one who called." She swallowed and glanced up the hallway. "Thank God you're here." She checked her watch. "You've got to do it before someone else shows up."

"Excuse me?" Cray asked. *Do what?*

The woman tapped Cray on the shoulder impatiently. "We don't have much time before folks start showing up. This is a closed casket service and I damned sure don't need anyone coming in with the lid up and you standing over him." She gave his clothes a quick up-and-down.

Cray couldn't blame her. He looked like he should be working on a carnival ride. "I'm not sure I know, ah, exactly what you want me to do," he said, wondering if he might just hand her the package and haul ass.

But before he could do anything, the woman opened the door to the viewing room and looked at Cray. "You're from the Voodoo Shoppe, aren't you? Well, get in there and put the powder on him. I promised him I'd have him protected. Whatever the hell *that* means." Then, to Crayton's dismay, she started to cry.

"Okay, okay," Crayton said. "I'll help you." He nodded and ducked by her into the room. It was set up with maybe twenty folding chairs around the perimeter. To one side was a small table covered in white linen, with a coffee urn, cups, saucers, cream and sugar, and a frost-beaded water pitcher and glasses. Small electric candelabras on the walls cast a pale yellow glow over the room. More soft music. Still sad, but with French horns instead of a string quartet.

In the front of the room was an inexpensive, buffed wooden coffin on a raised bier, the lid closed. He looked over at Janice Arcenet, who was standing some distance from the casket. "Oh, Daddy," she said softly, and another tear crept out of one eye.

Cray stared at the casket, hypnotized. He still had no idea what he was supposed to do.

"Well, come *on!*" she whispered harshly.

"Right," Cray said. With his Swiss Army knife, he slit the brown paper on the box containing the Five Finger Grass. He stared at the coffin. Other than attending a funeral for a classmate killed in a motorcycle accident back in high school, Cray had never been to a funeral. None of this particularly creeped him out—the gris-gris angle gave the whole thing a sort of spy-in-the-mortuary angle that would be sort of cool in a movie—but it was hard not to stare at a casket from two feet away. "I'm sorry about your father," he said. He pulled on the wrapping paper.

"Thank you." She sighed. "I don't want to offend you, but this whole voodoo thing's nuts. It's just that I promised Dad. He was scared they'd come for him."

"Scared who would come for him?"

"Daddy called it *Le Culte des Morts.* You must know, right? I mean, you're here."

"Oh, well, I just started at the shop. Still learning."

"I looked it up. The Cult of Death. Bad juju—literally. I mean, if they're real, they use corpses in their rituals. If they steal your body, supposedly your spirit can't travel to the afterworld. And so on." She barked a quick laugh of disbelief and shook her head. "See what I mean?" Then, as though she felt she owed Crayton an explanation, she added, "Daddy grew up out in the swamps. Voodoo is, ah, a big deal out there."

Cray was fascinated in spite of himself. "*Corpse* rituals?"

She looked tired and rubbed her eyes. "I know, right? I have a hard enough time with the wafer and the wine stuff." Then she gave him a look. "Anyway, don't you know all this? Go on and do whatever it is you do. That way I can at least say I kept my end of the bargain." She glanced at her watch and then at the casket, swallowed, and, as though making a sudden decision, said, "I'll wait outside. Close the lid when you're done. I left instructions with the funeral people that it stays closed from here on out. I've said my goodbyes." And she darted into the hallway.

Cray thought about it all. She was right. Freakin' crazy. At the same time, he supposed he felt kind of good about dusting the old dude with Five Fingers Grass. If it'd keep the corpse-robbers away, Cray was happy to do it—even if the whole idea was pretty fucking dark.

"Rightie-o," Cray murmured. Before he could think any more about it, he strode to the coffin and stood studying the bottle of Five Fingers Grass, a glass medicine bottle with a Xeroxed label that said FOR PROTECTION. *Like a prophylactic for the dead.*

Inside, it looked like any other dried herb. Twisting the cap off, he brought the bottle to his nose and sniffed. Smelled like old hay, if anything. He shrugged and reached under the recessed edge of the front half of the casket lid, feeling for a latch of some kind. Sure enough, it was there...and snicked open easily at Cray's touch. His throat went instantly dry as he lifted the top a few inches.

The room was totally quiet. When had the music shut down? And was that actually a smell of...*decay* wisping out from within the partially open box? He had to be imagining it.

All right, Cray thought, willing down his creeping panic and forcing himself to think rationally. *You open the lid, you sprinkle a little Five Finger Grass over the old guy. Hell, even mumble some half-assed prayer if you want—and you leave. You'll be hammering an oyster po'boy at Mandina's in thirty minutes.*

He raised the lid the rest of the way.

A roaring like harsh winds surged in his ears, and he stared in absolute disbelief, trying to process the desecrations before him.

Joshua Arcenet was dressed in some sort of African tribal gown that had been ripped open, exposing his chest. On his sunken breastbone, in what appeared to be ashes, someone had fashioned an intricate swirling design like a strange gray frosting pattern on a chocolate cake.

But Cray barely took note of that. Instead, he stared down at Joshua Arcenet's face, understanding at once why he'd smelled rot. Whomever the man had been afraid of—*Le Culte des Whatsis*—had definitely beaten Crayton to the punch.

They'd cut out Joshua Arcenet's eyes.

In each dark socket, someone had stuffed a dead baby crow. The birds were bloated with decay, their eyes squeezed into Xs, their tiny beaks frozen open, gaping at the ceiling.

CHAPTER TWO

Green Hopkins was watering one of the two plants he had, willing the fucker to stay alive. He had a lethal black thumb. He was supposed to be cleaning his apartment, but the process had drawn out. Green knew he was stalling when he ought to be working on his novel.

The St. Ignatius apartment needed all the help it could get. The complex was two stories of cinder block dwellings in a U-shape, surrounding a stale, envelope-sized pool, and the landscaping consisted of cracked concrete, sturdy weeds, and four weary banana trees. The units themselves were nothing more than Xeroxed cracker boxes.

The apartment was functional. Green tried to make it comfortable: well-stocked bookshelves and a big couch you could fall into and spend hours without feeling the need to move. There were framed photos of Tennessee Williams, John Kennedy Toole, and James Lee Burke positioned over his PC on the small desk in the living room corner. He wrote every day, no matter how busy or hungover, and his latest project, a thriller called *The Pagan Malt Shop*, was nearing completion of a comprehensible draft.

He'd majored in Creative Writing at LSU. Since graduation, he'd had a few short stories appear in college lit magazines, and last year *Oxford American* published an excerpt from *Malt Shop* in a "New Voices in Southern Fiction" feature. But even with those encouragements, Green knew it was an absolute long-shot profession. So he kept his day gig designing t-shirts at Pirate's Alley Gifts and wrote when he could, and until he scored a six-figure advance from Knopf and started palling around with Michael Connelly, he'd hunker down in the St. Ignatius. It was a rat-pit, but it was *his* rat-pit.

A pounding at the door interrupted Green's reverie. He set the watering jug on the coffee table, pushed his shoulder length hair behind the rims on his Ben Franklin glasses, turned the volume down on the Bluerunners, and peered through the fisheye peephole.

It was Crayton Breaux, a neighbor and, though they'd only known each other a few months, already a trusted pal. Cray's face was paler than usual and beaded with sweat. Green opened the door. "Dude, are you all right?"

Cray laughed nervously. "Hey, Green. Sorry to bother you." He shook his head. "The weirdest thing just happened. I don't know whether to quit my job or go to the police, or..."

"Jeez," Green said, "c'mon in out of the heat. You're not hurt, are you?"

Cray walked into the air conditioning gratefully. "No, I'm fine. I just didn't know who to talk to."

Green ushered him into a chair. "You look like you could use a beer."

"That would be greatly appreciated," Cray said, wiping the sweat off his brow with his forearm. "Hope I'm not interrupting you," he said again.

Green brought out two bottles of Dixie. "No, man, I'm just puttering around. Did a five-mile run earlier and vowed to not go out in the sun until October." Cray laughed shakily, took the beer, and inhaled from it.

"So. Why the police?" Green asked. "Somebody fuck with you at the Voodoo Shoppe?"

Cray took a deep breath and started talking.

An hour later, Green came back from the kitchen with their third Dixie each. "That's a fucking amazing story, amigo."

Cray was a pragmatist—or so it seemed. Green thought himself a prescient judge of character and had instinctively liked and trusted Crayton. In light of the bizarre story, he quickly reflected on what he knew of Cray's past.

Cray was from New Iberia. He'd attended Louisiana-Lafayette on a chemistry scholarship, but had dropped out after his sophomore year.

"It occurred to me," Cray had explained, "that not only did I not like chemistry, I didn't like *anything*. The idea of formal education seemed completely two-dimensional. I worked a few years in a hot sauce warehouse and one day, overnight, I just decided to move to New Orleans. I'd been up for Jazz Fest and Mardi Gras several times and always loved it. So, to paraphrase Jed Clampett, I loaded up the Camaro and hauled ass."

He'd scored the Voodoo Shoppe gig within an hour of hitting town and, after crashing at the YMCA a few nights, had found the St. Ignatius apartment. Green had come home from work and saw Cray struggling to unload a massive framed poster of Pete Maravich from the U-Haul and leant a hand. Green was a Maravich fan himself; Pistol Pete was the former LSU and New Orleans Jazz basketball star, a Louisiana hero and NBA Hall of Famer who'd died of a heart attack at the unlikely age of forty.

Now, Green tried to think of an explanation for the mortuary experience. "Voodoo *is* a big part of the town's lore. I mean, there really is voodoo. Came over from Africa with the slaves. People still follow it. Maybe this is just one of those aspects they don't exactly advertise in the tours and museums. *You* of all people should know that."

"I guess," Cray said. "It all seemed pretty fake to me—at least until today. Cosima and the Voodoo Shoppe, well, yeah, it's just a tourist thing. Back home, you'd hear about crazier stuff out in the bayou, but I just figured it was superstition."

Green swallowed some beer. "Hey, it's a religion. Who knows how real any of it is." He shook his head. "I don't know about the birds and the ripped-out eyes. I mean, we *assume* it's voodoo because you guys were called in to make a delivery. But it could be anything. A pissed-off employee, an enemy of the dead guy... Who knows?" He thought a minute. "And along with the birds in the eyes, there's some strange powdered design on this guy's chest?"

"Yep. It's the design that sticks with me most. I'll never forget it."

"Can you draw it?" He handed over a message pad and pen from his desk.

"I'm not much of an artist, but I'll try." His tongue poking out the corner of his mouth, Cray sketched for a minute, then handed the pad to Green. "That's the general idea."

It was a pinwheel sort of design, with what looked like harpoon spars at the end of each twisting spoke. At the compass points, though, the spar crudely resembled the fanged head of a serpent.

Green said, "I don't know what it means."

"I don't know what *any* of it means," Cray said.

Green tossed the notepad on the table. "So you just closed the lid and acted like nothing happened?"

"I *dropped* the fucking lid." Cray stared blankly at the Tennessee Williams photo and suddenly laughed. "I didn't know what to do. I damned sure wasn't gonna drag the daughter in to show her what had happened. I mean, as freaked as I was, two things were clear. The people her father was worried about are real. And two, they beat us to the punch. I just figured it was best to act like I'd done my job and shut the fuck up. What she don't know won't hurt her."

Green sipped his beer. "Then you hung around through the service?"

"I wanted to make sure she was right when she'd said no one was gonna open the casket. I didn't want anybody to accuse *me* of doing it."

"Yeah, but the daughter would have known you didn't have the time to pull all that off."

"Man, I was so freaked, I just thought I should cover my ass. I don't actually know what I woulda done if someone from the funeral home *had* tried to open it."

Green nodded. "And the lady didn't care that you stayed for the funeral?"

"She was honored, actually. I told her I felt like I'd contributed in some way." Cray shook his head again. "Then I called Cosima and told her I'd busted a hose and would be a little late getting back. And here I am."

Green had one more question. "You didn't tell Cosima about what happened?"

"Nope. What's the point? She'd just freak out. She's got a nice little tourist scam going here in the Quarter. No sense telling her there are actual voodoo kooks running around out there in Grown-Up Land. If it even *is* voodoo."

Green grinned. "You had to make sure everything was okay."

Cray leaned back and crossed his palms behind his gelled hair. "Well, yeah. And not just to cover my ass. I guess I wanted to see if any...*weirdos*—voodoo freaks—would show up at the service. I was a little worried about the daughter. But it was fine. Ten or fifteen old people, movin' slow and weepin'. About what you'd expect." He leaned forward. "There wasn't any graveside service. They loaded the casket in the hearse and headed straight to the cemetery. Private deal. So I hauled ass; they weren't gonna open the casket once they got to the cemetery." He looked at Green. "Basically, I just wanted to talk it out and see if I did right."

"Hey, man, I'm glad you came by," Green said enthusiastically. "I don't know if what you did could properly be called 'the right thing,' but if it makes you feel any better, I *hope* I'd have done it the same way."

Cray offered a small salute of thanks. Green added, "As you say, it all worked out. The daughter's happy and nobody knows..." He started laughing. "Unless the dead guy's a zombie and comes to your apartment tonight."

Cray winced. "Jeez, thanks for *that*, pal. Oh well, at least here in the Quarter it's hard to tell the zombies from tourists." He stood up. "Hell, I'd better get back. Even Cosima knows it doesn't take four hours to change a radiator hose. And thanks again for the beer and for letting me vent."

Green stood up from the couch and wandered aimlessly around the tiny room for a moment. "Sure... But really, what's your take on all this?"

Cray exhaled, picked up his empty bottle and peeled at the label. "It probably *was* voodoo," he finally said. "Given what the daughter told me, I guess he was just scared these...*cult* people would steal his corpse. It sounds ridiculous, but Christians worry about a red guy with horns, right?" He shrugged. "Do the birds mean something evil? Who knows. Maybe it isn't even anything bad. I mean, what if the birds were some grand message sending the old man off happily? How would we know?"

Green nodded. "I guess we wouldn't."

"Right." Cray adjusted his glasses. "But I doubt it. And this puts the whole concept in a bit more serious context than I'd ever thought about, working in the Voodoo Shoppe. But what happened in the funeral home...Someone wasn't kidding around."

"Doesn't sound like it," Green said. He brightened. "But think about it: One way or another, you'll probably never hear about it again."

Cray smiled grimly. "I hope not anyway." He crossed the room and opened the door. "I owe you some beer."

CHAPTER THREE

Lafitte's Blacksmith Shop was located on that part of lower Bourbon Street once ignored by tourists, and if that was unfortunately no longer true, well, the old bar was still Green's favorite watering hole in the entire world.

He walked in about midnight knowing he'd be just in time to catch Papa Hipolyte's late set. The cool, cave-dark interior of Lafitte's smelled of wood rot, fires long-dead, and the olfactory poltergeists of a million spilled cocktails and crushed out cigarette butts. A fireplace sat in the middle of the main room, angled from the bar and around the corner, hidden in an alcove, was a claustrophobic piano room where, nightly, one could still hear authentic New Orleans R&B.

In his earlier years, before he'd made his principal living drawing caricatures for tourists in Jackson Square, Papa had been a session pianist of some renown. He'd done a few dates with Earl King and sessions for Cosimo Matissa, though he'd never achieved the reputation of Professor Longhair, James Booker, or Prospero Godchaux. There was talk in the sixties about letting Papa cut his own album, but the opportunity never materialized. Once or twice a year, Papa might head out on a package tour of Deep South roadhouses. It was a relaxing, good time and a cool way to pick up a few bucks. But Papa was comfortable with his place in the hierarchy; he was a fine craftsman but no genius, and certainly not a star.

Still, Green considered it a privilege to watch him. He and Papa embarked on their unlikely friendship one night when Green was the only customer in the back room. He'd bought Papa a Dixie beer after the old man played an amazing original tune called "If It's August, It's Eileen." He'd taken a beer and a note of appreciation scrawled on a cocktail napkin up to the piano, and during the next break Papa brought two fresh beers over to Green's table to say thanks.

"Well, Lord, I never expected no fan mail on a night like tonight," Papa smiled. "Cert'nly not from a hippie white kid." He had that perfect N'Awlins accent, part-Deep South black guy and part-Irish Channel Brooklynese.

"And I never expected you to segue from Booker into one of your own tunes. That takes some guts in a town like New Orleans." James Booker had been one of the city's finest and most innovative R&B pianists. He had also been a junkie, alcoholic bisexual whose paranoid fantasies of CIA secrets contrasted an occasional sweetness of demeanor that caused even his most frustrated supporters to grin when they saw him. He was a true New Orleans legend.

Papa cocked his head, amused and impressed. "You dig Booker?"

Green shrugged modestly. "I dig Booker."

The old man stared for a moment, then laughed heartily and clapped Green on the back. "I'm Hipolyte," he said. "Mind if I sit down?"

That was two years ago. Green would drop by Papa's stand in Jackson Square, or Lafitte's to catch a set. Sometimes they'd grab a Sunday night dinner at the Gumbo Shop or Tujague's, where they sat in the bar and ate the boiled brisket of beef with horseradish sauce.

Green enjoyed Hipolyte's company and advice, and he knew the old man liked him. Papa was probably pretty lonely. He had no living relatives and he'd never married. Hell, somewhere in Green's apartment was a key Papa had given him to his cottage—"In case somethin' fucked up happens." Green considered that gesture the ultimate expression of the old man's trust. While Papa had met a few of Green's "regular" friends—though that was an admittedly odd way to think about it—the relationship was one of those unlikely things that seemed special unto itself and within unspoken parameters.

Papa Hipolyte was a small man the color of a pecan shell. His eyes were kindly under hooded, thick eyebrows, and his broad nose was flattened over a neat gray mustache. Rain or shine, indoors or out, he wore a hat, usually a shapeless, sweat-stained brown fedora. Though he despised the habit, he frequently smoked a corncob pipe, and he perpetually smelled of fruity tobacco.

Tonight, he nodded when Green walked around the corner and, as per their ritual, set a can of Dixie on the edge of the piano before retreating to a corner table to watch the set. Papa was cruising through "Junco Partner."

The old man was the only person Green knew who might have some insight into what Cray experienced, even though voodoo wasn't exactly a big conversational topic with Green and Papa. In fact, they'd talked about it precisely once.

They'd been walking on St. Ann early on a warm spring evening, headed to Mama Rosa's for a pizza, when, offhandedly, like a tourist guide, Papa pointed at a high mortar wall on the right side of the street.

"You heard of Marie Laveau, boy?"

"Sure," Green said. "The voodoo queen of New Orleans." Everyone in Louisiana knew who Marie Laveau was.

Papa laughed. "Actually, there was two of 'em. Mama 'n' daughter. Both of 'em voodoo queens. They used to live in a house right there behind that wall. It's gone now. I ain't sure what's back there. Don't make any difference, I suppose." Unconsciously, Papa crossed himself.

Green looked strangely at Papa, whom he knew was a devout Catholic. "Everything okay? Was the voodoo *real* or something?"

Papa started, almost as though he'd forgotten Green was there. Then he smiled, realizing Green saw the religious gesture. "There's strange things in the world, boy. Lotsa shit's magic, if you think about it the right way."

Green nodded, though he wasn't sure what Papa was talking about.

"What do you mean?" Green asked. "Are you actually telling me there's something to voodoo?"

Papa glanced at him out of the corner of his eye. They stepped around two drunks sitting hopefully in front of a liquor store. Papa said, "I grew up in a shotgun shack out by the Industrial Canal. It was a bad neighborhood then, it's *real* bad now. Lots of superstition and ignorance back then."

Mama Rosa's loomed just ahead. Papa paused, as though he wanted to finish his thoughts before they got to the restaurant. He absently kicked an empty beer can off the sidewalk. "Seven great religions in the world, boy, and there's something mystical and powerful about each one of 'em. Voodoo's a religion too.

"Growing up in my neighborhood, lots of folks followed voodoo. It ain't the zombie shit you see in movies. It's more a spirit thing, tied up in folk medicine, mixed up with the Catholic Church. The main idea is that your individual spirit carries on, and voodoo emphasizes the communication with spirits. But it's more than that too." Papa coughed.

"In the ghetto, see, it was hard for black folk to get medical help. You go to the Charity Hospital and wait fifteen hours, even if you're first in line, while the white peoples get treated immediately. So we rely on each other, on a lotta herbal remedies done been passed down from Africa and Haiti and through the slave days. All that stuff done mixed up with Catholicism once we got... *Americanized.*" He laughed, patting Green on the shoulder. "You're hungry, I know," he said. "I ain't trying to make a speech."

"Actually," Green said honestly, "I'm fascinated."

Papa nodded. "Well, it ain't something worth talking about over dinner, but I'll just say this. Voodoo, and the spiritual churches, that's community faith—all things to all folks—because we *needed* it, understand?"

Green nodded. "You're saying your family practiced voodoo."

Papa raised his hands in a "who knows?" gesture. "It's hard to know exactly *what* my mama and sisters was up to. I was the youngest, you know, and now I'm the only one left. But yeah, we done had our rituals and beliefs like anyone else." It was almost full dark now, and a flashing neon sign behind Papa cast a strange yellow glow over the old man's face.

"Thing is, Greenie," he said, "the power of the *mind* is an incredible thing. I've seen things no normal person would believe. Sometimes I ain't sure *I* believe 'em..." He spit on the sidewalk. "But so is the nature of greed. Lotsa hucksters claiming to be voodoo doctors and voodoo queens scamming poor folks. Which is where the Laveaus come in." He sighed and cleared his throat. This was quite a filibuster for Papa. "And in the middle, between where the mystical and the greedy meet, well, sometimes folks get caught up in stuff they don't understand, for all the wrong reasons. Power and greed ain't a good combination. Strong take advantage of the weak, right?"

Green nodded. "Yes, sir." He wasn't sure exactly how this tied in with voodoo, but there had been a perceptible shift in Papa's fervor and Green, who was certainly not C.G. Jung, could see that *something* in Papa's past, dealing with voodoo presumably, had left an indelible and unpleasant psychological scar.

Suddenly, it was gone. Papa smiled and grabbed Green's arm, tugging him toward the restaurant. "*E*-nough a that stuff. C'mon, boy, I'm hungry— and I don't like talking about voodoo. We'll talk about important stuff: Music and the Saints. Okay?"

It was the only time voodoo had ever come up.

Now, in Lafitte's watching Papa play, Green wondered what the old man would say about Crayton's story. After "St. James Infirmary," Papa retarded the tempo in a block of chordal clusters, then stood up and bowed in exaggerated fashion. He nodded at Green's one-man flurry of applause and, after a brief detour through the bathroom, flopped down at Green's table.

"I'm a tired old man." He pushed his hat back on his head. "And what brings your white ass out late on a weeknight? You ain't writing no novels tonight?"

"No inspiration," Green smiled, shoving a fresh beer across the table to Papa.

"I thought you were a regular ol' Steinbeck when it come to the muse." Papa cackled and lit his pipe. The air went immediately gray with the pineappley smoke of Papa's own secret blend. "Thanks for coming by. Always good to see you, Greenie."

Green smiled. "Well. There's something I need to talk about, and you're the only one I can think of..."

Papa raised his eyebrows. "Sounds sinister," he said, "since I know you ain't gotta ask an old man about womens."

"I always ask you about women," Green said. "I just don't have any right now. Not since Jana broke up with me."

Papa nodded and puffed at his pipe. He knew all about Jana and how much it'd stung when she dropped Green a few months back. "It'll come, it'll come," he said soothingly. He took a sip of beer. "So what do you want to know?"

Green scratched his head. "Okay," he finally said. "You know my pal Crayton? Tall, skinny, red-headed dude? Moved in next door to me a few months ago?"

"Yeah, you introduced us once, in Jackson Square."

"Right. Well, he's a good guy; we've become pretty tight."

Papa nodded.

"Cray's a clerk at the Voodoo Shoppe. I don't know if we told you that. You know it?"

"Voodoo Shoppe. That's the tourist juju joint over on Dauphine?"

"Right. He's only been there a few weeks, and he doesn't know anything about it. He's just a clerk. He needed a job."

"You're telling me he ain't no occult freak or nothing."

"Correct," Green said. "Anyway, this morning, his boss asked him to make a delivery—"

"A *delivery*?! From that joint? What he deliver, a t-shirt?"

"No," Green started. "Well, that's where it gets weird..." He glanced at Papa anxiously. "You got a minute?"

"I got time. What do you wanna know?" His tone was neutral.

Green told Papa what had happened, that the corpse's eyes had been removed and the sockets stuffed with dead birds. That there was a swirling, powdered pattern on the dead man's chest. He showed Papa Cray's drawing of the swirling design, adding that Cray remembered the pattern even though he'd been so scared he'd dropped the lid almost immediately.

He finished by adding, "That's it. Cray just let it ride. He didn't tell anybody—at the funeral home or at work. So far, I guess, no one's said anything about it." Green shrugged. "So I thought maybe you'd have some idea what it all means."

Papa leaned forward a bit and stared at him quietly. Finally, just as Green was starting to feel uncomfortable, Papa said softly, "Why you think I know anything about swirled designs and carved-up dead folks? 'Cause I'm a superstitious old black man?"

Green swallowed. "It has nothing to do with that." He looked Papa directly in the eyes. "I asked you because you're my friend, and because of that day we went to Mama Rosa's. You said some stuff about voodoo, about growing up around it. We thought maybe this was voodoo, since that's why Cray was there to begin with."

Papa took a deep pull on his pipe, blew smoke at the piano, and nodded. "All right. I apologize if I seemed rude. I told you, I don't like talking or thinking about the past. They were stupid times."

"I'm sorry, sir."

Then Papa waved in a gesture of repentance. "I'm a cranky old man, Greenie." He patted Green's hand and looked at his watch. He seemed to be thinking about something. "Bottom line: Yeah, it's probably voodoo. I don't know about no birds; that could mean anything. But the symbol? That's called a *vévé* sign. See, voodoo is about connecting with the spirits of your ancestors. Each spirit—or *loa*—has a symbol. These symbols, as part of ritual, summon the spirit."

Papa looked into the shadows, and the glow from the candle on the table lapped at the lines in his face like water. "I don't recognize that particular *vévé*." He chewed his bottom lip. "But the fact that it happened in a funeral home, to a corpse, well, that ain't good. Sounds to me like your friend just wandered into the wrong place at the wrong time. You sure he just closed it up and left?"

"That's what he said. He was pretty freaked out."

Papa thought. "I wouldn't worry about it, but tell him I wouldn't walk around telling about it like it's a joke neither. Who knows who's out there, listening?"

Then Papa drummed his fingers on the tabletop. "See, it ain't the *voodoo* that's the problem. It's the people *thinkin'* they got voodoo."

"I guess I'm not sure what you're saying," Green said.

"All right then." Papa sat there a moment, staring at the piano. He stood up. "You got a few minutes?"

Green looked up, puzzled. "Sure."

"Come on then," Papa said wearily. "This won't take long."

"What?" Green asked. "Where are we going?"

"Just come on. I wanna show you something I think you ought to see. Maybe it'll put all this into perspective."

CHAPTER FOUR

In that New Orleans way, a fine, almost imperceptible mist started. It should have seemed cooling, but it just made the night hotter. Typical hurricane season weather, wherein barometric pressure and humidity seemed to conspire like a whispered threat. Papa and Green walked in silence through the dark residential streets of the lower Quarter, blocks away from the bars and strip joints.

Papa finally said, "What I told you last year about voodoo? It was part of growin' up in our neighborhood. And it's a fact that some folks used it the right way and others used it the wrong way." A door slammed somewhere, and through the open windows of a balcony, classical music drifted into the streets.

"But there's a dark side to everything, Greenie," Papa went on. "Is evil a force with a capital E? Whether it's real, or whether the folks doin' it just *think* it's real, well, in the end, I don't guess it matters, does it?" They turned toward the river.

"I guess," Green said. It sorta made sense.

"Sure," Papa said. "So if someone actually performed a voodoo *sacrifice*"—he spat the word contemptuously—"not that I ever heard of *that* actually happening, what's the difference than if you kill someone 'cause he won't pay you some money he owes you? He's still dead, ain't he? It still evil, ain't it?"

Green thought. "But what Crayton saw today. Was that a spell? I mean, why'd the daughter call a Voodoo Shoppe?"

Papa laughed. "*Was* it a voodoo spell? A ritual? Well, probably, 'cause of the *vévé* sign. Who knows?" He sounded scornful in the darkness. "In my neighborhood, maybe you heard about people putting bad gris-gris on someone 'cause they were fucking around with someone else's woman... The idea was to prey on superstitious folk. You get word to someone they been hoodoo'd, then their own fear perpetuates the act. You follow?"

"Yeah." Green understood what Papa was saying, but not really *why* he was saying it. What did this have to do with where they were going? Papa was clearly circling around some kernel of logic he couldn't quite get to.

Just as quickly as it had started, the mist quit. Papa stopped at the entry to a narrow brick passageway halfway between Royal and Chartres Streets. Green didn't remember ever having seen it, but New Orleans was full of nooks and crannies.

Papa gestured down the walkway. "Down here," he said, ducking inside.

On both sides of the narrow sidewalk, dark brick buildings loomed two- and three-floors high—presumably the backs of apartments—and it was almost tar black. Overhead, a flash of white moon slithered out of the cloudbank for a moment but was quickly swallowed again by the shuffling sky. Green didn't know about voodoo, but they were certainly in a ripe spot for a mugging.

Papa Hipolyte seemed to sense Green's anxiety. "It's okay," he said. "Follow me." Papa grabbed a handful of Green's t-shirt, guiding him through the darkness with a slow, sure sense of direction. The passageway was so narrow that damp brick brushed against Green's arms on both sides. Suddenly, the alley opened into a cul-de-sac. Set back to the left was a two-story building with *faux* glass lanterns on either side of a massive wooden door. The rest of the small square was comprised of high walls and the rears of other buildings. They were more or less trapped, if you wanted to think about it that way.

"We're here," Papa said softly. He led Green up five steps to a small, tiled porch. Papa flicked his lighter under a brass plaque screwed into the door, nodding for Green to read the inscription. Green squinted to read faded, *bas-relief* letters.

ST. LYDWINE CATHOLIC CHURCH—STAR OF OUR SUFFERING
ESTABLISHED 1921

"Is this real?" Green asked. He was totally astonished. He'd had no clue whatsoever that there was a Catholic church hidden in a nondescript alleyway only five blocks from his apartment. The Quarter was only so big, and there was already a huge Catholic presence with the St. Louis Cathedral. Green wondered what possible demographic need there could be for St. Lydia of Whatever.

"Oh, it's real, all right," Papa said. He was whispering, though Green could discern no signs of life anywhere. "They opened it after World War I when all the soldiers were coming home. It ain't as old or pretty as St. Louis, but it's a good church. Lots of older folks like me, black folks from over in the Marigny, come here. Originally, they held mass in a storefront on Frenchmen, used to be a Laundromat. Then a rich old white woman named D'Arcy Dubrow left her house to the St. Lydwine church on the condition that the house be gutted an' used for a new church. Nobody knew her or knew why she did it. Left enough money to cover the costs of the renovation too."

"And no one knew who she was?"

"Just some woman in the neighborhood. She was the last one in her family though, and we never did find out exactly what was up. Lord works in strange ways."

Green gestured at the building. "And this was her house?"

Papa nodded. "Yep." He pulled out a key chain, selected one, and unlocked the heavy door. It swung open quietly, and Papa took a step inside and stood in the dark maw of the church. "C'mon. This is what I wanted to show you."

Green swallowed and stepped inside. The atrium was hardly larger than Green's living room and lit by dozens of prayer candles in front of a kneeling shrine to the Virgin Mary, a statue of whom gazed at them kindly. The floor was marble, and a holy water font was directly in front of Green, bisecting an entryway into the nave. That churchy hush enveloped them, as did a smell of wood polish and candle wax. From a pale tide of white light that reached toward them from high over the altar through the darkness, Green could see the church was tiny, with maybe twenty stained wooden pews to the whole thing. He turned to Papa.

"Are you a caretaker or something?"

Papa laughed. "Lord, Greenie. I ain't got enough jobs? No, I ain't a caretaker."

Green was embarrassed. "Sorry. The key..."

Papa smiled. "I been a member here long as I can remember. Everybody that's a member here has a key. Only about thirty of us. But it's our church, and it's important we be able to get in if we need to. In the old days—before crime got like it is today—Catholic churches were always left unlocked." He shook his head ruefully. "Not anymore."

Green was a lapsed Catholic, but it was cool these people had such a sense of spiritual community. He took a few steps further and looked around. Papa watched him check it out. Though it was dark, Green could see well enough to know the entire church had a stark dignity.

"This is beautiful," he breathed. He glanced back at Papa, who simply nodded.

Just to the right side from where they stood was an offset room that seemed at first glance to be little more than a dimly lit open closet.

"What's in there?" Green asked.

"That's one of the things we came to see." Papa eased around Green and stood in the doorway of the room. "Come here."

He crossed over by Papa and peered inside. The only light was from perhaps two-dozen glowing votive candles. A wooden ledge jutted out on the right, upon which the candles seemed to breathe, and behind that was a glass partition. It was the sort of alcove Green associated with exhibits in natural history museums.

Inside the glass, though, instead of a *faux* panorama depicting a mother bear and her cubs, was a cement sarcophagus. Green exhaled. "Who is this?"

He stared, transfixed, through the glass. Candle flames danced in the reflection.

Papa sighed. "Father Chet Darbonne. He was the first pastor here. One of the first black priests in New Orleans."

Green hesitated. "Is he a...*saint*?"

Papa barked a short laugh, but there was no humor in it. "No, he ain't no saint." He shook his head sadly. "But he was definitely a martyr."

Green could hear the emotion in Papa's voice. "I'm sorry, Papa. I guess I don't know who Father Chet was."

"Ain't no big thing, son. Not many folks do." He leaned his forehead against the glass. "Father Chet was a wonderful man. Father Timothy Choate's the pastor now. Been with us almost ten years, I guess."

Green looked back at the sarcophagus. He knew he was supposed to ask. "You said Father Chet was a martyr."

"Yep. Come here," Papa said mildly. He backed out of the mausoleum and led them down the narrow aisle that divided the pews until they stood right before the altar. Then he continued his story, staring at the white plank floor of the altar, just to the right of the podium. He pointed to an area with three large dark blotches soaked into the wood. "See them stains?" he asked.

"Yessir."

When he finally spoke again, Papa's voice was still quiet, but it had risen in pitch and there was a quiver of controlled rage to his tone. "In 1947, someone nailed Father Chet to the floor here—crucified him—and cut out his tongue. *A seventy-four-year-old man!*" Papa crossed himself automatically, and Green, horrified, found himself instinctively repeating the maneuver.

"Why?" Green whispered. "Was it voodoo?"

Papa turned and shrugged. "No, it wasn't voodoo, Greenie," he said tiredly. "It was racism. Couple of crackers done it, spelled out 'No nigger mass' on the altar in the father's blood. Two men from the Irish Channel. They were arrested but eventually walked. Not enough evidence." He shook his head. "Rarely was, back then."

"Jesus, Papa, I'm sorry." Green felt an odd sense of guilt just for being white.

"I know, boy. I ain't tellin' you this so you feel bad." Papa placed his palm on Green's shoulder. "I certainly don't blame you, Greenie. Or white folks, for that matter. I didn't bring you here to lay no guilt trip or civil rights lecture on you.

"Thing is, it *coulda* been voodoo. It *coulda* been Satanists. Coulda been Baptists or Hindus or Scottish Rotarians for Richard Nixon. Coulda been any of those things...

"What it *was*, though—what it *always* is—was human *evil*. No devils or voodoo gods responsible—probably just sad, deluded little men. And that, I guess, is why you're here. *That's* my point."

Papa crossed himself once more. Then he glanced out the corner of his eye at Green and they walked back up the aisle. After he locked the door behind them, Papa limped down the steps and toward the alley path, then stopped and turned back to the church. "One more thing, Greenie." He pointed up into the darkness toward the top of the church. Green strained to see against a night sky the color of a fresh bruise.

Now Papa sounded like a tour guide. "I don' know if you can see it up there," he said. "But there's a bell tower. It's visible during the day, of course."

In fact, Green could just make out a small square structure at the peak of the gabled roof. "Yeah, I think I see it."

"Well, that bell ain't rang since Father Chet was murdered."

Green thought for a moment. "That's a nice tribute."

Papa laughed. "You don't get it, boy. It ain't no tribute. It just stopped *workin'*. We had everyone from repairmen to clockmakers and bellfounders come and look at it. They can't find nothing wrong with it. You pull on the rope, the clapper hits the side of the bell, and *nothing*. It don't ring." In a sudden glow of moonlight, Papa's face was a mask of awe. "We finally just stopped trying."

CHAPTER FIVE

It was the Saturday after Crayton's lunatic experience in the mortuary, and he and Green were headed over to the annual Death of Summer party, hosted by J.C. Bitoun, who'd been one of Green's roommates at LSU. J.C. was a trust fund kid and Quarter character whose generous way with his money and seemingly effortless successes with women were subjects of admiration and legend. And while Cray was a newcomer to town, J.C. had instantly befriended him. As they approached the exclusive Pontalba apartments, where J.C.'s unit overlooked Jackson Square, Cray asked Green to keep the funeral home story between them.

They'd talked about it since the incident, of course. Cray had tried to do some clandestine research at the Voodoo Shoppe, and told Green he'd even discovered that the swirling pattern on the dead guy's chest was called a *vévé*—one of numerous voodoo symbols that apparently represented various gods. Of course, Green had found out the same thing from that Papa Hipolyte guy.

"But I didn't come across the specific one *I* saw," Cray had said glumly when they compared notes. Basically, Cray thought he'd like to just forget the whole thing. Besides, because he didn't trust anyone other than Green enough to confide in details, Crayton didn't really know what else he could do about it. Apparently no one was suspicious and, he guessed, the issue was—no pun intended—dead and buried.

Green had asked that old black guy, Papa Hipolyte, about it, but all he got was some speech about Evil being evil whether voodoo was real or not. Or something way too metaphysical, Cray thought, to be of any direct help.

The Pontalba apartments were highly exclusive, and the waiting list to get one was supposedly longer than the one to acquire Saints season tickets, though of course J.C. had a pair of those too. In terms of apartment décor, J.C. had avoided the Deep South overkill favored by so many of New Orleans' wealthy and went Southwestern. Indian blankets, potted cacti, rough-hewn timber furniture, and expensive Navajo art were placed throughout with a strategic nod to space. The floors were notched timber planks.

A buffet table was along one wall, opposite the floor-to-ceiling glass sliding doors which ran the length of the room and opened onto a narrow balcony overlooking the twilit Jackson Square. The food looked like Emeril's scrapbook. There was quail and andouille gumbo, crawfish etóuffée, barbecue shrimp, blackened catfish, and trout Ferdinand. A mime in a chef's hat carved from a tenderloin of beef.

Until he moved to New Orleans, Cray had never been around someone like J.C. Bitoun. He still felt intimidated by him, but he had to admit his host was cool and had been nothing but welcoming since they'd met. J.C. had a noble nose, a hero's chin, and sea-colored eyes that, according to Green, made women want to sing him lullabies. The story was, J.C. could adjust his soft-as-butter Louisiana drawl like a thermostat, and was expert at sweeping his blonde hair back so it would fall over his patrician forehead at the optimum angle.

J.C. came from old N'Awlins money and his only gig since college had been as a vaguely defined public relations guy for his uncle, State Senator Wallace Bitoun. The job seemed to require very little in the way of anything except hanging out—at which, Green emphasized, J.C. was particularly adept. He was quick to pick up a tab and always in the mood for fun. The word was, with Uncle Wallace gearing up for an actual run at a seat in the U.S. House of Representatives, J.C. might actually have to work.

They spied their host by one of the bar stations off the kitchen. His tanned arms were crossed and he was chatting with an amazing girl standing next to him. She was tall, with a toffee-colored pageboy, smoking a cigarette in an intriguingly amateurish fashion, wearing an oversized Better Than Ezra t-shirt tucked into new jeans. Crayton swallowed. She had a slender face with sharply defined features, though her green eyes had a soft, sad quality to them. A dash of freckles scattered across her nose gave a quality of mischief.

"Who's she?" he asked Green. "Is she new?"

"I think her name's Kay," Green said. "I ran into them at Le Bon Temps one night." Just then, J.C. spied them.

"Lord God, if it ain't Green Hopkins and Crayton Breaux!" he called, striding to meet them. J.C. held his arms out and gave each a brotherly hug. "Cajun Red, how you doin', bro?" J.C. said, ruffling Crayton's hair.

Then J.C. turned to Kay. "Honey, you know Green." She smiled and nodded. "And this here's Crayton, a true descendant of Huey P. Long."

"Pleased to me you, Crayton," Kay said, taking his hand. "I'm Kay LeMenthe." Her voice was like velvet.

Cray managed to say hello without his voice breaking.

"Cray, here, works over at the Voodoo Shoppe," J.C. drawled, his peculiar patois dripping with hot sauce.

Kay tilted her head at Crayton. "The Voodoo Shoppe? In the Quarter?"

"Yeah, on Dauphine," Cray said. Before he could think of anything else to say, J.C. clapped his hands decisively.

"Christ, what am I doin'?" he said. "Let's get you boys some cocktails. What kinda host you gonna think I am? Green, you give me a hand?"

"Sure," Green said, and they ambled toward a bar, leaving Crayton with Kay. He felt a moment of absolute panic. Fortunately, Kay spoke.

"So, what do you do at the Voodoo Shoppe?"

"Oh, uhm, voodoo," he said, nodding and rubbing his hands together briskly. "Garden variety witchcraft. That ol' black magic."

Kay giggled. "Cool. A wizard with a pompadour," she said, and he felt a refreshing jumpstart of new confidence—just an instant before an olfactory image crashed into his brain. *The stink of rotting feathers, followed by a snapshot memory of tiny beaks frozen in a dead man's hollow eye sockets...* He smiled back at Kay weakly, thinking, *Where the fuck did* that *come from?* and managed to say, "That's why we all wear those cone hats, to hide our hairstyles."

Kay laughed again, and then Green and J.C. were back with four bottles of Abita Amber. Cray sighed. He had no idea what to do around women, though, admittedly, J.C.'s seemed a fine place to practice.

"To good friends an' fine times!" J.C. intoned, holding up his beer in toast. They'd no sooner clinked bottles than a shrill war-whoop sounded from nearby.

Cray looked up to see Donny Pasqual and Huey Durand bearing down on them. Donny was a short, manic guy with George Costanza hair and a G. Gordon Liddy mustache. Every morning, Donny took the ferry across the Mississippi to Algiers where he worked as a tour guide at Blaine Kern's Mardi Gras World.

Huey—The H-Man—had a degree in philosophy which, he said, "Adequately prepared me for a gig as a day-shift burger flipper." He worked at Poppy's Grill on St. Peter, a notoriously cool Quarter coffee shop, and tinkered sporadically on a PhD thesis. The group fell into three or four tangents of conversation until J.C., glancing into the foyer, said, "Uh-oh." He took Kay's arm. "Y'all excuse us for a moment. I think Uncle Wallace just arrived, and I'd best go act like he signs the checks or somethin'."

J.C. escorted Kay through the thickening crowd, greeting guests and aiming for a short, rotund man in a navy suit with white wavy hair and gold spectacles. Cray thought Uncle Wallace looked like he'd spent a lot more time eating lunch at Galatoire's than legislating anything. He watched as J.C. introduced Kay to his uncle, then frowned as the old man kissed her cheek.

"Wow," Crayton said. "J.C. doesn't have any problems in the babe department, does he?"

Huey nodded. "I don't think he has any problems in *any* department, except ego," he laughed. "But yeah, Kay's pretty nice."

Cray exhaled. "What's not to like?"

Huey said, "Actually, we don't know that much about her. She's fairly recent, by J.C.'s standards."

Donny chimed in. "She's a senior at Tulane. A geology major, I think."

Huey went on. "Her parents own an antique conglomerate on Magazine Street. She seems pretty unaffected for a Garden District sorority girl, though."

Cray hesitated. "Are they, like, engaged or anything?"

Green snorted. "J.C.? Engaged?! *Right!* That's one of the reasons he stays so low-key at these parties. There'll be about five of his ex-girlfriends here, all glaring at him or at each other. And poor Kay'll get her share of death threats."

"Yeah," Huey added, "and all the while he'll be scoping out new ones."

A waiter replenished their beers and Donny announced, "I'll be damned if I let the rich people eat all the food. They can afford their own."

"I'm with you," Huey said, and they aimed at the beef tenderloin and a knife-wielding mime.

"Hungry?" Green asked.

"Naw." Crayton shook his head. He was still overwhelmed; it was reassuring to lean with his back against the wall and observe the madness. They sipped their beers, watching as fresh guests continued to come through the door. A blue haze of cigarette smoke formed over the room, and the sounds of a Junior Brown CD were slowly eclipsed by shouted conversation and laughter. He found himself watching Kay over by the bay window, still talking to Uncle Wallace.

Green must've noticed because he slapped Crayton lightly on the shoulder and said, "Kay's a hottie, brah."

Cray sighed. "She is that. *Way* outta my league." Then he grinned. "Am I nerd? Yes. But inside is the engine that runs my pile-driving ass!"

Green eyed him and laughed. "Why not, young man? As we were saying, she won't last with J.C."

Cray tried not to fan the flames of hope—and new confidence (where did *that* come from?)—licking within. He'd barely spoken to the woman. "Ya think?"

Green shook his head. "She's way too smart and independent for J.C." He took a sip of beer. "Who knows, Cray, maybe she's destined for *you.*" He affected J.C.'s drawl. "You livin' in Nu Awlins now, my man, not out onna bayou. Good things comin' you way."

With that, they integrated themselves into the swirling carousel known as party circulation, spending quality time at the buffet and various bar stations. Time passed quickly and Cray, who was squired gallantly by any and all of his new pals into various groups, found himself meeting nice folks and feeling surprisingly comfortable. One dude was a former Saints punter, and he also was introduced to a roadie from Cowboy Mouth. He was surprised when he glanced at his watch a bit later. It was after midnight and, looking around, Cray spotted Green standing by himself in one corner. He headed over.

Green waved a beer bottle. "My man," he said, his smile huge with alcohol. Cray chuckled to himself. In their short friendship, this was as drunk as he'd seen Green.

Cray said, "How you holding up?"

"Drinking too much," he said ruefully. "Kinda got the blues, thinking about Jana and all."

"Hey, I understand," Cray said, feeling like a moron for having dominated the conversation with his Kay fantasies. Here was Green, the walking wounded, still reeling from his longtime girlfriend breaking up with him. "What can I do to help?"

"No big deal," Green said. "I'm not much the maudlin drunk type." He frowned suddenly and changed the subject as Donny and Huey walked up. "Anybody seen J.C.?"

Donny knitted his brow. "I dunno. He keeps disappearing into the back bedroom. I think maybe Kay doesn't feel well."

Green blinked. "I hope she's not as drunk as me."

"Nobody drunk as you," J.C. said behind Green, emerging from his bedroom.

"How's Kay?" Crayton blurted. An odd sense of proprietary concern rushed over him, and he was afraid he blushed. He'd said, what, three words to the woman?

J.C. seemed not to notice. "She got a migraine."

"A migraine?" Huey asked. "Jeez, that's no good. Is this a regular thing?"

J.C. nodded. "You don' know the half of it. Technically, I guess they *ain't* migraines. But they're headaches and they're chronic, bra'. She's had 'em since she was a little kid. Been to the Mayo Clinic, M.D. Anderson in Houston. They worried she had a brain tumor at one point, but never could find nothin'. No one's figured out how to stop 'em."

Cray amazed himself by speaking up. It was as though his mind was operating independently of the rest of him. "I'll stop the migraine," he heard himself say. "But we gotta go to the Voodoo Shoppe." *Every time he blinked, the image of the* vévé *symbol on Joshua Arcenet's chest flashed behind his eyes.*

Green and Donny were looking at him strangely. H-Man laughed. "Well, why not?" he said. "Clearly, modern medicine ain't cutting it. Why not indeed? Though I can't imagine someone with a migraine—or any derivation thereof—getting out of bed to walk through the *French Quarter*, particularly on a sweltering August night."

But J.C. regarded Cray thoughtfully. "You got some herbal deal, right? Somethin' holistic?"

Cray didn't know *what* he had, other than a strange gut feeling—almost a premonition. The *vévé* symbol behind his eyelids was gone, but he felt an odd charge, almost as though he'd suffered an electrical shock. Cray couldn't even feel strange or frightened by it. He *liked* it... And now he was happy to follow the lead J.C. provided, saying, "I know how it sounds: holistic healing is a bunch of New Age bullshit, but..."

"No, no, I know where you comin' from," J.C. said. "Uncle Wallace always uses natural preventives and holistic stuff ever' winter. Claims he ain't had a cold or the flu in twenty years."

Cray smiled. "Well, yeah. I can give it a shot. But Huey's right. Kay may not *want* to get out, and the problem is, I can't exactly go forage the shop and drag a bunch of stuff over here. I guess you could ask Kay if she's up for it."

J.C. thought for a second. "I *was* kinda hopin' you could just bring the stuff here."

Crayton said, "Like I said. Besides, I'm not sure exactly what we have or what I'll have to do when we find it. And listen to this place"—he waved an arm to indicate the din of full-scale lunacy going on around them—"maybe it *would* do Kay some good to get some fresh air."

J.C. looked doubtful. "She basically lies down in a dark, quiet room till it's over. But I guess I can ask her." He nibbled his lower lip. "It ain't that late out. I'd go, but I don't know if I should leave the party. These people are animals."

Green then completely surprised Crayton by piping up, "Hey, I'll go with them." Everyone looked at Green; he was pretty blasted. "You know, just in case Kay feels weak halfway there or whatever. I can help out."

J.C. looked intrigued. "It'd probably do you good to get a bit of air yo'self, brah," he said, smiling. Then he said, "I guess *we* can talk about what Kay might wanna do all night, but one important aspect of this experiment might be to jus' ask her." He excused himself.

To perhaps everyone's surprise except Crayton's, who acknowledged to himself that, on some level, he'd known all along this was going to happen, it turned out Kay was ready to try anything.

CHAPTER SIX

The night was still hot, and the brick streets, moist with humidity and stinking of revelry, glistened in the multi-colored lights of the Quarter as Green led Kay and Crayton down St. Peter, through the clamorous inebriation of Bourbon, and then up Dauphine. He listened as Cray spoke softly to Kay, telling her goofy stories to make her relax.

"Here we are," Crayton said casually as they stopped in front of a darkened storefront on a relatively quiet block. He held a ring of keys up to the lambent glow of a streetlight as he searched for the right one. "You know," he said conversationally, "we don't even have an alarm system for this place." He found the key he wanted and fit it into the door. "The convict types are so freaked out by the whole voodoo thing that no one would think of ripping the joint off."

Kay smiled thinly at Green as they peered through the darkened windows at sinister display masks, amulets, and voodoo dolls. "*I* wouldn't want to break into this place," she whispered. Green patted her shoulder reassuringly. She was trying.

"Aw, Kay, you're just not the felonious type." Cray's demeanor was utterly calming and inspired a low-key confidence. A dim bulb came on over the checkout counter by the entryway and Crayton ushered them in, re-locked the door, and led them through the store to an empty wooden table against one wall. Boxes of unpacked merchandise were stacked next to it. Cray said, "This is far enough back so no one'll see us through the window."

The smell of patchouli was heavy. Cray looked around, thinking, then said, "Make y'all's selves at home while I rummage around in the back. Kay, you want some water?"

"No, I'm fine, thanks," she said, massaging her temple absently. Cray watched her for a second, then nodded and headed toward the darkness in back. It was museum-quiet, though Green could hear Cray digging around. Kay studied a wooden mask, still rubbing her temple. On the wall were framed pictures of Catholic saints. Green searched futilely for St. Lydwine.

"You ever been here, Kay?"

"Actually, no," she said. "Have you?"

Then Green remembered why they were there. "Sorry, does it hurt to talk?"

She smiled a bit. "Frankly, it hurts to *breathe*, but don't worry about it. I don't know what I was thinking, smoking one of J.C.'s cigarettes. Besides, I'd rather talk. It's almost too quiet in here." She picked up a voodoo doll from a display and said, "We had a black maid when I was growing up. Her name was Patience, and I asked her once about voodoo. I didn't know anything about it—still don't, actually—but we kids all thought, you know, if they're New Orleans *black* folks, why, of course, they must be into the hoodoo.

"Patience was insulted. She was Baptist, very devout, and sang in a gospel choir." She frowned. "Sometimes I hate the South."

Green nodded. "It can be backward. I read somewhere, though, that as much as thirty percent of New Orleanians practice some form of voodoo. And I live in the Quarter and I never *think* about it."

Kay shrugged. "I know exactly what you mean. On the other hand, I saw a ghost once." She glanced shyly at Green, as though he must certainly think her a lunatic.

"Hey, I've lived in this town long enough," he said. "I haven't seen spirits, but I *feel* them. There's a true energy about the whole city." He shrugged nervously. "When did you see the ghost?"

"When I was fourteen. I woke up one night and some figure was standing by my window, looking through the glass. At first I thought it was my father. Then I realized—just like the books, I could see *through* the figure, like it was—"

"All *right*," Crayton said, reappearing out of the rear of the store and setting a small box on the table. He pulled out two purple votive candles, a cone of incense, something that looked like a gardener's seed packet, and what appeared to be a tiny perfume sample in a glass ampoule. Then he took out a large knife.

Green and Kay looked at the knife and raised their eyebrows, and Kay actually backed up a step. Cray laughed gently. "Not to worry," he soothed. "We don't do blood sacrifices here. You'll have to go down the street to the Aztec shop for that."

"Whew," Kay said, looking relieved. "I was a little concerned there for a second."

"Myself," Green admitted, "I was thinkin', ol' Cray's learned something about voodoo he damned sure didn't know when he started here!" Green remembered telling Cray about the trip to St. Lydwine with Papa, and the whole idea of evil thriving without the help of any voodoo. And Kay with her ghost and Green's innate feeling that the whole city was on some different spiritual plane than other places. To be sure, that didn't alter what had happened to Cray in the funeral home, but both he and Cray agreed Papa had a point: Why jack around with voodoo if you want to fuck someone over? Just do it...

Now, here was Crayton actually claiming to utilize gris-gris, though admittedly it was of the white magic variety. He looked up from lighting the incense and the candles. A scent of sandalwood wisped through the air. "Actually, I'm learning as I go. Osmosis, I suppose. You can't help but pick up some of it." He placed the candles at either end of the table and busied himself with the packet.

"So, are you starting to believe in it or what?" Kay asked, watching the flames dance like tiny bonfires in the stillness. Green found himself mesmerized by the candles too, though he attributed this to his mountain-peak intoxication level and not to occult hypnosis.

"Do I believe in voodoo?" Cray asked, placing the open packet on the counter and turning his attention to the ampoule. "Well, like I've told Green... Sure, I believe in it. Just like I believe in water or popcorn or po'boys. What you're asking, Kay, is do I believe it *works*."

"Yeah," she said doubtfully. "I mean, do you perform rituals or healings or whatever you call it? Like, in your own home?" There was just the tiniest hint of tension in her voice.

Cray turned and smiled at Kay, tilting his head slightly. "That's what I'm doing now," he said, and suddenly tossed the powder in the air over her head. It had a green, sparkly quality, and dropped like snow, settling into Kay's hair and on her shoulders.

"Wha–?" Kay said, startled, and even Green's bleary eyes widened at Cray's action.

A thought sprang from somewhere silly in Green's mind: What if Cray accidentally put some *evil* spell on Kay because he didn't know what he was doing?

"Ssh," Crayton hushed Kay. Uncapping the ampoule, he dabbed oil on his fingertips and lightly traced a pattern on Kay's temples. Then he picked up the knife and pointed the blade at Kay's nose. She shrank back, but Cray soothed her. "It's all right, Kay, I'm not going to hurt you. Just stare at the knife point."

"But–" she started, glancing at Green with a gleam of anxiety.

Cray whispered, "Just concentrate." He held the knife steadily in front of her. Green held his breath, watching twinkles of candlelight reflected on the knife blade.Once more, Cray said, softly but firmly, "Kay, stare at the knife point. Do it."

She took a deep breath and focused on the tip of the blade. Green stared in drunken fascination. The woman had suffered migraines for years. The best hospitals and doctors in the galaxy couldn't help, and now here they were in some charm shop in the dead of night, lighting candles, tossing magic powder, and staring at knives. But Green held his tongue and watched.

Finally, as the tension peaked, Crayton suddenly pulled the knife out of the air, placed it on the table, and sighed. "Okay then," he said like a pediatrician who'd pulled a difficult splinter out of a child's foot. "You did good, Kay."

She looked at Green uncertainly. "That's it?"

Cray nodded. "That's it." He leaned over and blew out the candles.

"But, what about the headache?" Green blurted.

Crayton smiled. "Tell him, Kay. It's gone."

Kay put her hands to her head as though exasperated that she'd lost her car keys. She raised her eyebrows and looked from Green to Crayton. "It is?" she said. Then, "It *is*! It's *gone!*"

She held her breath tentatively, like maybe she'd forgotten what the pain felt like, or that she only imagined it was gone and was waiting for the sensation to come blazing back. The three of them stood for a moment. Cray smiled casually.

After a frozen pause, Kay let out a shaky laugh and tears started rolling down her cheeks. "It's gone," she said weakly.

Green could tell by looking at her face—the mix of anguish, relief, and even a hint of fear—that she was telling the truth. "Goddamn," he breathed. They stared at Cray, who grinned his farm boy grin. He handed Kay a Kleenex.

"I can't believe it," Kay said, daubing her eyes and staring at Crayton. "I... I..."

Cray tucked the envelope flap back into the powder packet and palmed the two snuffed candles. "Hey, that's what we came here for," he said. Then, eyes darting from Kay to Green, he laughed. "Close your mouths, both of you, before you start drooling."

Green asked, "Kay, you really don't have any pain?"

She actually giggled. "Green, it's really gone." She put her arm out, grabbing Cray's shoulder. Her hand shook and she looked like a little girl. "Thank you, Crayton," she said. "Thank you so much. But *how?*"

Cray scratched his forehead. Then he gently took her hand from his shoulder and kissed it lightly with aw-shucks gallantry. "How? Well..." He exhaled slowly and winked at Green. "Voodoo," he said.

CHAPTER SEVEN

Papa Hipolyte wandered across Esplanade into the Faubourg Marigny. Normally, unless he was playing the piano somewhere, he'd be in bed this late at night. Lately, events—*mind fucks*, Papa called them—conspired to keep him from sleep.

He turned toward the clamor of Frenchmen Street. It was the main thoroughfare in the big renaissance of the Marigny, crammed with restaurants, bookstores, and live music rooms, and on Saturday night it was as busy as Bourbon. He told himself he was walking to wear himself out, but he knew better. He could, for example, stop in Snug Harbor and nurse a beer. The great drummer Johnny Vidacovich and his trio were playing. But Papa knew that was putting off the inevitable.

Because he was *hunting*.

At some level, he'd known this would happen since the apparition appeared to him on St. John's Eve. He'd tried not to think of the woman rotting on his chair that night as a stress-induced hallucination. Then stuff started happening, what with Green's new friend stumbling into the gig with the eyeless corpse and the birds. *Well*, Papa thought, *that might be a coincidence and it might not.* But he suspected it wasn't, and he couldn't wait around any longer.

Suddenly, like some forgotten oddball math formula he'd memorized in school, a thought popped innocently into Papa's head. *You can't kid yourself any longer. You* know *who it is. Le Culte des Morts is back.*

Papa shivered. He was well aware that voodoo was still a force. The average person never heard about it because no serious mamba or *houngan* was going to open a novelty shop in the Quarter or perform wedding ceremonies for tourists. As Papa well knew, folks seriously into voodoo—at least *dark* voodoo—wanted zero publicity. And that for damned sure applied to *Le Culte des Morts*, which was a splintered black-magic outfit obsessed with power and darkness that utilized corpses in ritual—

"Careful, sir." A polite freak with a blue dreadlocks and a nose ring was trying to edge around Papa, who looked around and realized he was standing like an idiot in the middle of a crowded sidewalk.

"Sorry," Papa mumbled. He timed his step and kicked back into the flow, deciding that maybe he would sit down after all. He was damned tired all the time these days, and seemed to need to rest more and more. But the idea of resurgent activities by *Le Culte* didn't exactly pep him up. As he'd explained to Green the other night at St. Lydwine, it was a strange world:

beaucoup evil and an assortment of across-the-board nuts—he hadn't been kidding about that.

But one of the things he'd lied to Green about was that he knew damned well what the crows in the eye sockets signified. You steal the corpse's eyes so the spirit can't see to find its ancestors on the other side. Crows are the messengers of Baron Samedi, lord of the cemetery. You stuff the crows so the spirit can only do the Baron's bidding. Good thing the Crayton kid hadn't taken it upon himself to tidy up. Who knew what happened when you interrupted such a process.

Later, after some time period that depended on lunar cycles or eclipses or some such bullshit, they'd need to finish the ritual, and at that point it'd only *seem* like the crows stuff was twisted...

He'd also lied to Green about the murder of Father Chet. He didn't like lying to Green, but if he could quash the kid's curiosity about voodoo, maybe he wouldn't be drawn to examine things he was far better off leaving alone. And the sooner Crayton forgot about his experience, the better off they *all* were.

Papa's heart was racing and he felt weak and tingly. He stopped at a sidewalk beer stand and ordered a go-cup of Falstaff. It was the last kiosk in the city that still had Falstaff. He snorted back laughter; his town was dying in all sorts of ways—from voodoo to beer. Well, thank the good Lord for the law that enabled folks to walk around town with a drink as long as it was in a "go-cup." He took a deep swallow and trudged around the lazy bend on Frenchmen, only to stop again. Just across the street was a business he'd never seen before. It was a small, two-story restaurant Papa thought used to be a record store. Like, two weeks ago. With a poster of an old black-and-white photo showing Louis Armstrong serving as a pall bearer at the funeral for cornetist Buddy Petit. Now, someone had painted the building teal and built a nice outdoor deck with a garish orange and yellow canvas awning. A red, neon-scripted sign read GRIS-GRIS GUMBO. There was nothing about it that seemed out of the ordinary, but Papa felt drawn to the place. Which seemed stupid—or not...

Either check it out or go home, old man. He walked to the plate-glass window and peered inside: dimly lit, big crowd, red vinyl booths on a horseshoe upper-level that extended around the restaurant on three sides. Butcher paper spread over plank tables on the floor area, covered with galvanized pails of boiled crawfish and sausage and pitchers of draft beer; laughing folks slurping gumbo and eating oysters; Clifton Chenier's raw zydeco blaring over the speakers...

In the back was the swinging service door to the kitchen. A sweating waitress emerged, hoisting a tray, and was followed by a middle-aged, sturdy black woman wearing a do-rag. She carried a huge burlap sack of live crawfish under one arm.

Papa caught his breath. Her face was beautiful, the rich color of chocolate, and... *Was it her? It* couldn't *be...* He never knew anymore...

She paused, delivering instructions to a busboy, then turned and stared straight through the glass at Papa as though she'd known he was there all along. Her smile was Christmas-morning cheery, her liquid blue eyes laughing. Papa stared, frightened beyond description, calculating, trying to remember. Then she waved at him gaily with her free hand, shrugging at what he knew must be his clownish and pathetic visage—another wino, she probably assumed—then turned and started to wend her way through the tables in another direction.

It ain't her! he thought. *It's close, but it ain't her. Thank you, Lord.* He felt relief flood over him, and he started to chuckle over his loose grip on reality.

Out of nowhere, her face materialized on the other side of the window, no more than six inches away. She was still smiling tenderly and raised her hand, and Papa thought she was going to wave again. Instead, he saw she was holding a large, wriggling crawfish. She winked at Papa, opened her mouth, stuck the crustacean inside, and began to chew. He could hear the shell crunch through the glass, and a tiny pincer darted momentarily between her lips before she sucked it back in. A clear juice oozed over her bottom lip and coursed down her chin as she swallowed. Then she started to laugh.

Papa moaned. He spun away, his heart booming erratically, and stumbled past the deck of the restaurant and into the entryway of a well-lighted convenience store two doors down.

"Oh, Jesus!" he said, his voice a rasp. "Oh, Jesus!" Staccato breaths tore from his lungs and, hands shaking, he pulled the paper cup of beer to his mouth. He took a quenching draught, but spat it out even before his mind could register a hot, coppery taste quite unlike any beer he'd ever had. Papa whimpered. He wiped his hand across his lips, and a sticky, dark, viscous fluid came away on his palm. And just before the street began twirling and the harsh lights of the convenience store misted mercifully into a soft gray— just before he collapsed on the grimy sidewalk—he looked into the go-cup.

It was full of blood.

CHAPTER EIGHT

"I don't know about goofer dust, but goddamn, *this* is Big Voodoo." Green used both hands to support, vertically, a barbecue shrimp po'boy. He and Cray were eating lunch at the bar in Liuzza's by the Track, a magical place where Garden District rich ladies might sit next to Irish Channel bail bondsmen—all because the formula of the sandwich called for coring a crispy French loaf from the top, then pouring the titular crustaceans, sautéed in a buttery, tongue-spangling hot sauce, inside. It was best to eat from the volcanic opening at the crest of the loaf, lest all the goodness spill out due to gravitational forces.

"All powerful," Cray agreed, chewing happily. He, too, was working on one of the signature po'boys, and bowls with the dregs of a delicious, murky seafood gumbo sat on the counter in front of them next to frost-sculpted mugs of draft Dixie. It was the Tuesday after J.C.'s party, and Green was only just now getting over his hangover.

In fact, it had been Crayton who suggested Liuzza's after he started to worry Green would never recover. "Permanent damage, brah," he'd suggested. "Only one possible answer. Liuzza's by the Track." Green had at once agreed, and they'd hopped in Cray's Camaro on a blue-gray afternoon for the short hop out Esplanade.

It was on the ride over that Cray had explained about a gris-gris spell he'd read about at the shop called goofer dust. Comprised of graveyard dirt and church bell grease, you could supposedly utilize the powder to keep rivals away from the object of your affection. The Voodoo Shoppe didn't *have* any goofer dust of course, inasmuch as it was an actual, real voodoo component, but Cray thought Green might want some to win Jana back from her new boyfriend. Green had thanked him just the same, but spoke honestly when he told Cray he was committed to moving on beyond Jana.

Now, as normalcy crept back into his system, soothed by the scent of browning *roux* and the din of happy customers, Green set the po'boy on his plate and took a sip of beer. "Okay. In the context of this goofer dust thing, there's something I gotta know."

"Sure," Cray said.

"Kay and the voodoo Saturday night. What was that all about? Was that goofer dust?"

Cray grinned. "Wrong gris-gris. Plus, like I said, we don't have goofer dust. Besides, you were there. You saw what happened."

"But you had an exact routine: candles, *some* kind of powder, knives..."

Crayton took a pull on his beer and belched softly. "To be honest about it, I looked up the knife-point deal in a *Gumbo Ya-Ya* superstitions booklet while I was getting the candles, and–"

Green interrupted. "It had migraines listed?" A busboy wearing aviator sunglasses removed their gumbo bowls.

"Well, headaches. Actually, it called for stuff we don't have in the shop. Goat hair, shit like that. So I concentrated on the knife parts. As for the candles and incense and powder—which was just some green sparkly shit I found, by the way—I just thought it couldn't hurt to cloak the whole thing in ritual and mystery. I figured, psychologically, that if I made a big deal out of it, maybe I could pull it off."

"And you did," Green said. Across the room, a guy in a construction hard hat punched numbers in a jukebox and The Doors' dark carnival organ came over the speakers.

Cray shrugged. "How do we know it wasn't time for that particular headache to stop anyway? Besides, you know how magic works. Illusion and the power of suggestion."

"But the timing was incredible. And like you said, I was there," Green said. "And I definitely *felt* some kind of vibe."

Cray snorted. "Vibe's ass, Green. Any vibe was courtesy of the booze we drank and the fact that a voodoo store's a strange place to be in the middle of the night."

"Maybe. In any case, I'll bet Kay has a new respect for the gris-gris. You may have a regular customer."

Crayton smiled. "I wouldn't know about that, but she *did* call me last night to ask me to lunch."

Green gave him a thumbs-up. "For real? That's awesome. You're going, I hope."

"Yeah, absolutely. I mean, I did ask her about J.C.—to make sure—and she said they were just friends. I guess they *did* go out a few times, but..."

Green said, "Well, there you go. When's this luncheon gonna happen?"

"She's checking her class schedule." He shrugged and took a deep breath. "I'm just hoping it actually comes to pass."

Green slapped him lightly on the shoulder. "Of course it will. She called *you*, remember?"

Cray nodded. "You're right. You're right." He pointed at the jukebox. "I'll take it as it comes, just like Jimbo Morrison says. We'll see what happens."

Green nodded. "You don't even need goofer dust."

Cray laughed, popped the final crust of bread in his mouth, and patted his lips with a napkin as he swallowed. "Okay, I *do* got a voodoo idea though."

Green frowned. "Oh, lord, why do I feel weirdness coming on?"

"No, listen. I've been thinking some more about the shit that happened at the funeral home."

Green snorted. "I'll bet you have. Hell, I wasn't even *there* and I'm still thinking about it." Green tossed the final quarter of his po'boy on the plate in surrender.

"Right. Well, clearly nothing's going to happen. I mean, Joshua Arcenet's buried and the daughter's gone back to Ohio or wherever—and whoever did it got away with it."

Green's eyes narrowed. "Yeah. And your point is...?"

Cray shrugged. "I just figured, y'know, it probably had to be someone working in the funeral home. Like, the guy who embalmed Arcenet. That makes sense, right?"

Green thought for a moment. "Okay, makes sense. Sure. Someone inside. But, why do we care? I mean, we don't *want* to know these people, right?"

Cray straightened on his barstool and fixed Green with a beaming, ridiculous grin. "Well, here's what I was thinking..."

Thirty minutes later, after stopping at a Piggly Wiggly to pick up a bouquet of flowers and a thank-you card, which Crayton filled out with a credibly feminine cursive, signing Janice Arcenet's name to it, he pulled into Maddox & Sons Mortuary. A gleaming black hearse was parked at the rear of an otherwise empty lot. The sullen afternoon air was pocked with the promise of rain. The cicadas even sounded tired.

Green couldn't believe he was going along with this as he followed Cray up the flagstone walkway. "Are you sure this isn't insane?"

"Of course it's insane. But you gotta admit. It's fun."

Green wasn't sure it was *fun*, exactly, but there *was* a sinister aura of intoxicating menace to the whole thing. Still, Cray's plan involved nothing more than to deliver appreciative flowers—ostensibly from Janice Arcenet, who clearly would have had no idea her dad had been desecrated—to the mortician who'd prepared her father. What could go wrong?

On the other hand, Green had to ask. "And what, exactly, are we going to learn from this?"

They'd reached the entry foyer and Cray stopped and turned to face Green. His voice dropped to a gleeful whisper. "We're gonna see who *did* this."

"Who *probably* did it. And what does that get us? To look at this person?"

Cray grinned and sniffed the bouquet he clutched in his left hand. Green smelled chrysanthemum. Cray said, "I don't *know* what that gets us, brah. But it's gonna be cool to see what sort of nut would cut the eyes out of a corpse and stuff dead birds inside."

It was Green's turn to laugh, though he did so dismissively. "I'll tell you what sort of nut it is. It's a damned *serious* nut. And here we are, fucking around, raising his suspicions."

Cray shook his head with an expression of amused disdain. "He's not going to suspect anything. We're making a floral delivery. Happens dozens of times a day in this place."

Green sighed, reached around Cray, and pulled open the door. "Fine. Let's hit the corpse house."

Cray grinned and offered a thumb's up.

The air conditioning was mercifully set on Arctic, and Green recognized a surprisingly jaunty Brahms piece playing as background music. The floral reek of the place overwhelmed Cray's bouquet. They approached an information desk.

"Hi!" Cray said. "Remember me? From last week?"

The receptionist set down a Luanne Rice paperback and peered at Cray pleasantly. "Oh, yes, of course. How can I help you?"

Cray explained that he was training a new employee and that they had an unusual delivery. The daughter of Joshua Arcenet was now back home, out of state, and wanted to express her appreciation to the embalmer who had taken care of her "loved one." She had no idea, of course, who had done the actual embalming, but would it be possible for Crayton to meet the gentleman and give him the floral arrangement?

The lady smiled. "How thoughtful. Truth be told..."—she lowered her voice and glanced around as though to make sure no one was coming—"...no one *ever* remembers the embalmers."

Cray and Green both nodded enthusiastically. "Exactly," Cray said. "I thought it was awesome too."

"You know what? This is probably a perfect time." She was leafing through a notebook she'd pulled from a desk drawer. The Brahms had segued to something more melancholy. Debussy? Green couldn't be sure. "Okay, here we go. Yes, Marcus embalmed poor Mr. Arcenet and he's actually on duty. It's a slow day. There's just me; Tony in the office; and Marcus is in the back. I don't think he has any clients."

Green supposed "clients" meant "corpses." Cray smiled. "Well, it'd be great to meet him."

The woman adjusted her glasses and looked up at Cray from the notebook. "I'll just buzz Marcus. Or you can drive around back. You've made deliveries back there, right?"

"Perfect," Cray said. "We'll do that." He nodded toward Green. "He's gonna need to know where to go anyway."

They pulled the Camaro to the back of the parlor and parked where Cray spied a sign indicating where to make floral deliveries. "Jeez, you're pretty fucking smooth," Green said. "That whole exchange..."

Cray shrugged. "I don't know quite why this is so entertaining, but it is."

"And now we'll joke it up by giving flowers to a guy who ripped the eyes out of a cadaver and smashed rotten birds into the skull."

Cray had to laugh. "Exactly." He kept the flowers and handed the card to Green.

There was a metal fire door with instructions to push a red button. They could hear a buzzer sound inside. There also seemed to be a faint pattern of drums. Green said, "They must rock out when there aren't any corpses."

"Or even if there are," Cray said. "Maybe they're playing Oingo Boingo. *Dead Man's Party.*" He pushed the buzzer again, two quick bursts, but there was still no answer. Just drums.

Green muttered, "What is he? Ginger Baker, mortician?" and raised a fist to knock. But when he struck the door, it actually cracked open a bit. The drums—no accompanying instrumentation, just trippy, hypnotic jungle rhythms—were much louder. Green figured it must be soundproofed in the back; they'd certainly not heard any such percussion out in the foyer.

Cray called out, "Hello? We've got, uhm, a floral delivery for Marcus. Hello?"

Out of nowhere, Green had a sudden, spooky thought. "Is this what voodoo drums sound like?"

Cray paused, clearly thinking about it. "Interesting." He pushed the door completely open. "Hey, Marcus!"

They stepped inside what seemed to be a garage/storage area with concrete floors, sheetrock walls, and rows of industrial metal shelving. There were rolling body carts lined up neatly against the far wall, stacked cardboard cases of motor oil, orange traffic cones with FUNERAL printed in black, a spotless riding lawn mower and, on the shelves, rows of caskets wrapped in plastic sheeting. At the left end was a bay garage door with several floral displays organized in separate groupings just inside. On the wall next to the door, a clipboard hung alongside a purple and gold poster sporting the upcoming LSU football schedule.

Inset into the opposite wall was a freight elevator and two doors, one a conventional wooden door, though wider than normal—to allow access for caskets, Green supposed—and a stainless-steel number, presumably to a cooler where they stored bodies. The wooden door was open and the drums seemed to be coming from within.

"Jeez," Green said, taking it all in, his gaze lingering on the caskets. "You'd think they had dead people here or something."

Cray grinned, but he seemed less sure of himself than when they'd been outside. Still, he said, "Let's go find boogyin' Marcus and see what's up."

They crossed the floor, the smell of gasoline more powerful than the bunches of flora, and walked through the door into a well-lit, carpeted hallway. The drums pulsed with a droning, metronomic quality—and sounded disturbingly live. They weren't deafening, but you could certainly hear them. Cray tried again. "Hey, Marcus? Flower delivery. For you, man."

Green thought he heard someone shifting around from another open doorway, this one on the left side of the hallway. *A fuckin' labyrinth.* He tapped Cray on the shoulder, caught his eye, and nodded at the door.

They stepped over and peered inside.

It was all bright white, clearly one of those mysterious "prep rooms" civilians always wonder about. An angled porcelain table butted up against a sink next to something that looked like a water cooler. Intuitively, Green thought, *Fuck, that's an embalming machine...*

Oh, yeah, and utterly incongruous were the votive candles—dozens of them—positioned on three levels of steel counters, the flames shimmering in lazy time to the mysterious drumbeat. Green looked around for a stereo or jam box. Hell, for Ricky Ricardo and his congas. Nothing. Just the beat.

Through a side door emerged a tall, lean black man—Marcus?—head cocked at a slight angle, looking at them. Or, rather, oblivious, he seemed to be looking *through* them. He was dressed in a smart, well-cut black suit—as though he'd been on funeral director duty up front rather than dealing with body parts and formaldehyde—wore fashionable rimless glasses, and a neat goatee stylishly offset his shaved head.

In his right hand was a long pointed instrument attached to a suction hose, like some space-age gardening tool or barbecue fork. Marcus was moving it back and forth gently like a director's baton.

Cray took a tentative step into the room. "Marcus?" He proffered the bouquet. "Got some flowers for you." His voice sounded strained, but he had to speak loudly over the drums. Green exhaled and realized he'd been holding his breath. *Something's very, very odd here, bro.*

Marcus seemed to snap to attention. He grinned, but it was lopsided and off, as though he was attempting something he'd never tried before and couldn't quite get the hang of it. Still, when he spoke, it sounded normal enough, with a folksy resonance. "Fellas, what's up?"

Green and Cray glanced at each other, relieved by Marcus' easy tone. The drums pounded infectiously.

Hell, Green thought, *the lady out front said it was a slow day. Maybe this is how Marcus kicks back...*

Cray stepped forward, still extending the flowers. Marcus reached out and took them with his free hand. With his other, he held up the instrument in show-and-tell fashion. "This is a trocar," he explained.

"Okay, that's cool," Cray said, shooting Green an uneasy look. Marcus was talking *at* them, but not *to* them.

Marcus continued. "After you've flushed all the blood out of the body, you insert the trocar just under the navel and use it to puncture the stomach, bladder, large intestines, and lungs. Then you use the suction to withdraw the gas and fluids."

What? Green took an involuntary step backward. The multi-faceted weirdness factor had coalesced to a point beyond comfort. Cray kept his eyes frozen on Marcus, but slowly wiped his mouth with the back of his hand. To Green it was as though they had instinctively shifted into a mode where they were trying to avoid agitating a cornered and wounded jungle cat.

Marcus paused for a moment, looking thoughtful. A tear welled up in one eye. "I don't have any idea, man, what the fuck is happening to me today." He said it conversationally, like ordering tacos at a drive-through. "I'm glad you fellas happened along, though." He held up the bouquet and studied it for a moment. "And thanks for the flowers." He angled his head toward the arrangement as though to savor the scent—and selectively bit off the yellow bloom of a daisy. Chewing, he shook his head and said, "Y'all hear these fucking drums?" Marcus smiled and shook his head as though mildly disappointed by a weather forecast. He sighed.

With a quick precision that precluded any reaction by Green or Cray, Marcus fitted the spiny prong of the trocar under his chin. With a vicious thrust upward, he drove the tool all the way up into his brain.

Green gasped as Cray jumped backward and cried, "Mother*fucker!*" Marcus dropped to his knees and then toppled sideways.

Only later did Green realize it was at that precise moment the drums stopped.

CHAPTER NINE

Two nights earlier, Papa Hipolyte had opened his eyes and known at once he was in Charity Hospital. He could count the number of days he'd been sick in his life on one hand, but, in one familial situation or another, growing up poor, he'd done Charity countless times.

He blinked in the bright white fluorescence. He was lying on a moveable gurney in a tiny examining room. He was hooked up to an EKG monitor, and an IV tube was inserted in one arm.

The next question, Papa thought, stretching his free arm and moving his neck side to side in tentative self-examination, was, *Why am I here?* Then, in an only slightly delayed reaction, it all came back to him.

Slowly, grabbing the metal railing of the gurney, he pulled himself upright in a sitting position. He wished he had some water, preferably the kind that wouldn't turn to blood. But Papa suspected the creepy stuff was over for now. She'd gotten what she'd wanted.

Which was why he wasn't going to sit here and wait on a doctor so he could try to explain how his *beer* had turned to blood.

Papa studied his heartbeat on the EKG screen—a little fast; nothing to worry about—and took a few deep breaths. He'd rest a second, eighty-six the IV tube, and get the hell out of here. Which was, of course, the moment when the curtain slid back and a guy in a white coat with cropped brown hair strode briskly in with a chart on a clipboard.

"Well, hello," he said. "I'm Dr. Lemmon and you're back with us. And, by the way, I think you should be lying down."

"Thank you, Doc, for everything," Papa said, "but I'm fine and I think I'll be heading on home. If you can let me have my wallet and clothes, and point me in the direction of the cashier, I'll settle up and get on out of here."

Dr. Lemmon smiled briefly. "Hold on a moment, Mr. Hipolyte. I'm glad you're feeling better, but you can't just wander into the night. You were out for over an hour after all."

So it'd only been an hour...

"I'm fine, really," he said with a pleasant tone. "Y'all done good, but I'm gonna head home and take it easy."

Dr. Lemmon studied him wearily. "Mr. Hipolyte, no offense, but when they brought you in, we didn't just prop you in a corner so you could nap. That's not what we do. You fainted"—he consulted his clipboard—"on Frenchmen Street. You apparently threw up blood..."

Papa affected an air of studious contrition. He didn't bother to tell the doc the blood wasn't his. He knew that you just don't broach the subject of voodoo alchemy in the logical world of the modern hospital.

Lemmon went on. "We've taken your vital signs, Mr. Hipolyte, and there's cause for concern. We'd like to work you up a little more extensively. Have you been tired lately? Dizzy? Any chest pains?"

Papa wanted to say, "Doc, I was *born* tired," but he wasn't about to do that. The man seemed sincere and kind, if frustrated. The point was, Papa *had* been tired and dizzy lately. And yeah, some occasional burning in his chest. But with diet and an insistence on Crystal hot sauce with every meal... Plus, he'd also *counted* all of these symptoms since...since what happened on St. John's Eve. Stress'll do that.

All he said, though, was, "No, sir. I mean, I get tired, but I ain't exactly young anymore either." He grinned hopefully.

Lemmon pursed his lips, but his eyes remained kind. "Mr. Hipolyte, I think there's a very real possibility you've suffered some form of cardiac episode. Your EKG tracing indicates your heart muscle has at some point suffered some damage. We need to see how serious it is."

Papa felt like he'd been slapped. *Damage to his heart muscle?* "You mean I had a heart attack tonight?"

"I'm not saying that, sir. We don't *know* what the damage is, or how extensive. I *can* say that, if not tonight, then certainly within the past few months you've had some sort of cardiac episode. It may be that you have some form of heart disease, and we need to check. For *your* sake."

Heart disease? For a moment, Papa was tempted to let them go ahead with their tests. But that meant an overnight stay, at least. No, he *knew* what the problem was—at least as far as *tonight* was concerned.

"Dr. Lemmon," he said, "I surely appreciate your advice. But folks get old and die, and it's gonna happen to me someday. Maybe sooner, maybe later. And you can walk outta here thinking I'm the most ignorant SOB you've ever met." He grinned. "And I'll bet that's saying a lot –"

A faint smile appeared on the doctor's face. Papa continued. "But whatever my reasons may be, at this point in time, I don't *wanna* know." He held the doctor's gaze and crossed his hands on his lap.

Dr. Lemmon shrugged. "If that's your wish, Mr. Hipolyte, well, that's what we'll do. But I want to emphasize you're taking a major risk. I strongly recommend you reconsider." He looked like the old man had disappointed him. "Or I'll be seeing you *sooner* rather than later." He started to walk out the door and then turned back. "I'll have a nurse bring your belongings and you'll have to sign an AMA form."

"A what?"

"An Against Medical Advice form. All it means is that you're leaving against the suggestions of the doctors."

Papa nodded. "Ah, I see. Insurance liability?"

"Yes, Mr. Hipolyte. That's it in a nutshell. Hang on and a nurse will be right with you."

When Papa finally walked through the emergency room doors into the blast furnace heat of the pre-dawn New Orleans night, his biggest concern was whether he could find a cab. He was tired as hell, weak as a kitten, and didn't feel like standing around with the collection of freaks that clustered around the Charity twenty-four/seven, three-sixty-five. To his relief, Papa spotted a taxi dropping off a fare at the head of the big circular driveway and waved. He got acknowledgment from the cabbie and waited while the exiting fare paid up.

On the curb was a *Times-Picayune* box. Papa glanced at the early edition display copy—and got his next jolt of news. Dizziness washed over him again and he reached out to the newspaper stand to keep from falling. He looked again at the headline, hoping his eyes had played tricks on him in the dark. But he'd read it right the first time: *Convicted Cop Killer Prospero Godchaux Scheduled to Die Monday.*

Hands shaking, he deposited some change, pulled out a copy, and settled into the back of the taxi. Moving down Rampart, streetlights and neon signs flashed by at precisely the tempo, Papa realized, required to forge an ass-kicking headache.

He sighed, clutching the newspaper. This had been one long motherfucker of a night.

CHAPTER TEN

Bustling around, preparing to open the Voodoo Shoppe, Crayton felt cautiously optimistic for the first time since yesterday's bizarre funeral home suicide. After all, Kay had left a message saying she would call this afternoon to nail down a time and place for their lunch date, so *that* was big news.

With the money in the cash register and tunes on the stereo—a little Dr. John, the *Sun, Moon & Herbs* album—Cray started restocking the candle bins. He was jazzed about Kay, but he also kept flashing back on Marcus at the funeral home. It wasn't every day you watched some kook drive a...*trocar* into his brain. It'd been sufficiently disconcerting that he and Green had spent most of the evening drinking at the Maple Leaf, listening to the steamy funk of the Rebirth Brass Band in an attempt to sandblast the images out of their brains.

In the newspaper, the cops were saying it was a "suicide with suspicious circumstances," and an anonymous source alluded to voodoo. Two officers, both young guys, one white and one black, had questioned him and Green separately and together for two hours before letting them go—not that they were remotely suspected in the incident. Cray explained that the flowers were a gesture on behalf of Janice Arcenet by the Voodoo Shoppe, and that seemed to work.

The only thing no one could answer was the drums thing. There was no source for it and no reason to discount Green and Cray's assertion that they'd been clearly audible. The prep rooms were wired for stereo and television, but the only thing they'd found was an old Bill Withers tape in the cassette player.

After the police had finished their questions and told them they could leave, Green had paused at the door and asked, simply, as though he didn't really expect an answer: "So what *does* account for the drums?"

The cops glanced at each other. "Mr. Hopkins," the white guy said wearily, "you don't *want* to know what we see in this city that can't be explained."

Cray finished the candles and went in the back and pulled out a cardboard carton so he could check in and price a shipment of High John the Conqueror roots. He adjusted the price gun. Maybe it *was* this town. Clearly, the Voodoo Shoppe was a tourist place, but there were definite patterns to what people bought. For sure, the voodoo dolls were always a big item, as were t-shirts, incense, and postcards—stuff you'd expect to sell in the French

Quarter. But, Cray reasoned, there were *authentic* joints in the city where someone who really believed and knew what the hell they were buying could actually find the stuff they wanted.

Then it hit him, a common denominator: ordinary people—tourists and actual resident voodoo practitioners and maybe the folks in between—bought this stuff on the chance it might work. Like they bought lottery tickets. *On the chance that it might fucking work.* Maybe some were more serious than others and maybe some really *believed.* But...

Cray smiled. People were fucking nuts. Then another thought hit him: the bullshit ritual with Kay had worked, hadn't it? The headache *had* vanished. It'd been exactly like he'd told Green: he'd made it up and counted on a psychological reaction. It wasn't voodoo—except of the mind.

So what had gotten into *Marcus'* mind?

Cray priced the last root, looked at his watch and unlocked the front door, then perched on the stool behind the cash register. It was about twenty minutes later that a black woman glided in the door. She was obviously a local, and a decidedly odd one at that: stunningly exotic, large-boned and solidly built, with beautiful features and—very strange—swimming blue eyes. Was she wearing contact lenses? Her hair was pulled back in a twist, and she wore a simple, thin, floor-length shift of pale-yellow cotton. She was kinda hefty, Cray thought, but absolutely exuded sexuality. Too, though he did his best not to stare, it was hard to ignore the fact that her large breasts rolled free under the thin dress, and that her wide, dark areolae shone through in astonishing *bas-relief.*

A rawhide necklace hung around her neck with a silver fish pendant, and matching earrings dangled from her ears. She was carrying a basket of lacquered red straw in both hands, and its contents were wrapped in linen. There was a sense of power and timelessness about her that made Cray nervous; perhaps it was that she could've been anywhere from twenty-five to fifty—and the distinctive characteristics of youth and age seem to swirl within her features even as she just stood there smiling.

"How are you today?" the woman announced magnificently. There was a slight island lilt to her voice, and Cray at once thought she should be doing voice-overs for a cruise line.

"Just fine," Cray answered.

"Could I speak to the person in charge of ordering merchandise?"

"Uhm, that would be Cosima," Cray said. "She's actually off today. I just kinda work here."

"Ahhhh. That's okay," the woman said happily, as though Crayton had given her an unexpected award at a banquet. It was exactly the opposite reaction than what he'd wanted; despite her alluring chest, he'd hoped the comment about Cosima would serve as a deterrent to this person and whatever she was selling. Instead, she set her basket down on the counter as though she was going to share Easter eggs.

"Well, you see," she continued, pulling back the edge of the cloth teasingly, "I just happen to have some goofer dust today." She looked up and gazed directly at Cray, her blue eyes brimming with kindness. "Does the Voodoo Shoppe carry goofer dust?"

Cray froze, thinking, *goofer dust?!* Hadn't he just been discussing this shit with Green? "Well, no, I don't think we stock it..." *What the hell kind of coincidence was this?* He'd never *heard* of goofer dust till yesterday, a few hours before Marcus and the drums—and the *trocar*, don't forget that—and now here was some door-to-door weirdo, cruising in with her homemade stash of goofer dust.

Cray shivered; he could imagine this lady crawling around in cemeteries, filling vials with graveyard dirt while an equally spooky husband creaked along, fifty feet up in the moonlight, scraping grease off church bells...

The woman was talking. "You know about goofer dust, of course. How, in matters of romance, one might use it to defeat a rival!" She laughed gaily, as though at the corny premise of the whole thing.

"I don't know what to tell you," Cray said, reduced to absolute indecision by her presence. But before he could think of a graceful way to shut off her sales pitch, the woman pulled back the cloth covering the basket and showed several small glass bottles, like miniature spice containers, filled with gray/brown powder. There were no identifying marks—not handmade, homey scrawls in handwriting like for Cray's mother's file vials, or mass-marketed labels imprinted with GOOFER DUST logos.

"Here," the woman said, plucking a vial from the basket and offering it to Crayton. "You'll take a sample, okay?" Her voice was so rich with goodwill that he reached out his hand automatically. It would have seemed, well, rude to turn her down.

"I'll see that Cosima gets this," he said, staring at the goofer dust in his palm. Then he looked back at the woman. "Do you have, like, a card or a brochure?"

The woman laughed, full of carnival glee and warm autumn sunshine. "Oh my, no! I'm not so...formal, I guess you'd say. I'll just check back later."

This was increasingly strange. "Well, should I tell her your name? Have you two done business before?" He sat the bottle on the counter, glad it was out of his sweating hand.

"No, I'm new to the area. My name would mean nothing. But I'll check back." She started to pick up her basket, then seemed to think better of it. "I wonder," she said with slight hesitation. "Have you by chance any interest in seeing the Hand of Glory?"

"I'm sorry?" Cray was exceedingly tense now. This whole episode had gone on far too long and he realized that, from the moment this person had walked in, his central nervous system had rocketed into overdrive in some instinctual mode of attenuation. Now she wanted to talk about a hand of glory, which sounded to Cray like some *aide de fuck* from one of the porno shops on Bourbon Street. "A hand of what?"

"The Hand of Glory," the woman said, her features looking suddenly and remarkably young. At that moment, Cray would've sworn she was no more than twenty years old. She leaned forward to fuss with the basket, and Cray couldn't help but stare at her breasts. She glanced up at him, smiling, then teasingly pulled back the cloth on her basket, all the way, and spun the basket on the counter so the previously hidden side now faced Cray.

He looked down, certain she knew what he'd been staring at—and saw a severed human hand.

"*Jesus!*" He shrank back, then peered closer. The hand appeared, on inspection, to have been mummified maybe, and not some rubber Halloween prop, which, at first, Cray had suspected. It was certainly old: gray, dry, and withered, with a bit of jutting wrist bone, but none of the reedy tendons or fake blood one associated with joke store gags.

It was still pretty repugnant, but only because, for some reason, Crayton had the crawling suspicion that it was real.

"What is this?" he whispered, allured in spite of himself and the whirlwind lunacy of recent events.

"The Hand of Glory," the woman repeated. There was a bubbly awe in her tone, as though she was having a religious experience on a game show set. "It has many powers."

Cray looked up from the hand and stared at the woman. "This is, like, *fake,* right?"

"Oh, assuredly not," she answered.

"As in, this was once someone's hand?"

She nodded simply, meeting Cray's stare with an intensity that drew his energy like a magnet. Her cornflower-blue eyes were rimmed with what appeared to be pinstripes of shifting golden sand. Cray had to force himself to pull his own eyes away and back onto the severed hand—which was absorbing enough.

Against his own will—he wanted this creepo out of the store *now*—he spoke. "Where did it come from?" he asked, risking a glance at the woman's face. He blinked. Now she looked older again, as though harsh sunshine had flashed from behind a cloud outside, highlighting her age lines.

Just as suddenly, her girlish, teasing tone vanished. She seemed to have remembered something important, and glanced at her watch. "That...will have to wait for another time." She arranged the cloth over the hand and the vials and pulled the basket over her arm. She nodded at Cray with a final salesperson's smile. "Tell your boss about the goofer dust, eh?"

She reached and feathered the back of Cray's hand with her fingertip before sweeping into the morning. Crayton let out a sigh. "Jeez," he muttered, picking up the vial and holding it up to the light. How was he gonna tell Cosima about *this*? It wasn't like some ordinary sales call. And what about that fucking Hand of Glory—presumably with a capital H and a capital G. What the fuck was *that* about?

Suddenly, without knowing quite why he did so, Cray tucked the goofer dust into his backpack, next to the romance candle. He also decided not to broach this with Cosima. If she'd wanted goofer dust, he reasoned, she'd already *have* goofer dust.

Cray felt the tension ease. He supposed he'd expected shit like this when he signed on at the Voodoo Shoppe. It wasn't like being a stock boy at the A&P, where you knew the zaniest part of the day would be reconfiguring the canned spinach aisle. Then he laughed, feeling almost exhilarated. What else would you do when some nutso comes in, hands out samples of graveyard dirt, and lets you sneak a view of her tits—not to mention a severed hand?

Cray switched the stereo to something mellower—Ellis Marsalis' *Twelve's It*—then reached under the counter for the house books on voodoo superstitions and spells. He was looking for something called a Hand of Glory.

CHAPTER ELEVEN

The next morning, Green rose early for a long run in the hopes of clearing the Maple Leaf cobwebs. Instead of loops through the Quarter though, he'd head into the warehouse district, then to the main branch of the New Orleans library at Tulane and Loyola streets. He took off and headed up Toulouse toward Canal.

Since the night Papa took him to St. Lydwine, Green had had an irrepressible urge to wax Clete Purcel and check out the story on Father Darbonne's murder. Not that he didn't trust Papa Hipolyte—he did—but the more he thought about it, there was something out of proportion about the drama of Papa's presentation given the relative insignificance of Green's questions.

He cut on Canal toward the river and angled up through the Warehouse District to Poydras, sweating out his fear. Because—oh, yeah—yesterday's events at the mortuary had gone a long way toward darkening Green's worldview. He *thought* he'd been drunk enough after the Maple Leaf to at least go to sleep last night, and indeed he would doze off—only to jerk awake, gasping, from jagged images of the ludicrously smiling Marcus and his brain-mix trocar.

Hell, in context, even Kay's vanishing migraines were giving *him* migraines. Green was happy for her, but all these events had conspired in a very short time to knock his life out of balance. He felt restless not trying to explain at least *some* of this stuff.

He ran up Poydras, past a line already forming at Mother's for the early lunch rush. Green smiled in spite of himself at the nuances of his city. As far as the St. Lydwine homicide, Green could probably have found something on the Internet, but the *Times-Picayune*'s online archives were notoriously incomplete and so he figured a search through microfilm might help.

By the time he got to the library, Green had worked up quite a sweat. The air-cooled foyer felt sweetly antiseptic as he stopped by the microfilm desk for help. A pleasant woman retrieved the reel and Green settled at a viewing station, looking for anything he could find on the murder of Father Chet Darbonne in St. Lydwine, sometime in 1947.

To his initial relief, he found the story almost at once, though the headline caused him to pause: *Police Investigate Possible Occult Slaying of Priest.*

"Occult?" Green mumbled. *What about the white trash bigots?* Confused, he read on. The killing happened in March and, as Papa had described, the priest had been crucified on the floor of the altar. But nothing was said about a racist message scrawled in blood; indeed, the article quoted a department spokesman who said certain aspects of the murder were consistent with occult or voodoo ritual.

Fuck. Green frowned. Though police refused to release many details, the spokesman never even suggested race as a possible motivation. Reading several weeks' worth of increasingly brief stories, it became obvious the killers had never been found, though the occult angle continued to be played up heavily. Eventually, the story dropped out of the papers, presumably unsolved.

Green couldn't believe it. He felt a hollow sense of betrayal. This was light years away from Papa's account. In fact, the details seemed to only lend credence to the very thing—dark voodoo—the old man was trying to lead Green away from.

Still whirring through the reel, just because he was there, Green spied a small feature dated three months after Father Darbonne's death: *Church Bell Silent Since Priest's Murder.* Green read it and took a deep breath, thinking, *Well, at least Papa ain't lying about* that. The only other thing of importance was the reporter's reiteration that the murderer(s) had never been apprehended.

Green turned off the machine and sat for a minute. He couldn't believe the trouble Papa had gone to convince him the murder had been an act of racial intolerance—and to what end?

Eventually, he began his jog back to the Quarter. He felt hurt by the misdirection and, as he ran along, he decided to approach Papa, tell him he'd been interested in Father Chet and had gone to the library—and take it from there.

Then it hit him. *Misdirection.* Of *course* it was. Papa had gone to great length to steer him *away* from voodoo. The priest murder was damned dramatic—particularly if Papa altered the facts to fit his purposes, never figuring Green would actually check the story out.

"Jesus, I am certainly dense," Green panted, headed down Bourbon. "So those goddamned birds meant something after all." In conjunction with Marcus' suicide, Green felt he had to ask Papa about everything. Who else might know?

CHAPTER TWELVE

Coming into Jackson Square, Green spied Papa among the fortunetellers and mimes in his normal spot perpendicular to the cathedral. Oddly, Papa was drinking a Cafe Pontalba Bloody Mary, instantly recognizable by the distinctly logo'd go-cup. It was a bit early in the day for Papa, who was sitting under his umbrella facing the statue of Andrew Jackson. A virgin square of sketch paper was fastened to his easel, and leaning against the wrought iron fence were portraits of Papa's bread-and-butter art: *People* magazine weasels like the *Sex in the City* babes or Brad Pitt or old standards like Elvis or John Travolta in *Staying Alive*. A flutter of wind blew one corner of paper from the easel, but Papa seemed oblivious.

Now that he was here, Green wasn't sure how to proceed. He'd never actually been *angry* with Papa before. In fact, just seeing the old man, he was more confused than anything else. Finally, he just acted normal.

"Got any pictures of Al Hirt, Mistah?" Green asked in a disguised baritone.

Papa started, turned, then smiled. "Say, Greenie, how you doin', boy? You done give me a turn."

"Didn't mean to, sir," He tried to hide his shock at how old and washed-out Papa looked.

"Naw, just thinkin' about old times," Papa said, stretching out a hand which Green shook. It felt bird-like in its frailty. Still, the old guy sounded okay.

"How's biz? Selling any art?"

Papa shrugged. "Not bad. Gotta get more current. Need some of those—what do you call them?—pop culture people."

Green decided to start slowly by mentioning Cray's discovery of goofer dust.

"Say, Papa, I was talking to my pal Crayton, the guy at the Voodoo Shoppe. He was talking about something called goofer dust."

Papa stared at Green incredulously. "*Goofer* dust?! What the hell you doin' now, Green? I thought we cleared up that voodoo stuff." He took a big drink of his Bloody Mary and, for a lightning-flash instant, Green thought he'd really screwed up. Papa's eyes seemed to sag with an almost whipped sense of capitulation.

"Papa! Are you okay?"

Papa clenched his eyes shut—then, to Green's relief, laughed. "I'm okay, boy. Just ain't one of my golden days." He opened his eyes. "Hell to get old, boy. Hell to get old." The go-cup shook in his hand. It was the first time Green remembered Papa's hands shaking ever.

Green was desperately sorry he'd brought up the goofer dust. "I'm sorry, Papa. I *know* what you told me about voodoo stuff, and, in fact..." Green hesitated. Now was the time to talk about what he'd found in the *Times-Picayune* files. Or about Marcus and the trocar. Still, Papa was just not looking great. Finally, he said, "Well, Crayton says..." Concerned, he stopped to study Papa, who smiled tiredly.

"Go ahead, boy. I'm okay. And I know what you're fixing to ask. Does goofer dust work?"

Green gaped. "How'd you know?"

Papa reached out and patted Green on the arm. "'Cause goofer dust does many things. Supposedly. But yeah, it'll help you get your girl back. Jana done broke up with you, and your buddy is trying to help."

Green nodded. "Right."

"You don't need goofer dust, Green. You're young and strong. New Orleans got twelve-billion beautiful women."

Green wanted to reassure him. "I wasn't going to use it anyway, Papa. Cray just read about it at work. I don't want him getting into shit he shouldn't get into—and certainly not on my account."

Papa pulled a handkerchief from his back pocket, daubed his forehead, then squinted up at Green. "You read the papers, follow the local news?"

Green shrugged, unsure where this was going. "I guess."

"Hear about 'em executing Prospero Godchaux down to Angola Monday night?"

"Sure," Green said. "Very sad." Everyone in Louisiana knew about the Godchaux case. Prospero Godchaux had been a promising rhythm & blues pianist, a contemporary and friend of Professor Longhair and James Booker. The story was that a white policeman claimed the musician was driving erratically and had pulled over Prospero Godchaux on Airline Highway. The cop searched the car, found a baggie of marijuana, and arrested Godchaux.

Prospero made bail in spite of two prior felony convictions and, four days later, astonishingly, the charges were upgraded to possession with intent to traffic. Prospero was looking at life without parole in Angola. The next evening, the arresting officer was shot in the face and killed as he got out of his car at his apartment complex. Prospero was arrested an hour later in a bar less than a mile from the homicide, and a witness in the complex parking lot picked him out of a line-up.

Despite the absence of a weapon, Godchaux was convicted and sentenced to death. The case caused a huge racial rift in the community, enraged the New Orleans music scene and, over the years, as appeal after appeal failed, ended up thoroughly demoralizing Prospero Godchaux. Eventually, he fired his attorneys, refused to see his old friends, sent back the monies from the countless benefits performed on his behalf, and begged to die.

Monday night, Prospero had gotten his wish.

Papa was saying, in a voice taught with emotion, "Prospero was a friend."

"Jeez, Papa, I'm sorry," Green said. No wonder Papa looked bad. No wonder he'd decided on a cocktail.

Papa nodded. "Thanks, Greenie. We weren't close or nothing. But I knew him. We did a few tours together; shared a gig or two around town. I wasn't in his league..."

He paused. "When he was on death row, I tried to help him for the longest time. He finally sent us letters saying he didn't wanna fuck with it no more, and to stop coming to see him or trying to contact him. Said he wouldn't answer or speak with us."

Papa drained the last of his drink and carefully set his empty cup on the ground. A pigeon landed about four feet away, eyeing it with a wizened eye. Staring at the bird, Papa said, "Didn't you once tell me you wanted to go to a real, old-time N'Awlins jazz funeral?"

Green said, "Sure. I mean, there's a lot of history in those things. But don't you have to be in one of the benevolent societies or social clubs?" A student of New Orleans history, Green knew that such organizations had cropped up starting after the Civil War, when it was impossible for blacks to get insurance. They joined neighborhood clubs which not only took care of their own, they gave birth to the whole parade tradition and served as a conduit that allowed brass bands to serve significant roles in the creation of jazz.

Papa shook his head. "Don't have to be a member to second-line. And anymore, not if you're with someone *in* the secret society."

"Who's funeral are we going to?"

Papa raised his eyebrows in mild exasperation. "Why, Prospero Godchaux's, of course. That is, if you still want to go."

It took Green about a millionth of a second to decide that All Things Voodoo could wait till another day. "Absolutely I want to go." Then, because he didn't want to appear like a selfish jerk attracted solely to the celebrity of the affair, he added, "I'd be honored, Papa. I mean it. *Dauphine Street* is one of my favorite albums," he said, alluding to one of Godchaux's releases.

Papa smiled faintly. "I know you'd do it in the right spirit, Greenie. I wouldn't ask if I didn't know that."

Green swallowed, gratified by the old man's confidence.

"Now, it's today, you know. You clear with that?" Papa asked.

"Absolutely. I've got the day off. I've got clean, appropriate clothes." He knew he sounded like an eager Cub Scout, but he couldn't help it.

This time Papa actually laughed. "All right, Greenie. All right." He thought for a moment. "Tell you what. I've got to go to a private viewing over to the funeral home, so...what say you meet me on the neutral ground in front of Buffa's. One-thirty okay?"

"You tell me."

"I'll see you then."

"Yessir." For a moment, the image of a private funeral home viewing caused visions of dead birds and empty eye sockets, or of a suicidal mortician and mystery drumbeats, to bubble in Green's mind, but he shrugged them off. He took a deep breath, saluted Papa, and turned to blast through his errands so he'd have time to iron a shirt.

"Green?"

He turned back. "Yes, Papa?"

"This friend of yours. Cray?

"Yessir?"

"He ain't messed up in this, is he? Y'all didn't make any goofer dust, did you?"

Now was the time to describe Marcus and ask about St. Lydwine. But the funeral... Green said, "No, sir. We were just talking. It was just something he read about because he's, well, he's just a cashier in a voodoo store."

Papa nodded, pondering a moment. To Green's surprise, he started chuckling. "Goofer dust," he said. "Lord God, if that's all we had to worry about..."

CHAPTER THIRTEEN

Papa was standing on the neutral ground across from Buffa's under a huge oak tree whose roots had chewed through the curb. He'd changed into a shapeless but clean black suit, and Green suspected it was the only one he owned. Which made him one-up on Green, who was wearing khakis, a dress shirt, and a rep tie—all he had.

He asked, "How was the viewing?"

Papa shrugged as they walked across Esplanade. "He looked pretty good actually. Older, of course. Lord, much older and smaller than I remembered. 'Course, he'd been in prison too. But at least he wasn't all tarted up."

Papa thought a moment. "Had his hands folded up on his chest." He looked meaningfully at Green. "You know about the ring?"

Green smiled. "Absolutely."

Anybody who knew anything about New Orleans music knew about Prospero Godchaux's ring. A star-shaped monstrosity with a gaudy heap of tiny emeralds, rubies, and diamonds, Prospero's ring was perhaps his most famous affectation. During insanely tempo'd scales and boogie figures, he'd grin hugely and hold his ring hand up to the crowd, middle finger extended in a timeless gesture made somehow playful in the Godchauxian context, the singular piece of jewelry sparkling with a dozen white-hot pinpoint fires in the spotlight...

"He was wearing the ring?" Green asked.

Papa nodded happily. "He was wearing the ring."

With that bit of buoyant information, they strolled in companionable silence toward Tom's Bar. It was a weather-punished tarpaper box at the corner of Burgundy and Touro, a largely poor residential section as yet untouched by the renaissance closer to the river. An ancient Jax beer sign, spelling out TOM'S below the logo, jutted perpendicularly from an old metal pole next to the building. Across the street was a coin laundry, but the rest of the block was stuffed with small shotgun shacks and cheap frame houses in varying states of disrepair.

A few crews from local television and radio news affiliates were clumped together on the periphery of the corner, scoring footage from an overflow crowd of mourners milling out from the screen door: mostly older black folks dressed in their church finery with a few recognizable younger white artist- and musician-types, all talking in low voices and clutching cans of Dixie beer.

Green had speculated that, given Prospero's status as a minor R&B legend, the crowd could number maybe a thousand. There was nowhere near that many. *Well, the guy was a convicted cop killer.*

"Not as many folks as I'd expected," Papa muttered, eerily echoing Green's thoughts. He surveyed the crowd, then said, "C'mon, boy, let's get us a cold one." He took Green gently by the arm and led his glaringly white face into the throng.

Tom's had been Prospero's hangout just like, in his later years, James Booker worked the Maple Leaf. Prospero had lived in an apartment nearby, drank at Tom's daily and, on Wednesday nights, sat at the dilapidated piano in the corner and let it flow. *Live Cool in the Marigny* had been recorded at Tom's on a cheap cassette recorder through the beer-stained house mixing board, but it was another of Green's favorites.

Age-old traces of smoke, sour beer, and the sweat of blue-collar labor seemed to have sandblasted onto the walls. Mahalia Jackson was on the house stereo. An older waitress, tears running down her face, broke into a smile at something a customer said as they embraced. The mood was sad, but oddly cheerful too, and Green could tell this was a close-knit crowd and Prospero had been much loved.

He figured Prospero's passing was viewed by this group of working-class New Orleans blacks as the sort of occupational death by misadventure that was an inherent possibility simply by societal definition: by virtue of having been born Negro in the South in the forties or fifties—hell, in the *nineties*, for that matter—meant you were subject to the whims of Southern justice.

Papa led him through the crowd, shouting hellos at folks. Tall stools lined one wall opposite a plywood bar running the entire length of the room. That left just enough space down the center for one row of four-top tables. At the far end was a pinball machine, and a few of the tables had been pushed together so a small buffet of lunchmeat, cheese, and bread could be spread out on top. A massive, dented pot of gumbo simmered next to the cold cuts.

A spotlight focused on the piano, across which was a spray of sunflowers. A framed booking agency glossy of Prospero, smiling with sleepy-lidded seduction, was perched in front.

For an hour, Papa circled the bar and introduced Green to perhaps a dozen people. Though Green felt an initial onslaught of anxiety at being one of the few white people in the room, everyone treated him like kinfolk. He supposed that, not only was Papa extremely respected, but also a new face, white or otherwise, represented a great excuse to tell stories about Prospero. By the time the hearse pulled up, Green felt at home and as though he'd known the man.

They gathered outside the bar and, at some invisible signal, the Creole Wizards Brass Band, dressed in navy and gold uniforms, congregated behind the hearse and began an exquisite take of "What a Friend We Have in Jesus." The sun sparkled off the horns, and the rich sounds of the brass pounded like a big heartbeat in the thick air.

The walnut casket filled the back window of the hearse, and red and white roses layered the coffin like icing on a Valentine's Day cake. The band began to follow in a syncopated march, somber but funky. The second-liners fell in, including a staggering array of famous New Orleanian musical luminaries.

Several mourners were carrying handkerchiefs and parasols adorned with black crepe paper and someone distributed a variety of percussion instruments and beer. Green, armed with a tambourine and a Dixie, fell into a self-conscious shuffle.

Two tiny women in black were directly in front of Papa and Green—they must've been eighty—and wielded their closed umbrellas like conductors' batons, singing in glorious, full-gospel voices. There was a remarkably mellow and benevolent vibe to the whole parade, and Green supposed that was the whole splendid idea.

CHAPTER FOURTEEN

As the hearse parked just inside the gates of the River of Life Cemetery and they waited for the pallbearers to carry Prospero's casket to the gravesite, Green was astounded by the pastoral beauty. The high, fragmenting walls of patched mortar and cement pretty much hid the view from the street.

Only in New Orleans, where they called them the "Cities of the Dead," are cemeteries considered an architectural art form.

For one thing, all the burials are above ground. New Orleans is below sea level and, for years, any graves that were dug filled with water. A heavy rain resulted in a river of corpses coursing through the streets. Cities of the Dead, then, sprang up by necessity, particularly after a yellow fever epidemic in 1788 littered the city with cadavers.

The cemeteries were beautiful in a haunting way, and the River of Life was no exception. Tombs ranged from moss-caked vaults of crumbling brick and mortar to elaborate marble shrines and statuary. There were *faux* cathedrals, a Tara or two, museums, even a Taj Mahal replica...

And, like the actual city they mirrored, there were "poorer" districts: clusters of high-rise mausoleums or small tombs with whitewashed marble doors, lined up in rows with cinder pathways crisscrossing like neighborhood streets.

The funeral procession followed the casket and stopped in front of a small crypt almost all the way across the cemetery. There was a rustling as everyone got settled. Then a preacher started a prayer and Green bowed his head.

Then a swaggering, bucktoothed woman stepped up by the casket and cleared her throat. Green recognized City Councilwoman Sharonda Davis, a radical activist and staunch police reform advocate.

Papa nudged Green. "Uh oh," he whispered. "That woman'll talk all day and turn this into a political rally. Let's take a break. I wanna show you something anyhow." Papa discreetly peeled off from the periphery and crept down a path. Green followed him around a curve and behind a granite statue of St. Francis. Only then could he see that the cemetery was L-shaped, and that a line of four large oak trees hid the smaller wing from the entrance.

They walked about thirty yards before Papa paused. There, tucked in the near corner, the size of a backyard tool shed, was a crypt of chipped, whitewashed bricks built to resemble a country chapel. The structure sat at a drunken angle where one side of its cement slab had sunk into the earth.

On top was a wooden belfry with a cracked steeple pointing crookedly at the sky like an arthritic finger. The frame of the bell works was draped with cobwebs, and the old iron bell was orange with rust. A marble tablet sealed over the door bore a weathered, carved inscription obscured by time and the elements.

Papa tamped some tobacco into his pipe and lit it. He exhaled smoke and stared at the bell tower. Then, casually as commenting on the weather, he said, "Once, in another cemetery, when I was much younger, and thought I needed me some goofer dust, why, I climbed into a tower just like that one, under an October moon. And I got me some bell grease."

Papa smiled faintly, his eyes hidden behind a pair of dime-store sunglasses. "'Of course, I don't figure anyone's greased this one in a while. Anyhow"—he shrugged—"it ain't the goofer dust, it's he who makes it..."

Green felt prickly. A collective chuckle washed over from the funeral, and Papa looked over and nodded as if he knew what they were remembering. Green knew this was the time to broach the subjects he'd wanted to talk about. Instinctively, he started with Marcus' suicide rather than the St. Lydwine lie. He blurted it out in a few sentences as Papa listened, occasionally sighing.

When Green finished, Papa shook his head. "Suicide and drums, huh?" He paused, took a sip of beer reflectively. "Okay, bear with me," he finally said. He pointed at the tomb with the bell tower. "At one time, a Catholic priest was buried in this chapel. Name was Darbonne."

Darbonne?! Green started. "But isn't that...?!"

Papa nodded, somberly. "That's right, boy. Father Chet was the priest at St. Lydwine's, the one who was murdered on his own altar. He was buried here, in that chapel, till somebody stole his body three months later. Sexton found it in another part of the cemetery." He gestured at an unkempt corner overrun with vines. "That's when they had him re-interred at the church. So they couldn't get at him anymore."

Papa took a deep breath. "Greenie, forgive me, boy, but I lied about the killing of Father Chet."

Green, open-mouthed at this unexpected revelation, decided not to mention his library research—at least for the moment—and asked, "What are you saying? He *was* killed, right?"

"I'm sorry I lied to you. A man don't do that to his friends."

"I don't understand—"

"It was a ritual murder, Greenie. May *have* been voodoo. Probably was. I don't know who done it," Papa said, "and that's the truth." He waved his pipe helplessly. "I only lied because I didn't want you boys to get *more* interested in voodoo. The idea was to turn you *away* from it. I don't know"—he shrugged wearily—"I just figured if it sounded, well, *exotic* or whatever, you and Cray might get even more curious. And I thought to show you the bloodstains, and then give it a real-world explanation... I'm sorry, Green. I was wrong."

Green looked into Papa's sunglasses. "Apology accepted. I see—I *guess* I understand—what you were trying to do. But why the big production? I mean, wouldn't it have been easier just to blow it all off while we were in Lafitte's?"

"Probably." He sighed. "But maybe y'all would just keep digging around too. And you did. Went back to that funeral home—and look what happened. So my plan didn't work."

"But what *did* happen? Why did he commit suicide? What exactly did we see? Was it connected to the first time Crayton went there? And for that matter, is it the same stuff that happened with Father Darbonne?" Green pointed at the chapelesque tomb. He felt a slight hysteria. "Here we are, taking a casual walk through a cemetery, in the middle of a funeral, and you're telling me you used to make goofer dust." He wiped sweat off his forehead. "And that the body of Father Chet, who was murdered by persons unknown, was torn out of its coffin."

Green actually laughed. "Hey, look, I've always known there was voodoo. I mean, this is New Orleans. But has this shit been going on all along? And we just don't see it? And—" Green knew his voice was rising and he forced himself to quiet down. He actually spun in a small circle, stopping to face Papa once more. "*Who* wanted the priest's body? And why?"

Papa sighed wearily, as though he'd opened an irrevocable can of worms and was forced to play it out. He gestured again at the far corner. "Rumor was, this was a popular spot for certain voodoo ceremonies. Folks conducting rituals to Baron Samedi. Wouldn't do to have no Catholic priest buried here."

"Baron *who*?"

Papa knocked his pipe against the wall of a crypt, then poked it in his shirt pocket. "Baron Samedi is the Lord of the Cemetery." He pulled two cans of Dixie from his jacket and offered one to Green.

Green nodded and felt an odd sort of resignation take over, as if it was now his lot to sit around in graveyards discussing voodoo gods of the dead on a regular basis. He took the beer, snapped it open, and helped himself to a well-deserved swig.

From Prospero's grave, Aaron Neville's voice could be heard singing "Amazing Grace." They listened for a moment, but Green was hooked by what Papa was saying and had to know more. "So, first things first: Did Cray walk into some Baron Samedi thing? What will have happened to that body?"

Papa sounded weary. "I don't know, Greenie. I got out of it before I learned anything about those rituals."

Green froze. *Got* out *of it?!* So Papa had not only been involved in voodoo at some point, he'd actually dabbled in the dark shit! He whispered, "What happened to Father Chet's body?"

Papa looked up at strips of dead white clouds hunkered tiredly in the pale sky. "They found it on a grave," he said tonelessly. "Over there." He pointed to the same corner.

Green stared in horror. "Good God. So..." He considered his words. "I guess you're saying, maybe, you were pretty heavily into this thing at one time." Strangely, Green didn't feel frightened or repelled by the possibility that Papa had dabbled in grave robbing or corpse desecration. For one thing, it seemed too distant—as though Papa as a young man was a different person than the one standing before Green now.

Papa smiled briefly, humorlessly, and pulled at his own beer. "Yeah, I was into it. But not enough to steal the corpse of the body of the priest at my own church. What happened to Father Chet happened a long time after I'd been outta the voodoo." He scratched the back of his neck, then said, "Come over here and look at this."

He led Green into the far corner, where he said the sexton found the father's body. Papa pointed at two towering marble angels gazing down from either side at a modest, flat-topped brick crypt slightly taller than Green.

"In voodoo," Papa said, "women are as powerful as men. More so. They call 'em Reverend Mothers or mambos. Marie Laveau was the most famous ever. Right?"

Green nodded slowly, still reeling from Papa's series of bomb-drops.

"But there are dozens of 'em," Papa continued, "even today. Some of them fine people. Saints. Others ain't so fine. They get caught up in the power; get greedy. They get seduced by Evil. Capital 'E.' Sounds corny. It's not."

It was clear Papa had been afraid that Cray—and, by extension, Green—might have gotten somehow involved or vulnerable by stumbling into the rite in the funeral home, and then later by being there for Marcus' death. Now, Green figured, Papa thought the *truth* would serve as a warning. It was damned effective. Robbing graves was pretty out-there, but hell, who knew what high school kids were doing right now because they thought it would please Marilyn Manson?

"Power and evil," Green mused. "No disrespect, sir," he went on slowly, "but couldn't you say the same stuff about politicians? Seduced by power and evil, I mean? The Vietnam War."

Papa chuckled. "Ain't that right? But let's look over here a minute." He led Green off the path, onto the gravesite itself, next to the two statues. Up close, the carved faces of the two angels showed no signs of the compassion and comfort one expected from graveyard statuary.

Instead, the visages, flawlessly crafted, were grotesque. They reminded Green of gargoyles. They were human enough, but something was horribly wrong. One face was laughing, yet the eyes were livid in absolute ferocity. The other was pathetic in defeat; a cringing, weeping mask. Green took an involuntary step back. "Jesus!" he breathed. "What the hell are they?!"

Papa leaned over and stared into the face of the laughing statue, as though studying it for secrets. "I knew a Reverend Mother once—doesn't make no difference what her name was now—she became seduced by this power we talkin' about. Just like them politicians you mentioned.

"Anyhow, she told me these statues right here"—he tapped the laughing angel on the nose—"they represent Cruelty and Despair."

Back over at the service for Prospero, the band started into "When the Saints Go Marching In."

Green asked hoarsely, "Who's buried here?"

Papa shrugged and pointed at the worn marble tablet over the front of the crypt. They could make out a few letters, but most of them were too faded. "This is New Orleans," Papa said. "Lotsa folks been buried here, I guess."

He was referring to the tradition that, a year and a day after interment, the remains of a body are swept to the back of the vault, the husk of the casket removed, and room is thus created for the next body. There's only so much space.

"Well," Green said, eyeing the angels, "this just isn't...*normal.*"

Papa took a deep breath. "We need to go. It don't make no difference who's buried here or who made these statues or what they're doing here.

"But the Reverend Mother that showed me this place, well, one night, not far from this spot, I saw her lay her hands across a dead baby gator an' bring it back to life."

Green wasn't sure he heard correctly. But beer roiled like warm grease in his gut, and he knew that, in fact, he'd heard just fine. Worse, in spite of Papa's earlier fibs, he believed every word—or, at least, that the old man himself believed it. And somehow that was just as bad.

Papa was breathing shallowly but was absolutely lucid. "I know it was dead," he continued, "'cause I killed him myself, over in Bayou St. John. Then I threw him in a red flannel bag and brought him over here." Papa removed his sunglasses and blinked his eyes shut, remembering. "Revered Mother dumped him out on this very grave and ran her hands down his cold belly, and he opened his yellow eyes and mewled like a kitten. Then he rolled over and slithered into the darkness."

Papa brought his face two inches from Green's nose. Green smelled traces of beer, liniment, and pipe tobacco—but he also smelled fear. When Papa spoke, his voice was a rasp. "I tell you what, boy. I never seen no politician do *that.*"

Second-lining back into the Marigny, Green had to remind himself to keep up with the dancers, whose parasols were now open and twirling in cyclonic fashion. The Creole Wizards were absolutely cooking, and the funeral had shifted to the celebratory. Papa Hipolyte seemed to have forgotten his eerie graveyard diatribe—maybe in the liberating sense of having gone to confession—and jacked into a stone groove during "Tailgate Ramble." Green, tired and partially drunk and more than a little freaked out by what he'd learned and the implied connection of everything they'd talked about, felt he was moving in slow motion.

The streets slid by and the Creole Wizards roared through "Clarinet Marmalade" and were into "Down by the Riverside." Someone skipped backward through the crowd, dispersing Dixies. Papa took two, spun around, and held out one to Green.

"Goddamn, for someone who always runnin' they ass off every day, you sure don't have much energy! You all right, boy?"

"Yeah, I'm fine," Green called, taking the beer. A black kid came off the porch of a yellow shotgun shack—he couldn't have been ten—and back-flipped down the street in time with the music.

Papa laughed at the kid's antics. "I wonder if he'd teach me to do that?"

At that point, Green had zero doubt the old man could pull it off. In fact, nothing he said or did would surprise him anymore. "Say, Papa?"

Papa looked at Green, his head bobbing in time to the music like a fishing cork. "Yeah?"

"What happened to the Reverend Mother? The one with the alligator?"

Papa actually slowed down to walk. He looked at the second-liners around him to see how many could hear him. Green leaned in.

"Greenie, she's been dead for years. And it sounds goofy, but Evil lives on, you know. You find out why that man killed himself, you'll find something Evil behind it."

Green nodded. *I figured as much. Evil with the capital "E."* The band turned onto Frenchmen.

"I been away from that stuff for years now," Papa said solemnly. "I'm Catholic now, and I'm serious about it."

"I know that."

Papa frowned, perhaps wondering how much to say. Finally, he spoke. "I still hear things." He pointed ahead. "In fact, you see that restaurant there? On the corner?"

Green looked up the street and saw a small, neatly painted teal cottage with an orange and yellow awning over a deck full crowded tables. An art-deco neon sign at the top of the French doors proclaimed GRIS-GRIS GUMBO. Green had heard of the place. It was new.

"Gris-Gris Gumbo?" Green asked. "What about it?"

"Well," Papa said, studying the restaurant as they marched toward it. "The Reverend Mother we were talking about? Her daughter owns that place."

Green took a sip of beer and studied the old man's face. Papa didn't look frightened, necessarily, but definitely wary. The band segued into "Indian Red" and the second-liners reached the near-boiling point of ecstasy, but it might as well have been happening blocks away, given the sense of intense isolation Green felt at that moment.

Green spoke. "And the daughter's carrying on the tradition?"

Papa took a deep breath. "Maybe. I just stay away and try not to worry about it. There's plenty of places to eat in New Orleans. You may have heard that." He smiled briefly. "No need to be coming over here."

Green lightly grabbed Papa's shoulder. It was taut with muscle. "Where do you hear this stuff?"

Papa smiled briefly. "Age ain't necessarily like the stereotypes, boy," he said, twisting Green's question. "You get to be my age, sometimes your hearing's a lot better than it was when you was young. Leastways, if you know what to listen for."

They drew even with Gris-Gris Gumbo and Green looked over at the restaurant deck. What he saw made him stop in his tracks, and straggling second-liners had to shift in their momentum to get around him.

Seated at a far table, engrossed in conversation and oblivious to the parade, were Crayton and Kay.

CHAPTER FIFTEEN

Several hours later, in a different graveyard, another sort of rite was taking place.

It was just past midnight, the flat-black sky speckled with stars, and a quarter-moon carved of ice hung at precisely the apex of its journey. To the west, over high mortar walls and silhouetted rows of banana trees bordering the cemetery, a wash of pale light quivered over the Central Business District.

There were no clouds, and it was extremely dark inside St. Roch's Cemetery. The pregnant air was pocked with the scent of quiescent water, clammy earth, old marble greasy with humidity, and a mélange of decaying vegetation. In front of one vault by the rear wall, flames from two torches capered in a hot breeze, casting fragmented shadows across the geometric mosaic of the nearby tombs.

The torches were positioned on either side of the entrance to the tomb of the Arcenet family, and the flickering light was just luminous enough for five figures to maneuver comfortably in the direct vicinity of the moderately sized walk-in structure. The mausoleum was whitewashed brick with a gabled roof atop which sat, at the very front, a squat marble cross. Draped upside down over the heavenward point of the cross, for tonight's purposes—for after all, St. Roch was the patron saint of dogs—was the carcass of a large black pit bull that had been torn open and drained; the beast's head, twisted at a skewed angle, was pointing at the ground.

Over the entrance, ARCENET was spelled out in carved letters that had worn almost smooth in service to almost four generations.

It had been exactly one voyage through the lunar cycle since Joshua Arcenet had been memorialized in a brief ceremony attended by perhaps a dozen mourners, only one of whom, Crayton Breaux, had any idea that the dead man's eyes had been removed. And Cray didn't know the procedure was part of one of the oldest and most central rituals of *Le Culte des Morts*—the Cult of Death. Tonight, the perpetrators of the deed had arrived in St. Roch's Cemetery to complete the rite.

It was the posthumous realization of Joshua Arcenet's worst nightmare; in the increasing and superstitious fear of old age and infirmity, he had implored his daughter to provide posthumous protection against just such black gris-gris. A rash of late-breaking and sinister graveyard disturbances in Orleans Parish, bearing tones of voodoo, had frightened the elder Arcenet.

But however well-intentioned his daughter's too-late ministrations were, the simple fact that they'd chosen Maddox and Sons Funeral Home, where Marcus had worked, had guaranteed that Joshua Arcenet's corpse was subject to being used in ritual. Joshua Arcenet could not have known this. With Janice's assurance that she would arrange for the proper ritual, he had died confident nothing bad could happen to his mortal remains.

He'd been wrong.

It took two men, clothed comfortably in black and wielding chisels, about five minutes to remove the seal on the Arcenet tomb. Two other men stood by, unconsciously moving in time to the languorous sounds of drumming that throbbed throughout the cemetery. There was an organic, pervasive force to the snaking beats, steady and reassuring, and they seemed to rise from the moist earth beneath them. That there were no drums to be seen, and no one around to play them, bothered the group not at all.

Meanwhile, a mambo called Maman Arielle oversaw other preparations with the sort of quiet scrutiny and economy of movement one would associate with a mountain climber. A handsome, large black woman with bright blue eyes, she wore a collarless scarlet jersey, a loose black skirt that hung to mid-calf, and her hair was tied in a black handkerchief. She was barefoot.

This was a familiar ritual for her; Baron Samedi, the god of the cemeteries, the doorman to the dead, so to speak, walked the streets of New Orleans at the bidding of the followers of *Le Culte*—and must be sustained. To that end, though none of her followers knew it, Maman Arielle herself was negotiating the tender space between the living and the spirit world in ways they never would have suspected—only because the Baron *allowed* her to do so. Which made tonight's ceremony doubly important...

The path in front of the vault was further lit by parallel rows of black votive candles, and at the four compass points around the plot sat bottles of rum spiced with the blood of the dog on the cross. Periodically, the bottles were passed around for communal drink.

Incense burned in low bowls and, where the path to the Arcenet tomb ran into the wider brick walkway bisecting the cemetery, Maman Arielle took a vial of grayish white powder and swiftly drew an intricate, swirling pattern flourished with crosses and arrows—a *vévé* symbol—which, once completed, pulsed faintly with thousands of blood-red pinpricks, as though someone had drizzled neon scarlet sparkle on top of the design. By daylight, the symbol would look only like cornmeal. It was, in fact, ground and consecrated human bone, the skeletons of murder victims.

Normally fashioned of ash or flour, the *vévés* communicated something else entirely when comprised of human bone. *Loas*, the group of divinities that interacted with the living, were solicited by the *vévés*, and Maman Arielle had a unique motivation for doing so, even within the closed ritual of *Le Culte*.

Finally, from a canvas shoulder bag, she extracted a series of plastic medicine bottles and, kneeling, set them carefully on the path. From each, she took tiny amounts of powders and herbs and, mumbling incantations, tossed them into the air, from which they settled onto the ground in front of the grave.

When finished, Maman Arielle looked at the four men, who now stood together in single file, still nodding in time to the soothing heartbeat of the unseen drums. Maman smiled faintly; with their easy rhythms, they looked for all the world like a well-choreographed street corner doo-wop group.

Of course, Marcus was missing. He'd killed himself. Or so the others here thought. After all, he'd driven an embalming instrument into his own brain. But they were also aware of Maman's powers and, to be sure, they had to be at least somewhat curious. And that was okay too. Uncertainty was not a bad thing sometimes, and in any case, she was pleased at how silently and obediently they were carrying on.

Now, she nodded once and gestured toward the inside of the burial vault. Without a word, they slipped inside and returned moments later carrying the coffin of Joshua Arcenet. The casket was laid out on the path; one of the men quickly snapped the hasp with a chisel and, with only a momentary hesitation, raised the lid. A small assortment of vermin skittered into the darkness, and one of the men uttered a guttural sound of disgust as he flipped a large beetle off his hand.

The smell was awful—a foul, saccharine reek like moldy marshmallows and crabs left too long in the summer sun—and took hold of the night. Had Arcenet been embalmed, the ripe confluence of decompositional gasses and biological decay would have, after four weeks, passed the peak of their olfactory powers.

With all the rotting organs intact, though, as well as the blood and bodily fluids, everything followed the prescription of gravity and pooled in a reeking stew at the body's lowest point; the corpse was a sodden, disfigured lump, caving in like a rain-filled Jack-o'-lantern well into November. Still, while the odor was almost suffocating, no one standing around the coffin seemed particularly bothered by it. They'd smelled such things before.

Then, as one of the men shone a tiny Maglite into the box, they glanced at one another in rapid assertions of surprise. Though Joshua Arcenet's head was now almost completely disfigured, resembling splotched, wet cookie dough more than anything human, it was still possible to tell they were looking at what had been someone's face.

But something was missing.

"The birds are gone," one of the men said in a tone of low urgency. They all looked immediately to Maman Arielle, standing at the foot of the coffin, to gauge her reaction to the fact that somebody had removed the dead crows from Arcenet's eye sockets. *This* would indeed make the men suspicious, Maman knew, because Marcus was the funeral home connection.

But she was already aware of what had happened. The Baron had told her. A young man named Crayton Breaux had taken them the day of the funeral. And though it slightly altered the ultimate meaning of the series of rituals, it would not affect why Maman Arielle was here tonight. That Marcus would be punished for his inattention to detail was something she'd had to set in motion inasmuch as it was unacceptable.

The removal of the baby crows had opened a world of power to Crayton Breaux—an outsider—even though he had little clue as to the opportunities. It was like someone buying an old painting at a yard sale because the frame was quaint, not realizing the picture was a lost Caravaggio. Had he simply left the birds where they were, Crayton Breaux would not have disturbed a procession already set in motion. Instead, he'd inserted himself into a chain of actions and reactions by his spontaneous decision at the funeral home.

Maman knew this, of course, and infused slight glimmerings into Crayton's being—piqued his subconscious curiosity, one might say—simply to see how he'd respond. It was possible someone might blunder into a situation like this and have no reaction whatsoever, rather like touching jumper cables to a completely dead battery.

This fellow with his gout of red hair, though, showed some spark. Not a lot, admittedly, but some. Maman even made a visit to Crayton Breaux at that ridiculous Voodoo Shoppe, tempting him with trifles like goofer dust and introducing him to a more powerful concept: The Hand of Glory. It remained to be seen if young Mr. Breaux had the internal and spiritual chemistry to recognize the possibilities of the *power* that festered like a fetus within himself.

There were, she thought, signs it might be happening. Just today, the young man had shown up at Maman's restaurant with a pretty young girl. Who could say whether he simply chose Gris-Gris Gumbo because he'd heard it served good food? All that mattered was that he'd shown up...

But Crayton Breaux and his attuned sensitivity were matters for another time, and so Maman Arielle quietly soothed the men gathered around the casket. They seemed nervous over the absence of the birds, and were no doubt wondering if this fact was connected to Marcus' suicide. Well, she wouldn't broach it. Let them wonder a bit...

Again, Maman Arielle permitted herself a small smile. In a certain context, it was intriguing to think how amusing these rites could be. In spite of, or perhaps because of, their dark purposes, they were stuffed with irony and enlightenment. When dealing with the spirits, there was always the element of chance. As with Crayton Breaux—*or* Marcus.

"We cannot worry about the birds," she said quietly, and her firm tone was sufficient to halt all rustlings of curiosity. "We have other duties as well." Again, she nodded, and a man called Henri, distinguishable only by his wire-rimmed glasses, withdrew a ceremonial knife. The invisible drums picked up in their intensity, as though attempting to speed the pace of the activity.

Working with the skill of an urban pathologist, Henri focused on another *vévé* symbol. It was the one he'd drawn on Joshua's chest, the one that had burned into Crayton Breaux's mind despite his shock over the corpse's horribly disfigured face.

At Henri's first incision, a far crueler stench than had already suffused the area rose from the body cavity—a choking, intense miasma like boiled blood and a sour pork loin—and this time the attendants had to fight not to pull away from the coffin. Maman, ever concerned, passed a bottle of the rum mixture among them.

"Be quick," she soothed, imploring Henri with her eyes.

He nodded and slipped on a pair of surgical gloves. As one of his compatriots held the flashlight over the yawning body cavity, Henri assiduously went about the task of removing the putrefied heart.

It took perhaps a minute and, with a murmur of satisfaction and a final tug, he held the muscle up in the palm of one hand. After weeks in the grave, Joshua Arcenet's once-beating heart looked only like a shriveled, raw oyster someone had dropped in gray mud.

Rife with bacteria, it was like any other piece of rotten meat in that it was extremely poisonous—a fact that didn't bother Maman Arielle in the least. By this point, she was beyond such earthly concerns.

It was with the fluid economy of one who must negotiate a mildly unpleasant but necessary task that Maman Arielle plucked the heart from Henri's hand and ate it.

As she swallowed, the drums suddenly stopped and, in the paradoxically harsh silence, across the length and breadth of the cemetery, fresh memorial flowers, recently placed by mourners on new graves, turned black and curled unto themselves. A shard of blue lightning crackled, spinning across the sky. The crisp scent of burning copper mingled with the smell of decay, and even the men around the coffin started and gaped, wide-eyed, as Maman Arielle began to laugh.

On top of the Arcenet vault, the carcass of the pit bull twitched. Had an outsider witnessed this last phenomenon, he would no doubt have rationalized it by postulating that the lightning's electricity had somehow triggered the movement of the dead animal. Which might have been believable—at least until the dog slowly opened two lifeless yellow eyes and began to howl.

PART TWO

CHAPTER SIXTEEN

Six weeks later

Crayton Breaux was wondering what the hell was wrong with him. He was laying in the sweaty gloom of his bedroom, staring at the ceiling by the flickering light of a wasted candle, and next to him Kay LeMenthe was breathing deeply in post-coital slumber.

If you'd told Cray at J.C.'s, when he first saw Kay and thought she was the most ravishing creature currently breathing in the solar system, that by October he'd be sleeping with her, he would've asked you what chemicals you were huffing.

But that wasn't the weird part. If you'd told him he'd be sleeping with Kay and wanted *out* of the situation, well, *that* was insane. Yet here he was, only an hour or so after spirited sex with that exact woman—and he wished he was somewhere else.

Cray turned his head and looked at Kay in the sputtering glow. She was on her back with the sheet drawn up between her thighs and just across her stomach. One bare, sculpted leg angled over the edge of the double bed, and she'd thrown an arm across her forehead. Her wondrous breasts rose and fell like waves with her breathing.

On their first lunch date together, when Kay told him to choose any place he wanted to eat, he'd remembered a matchbook left on the counter by the woman who had dropped off the goofer dust sample. Gris-Gris Gumbo, the place on the matchbook was called.

It was as magical as the name implied. He and Kay lingered over jambalaya as the noon crowd thinned out, and they'd even seen a real jazz funeral bopping down Frenchmen Street.

By then, Crayton figured out that, for whatever reasons, Kay liked him. The next time it would be a real date, not a debt paid. He just had to ask her.

Green, Donny, and the H-Man uniformly advised Cray to go for it. J.C.'s entourage of women was an established fact, and one more or less wasn't going to make much difference.

Crayton agonized for days, and actually thought about bringing a Rose of Jericho home from the Voodoo Shoppe. He'd been burning a pink Success in Romance candle, which seemed sort of stupid, though he was surprised at the low-key confidence it inspired. But the Rose of Jericho was expensive and, besides, it seemed to offer the same romantic promise of the candle.

Then he had another idea, and he realized it had been simmering in his brain all along. So, a few days after that inaugural luncheon with Kay, when J.C. asked him and Green, Huey, and Donny over for an evening of poker, cigars, and whiskey, Cray decided it couldn't hurt to take along the vial of goofer dust from the Voodoo Shoppe.

It'd been easy enough to sprinkle some of the powder around J.C.'s bed. Cray waited until the guest bathroom was occupied, then asked J.C. if he could use the facilities in the master bedroom. Once there, he'd applied a light, indiscriminate dusting around the periphery of the huge bed. The room was a mess and the carpet a lush gray flecked with cigarette ash and littered with old newspapers. He was certain J.C. would never notice.

To be honest, Cray felt like an imbecile with the dime-store voodoo shit. First he was curing headaches, then he was burning candles and sprinkling goofer dust. What could it hurt?

Besides, when you thought about Marcus—which he still did, nightly—there was a lot weirder shit going on than goofer dust. But that wasn't all. A few weeks ago, he'd read in the *Times-Picayune* about a disinterred body found in St. Roch's Cemetery. The paper didn't describe the mischief, but identified the remains as Joshua Arcenet. Now *that* was a name Crayton would never forget. He felt bad for the Arcenets, but he'd also been cringing through work, waiting on word from the old man's daughter—or maybe her lawyers.

Cray rubbed his eyes and wished he could go to sleep. But there was too much coursing through his brain. There was also the stuff Green told him about the River of Life Cemetery, with the Cruelty and Despair angels and Papa's story about the back-from-the-dead alligator. Jeez, at times, Cray thought he didn't *want* to know any more...

Sprinkling goofer dust was one thing, but grave-robbing and the Hand of Glory the voodoo woman showed him, well, it was all good *Creepy* magazine stuff, but real-life application in your very neighborhood... Cray shivered despite the heat of his bedroom. Kay suddenly shifted onto her side and a nipple brushed against Crayton's shoulder, causing a trace shock of excitement to course through him.

Well, by God, for whatever reasons, here he was with Kay. Maybe the goofer dust had worked, and maybe it hadn't.

Maybe it'd all been J.C. Kay might not be here right now if J.C. hadn't called out of the blue a few days after Cray and Kay had lunch together—*before* the goofer dust deployment, gris-gris fans—with a most astounding offer.

"Cajun Red," J.C. drawled over the phone, "I got two seats I ain't usin' for the Saints/Bengals game Monday night. You want 'em?"

Crayton was flabbergasted. "Jeez, J.C., that'd be terrific. But...you don't want to go to the game?"

J.C. laughed. "Oh, I'll be there. It's just that Uncle Wallace done asked about twenty asshole politicos up to his private box an' he wants me there to distribute liquor an' such. It's an election year, after all, an' he's trying to make the jump to the U.S. House of Representatives.

"He don't ask much, so when he says *hop* I'm the fuckin' Easter rabbit. As such, my tickets are available."

"Damn," Crayton said, "Saints tickets'd be pretty great."

"An' don't blow these babies on Green or Donny or Huey," J.C. warned. "Them assholes done seen enough games, and Donny'd just take drunk an' embarrass your ass." J.C. paused. "Hey, why doncha ask Kay?"

Crayton was flabbergasted. "Kay?! Are you serious? I thought you were, like, *dating* Kay."

"Naw, she's just a good buddy. We known each other for years. She's a lotta fun."

Cray couldn't tell if there was a touch of royal benevolence in J.C.'s suggestion, as though he was tossing a faithful hound a filet mignon he thought was slightly overcooked. But he didn't really care either. "Thanks, J.C. This is pretty thoughtful of you."

"Don't mention it, son. Just have a large time."

Since then, Kay had spent the night five times. At first, Cray was rejuvenated through a sheer overdose of raw carnality. Which was good because, frankly, at just about the time they did it that first time, it was dawning on Cray that the only reason he was still interested in the relationship was because Kay was so damned good looking.

Otherwise, he'd sort of run out of things to say to her—and she wasn't exactly dazzling him with conversational jewels either. It wasn't that Kay wasn't smart; their interests and natural chemistry just didn't fit. Frankly, Crayton thought Kay would be ideally suited to Green. But how do you broach *that* with either of them?

Cray yawned and reached on the nightstand and took a swallow from the pre-sex bottle of Dixie he'd been drinking. He grimaced; the beer was flat and warm, and Cray supposed he ought to brush his teeth. But that would require getting out of bed, which would wake up Kay and she might want conversation. And he was too tired. He'd just have to go to sleep with lousy breath.

Now, sliding toward slumber, Cray reflected, in a thought that seemed to stretch out over a month, that at least Kay hadn't been bothered by migraines anymore. *That* was good...

Crayton was asleep. Moments later, the tiny remains of the Voodoo Shoppe candle flickering feebly on the nightstand burned out, and whatever magic it might have held dissipated in the stale night.

Tomorrow, Crayton, not wanting to throw it away for reasons he wouldn't fully understand, would tuck the waxy glass container behind some pillows on the third shelf of his closet, next to the shoe box in which he'd hidden the bodies of the baby birds he'd removed from the eye sockets of Joshua Arcenet.

CHAPTER SEVENTEEN

The next afternoon, Crayton and Green were watching the Saints/Jets game and sipping Abita beers at Lafitte's. The Saints were still unbeaten, and Cray and Green were as ecstatic as the rest of the city. They were seated at a table by one of the open-air French windows facing Bourbon. A breeze pushed in from the Mississippi, and through the windows crept hints of cinnamon and coffee, old fruit and puddles of warm rain. Crayton tossed a *Times-Picayune* on the table. A red bandana tied in seven knots, the points sticking into the sky, obscured his hair. The bandana gig, he explained to Green, was an obscure contrivance of Marie Laveau's he'd read about at work.

"I like it," Cray said. "It looks more interesting than the Axl Rose way, who, by the way, is the last white person I remember who actually wore a bandana in public."

"Hmm," Green said, studying the scarf. "I dunno. With those points sticking up, it looks more like one of those cardboard crowns from Burger King. Maybe you should try another color."

"It's got to be red for the magic to work."

"Magic, huh? And what is that exactly?"

Crayton shrugged. "I don't know. It's just...voodoo."

Green laughed. Crayton's slipshod approach to voodoo lore seemed to be based as much on fashion as anything of theoretical importance. More and more, Cray was obsessed with gris-gris accouterments. Personally, after Marcus' suicide and Papa's speech in the cemetery, Green had had all the fun he wanted digging into voodoo. But he had to admit there was a certain increased *awareness,* you might call it, or maybe a healthy respect for voodoo. At the same time, Cray's approach seemed to be to embrace the whole thing humorously.

"What if you inadvertently put a black magic spell on yourself?" Green asked.

Cray scratched his chin, where a sparse patch of whiskers had sprung up over the weekend. "Hadn't thought of that... Let me know if I turn into a lizard or something." He pulled the bandana points to ensure they were standing up properly.

As Green was returning from the bar with two fresh beers, the Saints quarterback threw an interception that was returned for a Jets touchdown. Crayton swore and, in contempt, hid his nose behind the *Times-Picayune.*

After a few minutes, during which Cray pointedly ignored the game, he spoke from behind a wall of newsprint. "Hey, did you hear Stream Forester died?"

Green didn't bother to turn away from the television set. "Who the hell is Stream Forester?"

"You know, that *wunderkind* actor. He was the star of that television show, er, *Tommy Perkins, Teen Homicide Cop.*"

That triggered an image for Green. "Oh, the surfer-guy-turned-thespian?"

"That's him."

"He *died*?"

"Yeah. The paper says he stumbled out of a Manhattan night club, saluted the bouncer, said—and I quote—'I'm going down, dude,' and collapsed. He was DOA at the same hospital where they took John Lennon..."

"Jeez, that's a drag," Green said. A rustle of excitement buzzed inside the bar as the Saints completed a long pass. "What was the cause of death? Drugs?"

Crayton lowered the newspaper enough for Green to see what an idiotic question he thought that was. "Stream's girlfriend told police they'd been up for three days shooting a mixture of animal tranquilizer, speed, and picante sauce."

Green smiled. "That might cause some problems."

A roar erupted as a Saints tailback broke two tackles and sprinted 20 yards for a touchdown. The whole Quarter exploded; you could hear revelers as far away as Decatur Street, and for a few minutes Green and Cray forgot all about the proclivity of the young and famous to ingest heart-exploding mixtures of drugs.

At halftime, though, the faint scent of a Lucky Dog cart caused Green and Cray to march a block up to Dumaine to buy a few of the iconic wieners. They stood on the curb, chewing happily, and Crayton swallowed and shook his head.

"What?" Green said, stifling an onion and mustard belch.

"I can't get over that idiot Stream Forrester."

Green shrugged. "Probably a dozen young people die of ODs a day in this city alone."

"But he was famous. That makes it luridly fascinating." He crumpled his hot dog wrapper and deposited it neatly in a trash container.

"I suppose so, but—"

"Hey!" Cray interrupted, laughing. "What if we had one of those, y'know, ah, dead pools?"

"A what?"

"A dead pool! Where we try to predict who's gonna die in the next year or whatever. We have a roster of draft picks and everyone throws in some cash and, after twelve months, we total up the carnage. So to speak."

"Seriously? A dead pool? That's sorta dark."

"But fun. Big fun, right? We could get J.C. and Don and H-Man. We'd be bigger than the NBA." Cray was clearly jazzed by his idea.

Green wasn't so sure. "I mean, it *does* sound kind of hilarious. But I'm not convinced we could talk the others into it. Particularly not J.C. He's a bit weird about death."

Cray looked at his watch and nodded his head back toward the bar. The second half kickoff was any moment. "Well, maybe not J.C. But ya never know. It can't hurt to ask."

Green shrugged and then he laughed too. "No, I suppose it don't hurt to ask."

CHAPTER EIGHTEEN

The draft for the inaugural season of what Donny dubbed the Vieux Carré Fantasy Death Society was held, appropriately enough, on Halloween day. Furthermore, in said spirit, when the H-Man suggested they stage the event in the old St. Louis Cemetery #1, across Rampart and Basin Streets from the Quarter, the idea was met with unanimous approval.

It was actually chilly and overcast that morning. Green trudged lakeward on Rue Conti in a denim jacket, carrying a bag of muffalettas from the Central Grocery, and the heady scent of the signature olive mix was almost like riding an olfactory magic carpet. Greatness. He was the newly elected commissioner of the VCFDS, and his first official duty was to supply draft day sustenance. His second official duty had been to order the rest of them to chip in and buy beer.

Green supposed he ought to feel a bit odd about the cemetery concept, given that the last time he'd been in one was with Papa Hipolyte, at Prospero's funeral. But the fact was, Green found the whole idea of a rotisserie *death* league so outrageous, so hysterical, that he kinda liked the idea of going back into a graveyard.

As for the River of Life experience, well, he'd only seen Papa once since, when he dropped by Pirate's Alley Gifts to say hello and that he hoped Green understood about the St. Lydwine thing. He'd simply wanted Green to know there *were* people who took voodoo to a truly bad level, and it was nothing to be trifled with.

Green told Papa he more than appreciated it, that indeed he'd learned as much about voodoo as he needed in this lifetime, thank you.

"You understand where I'm coming from then?" Papa said.

"Absolutely."

Papa smiled. "All right." He held up an index finger sagely. "So you're keeping Crayton on the straight and narrow then."

Green grinned back. "I won't let him join any voodoo cults on us, Papa."

The old man saluted as he headed out into the afternoon. A few days later, Papa called to say he was going out on a hastily arranged R&B package tour of the South, a sort of Prospero Godchaux memorial gig. It was a cool opportunity to play some nice clubs and pick up some cash.

Green shifted the sack from one arm to the other as he reached Rampart Street. Thinking of Papa, Green was glad the old man wasn't around so he didn't have to tell him about the Halloween party he was going to. Cray was invited to some voodoo-themed soiree over in the Marigny by his boss, Cosima, and asked Green to go along.

Why not? The Quarter was a zoo on Halloween, and it wasn't like he had a date. Cutting by the old St. Jude shrine and mortuary chapel, with its way-cool candle grotto, Green spotted the others standing by the cemetery wall, laughing and joking. He stopped in front of them and grandly intoned, "Gentlemen, let the games begin!"

In spite of the graveyard's location in the ominous shadows of I-10 and the Iberville projects—described by many prominent criminologists as one of the premiere murder training grounds in the free world—the charter death league members felt safe enough. There was a scattering of New Orleanians in the cemetery, cleaning family crypts for All Saints Day, when citizens all over the city would flock to the graveyards with thousands of chrysanthemums for loved ones' tombs.

They settled in a small area where five paths converged at a waist-high tomb shaped like the Astrodome; it would serve admirably as a dining table as well as a writing desk for Green, whose job it would be to record their draft picks.

The mood was festive as they broke out the po'boys. Huey was punning at top speed in a sport coat. J.C., already swilling Dixies, was wearing a *Wizard of Oz*-style witch hat. "Y'all eatin' with the Lord of the Dead!" he kept saying, and apparently his initial queasiness over the death league concept was dissipating in a wash of beer.

Crayton was removing olive slices from his sandwich and sailing them indiscriminately across the corpsescape like tiny green UFOs, and Donny sat wolfing his food on the steps of a tall crypt across one of the paths, sharing his space with a marble angel whose arm was poised to knock on the grave door like some heavenly bill collector. Green couldn't help but think of the Hatred and Fear statues.

Some twenty yards away was the grave of voodoo queen Marie Laveau. It was a set white slab consisting of three crypts and a holding vault and, even from a distance, they could see graffiti'd crosses etched in red brick dust, various gris-gris offerings, and the remnants of incense and burnt candles believers still placed at the perimeter of the grave.

While they ate, Green went over the rules: a ten-round draft; selections occurring in reverse order on successive rounds; and the only requirement of the draftees was a majority agreement that the selection was in fact a public figure or someone known to all in some larger-than-life capacity.

Scoring was simple: six points for a death, and a four-point bonus if the corpse happened to be under forty years old. Therefore, if the H-Man chose Robert Redford, John Madden, and Ross Perot, and they all died within the three hundred and sixty-five day season, he'd score eighteen points.

But, say J.C. had successfully chosen Edward Kennedy, Dick Cavett, and Drew Barrymore, he'd tally twenty-two points, with young Barrymore kicking in the bonus. As Donny observed, it was one thing to correctly predict that someone in their sixties or seventies would die; it became considerably more difficult with the youngsters.

With the sandwich wrappers placed in a trash bag and a fresh round of Dixies cracked, each franchisee handed over his twenty-five-dollar wager, which Green tucked into a bank bag. The pot would be sweetened over the course of the year, of course, by trades or by guys dropping picks and replacing them with newly inspired choices—all transactions at five dollars a pop. Next Halloween eve, Green would calculate the destruction and distribute the winnings: seventy-five percent to the first-place finisher, twenty percent to the runner-up, and five percent to Green for administrative fees...

It was time. In a prior drawing, it had been determined that J.C. had the first pick.

"Everybody ready?" Green asked, his Bic pen poised to record the ignominious first name.

"Hold on a second," Crayton said, slapping himself lightly on the forehead as though he'd forgotten something important. "I'll be right back." He pulled a small red flannel pouch out of the pocket of his windbreaker and trotted off through the tombs. His trellised hair bobbed like new fire.

"What's that kook doin' now?" J.C. muttered, fingering the brim of his hat.

Green shrugged, but he suddenly realized Cray was headed to Marie Laveau's crypt. They watched in silence as, sure enough, Crayton stopped and dusted off a spot at the base of her grave. Kneeling, his head bowed as though against a strong wind, he sat his pouch against the wall of the tomb. Then he stood up, dusted off his hands, and jogged back.

"Sorry." Cray smiled slyly. "Let's do it!"

Everyone looked at Cray. Even Green found the maneuver peculiar.

"What the hell were you doin' at that...that *witch's* grave?" J.C. demanded.

Cray laughed. "Witch? You're the one with the hat, dude."

J.C. glared. "That's Marie Laveau's grave, Red. You was over there with some gris-gris bullshit."

Cray held out his hands in supplication. "Hey, relax, guys, it was just a joke, okay?" He tried a laugh.

J.C. cut in. "You over there casting spells an' shit."

Cray looked at Green as though for support. "Like I said, I was just joking. Go look in the pouch if you want. It's empty. It was just a pre-draft psyche-job."

"Well, I don't find it amusing," J.C. said sourly. He addressed Green, Donny, and Huey. "First we start a fantasy death league, which is bad enough, then we gotta have the draft in a friggin' cemetery. An' now Voodoo Red takes some...*bag* over to Marie Laveau's grave, and he's gonna tell us he's joking around?!" J.C. spun to face Crayton. "Listen to me, pal, that stuff's nothing to fuck around with!"

Cray fixed J.C. with a harmless smile. "Like I said, J.C., there's nothing in the bag. Go check it out if you don't believe me."

"Dudes," Donny implored. "What are we arguing about? It's Halloween. It's a death league. And J.C., this is New Orleans. It's the goddamned *home* of voodoo!" He smiled broadly, all reason. "I think it's pretty funny."

Cray nodded gratefully at Donny. "Right. Hey, I work at a voodoo joint; I'm just playing around."

Green extended a new Dixie to J.C., who finally took it. "Jeez...all right...I'm sorry." He grinned weakly at Cray, then glanced around. "I guess ever since you fixed Kay's migraines, I've been thinking maybe there's something to the whole voodoo thing." He looked embarrassed. "There's strange shit in the world, right?"

"Hey," Crayton said as he and Green shared a quick, secret glance, "maybe she outgrew them. Look: anything I could do to help, I was glad to do. But it wasn't voodoo."

Huey crumpled a can loudly. "Excuse me! If anyone's interested, I actually have to work tonight."

J.C. exhaled. "It's been a long week and the election's coming up." He then broke into his cocky grin. "With that, then, I draft George McGovern!"

Laughter exploded then. H-Man was pissed. "McGovern's a sure-thing corpse!" he said. "I had him on my list!"

"Relax," Green soothed. "There are plenty just waiting to die."

It was Donny's turn then, and he opted for Dick Van Dyke. They were off.

The afternoon grew giddy in the sheer audacity of the project, lubricated with Dixie and punctuated by wild howls of disbelief at some of the selections. Most of the choices were predictable enough, but affected one or more of them on purely sentimental levels. No one, for example, wanted to see Paul Newman die. But later, when Huey chose him in round two, everyone had to agree he'd made a shrewd selection.

Only Crayton's picks defied logic. He started off with Sammy Gallagher.

"Sammy Gallagher?!" Green said incredulously. "He's thirty-two years old and in perfect health!"

"Who the hell is Sammy Gallagher?" H-Man demanded.

"He won the Ironman Triathlon in Hawaii the last four years," J.C. said, looking at Crayton strangely.

"You found out he's got AIDS, right?" Donny asked hopefully.

"Not that I'm aware of," Cray said. "My strategy as a franchise owner is to go for the youngsters and pile up the bonus points with fewer corpses." He smiled peacefully and reached in the ice-chest for a fresh beer.

"Hey, why not?" Green said admirably. "A few long shots and you're all set."

Cray grinned and, in an "aw shucks" gesture, pawed the path with his toe.

"*Long shots* is the operative phrase," Donny said aggressively. "I'm going for the guaranteed embalmees and, since it's my turn, I choose Rosalyn Carter."

There were good-natured groans of disgust, but they were all aware that people get old and hearts stop—no offense intended from the members of the Vieux Carré Fantasy Death Society. It was simply their humble and collective duty to correctly predict who the dead folks were going to be.

CHAPTER NINETEEN

By the time Crayton and Green arrived on foot in front of a walled fortress in the Faubourg Marigny that night, a cheddar moon hung low over Algiers and the afternoon's cloud bank had shredded into dark gray wisps inlaid against the navy-blue carpet of night.

The street was abuzz with Halloween activity. Clusters of tiny maskers darted like waterbugs from house to house, shouting with glee at each new treat while parental silhouettes stood guard on the *banquette* with flashlights.

"So, exactly whose party is this again?" Green asked. As per the instructions on Crayton's invitation, they were dressed casually; the only request had been that guests wear Mardi Gras carnival masks. Green's was an orange sparkle job that flourished into butterfly wings; Cray had opted for a more traditional, black Lone Ranger number.

"Actually, I'm not sure," Cray laughed, squinting, trying to read the invitation by the mellow glow of a streetlight down the block. "Insane, huh? All I know is that invitations arrived at the shop addressed to Cosima and me. She says it's a *patron* of the Voodoo Shoppe. Like it was the Medici family. But I don't think she actually *knows*, to tell you the truth."

Green shrugged. "Hey, with our popularity profile, I'd say we're damned lucky to *be* at a party."

They laughed and Cray rang a bell next to a scarred wooden gate. "Let's check it out," he said. "Who knows what evil lurks?"

After a minute, a tall black man in a white jersey and white jeans opened the gate. His mask was red satin, and he had a glass of white wine in one hand. He smiled hugely. "Happy Halloween! I'm Henri. Please come in!"

"Uhm, I'm Crayton and this is Green," Cray said, proffering his invitation. "I work with Cosima."

Henri pocketed the invitation without a glance, grinned, and said, "Right! Glad to know you guys." He led them through a small garden courtyard and inside what appeared to be a large, two-story Creole house. Directly inside the door was a brightly lit living area. Perhaps thirty people, black and white, were milling around with cocktail glasses. They appeared to be young professional types, though their masks made it difficult to tell with certainty. Conversation buzzed warmly over light jazz playing in the background, and it seemed to Cray he'd walked by mistake into some church social function.

The room was expensively furnished in red and gold, and over-stuffed white sofas and chairs fit snugly against bookshelves and tables of polished walnut.

"There are drinks and hors d'oeuvres in the kitchen," Henri said, pointing through an alcove. "Make yourselves at home." He ducked through a side door into a darkened hallway. The crowd continued chatting pleasantly.

Looking around, Green murmured, "This is a voodoo party?"

"I'm with you," Cray said. "Bore-ville." He nodded toward the alcove. "When in doubt, find the beer."

The kitchen was spotless in gray and white tile, with a variety of knives and cooking implements hanging over a massive butcher block in the center. People were gathered around a keg in the corner, and a black woman was carving cheese from a wheel next to a bowl stuffed with iced boiled prawns. A wet bar was set up on the counter by the sink.

As Crayton was triggering beer into Green's cup, a brassy woman's voice called out.

"Crayton, is that you, you space alien?"

They turned to see a skeletal woman in a yellow gown, beaming through a leopard-spotted mask. Cray said, "Cosima, we were beginning to wonder if we were in the wrong place. This is my friend, Green Hopkins."

Green said, "Hi, Cosima," and offered a hand, which Cosima clasped in both palms.

"Oh, Green," she said, "nice to finally meet you. Say, have you two been into the absinthe yet?"

"Absinthe?" Cray looked puzzled.

"*Real* absinthe? As in wormwood?" Green asked.

Cosima nodded enthusiastically. "Oh yes. Out in the courtyard."

Cray looked at Green. "The Green Fairy of lore?"

Green grinned. "Baudelaire, Rimbaud, Van Gogh—bastions of sanity."

Cray checked Cosima, beaming like a neon sign advertising eternal bliss. "Have you had any, Cosima? Is it real?"

She nodded sagely. "Oh my, yes. I think both of you should have a sample. We'll all need to heighten our sensibilities for the ceremony."

Cray and Green traded glances. "Whaddya think?" Cray asked.

Green thought a moment and laughed nervously. "Yeah, why not? Might as well. College was the last time I've done anything remotely hallucinogenic. We can at least check it out."

Suddenly a tall woman in a powder-blue outfit and matching mask grabbed Cosima, sputtering about someone whose spiritual awareness required immediate counsel. Cosima waved and Crayton and Green stepped into a deeply shadowed courtyard lit only by the sputtering flames from four tiki lamps. Bordered on all sides by two- or three-story dwellings, the brick red courtyard was about the size of a tennis court. In the dappling light, it was difficult to tell if the buildings were all part of the same structure—in which it was a considerable mansion, or separate, tenement-styled apartment buildings facing onto four different streets.

Around the circumference of the courtyard, banana and palm trees towered overhead, their autumn-cured leaves rustling dryly in the sudden breeze. At the far end was what appeared to be a small altar. A variety of dark objects were placed on or near it. They were shrouded with dark cloth. A few guests were gathered around a table in one corner, smoking cigarettes and performing some task involving a giant punch bowl.

Suddenly, a light came on in one of the windows on the second floor opposite where he and Green stood. Cray saw a large black woman staring down on them, perched on an interior window ledge like a Storyville hooker.

Cray stared. She bore a remarkable resemblance to the person who'd come into the Voodoo Shoppe with the goofer dust and the Hand of Glory, but she looked older than the lady in the shop. The backlighting made it hard to see.

"Who do you suppose that is?" Green asked.

Crayton hesitated. "I think I've seen her before, in the Voodoo Shoppe," he said. For obvious reasons, he hadn't told Green about spreading goofer dust around J.C.'s bed, or where he got it.

"Maybe this is her party," Green suggested. "If there's going to be some sort of voodoo ceremony, maybe she's the voodoo queen or whatever."

Cray shrugged. "Makes sense." They looked back up at the window, but already the light was off. Cray said, "That's peculiar." He tried to ignore the prickly sensation that had pulsed over him since they'd spied the woman. He couldn't shake the feeling he was *supposed* to see her. Intent on getting his mind off the subject, he turned to Green. "So, what about this absinthe?"

They walked over to the group clustered around the table, on which was arrayed expensive looking bottles with labels that read *Sauvage 1804*, notched spoons, napkins, and glasses filled with what appeared to be water. Cray thought the whole thing seemed rather sinister, but, flowing on the tide of the day's beer, piped up, "Hi, I'm Edgar Allan Poe, official absinthe taster." He pointed at Green. "This is my raven. Nevermore, my ass!"

Several chuckles arose from the crowd, and a man in a feathered mask said, "You're in the right spot," he said. "Can I help you get started?"

Green and Cray looked at each other, shrugged and nodded, then watched as the man, explaining as he went along, poured the liqueur over a perforated spoon full of sugar into the glasses. After the mixture clouded up, he grinned and nodded as the crowd around the table offered encouragement. Both took cautionary sips. Cray shivered; it tasted a bit like licorice and mint, with a heavy alcohol aftertaste.

"Whaddya think?" Green asked, swallowing with a faint grimace.

"Hmm," Cray said, holding up his glass against the wavering torchlight as though studying a vintage wine, "I guess we'll find out."

CHAPTER TWENTY

At some point, Green noticed, the wind blowing in from the river picked up and a new cloud cover swallowed the moon. A light, lush mist started to fall, looking like shredded silver in the flickering orange glow of the torches.

They stood around the absinthe table for a while, discussing with others the properties and histories of the liquor. Gradually, as more people came into the courtyard, Green and Cray moved off to one side, giggling and comparing notes as the Big High came on. Then Cray went back to the kitchen to refill their beer cups.

Green, who'd been tired and slightly skeptical on the walk over, was feeling much better. The absinthe seemed to be working in neon ways ordinary liquor couldn't replicate. He spied Cray heading back, laughing and talking to a short, thin blonde girl in an elaborate blue glitter mask.

"Hey, Green, this is Eliza Stewart," Cray chirped, handing Green his beer. "I just met her at the keg. Eliza, this is my friend Green Hopkins."

They shook hands and Cray explained that Eliza had recently moved to New Orleans after graduating from Georgetown University. She was a D.C. native who'd fallen in love with New Orleans after a visit to Jazz Fest.

"The town'll do that to you." Green smiled. It was hard to tell with the mask, of course, and in the dim light of the courtyard, but Eliza seemed a hottie. She was wearing wheat-colored jeans and a green and white checked fitted shirt. Her skin was pale, but Green could see big blue eyes behind the mask, and a small mouth and pouty lips set off her upturned nose. Her short brown hair was moussed back from a part in the middle and flipped under at the base of her neck. She wore three tiny hoop earrings in each ear.

"I love this city!" she said. "But then, I've only been here six weeks."

"Hell, I haven't been here much longer than that, and I'm running for mayor!" Cray said.

They laughed and Eliza told them she'd gotten an invitation to the party because she worked for the florist providing flowers. "Ordinarily I wouldn't dream of actually showing up; I don't know a soul here. But Henri was so nice when he was in the shop, and I was sorta lonely, and I thought, 'What the heck?' Plus, I wanted to see what the voodoo stuff was all about." She looked at Green. "So of course I meet Crayton and he *works* at Voodoo Land."

"The Voodoo Shoppe," Cray corrected, "and it has about as much to do with voodoo as a flower shop."

"So you're a florist?" Green asked Eliza.

"Well, I work for one at the moment. I needed a job when I got here and that's what was out there. My degree is in marketing and advertising though, and I'd like to catch on somewhere as a copywriter at some point."

"Cool," Cray said. "Green's a writer."

Eliza looked impressed. "You are?"

Green shot Crayton a look. "In a very small way." A massive chill ran down his spine, and he thought to ask Eliza, "Hey, have you, uhm, tried the absinthe?"

"Actually, no. I thought about it when Henri told me, but I didn't want to freak out since I don't know anybody. Did you guys do any of it?"

Green whistled. "Yeah, and it's starting to work big time."

Cray laughed. "I'd say you're right. It's a pretty nice rush." He held an arm out to Eliza. "Whattya say, ma'am, now that you know someone, would you like a small sample?"

She hesitated, then giggled. "You think it'll be okay? I've only smoked pot, like, five times."

"We'll take care of you," Cray said. "I promise. It's pretty mellow." And with that he led her over to the absinthe table.

Green smiled and watched as, this time, Cray prepared a glass. Green took a deep breath. His ears popped and he looked around the courtyard, realizing that several more torches had been ignited and the patio shimmered with the jumping light of flames spitting in the mist. He could hear a subtle, vaguely familiar rhythm like the hypnotic sound of distant cicadas on a childhood summer night.

It took Green a few minutes before he was even aware that the sound was drums—and even longer before he realized that the drums were *live*. He felt an instant of panic, flashing back to the drums and Marcus' suicide, but craned his neck and spied two tall congas at the far side of the crowd. Henri and another black man beat on the drums. They were leaning into their work and staring just over the heads of the rustling crowd; the other fellow was thick-set with eyes that looked like ink spots through the eyeholes of his mask. Green, shivering as a new wave of absinthe washed over him, felt reassured that he could see the source of the drums.

The evening, it seemed, was metamorphosing from a late fall cocktail party to a steamy, funky rite. And then Cray and Eliza were back. Cray pointed at the shrine: now undraped, it, too, was lit by torches. There was a large cauldron, suspended by triangulated iron rods over a small fire, and a shelf ran along the back of the altar with dozens of lit black candles. The quivering flames were protected from the elements by an overhanging shelf, on which Green could make out wooden statues of a wolf, a bear, and a lion interspersed with framed pictures identified by Crayton as St. John, St. Barbara, and the Indian chief Blackhawk.

"Patron saints in voodoo tradition," Cray whispered to Green and Eliza. She smiled at Crayton with something akin to hero worship, and Green felt pleased for his friend. This voodoo stuff worked wonders with the women.

A sudden movement on the top shelf of the altar grabbed Green's attention. There, tethered by a short length of rope, its beak wrapped with twine, was a skittering black rooster.

Then a pretty white woman in a diaphanous gown danced out of the dark crevices at the back of the courtyard. She was probably in her early thirties and wore a pearl gray mask, and her ash blonde hair was tied on top of her head with a white handkerchief. She was shaking a calabash that had been filled with pebbles, and its drone meshed with the throbbing of the drums. She slunk like a drugged reptile into the light and around Henri and the other drummer, moving in sensual fashion.

"Where'd she come from?" Cray asked, bobbing to the beat.

"I don't know," Eliza laughed, "but she's not wearing a lot of clothes for late October, is she?"

The woman, still shaking the gourd, was running her free hand lightly around Henri's head and neck, duplicating the maneuver on the other drummer.

Two thin black women, dressed in identical gowns with gold opera masks, skipped grinning through the clumps of guests from the direction of the kitchen. They stepped up on the altar and stood at the cauldron, calling out in some pidgin Creole dialect. One tossed a handful of black powder inside, then the other a pinch of white powder. After a moment, with a series of small explosions, clouds of blue, gold, and red sparks popped out of the cauldron and floated into the air. The crowd shifted in focus toward the altar, *oohing* and *ahhing* like kids on the Fourth of July.

A collective awareness seemed to rustle through the crowd that *something* was evolving. The patterned beats of the drums began to quicken as more and more of the guests gave in to the pagan urge to dance.

Suddenly, from a dark corridor just beyond the drums, came four heavily muscled black men wearing only white loincloths. They were carrying goblets of flaming liquid, and as several women in the crowd whooped and whistled, the men dipped their fingers in the wet fire and tossed squiggling tadpoles of flame over the dancers. As they reached the center of the crowd, they split up and aimed respectively for each of the four corners, arcing drops of burgundy fire over the joyous mob.

It was marvelous spectacle. "Any of this mean anything to you?" Green asked Cray, cupping his hand to his mouth to be heard over the increased volume of the drums.

Cray pulled Eliza in where they could both hear him. "Well, the four guys went to the four points of the compass, and the flaming liquid is probably a brandy and molasses mixture."

Cray's voice was unnaturally high-pitched. Green wanted to compliment Cray on his knowledge, but was too busy staring at the tracers of flame. Green's high was at a zenith, and much more would overload his circuits. He took a deep breath of thick, moist air and felt his ears pop. The rhythm of the drums sounded like panting animals and seemed, somehow, to emanate from under Green's own skin.

Eliza tugged on Crayton's arm and dragged him into the percolating vortex of dancers. The black guys lifted their flaming snifters and swallowed the dregs of the glowing liquid, and shouts and cries rose over the sound of the congas as a large black woman materialized from between the drummers, singing an ethereal, wordless melody and holding a large fish, perhaps a yard long, overhead between her outstretched arms.

She was, Green realized, the ceremony's mambo Cray had speculated about: the woman in the window. He couldn't take his eyes off her. Though heavy, she emanated a profound sexuality, grounded in soft, little girl features and a sharply defined, buxom figure. She was barefoot, wearing a long yellow shift and white feather earrings, and her thick long hair was anchored in a French twist by a large piece of turquoise jewelry.

Green shifted his stare to the fish she aimed at the sky. Its frozen eyes gleamed and the scales along its back glowed with a dozen twinkling colors in the firelight.

The guests roared at the woman's slithering dance. She stood in front of the altar now, swaying and moaning with more tangible charisma than any rock star Green had ever seen, her eyes clenched shut and a mystical expression of pleasure etched across her face.

Green started to pant; he was aware that he was losing the battle with his own anxiety. He started to dance in place like a reluctant puppet, trying to force some form of funky syncopation with the clamorous rite unfolding before him. Two of the black men appeared from their corners and took the fish from the voodooienne's hands, and she started to cry in a curious sing-song:

L'Appé vini, le Grand Zombi,
L'Appé vini, pou fe gris-gris!

Then the voodoo queen began a recurring chant, exhorting the guests to shout out in unison:

Danse Calinda, boudoum boudoum!
Dance Calinda, boudoum boudoum!

The sheer mob energy was overwhelming; Green felt like an impostor at some mystical event where everyone knew a secret but him. He gulped, fighting for control. *Too much absinthe?*

Sweat and mist leaked behind his mask and into his eyes and, for one horrifying moment, Green couldn't even be sure he wasn't crying. Thousands of jumbling and ominous thoughts confetti'd through his brain: *Were all these people actual followers of voodoo? Had Cray known this was going to happen all along? Had he somehow stumbled into some sort of* Rosemary's Baby *block party?*

Green tore his mask off and dropped it onto the courtyard bricks. He mopped his brow and looked through the kaleidoscope of dancers, trying to spot Crayton and Eliza, but he couldn't see them.

Danse Calinda, boudoum boudoum!

Danse Calinda, boudoum boudoum!

The crowd settled into the chant, calling it out, over and over, to the hammering of the drums. People were swaying and dancing and clapping their hands, and to Green the din seemed so loud it could be heard all the way to the Garden District. Didn't the neighbors ever call in noise complaints? Of course, they were in the Marigny, where a little loud yelling wouldn't impress police officers as the major crime problem on Halloween night. Plus, this entire fortress *was* a self-contained unit. Whoever this Maman was, if this was her place, she had a helluva spread. The voodoo business must be good.

She was standing in front of the altar, sipping from a bottle of white rum, smiling as the cyclonic mob moved and chanted. Green tried again to find Cray in the gris-gris mosh pit, but it was pointless; images tended to blur on the edge of his vision, and the rain and torchlight and shifting colors were nauseating. He closed his eyes and tried to relax, but the drums echoed in his head like a pneumatic drill. Sharp explosions of hell-red and egg yolk-yellow pulsed behind his eyelids, and Green was overwhelmed by a feeling of dread. *What the hell was he doing here after all Papa had told him?* Fuck *voodoo!*

Just as he was seized with the urge to march through the crowd, find Cray and drag him back into the spacious, normal territory of the Quarter, the drums and chanting abruptly stopped. Green jerked his eyes open and found himself staring at the altar.

Henri had moved from his drum and was now carrying the trussed black rooster from its perch on the shelf to Maman. The silence was eerie, and Green heard the party guests breathing heavily like ballplayers gathered after practice to listen to a coach's reflections.

The voodooienne took the rooster from Henri, holding it overhead like a newborn child, arching her back in religious ecstasy, mumbling:

Je suis Arielle,

Je suis Arielle...

Green remembered enough high school French to know she was saying, *I am Arielle, I am Arielle...*

As though controlled by a Hollywood special effects unit, the drizzle stopped. Steam rose like woodsmoke off the panting guests, twisting into the sky. The sense of expectation hung over the horde like wet towels, and Green could hear the random raindrops fall off the dead banana leaves and plop onto the bricks.

His heart was pounding and blood rushed in his ears like floodwater. His palms were greasy with sweat and, realizing he was only moments away from a panic attack proper, Green bit into his gums in some ludicrous and final attempt at self-control.

Maman Arielle lowered the rooster in front of her face and stared at it tenderly—just before she opened her mouth and tore the bird's throat out with her teeth.

Green's scream went unnoticed as the drums kicked in and the crowd roared its frenzied delight, and as he bolted from the periphery of the ceremony into the nearest darkness, he saw Maman Arielle holding the carcass of the bird like a puppet, spraying scarlet gouts of blood first into the cauldron, then over the heads of those nearest to her as they raised eager faces to catch their fair share of the gore.

Green flung open a door he found in the rear of the courtyard, hidden in a small, ivy-cloaked pathway off the main patio. Then he was inside with the door closed, leaning against a dark, cool wall, hyperventilating.

Outside, he could hear chanting again—*Arielle est voudon*—but frankly Green didn't give a shit. He'd had all the absinthe-laced voodoo lunacy he could take for one Halloween night, and he just wanted to lean against the wall until he got his act back together. Then he'd find Cray and they'd get a taxi and go back to the world.

After several minutes of taking deep drafts of the dank air, Green felt better. He realized he was across the courtyard from the main house. There was a dim, wavering light up the corridor, and he could smell an intriguing scent like gumbo or maybe jambalaya. At first, it made him queasy in its well-seasoned richness, then he realized he was famished and the idea of food was irresistible.

He hesitated. What if this was someone else's pad? No. It wasn't. He remembered someone chatting at the absinthe table saying this was all one property. He started cautiously in the direction of the wafting scent. Maybe he was just closing in on the post-ceremony food spread. If so, given his night so far, it couldn't hurt if he got a bit of a head start.

Green reached a partially open wooden door behind which the light ebbed and flowed. His breathing back to normal, and the sounds of the ceremony receding in his new exploration, his confidence grew that the worst of the absinthe-laced panic had abated.

The heady smell of gumbo—he was sure that's what it was now—was overwhelming, and Green smiled to note he was salivating. No wonder he'd lost his shit out there: drinking all day, absinthe, some maniac ripping a rooster's throat out with her teeth... Who *wouldn't* freak?

Green knocked. "Hello? It's just me, from the party." He swung the door open and saw an industrial kitchen of some kind, lit by dozens of black votive candles. He was apparently in the back of some kind of restaurant; there were two eight-top gas stoves, a huge broiler and prep area, and a walk-in refrigerator. The gumbo that enticed him down the hallway sat gurgling in a huge cast iron vat over a flickering burner. Across the room were two service doors and a bay with a wire where waiters could hang orders.

Where the hell am I? Green wondered. He took another step, calling again: "Hello? Anyone here?" It was silent.

All he could figure was Maman Arielle owned a restaurant or a catering service. Maybe the voodoo business *wasn't* all that hot, and she supplemented the gris-gris with a food services gig. Or maybe voodoo was simply her religion. Green shuddered.

He spied a pile of paper cocktail napkins on one of the counters and picked one up. The teal and orange logo printed on the napkin said GRIS-GRIS GUMBO.

It hit him: he was in the kitchen of the restaurant Papa Hipolyte pointed out the day of the jazz funeral—the one owned by the daughter of the evil voodoo queen. *Christ, listen to yourself,* Green thought. *Evil queens.* He sounded like *Alice in* fuckin' *Wonderland...*

Still, it *did* all fit together. This side of the fortress must border on Frenchmen Street then, meaning Arielle was the priestess Papa had warned him about. Which in turn meant the goddamned ceremony he'd just witnessed was real! Green felt a resurgent tide of fear and forced himself to remain rational.

No need to get hysterical. Why *couldn't* tonight's display have been a party deal? A sort of rent-a-ceremony for the entertainment of Halloween guests? Or another possibility: maybe it *had* been legitimate, but Maman Arielle also had a darker offshoot sect she ran in secret? The one Papa worried about...

Green sighed. Whatever he'd seen or experienced tonight—and the absinthe hadn't exactly clarified the whole thing—the antics with the chicken seemed less sinister in this clean, warm kitchen so completely infused with the seductive aroma of bubbling gumbo. The black candles were a bit odd, but Green's own apartment was heavily reliant on candlepower, so...

He hesitated, then moved to the stove. He couldn't resist and grabbed a large, silver ladle next to the vat, picking up the lid with a hot pad, and opened his nose to the vapor trails of fragrant steam jetting to the ceiling. *Maman Arielle might be hell's demon on earth,* Green decided, *but her gumbo smelled amazing.*

He dipped the ladle into the thick brown *roux* and stirred it. It was hard to see in the faint, unsteady glow of the candles, but Green thought he spied a pink shrimp and a brown coin of Andouille sausage murmur to the surface. He dipped just a bit of the broth, pulled it up, savoring the scent, blowing to cool it off. When he slurped into it, the explosion of flavors was absolutely the finest he'd ever put in his mouth.

Green looked around the stove area for a bowl—he figured he deserved this after what he'd been through—meanwhile dipping the ladle deep into the vat and paddling around in it to stir up the seasonings a bit. Then his spoon hit something too *big* to belong in a pot of gumbo. He frowned and poked at the shape in the depths of the vat. An entire link of Andouille to be carved up later? The world's largest prawn?

He fished around under the object with the ladle and pulled upward. It felt like he was reeling a trotline through muddy river water. The turbulence stirred up the gumbo's ingredients and, suddenly, Green's hunger somersaulted into a wave of nausea. The savory scent vanished and was replaced by a horrible smell of boiling blood and summer-heat-decay. His breath caught and, despite the shadowy gloom, he could easily identify the bodies of dead scorpions and centipedes as they churned to the surface of the gumbo—along with a severed human finger.

Before his brain could even short-circuit the momentum of his hand, Green finished tugging the dipper upward, realizing with horror what it would have to be. He stared at the ladle frozen in his hand, speechless at the sight of the thick black snake that had been simmering at the bottom.

CHAPTER TWENTY-ONE

On November 11, the day before Crayton turned twenty-five, Green got a late afternoon phone call from J.C., who was drinking his lunch at Galatoire's. It had been a hectic social week for J.C. Uncle Wallace had been elected to the U.S. House of Representatives in a landslide, and J.C.'s gossamer position as a "PR guy" suddenly blossomed into a bona fide job. J.C. was actually going to run Uncle Wallace's New Orleans office when the old ward heeler took his act to D.C. The celebration had been ongoing since the polls closed.

"I guess I got to learn the fine art of the Big Graft," J.C. had joked election night. It seemed to Green the sort of thing the Bitoun family gravitated toward anyway, and he supposed it was time J.C. grew up and contributed to the family power structure.

Green was finishing work on Cray's birthday present when J.C. called. Raucous conversation and the clattering of silverware sounded in the background.

"I am interruptin' a headlong dive into a platter of Buster Crabs Amandine to give you very important news," J.C. said.

"It sounds like you're diving into a gin bottle," Green said.

J.C. laughed. "That too. Now, what I called to tell you, in case you ain't heard, is that the honorable Supreme Court Justice Allwyn K. Dysart is dead."

"You're kidding." It wasn't that Judge Dysart was dead that shocked Green. At 83, he'd been hooked to a respirator since the Carter Administration. It *was* surprising that the judge was on J.C.'s death league roster.

Green actually hadn't thought much about the corpse league since, well, the night of the Halloween party—when the sordid ingredients of the gumbo surfaced out of the bubbling *roux* and Green absolutely lost it. He'd hauled ass out a side door in the back of the restaurant and sprinted back to his apartment, where Crayton and Eliza found him an hour later.

He'd explained what had happened, playing down the smell and the insects and human finger and emphasizing it could have been an absinthe-based hallucination. To his eternal gratitude, both Cray and Eliza were supportive, and Eliza didn't seem particularly freaked.

In the voodoo context, Cray said he'd never heard of any sort of vermin gumbo in his brief studies. He'd also checked at work with Cosima. She told him she'd never heard of such a thing, either, but that voodoo—even so-called "white magic" voodoo—often employed ingredients that might bother the squeamish. She suggested Green shouldn't worry too much about it. Cosima, who'd left the party early to go another soiree, also told Cray the whole ceremony was indeed a booked-party sort of event, like hiring a clown for a kid's birthday party. New Orleans, she said, was full of such "professional voodoo folk," and even the bloody chicken routine wasn't unusual.

For his part, Green of course wished he could speak with Papa, about the gumbo if nothing else. But of course he couldn't—not while the old man was out on tour. Plus, since Papa had gone to bizarre lengths to dissuade Green and Cray from delving into such things, Green wouldn't have relished telling Papa about this latest episode, no matter what he might learn. Bottom line: get over it. Crazy shit happened every day—particularly in *this* town.

By agreement, Green, Cray, and Eliza also kept the gumbo anecdote secret from Huey, Donny, and J.C. Green's instinct had been to get on the computer and find out what the hell he'd stumbled into. But where to start? You sure as hell didn't do web searches for Entomologist Gumbo recipes.

Green snapped to the present—here was J.C. calling, with news of an actual corpse for the death league. Already. J.C. brayed like a donkey. "Son, ain't you gonna congratulate me?"

"Uh, sure. Congratulations, J.C.," Green said. "You're on board first."

"Precisely," J.C. said. "Tell that flame-headed voodoo nut his magic spell ain't happening! I am the Lord of Death!"

Green had to laugh. He tucked the phone between his shoulder and jaw and held up the t-shirt design he was working on so he could see how it looked. "It's a long year, J.C.," he said, "but I'll certainly pass on the word to everyone that you've scored."

"Chime them funeral bells, Greenie!" J.C. said. "My man's already embalmed!"

"Absolutely, J.C." The design looked pretty damned good. Cray would be jazzed.

J.C. shifted gears. "Now, we still on for the All-Stars?" Cyril Neville and the Uptown All-Stars were playing the Rock 'n' Roll Church Monday night, and everyone was going.

"Planning on it," Green said. He was thinking, J.C. sure pulled a one-eighty on his enthusiasm for the Vieux Carré Fantasy Death Society. All it took was one dead body and the burgeoning politico was a bloodthirsty fiend.

Green got up, tucked his design into a cardboard mailer for protection, and headed out into the balmy day, aiming for Pirate's Alley Gifts. He needed to drop into the back room of the shop and make Cray's sweatshirt. The idea was to meet Cray and Eliza for a birthday breakfast at Café du Monde tomorrow before Green had to work, and Green needed the shirt finished and wrapped.

The next morning was textbook autumn, with the sun shimmering over the Mississippi, the spire of the cathedral across Jackson Square bright white against the cobalt sky, and brisk air redolent with chicory coffee. He and Cray and Eliza had one of the wrought iron tables on the patio. Cray had arrived with one arm draped around Eliza's shoulders. In his other he was carrying a grotesque, carved walking stick with a snake's head—a birthday present, Cray had told Green the night before, he'd bought for himself. He was also wearing some weird feather-and-tooth necklace around his neck— voodoo stuff, what else would it be?—but as long as he didn't shove the cane through his throat, Green was cool with it.

Eliza looked terrific, her face bright with happiness and her hair tucked under a gray, long-brimmed fishing cap. Green again felt a twinge of longing. Cray was lucky; Eliza was really cool, bright and funny, and she and Crayton had hit it off well in a natural way that bore little resemblance to Cray's angst-ridden pursuit of Kay. Green didn't really know why that earlier relationship didn't work; Cray hadn't explained and Green hadn't seen Kay in a while. Which was a shame. Kay was pretty amazing.

After a waiter in a white jacket and white paper cap brought hot coffee and a platter of the cafe's signature crusty, powdered-sugar beignets, Green held out a manila envelope and a package wrapped in orange foil. "Happy birthday, brah."

Cray grinned. "I do so love presents," he said, setting the envelope on the table, holding the gift-wrapped box up and giving it that slight maraca action against his ear.

"Open it," Green said, catching Eliza's eye and winking at her. She smiled back easily. "Has he opened your stuff yet?" Green asked her as Cray began tearing at the scotch tape securing his gift.

"Some," she said. She winked back. "I'm saving *one* for later." Cray had his head down, studying Green's present, but Green thought he could see that his pal was blushing. Eliza went on, "Plus, I got him a CD he wanted that you told him about. A live recording by that guy they just executed."

"Prospero Godchaux."

Eliza nodded. "Yeah, that's him."

"Nice," Green said. "My friend Papa Hipolyte's out on tour with a Prospero Tribute show. I just got a postcard from him at Graceland."

Eliza swallowed a tiny bite of beignet. "Cool. I'd love to hear him play."

"Papa's the real deal," Green said. "We'll go hear him when he gets back."

Green watched a small girl, maybe three, race out of the Café du Monde dining room and steamroll into the outdoor patio. The kid's parents, if they existed at all, were nowhere to be seen.

"I'm cleaning up," Cray said as he looked up from decimating the package. He pulled out a purple sweatshirt, hand-crafted with a stark white line drawing of Pistol Pete Maravich spinning a basketball on the tip of his index finger, smiling that boyish smile.

"Ohmigod, this is unbelievable!" Cray breathed.

"Wow!" Eliza said. "Green, did *you* do that?"

Green shrugged. "I guess."

"Goddamn!" Cray bubbled. He was clearly buzzed. "Pistol Pete!"

Green knew Maravich had been *the* boyhood hero to Cray. There was the shrine-poster in Cray's living room, and they'd also spent more than a few evenings at the Old Absinthe House bar on Bourbon Street, where Cray stared at one of Maravich's moldering New Orleans Jazz jerseys that hung, amongst dozens of items of memorabilia from Louisiana sports history, from the high, pressed-tin ceiling.

"Too much," Cray said, awed. Then he remembered the manila envelope. "And what's this?"

"Well, it's presumptuous, is what it is," Green said. "You keep asking how my writing's going, so I decided to give you a scene from my work in progress."

Cray's eyes widened. "You're kidding! Really?" He opened the envelope carefully, withdrawing a sheaf of typed pages. "Jeez, Green, this is great!"

Green shrugged at Eliza. "I don't know. I just thought..."

"That's awesome," Eliza said. "Cray said you wrote fiction. Is this a finished novel? Can I read it when Cray's done?"

"Uhm, sure. If you want. And yeah, it's pretty much done. Enough, anyway, that I sent two chapters off to the Tennessee Williams First-Novelist competition."

"Dude, that rocks!" Cray said, flipping through the pages. "So it's called *The Pagan Malt Shop*?"

"Yep."

Cray tucked the pages back in the envelope and looked at Green. "This is an honor, my man. A privilege." Cray tapped on his water glass with a fork. "And now," he said, reaching inside the backpack he'd set by the table, "I've a few tokens of appreciation for *you* fine folks." He presented two gift-wrapped boxes, holding one out to Green and one to Eliza. They looked at each other.

"What's this?" Eliza asked.

"Yeah, it's *your* birthday," Green said. The little girl raced back through the patio like a speedboat.

Cray bowed his head slightly. "I *like* giving gifts on my birthday—to my two favorite people." Cray's tone was light, but Green could hear a catch in his throat.

"Good enough," Green said.

Eliza opened hers first: a gorgeous set of gold earrings. "Oh, baby!" she said, giving Cray a healthy kiss.

Then Green pulled out a hardback copy of *Memoirs*, Tennessee Williams' autobiography. "No way!" he said, opening the book. "A signed first edition?! Jee-zuz, Crayton." He looked up in disbelief.

Cray shrugged. "It's not such a big deal. There's no dust jacket, the spine's bent, and the critics hated it."

Green laughed, but he was almost speechless at Cray's graciousness. "Maybe, but... Cray, you shouldn't have done this—" It wasn't just that the book cost some serious cash. More than that, Crayton had really *thought* about a gift that would mean something.

"Well, you shouldn't have done the Maravich shirt either," Cray interrupted. "But we did. Here's to heroes, right?" He raised his cup in toast, and Eliza lifted hers.

Green looked at them, raising his water glass. "And to friendship."

At that moment, the marauding little girl dashed around a table and cycloned right into Green, who instinctively put out his hand to cushion the collision. Unfortunately, it was the hand holding his water glass, which shattered on the table edge.

"Whoa!" Green breathed, holding up his hand and staring at it. A fine triangle of glass was imbedded in his palm, and deep red drops of blood began to ooze to the surface and crawl down his wrist. A drop plopped on the open copy of the Williams autobiography, landing directly on his signature.

The kid, unhurt, giggled and ran back inside. People at nearby tables glanced at Green, muttering sympathetically.

"Oh, man," Green moaned, looking at the book. "I bled on Tennessee's signature."

"Don't worry about the book," Cray said. "That looks like a nasty cut."

Eliza said, "Let me see your hand."

After a frozen moment in which Green stared at his palm as though it belonged to someone else, he reached out with his good hand and plucked the piece of glass out of the flesh. Wincing, he laid it gingerly on the table.

"Here," Cray said. He proffered a white handkerchief from his shirt pocket and daubed it with ice. "It's clean. Washed it this morning."

Green nodded and began swabbing his hand. "Thanks, dude."

The customers in the immediate vicinity were still buzzing, like downwind antelopes. A waiter arrived with hydrogen peroxide and more napkins, concern etching his questions for Green's well-being.

"Everything's cool," Green said. "It's just a scratch."

"Let me see it," Eliza commanded again, and Green held his hand out. She studied it a moment. "Well, it's not just a scratch, but I don't think you'll need stitches." She handed Crayton his bloodied handkerchief, then doused Green's hand with hydrogen peroxide and wrapped it in paper towels. "You head home and bandage this and you'll be fine."

"But look at my book," Green pouted.

"Not to worry," Cray said. He grabbed a clean corner of the handkerchief and dabbed at the page with surgical precision. "There. You can still see the signature. There's a slight pink smear across the top of his last name. When you think about it, ol' Tennessee probably *liked* pink."

They had to laugh. By now, people had gone back to their beignets and coffee. "Thanks for the help, guys," Green said. "I guess I'd better get home and clean up before work."

They exited the restaurant, and Green said, "I'll buy you a replacement handkerchief this afternoon."

Cray said, "Are you kidding?" He waved the bloodied cloth. "I'm framing this baby. When you sell your first novel all I ask is that you sign it for me."

Green grinned at Eliza. "We gotta lot of bloody autographs around here." He hefted his Tennessee Williams book and shook it like a Super Bowl trophy. "All right, you got a deal."

They walked down Dumaine toward Chartres, where Green would split off for home. A chilly breeze picked up and tattered New Orleans Saints flags flapped on the wrought iron balconies of apartments. A pigeon screeched from overhead, fluttered down to the corner, and perched on a *Times-Picayune* coin box. Green glanced over at the bird and did a double take when he saw the banner headline announcing the death of Justice Dysart.

"Hey, Crayton, I forgot. We haven't talked about Judge Dysart kicking off."

Cray looked puzzled. "The Supreme Court guy?"

"One and the same."

Eliza rolled her eyes. "Jeez, Cray, it's only been on every news show for the last 24 hours."

Cray scratched his chin. "Hey! Didn't J.C. draft him?"

Green said, "You got it. He said to tell you that he's the Lord of Death, and that your juju ain't working."

"Wow," Cray said. "*That* was quick. Truth told, what with Eliza and all"—he winked at her—"I'd kinda forgotten about the ol' death league. I'll have to dust off my roster and see who's on it."

"What are you two talking about?" Eliza demanded.

"Sorry," Crayton said. "I guess you don't know about the, uh, Vieux Carré Fantasy Death Society."

"The *what?*"

They filled Eliza in on their new hobby. Given the morbidity of the project, she seemed fairly amused—a reaction that obviously relieved Cray. He gave Green a look: *Who knows what the average woman is going to think of something like this?*

"So your friend J.C. scored first, then, when Dysart died?" she said, putting it all together.

"Precisely," Green said. "It figures. This sorta stuff always seems to work out for J.C."

"Who did *you* draft, Crayton?" Eliza demanded, poking at him with his walking stick.

Cray rubbed his new sweatshirt with *faux* modesty and winked at Green. "Well, babe," he said, "just some people who are gonna die soon."

CHAPTER TWENTY-TWO

Cray hadn't lied when he told Green that, since draft day, he hadn't thought much about the Vieux Carré Fantasy Death Society; that, in fact, he hadn't thought about much but Eliza.

Now, the morning after his birthday, Eliza had just left for work. Cray liked the casual sound of implied domesticity: *Eliza just left for work.* Like they were, well, co-habitating. He turned on his new Prospero Godchaux CD and wandered around the apartment, lighting his daily candles and incense sticks, generally digging the whole birthday aftermath.

Because, last night, they'd actually slept together—a bona fide fireworks display as conducted by the surprisingly wild Eliza Crane. And this morning, when she got out of his narrow bed and padded naked, yawning, to brush her teeth, and emerged wearing the Maravich sweatshirt he'd draped over the towel rack, it was a perfect exclamation point to the best birthday of his life.

Since he didn't have to be at work until two, he went into the kitchen to make hot chocolate and spied the death league rosters attached by a magnet to the refrigerator. *Oh, yeah.* J.C.'s judge died. *Unbelievable.*

He pulled the rosters off the 'fridge and set them on the counter. He ripped open a bag of Swiss Miss, poured it into the cup, added hot water and, balancing the saucer in one hand, picked up the rosters and headed for the living room couch. Cray thought back on the draft session in the cemetery. J.C. had freaked when Cray went to Marie Laveau's tomb and did the whole gift-offering shtick.

He'd done it for laughs—*except it wasn't* entirely *a joke, was it?*

Cray supposed that, if you wanted to look at it technically, the offering he'd left at the base of the Laveau tomb *was* kinda real—at least insofar as Cray was capable of discerning what was real and what wasn't in "voodoo." But now J.C. was the one with a corpse. So much for magic.

Except it wasn't a death charm at Marie's grave.

Cray frowned. Where were these mental counterpoints coming from?

The fact was, Cray *wouldn't* know a death spell. *Were* there death spells? He'd simply placed a "Get What You Wish For" gris-gris bag at Marie's grave.

Cray chuckled and shook his head. This voodoo stuff really was an out-there concept. And Cosima's speculation that the Halloween party gumbo was just folk symbolism was too lame. In Cray's opinion, throwing scorpions and a fucking snake—and, oh yeah, a human finger—into the gumbo was going a little too far for trick or treat comedy. Besides, the gumbo hadn't been served at the party—at least not while Cray was there.

He blew on his steaming cocoa, hazarded a small sip, and thought. In idle time at the Voodoo Shoppe, he'd root around in the inventory and read whatever "literature" they had. Not *once* had he seen anything like Vermin Gumbo. In conjunction with the birds he'd found in the corpse's eyes, and Maman Arielle's goofer dust, the Hand of Glory, and *maybe* the suicide in the funeral home, it seemed plenty of folks around New Orleans took voodoo a lot more seriously than Cosima. Like Maman Arielle.

Cray sighed. Did he really *want* to know any more about her? It was one thing to buy a Papa Legba walking stick or wear an ankle charm as sartorial affectations. But what sort of person actually broke into a funeral home and tore the eyes out of a dead body? And to what ultimate end?

Well, he didn't know. He took another swallow of cocoa and glanced down at the fantasy rosters. Now, the death league was also absurd—but in a more wholesome context. There were plenty of Internet death games where people picked celebrities who might die. As he looked through the rosters, it occurred to him that the strategy of drafting only youngsters was particularly stupid. There was no way even two of his kids would die in a year's time.

He walked into the bedroom to dress. "Fuckin' J.C.," he grinned. They'd practically had to drag J.C. into participating, and now he was leading the league. Cray pulled on a pair of jeans. It'd been, what, twelve days since they'd drafted? And someone was already dead?! What were the odds of *that?*

The Otherwordly Cray voice whispered again.

What sort of magic did J.C. spin to pull it off?

Crayton laughed; which cobwebbed corner of his mind was this coming from? Still, he answered his own question: There wasn't any magic. People just died. That was why Cray thought of the death league: the entertainment value of random death.

He stepped into the bathroom to gel his hair. *Nope, no magic.* J.C.'s early tally on the death board was nothing more than chance. Just like Cray's moving to New Orleans, meeting Green, and dating Kay had been luck. Cray buttoned up a white dress shirt and went to the dresser to leaf through his voodoo charms for today's selection. He was fingering a silver necklace with a small Sacred Bark pendant when the next question came from the game show host in his brain: *But had dating Kay actually* been *luck?*

After all, he'd burned the romance candle and he'd sprinkled goofer dust around J.C.'s bed and...

And you got her.

But maybe Kay just dug him.

He fastened the Sacred Bark necklace, which was an item he'd found in the Dixie Apothecary over in the Ninth Ward. A *real* voodoo shop. There was no point in shopping for authentic voodoo shit in his own store because there wasn't any. According to the Dixie clerk, this necklace would appease the spirit of the Indian chief Blackhawk. Cray didn't know why, precisely, one would want to appease Blackhawk, or even why the chief was a big deal to voodoo folks—something about Native Americans helping runaway slaves—but it was a cool necklace.

He glanced over in the corner at the Papa Legba walking stick. He didn't really know why he'd bought that either. He picked it up. The oaken barrel was covered in intricately carved *vévé* symbols—much like the one he'd found drawn on the corpse's chest—and culminated in a wide-fanged serpent head.

As for Papa Legba, Cray *had* read about him in the Voodoo Shoppe. Legba was the spirit ruling the crossroads between life and death, and a servant to loas, the divine spirits. Spirits were a big deal in voodoo. Apparently, if you knew what you were doing, you could get the spirits to watch over you and protect you. They were all around—depending on which discipline you were talking about.

Voodoo mythology was rather complex and had splintered over time. There were other disciplines: Santería, Palo Mayombe, Santa Muerte... And some of them were damned creepy. But that wasn't the point. Cray was interested in looking cool—and even Eliza liked the Legba cane. He went back into the bathroom and was brushing his teeth when the next intrusive thought hit:

What if you were meant *to meet Eliza at the Halloween party?*

He groaned. As in, just because he hadn't wished for someone to die at Marie Laveau's tomb, that didn't mean the amulet hadn't worked; *You get what you wish for,* the gris-gris bag had promised. And hadn't he been wishing for a girlfriend?

Only my whole fucking life.

The truth was, though, these weren't the only things he'd bought at the Dixie Apothecary either. There was, well, a shelf in the hall closet *full* of trinkets and herbs and beads. And why? Because they came from the Dixie and were supposed to be "real"?

What does that *mean*? Cray spit toothpaste into the sink. What *was* "real" anyway, and what was the point? That voodoo *did* have some power? Cray studied his visage in the mirror. What the fuck was wrong with him? Here he was, not an hour after the most erotic night of his life, and what was he thinking about?

Voodoo.

He opened the closet. Christ, look at this stuff: bottles of consecrated rum—what the hell were those for? He reached out and touched a small box of ouanga bags. Those were extremely valuable, considering Cray had *no fucking idea what they were or why he'd bought them!*

He reached up to the top shelf and pulled down an old Converse High Tops shoebox. And here was something he *hadn't* bought at a voodoo joint—and yet, it was perhaps the most disturbing thing he'd collected.

At least the smell was gone. For a while, after he'd brought it home, it'd gotten pretty funky. Which was probably when Crayton had dived head-first into the incense and scented candles concept.

Then, as he did only rarely, he removed the lid from the shoebox. Inside, lying on a bed of tissue paper, were the birds he'd pulled from the eye sockets of Joshua Arcenet. Well into the decomposition process, they were shrunken and looked cured in some pre-mummy sense of the word.

One thing was certain: if he were going to keep all this stuff, he'd have to find somewhere else to store it. If Eliza kept coming over and spending the night, as he certainly hoped she would, and she somehow discovered this crap, she'd have to think he was a little nutty. Particularly if she came across a shoebox full of rotted birds. He could imagine how lame it would be if he explained that he didn't even know what half the shit was or what it was for!

I'll show you what it all means.

This time the voice in his head wasn't his own. Cray swallowed and felt sweat bead on his palms. This time, the voice was feminine, low and sultry and faintly accented; somehow familiar in its whispery promise of sinister fun.

Then of course it hit him. He'd heard the voice before, when it had lulled him with secrets of goofer dust and spoke of the Hand of Glory; and when it had shrieked ritual Patois in misty Halloween firelight.

It was Maman Arielle.

He swallowed and at the same time heard a whispery flutter from inside the closet. *Had something fallen from the shelf?*

Cray didn't hesitate. He yanked the door open, rather more forcefully than he planned to—

—and dropped to the floor, stunned, as perhaps twenty crows flew out of the cramped space and spiraled randomly into various rooms of the apartment. Like someone reacting to sudden gunshots from an unknown location, Cray rolled over, scuttled back against the hallway wall—and then tried to absorb his overreaction, or perhaps his miscalculation, to what was happening and what it might mean.

In context, he had plenty of time to take it all in, because it wasn't just that live birds had materialized in a closet *he'd just examined.* Though, yes, that was without question a strange development.

But that wasn't all. No, Maman Arielle—and instinctively, without thinking about it, Cray *knew* she was responsible for this display—had gone a step further.

Because the crows were flying in *slow motion.*

As in: footage from some peaceful nature video of Canada geese winging majestically against a burnt orange sunset, the sort that came with a soothing Yanni soundtrack. And with a Captain Big Voice narrator grandly intoning the miracles of God's flying creatures...

Only this wasn't a video, this was Cray's fucking apartment, and the slo-mo crows—and there's *a band name for you,* he thought hysterically—*the slo-mo crows were delicately winging out of his sight line and through the tiny rooms of his living quarters with their glossy black wings moving in half-time as though powered by dying batteries...*

...And all at once, just like that, Cray felt fantastic.

Oh, he was freaked out too, no question about that—but absolutely exhilarated all the same. Because he *knew* he was watching something—some... *power*—that Joe from Popeye's Chicken wasn't remotely privy to. He shook his head and managed a small grin as he quantified what was going on. For whatever reason, Maman Arielle was putting on a show for his express benefit.

"Cool," he finally said, and, yep, that was buoyancy he heard in his voice—not fear or lunacy. After a few moments, Crayton rose to a sitting position, then got to his feet. He made his way from room to room looking for the birds.

Everywhere, the floors were clotted with dead crows.

CHAPTER TWENTY-THREE

On the Monday night following Crayton's birthday, Green, H-Man, and Donny trudged through a cold, steady rain toward the Rock 'n' Roll Church. The Uptown All-Stars were Cyril Neville's permanent side-project, an infectious outfit melding reggae with funk, soul, and hip-hop. Passing through a gift shop into the main room, they spied J.C., who'd secured a large round table with an optimal view of the stage. He was the clichéd image of the political wizard after long hours: the tie loosened, tall scotch in his left hand, Marlboro Light clenched in his teeth FDR-style. Walter "Wolfman" Washington issued from the house speakers.

They reached the table, discarding rain gear, and only then, in the gloom, did a woman seated next to J.C. spin away from the stage and face them. She seemed a synthesis of every model in every glam-metal music video: leonine white-blonde hair, a face so pretty it hurt to look at it, and wearing what appeared to be an infant's t-shirt pulled over two pumpkins. J.C. introduced her as Darby. She waved, smiled, and took a sip from a frothy green drink with a blue plastic shark stuck on the rim of the glass.

"I done tol' y'all about Darby, right?" J.C. asked. He hadn't, but they knew J.C.'s routine.

"Absolutely," Huey said.

"Met her at a fundraiser for Uncle Wallace," J.C. said. "She's a model. Ain't that right, darlin'?"

Darby flashed another grin and nodded. J.C. peered around as they got settled at the table.

"Where's Voodoo Red?" J.C. cawed. "I ain't yet had the opportunity to discuss this death league situation with him, in particular that I'm in the lead an' all."

"He'll be here," Donny said. "He was waiting on Eliza."

"That's right," J.C. beamed. "I guess this means I'm finally gonna meet this new Wonder Woman he's got."

A waitress arrived and took drink orders. General conversation splintered into sub-topics, with J.C., Donny, and Huey arguing about football and, because he was seated next to her, Green tossing biographical softball questions to Darby. She seemed nice enough, vaguely describing her burgeoning modeling career.

A few minutes later, to his surprise, Green spotted Kay sitting with another girl at the front bar by the entrance. She was laughing and drinking beer. Her hair was shorter now, and she looked terrific in a gold sweater. Her black jeans were tucked inside her cowboy boots.

She obviously hadn't seen them, which, given the size of the crowd and the club's dim lighting, wasn't all that surprising. Still, as Green talked with his friends, he couldn't keep from checking her out. It was sort of odd: she'd been out of sight and mind but, watching her secretly from across the room, he was reminded how much he'd envied first J.C. and then Crayton when they'd had a chance to hang around her.

Finally, when Kay's friend got up and headed toward the restrooms, Green excused himself and made his way across the club. As he climbed the steps to the bar area, Kay turned to look at the stage area and saw him.

"Ohmigod! Green!" she said, climbing off the barstool to give him a hug.

"It is I," he intoned in mock solemnity, returning her hug and feeling quite excellent about it.

"How are you, darlin'? You look great," Kay said.

"I'm fine, thanks," Green said. "*You* look terrific! How's school and everything?"

"Fine. Boring." Kay laughed. "Sit down?"

"Uh, I thought I saw you with a friend."

"You did. A sorority sister. But she left. We ate at the Napoleon House and popped over here for a beer. She went back to study and I was too restless to go back to the house." She pointed to the empty stool and Green sat down. A bartender with a stern flattop came by and ignored them.

"So. How's everyone?" Kay asked. "Are you still hanging out with Crayton? And I haven't heard from J.C. in, oh, I don't know when."

Green pointed over his shoulder at the buzzing crowd. "The gang's all here. Or will be," he said, remembering Cray and Eliza hadn't arrived yet. Hopefully they wouldn't walk past them in the next minute or two. That would be awkward.

"Big Cyril Neville fans, huh?"

Green nodded. "That's a law in this town, right?" Kay smiled again. A sudden thought hit Green. "Hey, you still headache free?" he asked.

"Absolutely." She looked almost guilty. "Isn't that the strangest thing?"

Green reflected on some of the things he'd experienced lately. "Yeah, I guess so... That was a bizarre evening."

Kay took a sip of her beer. "Do you know I dream about it? Being in that voodoo store late at night?" She giggled self-consciously. "It's always too vague and shadowy and I don't remember details. It's not nightmares, exactly, just...a bit disconcerting."

Green nodded. "Oh, I can believe it. I guess the important thing to remember is that you're not having migraines."

"There's that—and believe me, I'm grateful."

At that moment, the houselights went down and shouts and whoops rose up from the crowd. "That'll be Cyril," Green said over the applause. He paused. "Would you like to join us?"

Kay smiled sadly. "Maybe not this time." She met Green's eyes. "You understand, right?"

An explosion of drums crackled onstage, segueing into a second-line rhythm, and a spotlight trained on Cyril Neville, magnificent in swirling feathers and tribal colors of purple, gold, red, and aqua. The All-Stars cranked into a Jamaican-flavored version of "Wild Injuns," and the crowd ignited.

Green turned from the spectacle to find Kay standing by the bar, purse in hand.

"You're leaving?" he called over the music.

She nodded. "Yeah, I think I'll head home after all." She seemed nervous. "It's been good seeing you, Green."

"You too." He felt a burst of desperation. "Hey," he said. "What if I called you? To do something, I mean." *I sound like an idiot.*

To his relief, Kay smiled and leaned over and kissed his cheek. "I'd like that."

The All-Stars had finished a blazing first set and a Mose Alison tape was playing over the P.A. when Crayton and Eliza showed up carrying Dixies. Cray had a mellow grin on his face as he helped Eliza out of her raincoat.

J.C. made a big production out of introducing himself and Darby. He went so far as to kiss Eliza's hand—a transparent maneuver that was vintage J.C., though Eliza smiled and seemed to blush. Then he turned to face Crayton, who still wore his enigmatic smile. Cray held out his hand. "It's the Lord of Death."

"You got *that* right, my man!" J.C. said, gripping Cray's palm and pumping enthusiastically. "I ain't heard from you since ol' Judge Dysart passed on." He winked at the table. "Since you done picked all them youngsters on your death team, I was wonderin' if you wanted any advice on roster moves from the Corpsemeister."

"Well, not really, but thanks. In fact, that's why we're late. We were watching ESPN, so I guess you guys haven't heard." Everyone looked at him and Cray raised his bottle up like a microphone and did a fine Howard Cosell: "Five-time Hawaiian Ironman champion Sam Gallagher died today of massive brain trauma after a tragic accident during a bicycle training ride. He was twenty-eight years old." Cray put his arm around Eliza, beaming like a proud papa.

J.C. looked like he'd caught a wino peeing on his newly shined shoes. Donny cleared his throat and said, "He's *dead?*"

Cray got serious. "Yeah. I couldn't believe it. I mean, I never expected him to actually *die.*"

J.C. couldn't believe it either. "Wasn't Gallagher your first pick?"

Cray thought for a second. "You know, I guess he was." He looked puzzled, then scratched his forehead. Around the room, bottles and glasses were clinking and conversation was humming. Mose Alison started singing that he was smashed.

Green knew what everyone at the table was thinking: What were the odds that a championship athlete, in the prime of his life, would die? Furthermore, what were the odds that a guy's first-round draft pick would also happen to be his first corpse? The entire voodoo issue tried to swirl through Green's brain like a gust of cold wind, but he forced himself to think rationally.

"Well, you're on the scoreboard, dude," he finally said. "Congratulations."

Crayton chuckled self-consciously and sipped from his Dixie. "I guess I am. So, anyway, J.C., when you figure in my bonus youth points, that means you're in *second* place. At least until we see who dies next."

CHAPTER TWENTY-FOUR

Natchez, Mississippi

With a wooden spoon, Papa Hipolyte stood in the kitchenette of a Road Rest hotel, slowly stirring flour and vegetable oil in a deep-bottomed cast-iron skillet. He was wearing reading glasses, house slippers, baggy jeans, and a frayed Tipitina's sweatshirt.

Today was his day to cook, a duty Papa frankly relished. Gumbo requires a series of methodical, time-devouring procedures the old man found soothing, and making the *roux* was perhaps the most surgical of maneuvers. The precise timing always gave him a secret thrill, though he supposed such an admission to anyone else would probably result in blank stares.

He studied the smoking, thickening mixture, zeroing in to spot any black specks that meant he'd burned the *roux*. A heavy smell of hot vegetable oil and heating flour stuffed the room, mingling with the earthy aroma of chopped okra and the fruity tobacco from Papa's pipe. It was stifling but wonderful.

Most days, since the gig towns were so close together, the musicians rotated cooking; it was too expensive to eat every meal out, and though the clubs always had contract rider deli trays or a hot meal backstage, it was logical to prepare their own food. It was a reality dating back to the Chitlin' Circuit era when black musicians never knew whether they'd find a restaurant that would even serve them—and everybody remembered when Fats Domino used to make and carry his own giant pot of private-recipe gumbo from town to town, tucking it next to him on the front seat of his Cadillac like a pet bulldog.

Papa sighed happily. When he'd signed on for the *Legends of New Orleans R&B/Tribute to Prospero Godchaux* tour, he'd had some doubts. Though he'd done package tours before, they'd been two-week junkets—and this one was five weeks. That was a long time for an old man, set in his bachelor ways, to voluntarily live in cramped hotel rooms, travel in crowded sedans or stale vans, and stay up late drinking too much beer and whiskey.

Which was another consideration: his health. The doctor back at the Charity had warned that Papa was probably facing some bad heart shit. Papa dismissed it at the time, figuring the stress from St. John's Eve and at Gris-Gris Gumbo caused the erratic physical symptoms...

The *roux* was just right, and Papa chuckled, recalling his mother's long-ago advice on how to tell when your *roux* was the precise color. "It gots to be deep, deep gold," she'd say in matter-of-fact tone, "right ready to fall off the cliff of chocolate brown. *That's* when you *roux's* done."

Well, Papa's was falling off the cliff. He lifted the skillet off the flame with one hand, stirring continually with the other, and set it down on another burner with a pre-adjusted, lower heat. Then he reached for a plastic mixing bowl in which he'd put his celery, okra, onion, green peppers, Andouille sausage, tomatoes, and various spices, and dumped them in...

The tour had been fun, and Papa was enjoying the camaraderie more than he'd expected. The guys were wonderful, the music always a pleasure, and the crowds receptive and respectful. To be sure, some of his enjoyment was because the tour took his mind off weird shit back in New Orleans. That was a major reason he'd signed on.

What alarmed him, though, was that the symptoms he'd been experiencing before they left hadn't abated. He'd experienced some chest pains, some dizziness, had one bout of arrhythmia... It wasn't daily—then he'd be truly alarmed—but enough to think the doctor was right. When he got back, he'd get checked out proper.

"What you cookin', Papa? That *roux* I smell?" Chief Spencer, the bass player, wandered out of a bedroom, rubbing his eyes sleepily. He was a tall, stooped man with a shaved head who'd been around for years, supplementing his gigs with dock work. In the early sixties, he'd played with Gatemouth Brown and was a reliable veteran of hundreds of studio sessions over the years.

"Mornin', Chief," Papa said. "Got some gumbo workin'."

"That smells pretty fuckin' delightful," Chief said mildly, "if you don't mind such language this early in the morning."

"Yes, I do, but you're right, the gumbo's gonna be fuckin' delightful, Chief, it surely is," Papa said, never taking his eyes from the alchemic duties before him.

Chief peered over Papa's shoulder without disrupting the process. "You gonna put some shrimps in that?"

"Got some fresh catfish, brother."

Chief nodded, yawning. "Where is ever'body?"

"You and me the only ones awake over here."

They generally stayed in two or three hotel rooms in budget inns that catered to traveling salesman types. Typically, such hotels had quasi-suites, like this one with two bedrooms and a kitchenette. With folding beds and the couch, and another standard double room, there were adequate sleeping possibilities for nine musicians, a sound engineer, and a roadie.

"You were hot last night, Papa," Chief said. "Dug that Booker stuff."

"Thanks." Papa grinned. He adjusted the heat under the skillet, then moved over to a cutting board and his catfish fillets.

"Where we going tonight? Someplace fairly close?" Chief asked, rummaging through the detritus of food sacks and coming up with a handful of Fritos.

"Jackson."

Chief nodded and stretched. "Well, I'm gonna walk down to that drugstore on the corner and get some razors. Need anything?"

"Naw, I'm set. Thanks."

Chief shuffled out the door, admitting a spear of morning sunlight. Papa set about chopping the catfish fillets into bite-size squares. He thought for the hundredth time he ought to call Green, see how he was. He'd sent him a postcard, but he still felt guilty. Green was a good kid and Papa had just upped and hauled ass after laying all that voodoo shit on him. He scraped the catfish pieces in a bowl. Then stirred the pot. He slurped a taste; the flavors were coming together.

Papa wiped his hands on a paper towel. Now all he had to do was let it simmer for a while. Since Green was on his mind, he decided it was an excellent time to call. Who knew? Maybe Green and Cray didn't have plans for tonight and might wanna drive over for the gig...

He'd just punched in the New Orleans area code when it happened. A searing, electric sensation rolled through his left arm like someone had run a hot wire into his biceps and down the bone to the wrist. Papa staggered. Just as he framed the thought that some type of insect must have stung him, he felt a second shock, as though he'd been kicked in the chest with a heavy work boot. The force of the invisible blow drove him backward and he fell over. Before he lost consciousness, it occurred to him how absurd he must've looked, tottering around like some huge puppet.

The next thing Papa knew, the door to the hotel room was opening. He was conscious that great tides of pain were washing through his ribcage, and that a creepy, disjointed pounding was pulsing in his ears. A hazy golden light poured through the door, and the shadowy figure of Chief Spencer was suddenly over him.

"Papa! Papa!" he could hear Chief cry, though it sounded somehow far away. "Hey! Hey, Lou! Morris! Wake up! Papa's down!"

The room seemed to be darkening, and the smell of the *roux* was suffocating. "Stir the gumbo!" Papa wanted to tell Chief, but there was a great weight pressing on him from above and he couldn't get his voice to work. Some part of his brain acknowledged that he'd had a heart attack and that Chief was performing an impromptu CPR procedure. Papa closed his eyes against the pain.

"It ain't working," he tried to say. "Chief, it ain't working..."

Papa squinted through swirling light that suffused the room like smoke—and realized that it wasn't Chief after all. It was...it was...

Maman Arielle!

Papa felt terror overtake him. Arielle's face was inches away, just like at Gris-Gris Gumbo, when she'd laughed at him, crunching the live crawfish scornfully. And now she'd come to kill him! Papa gasped for air, choking, suffocating...

As he struggled to keep her in focus, to somehow slither away from her, he realized how incredibly young she was—a child, really—and that her luminous blue eyes were misting with concern. In the heavy Franco/island accent she'd picked up living off and on in Haiti, she murmured, "Don't be afraid, old man. Ever'ting is all right. Ever'ting will be fine..."

He was sinking deeper. A loud silence overwhelmed all other senses, and finally all he could see were her fathoms-deep eyes caressing him like a three-dimensional lullaby. It hit him that he was probably dying—and that, somehow, was okay too. It hurt too much, it was too...

Astonishingly, the pain began to ease and the room began to come back in focus. Papa opened his mouth and greedily drank in cool air. What the hell was going on? He looked around for Arielle but couldn't see her.

"The ambulance is here," Papa heard someone say.

Then Chief was looming over him again. "You back, brother," he said, fear and relief intermingled in his words.

Papa tried to speak, to describe how Arielle had come to take him—

"Sssh," Chief said softly. "You gonna make it, Papa."

Papa didn't know how it had happened, but apparently Chief had driven Arielle away. "Thanks," he whispered. He wanted to say more, but suddenly two white men were kneeling by him, doing that medical shit they do.

"Just try to relax, sir," one of them was saying, sliding an IV needle into Papa's arm. "You're going to be fine."

Papa wasn't so sure about that. But there was so much to think about. Arielle had frightened and confused him and...*comforted him*?

CHAPTER TWENTY-FIVE

New Orleans, Louisiana

Cray grabbed his shoulder bag and walked out into the black-gray dawn. Eliza, who stayed almost every night now, had just dashed off to her place to get ready for work. She had a new gig over in the CBD as a copywriter in the marketing department at Crescent City National Bank, one with a real person's hours, so these early mornings were becoming something of a regular habit.

The automatic St. Ignatius porch lights were still on and would be for another half-hour. Otherwise, the apartments except for Cray's were silent and dark. He quietly unhooked the wrought iron gate and trudged through the archway. Just to the rear of the complex was the apartment parking area, which was kinda useless since Cray and one old woman across the courtyard were the only two tenants with cars. The lot was a secured gravel-and-weed space cluttered at the far wall with scrap wood and stacks of castoff St. Ignatius sinks, toilets, and window frames. In the corner diagonally across from the gate was a storage shed of weathered plywood that originally served as a maintenance closet. Years ago, a newer shed had been erected in the courtyard next to the pool.

Crayton seriously doubted that anyone at the St. Ignatius had any idea the old shed existed. Or that, if you could fit between the side of it and the apartment wall and inch your way to the rear, you'd find that the back of the shed wasn't set flush against the brick wall marking the property. There was actually a crawl space and closet on the *back* side of the shed.

Cray, with his skeleton's build, discovered the damned thing out of desperation when he needed jumper cables one September day. The closet was probably three feet deep, with a sliding door, which was convenient since a swinging one wouldn't have completely opened in the narrow space. There was now a padlock on the door, purchased by one Crayton Breaux and necessary because he didn't want anyone bumbling around and accidentally discovering his private little warehouse. He stood in the cramped back space and shivered in the cool chill of the morning, absently fingering the lock. Why *was* he here? If he felt creepy and guilty about Sam Gallagher, *why* was he here?

Well, because of the *exhilaration* and because he had to know if it was all a coincidence. Frankly, until recently, the whole voodoo deal, from Joshua Arcenet to Kay's migraine, the goofer dust and the vermin gumbo,

the Hand of Glory and the tour of the cemetery Papa Hipolyte gave Green—
had all seemed somewhat hollow, as though they were elements of validity
like croutons in a salad of New Orleans hogshit.

On the other hand, Cray couldn't deny that there were a helluva lot of
croutons, almost as many as there had been dead crows he picked up in his
apartment. So maybe it wasn't *all* hogshit. And *that* was why he was
sneaking around behind a cobwebbed tool shed at six in the morning while
the rest of the world slept.

He unlocked the door and edged in, clenching and unclenching a packet
of matches in his hand, staring into the darkness of his secret place without
really seeing anything. Almost as an afterthought, he struck a match and,
guarding the flame against the November wind, leaned and lit a black votive
candle—one of dozens of multi-colored ritual candles that partially
constituted his voodoo altar.

The light cast leapfrogging shadows in the damp space, and the feathers
and bones, incense and herbs, High John the Conqueror root and sundry
other charms sat on plywood shelves like so many *National Geographics* in
an old-timer's garage.

There wasn't much method to Cray's altar. He'd studied an exhibit at
the Voodoo Museum over on Dumaine. Various renditions of altars had a lot
of the same stuff, and Cray took notes. If he'd figured out anything about
voodoo, it was that there was a lot of individual interpretation.

To be sure, he even got on the Internet at work. The variety of answers
was overwhelming. Voodoo wasn't exactly a cut and dried deal. Still, there
were enough recurring characteristics that Cray decided to forge ahead.
Indeed, the more he found out, the more it seemed an individual twist was
actually *good*.

And here he was. There were four stones at the compass-point corners
of the bottom shelf, rinsed in anisette. There was a bottle of rum amidst the
flickering candles and beads. There was graveyard dirt in a wineglass, and
the top shelf contained photos of various saints. There was a glass of water
to soak up bad energy.

He didn't know why, precisely, any of these things were significant in
the big scheme of Gris-Gris Proper, but they'd been for sale at the Dixie
Apothecary, so he figured they probably meant something to somebody. Or,
more properly, Somebody.

He knew he was missing stuff—almost all the altar info he could find
showed a skull in a top hat, but who knew where he could score one of
those? But looking at his altar with a non-jaundiced eye, Cray was pretty
impressed.

And why not?

Swallowing nervously, he looked at the middle shelf. In the center were
three black votive candles, all burnt down now. Behind them, propped up
against the back wall, was a smiling picture of Sam Gallagher from the cover

of a recent *Triathlete Magazine.* Crayton had used cuticle scissors to clip out the area where Gallagher's heart was, and with a black Marks-a-Lot obliterated the athlete's eyes.

According to what lore he *could* find, there was other stuff you did if you actually wished someone harm, kooky chants and rituals calling for things that made no sense at all: red peppers, odd leaves, human hair, animal parts... But there were no clear-cut instructions. At least none that he could find. So a lot of it Crayton just made up as he went along, like some wizard chef improvising as he strolled through a stranger's kitchen.

Yes, Cray *liked* it here. There was a feeling of quiet power, a slightly electric hum that seemed to vibrate just under his skin, as from a battery-powered contraption a massage therapist might crank up for those really tight muscle clumps.

Cray fingered his hunk of John the Conqueror root. The Gallagher *curse,* if that's what you wanted to call it, had been a whimsical burst of inspiration, a nutty idea that turned into a fun project. It was like those New Age zealots Cray had read about. They made vision boards sporting cutout magazine photographs of their every desire, and hung them on closet walls. Then, every day, they visualized and meditated over them, swearing to friends that, eventually, it all came true.

Crayton could dig it; it might be nonsense, it might not. But the excitement was actually in the *waiting*—just to see what *might* happen. Because, in this maniac's world, you just never knew.

Cray couldn't really blame himself, then, for feeling a little giddy and, at the same time, nervous about the whole thing. After all, the bottom line was that, 2,000 miles away, Sam Gallagher had a bicycle accident. He was dead. It had *happened.*

Yet that still didn't answer whether the whole thing was a one-time coincidence. And *that* bugged him. Cray didn't really want anyone else to die, at least not if they weren't going to do so independently of his garden-shed ministrations—his moccasin fang and chicken-claw vision board, if you will. But there was only one way to know.

So it was with another set of seemingly incongruous emotions—dread and anticipation—that he dug into his shoulder bag and pulled out three fresh black candles and a fine *People* magazine photo of draft choice number two: a sixteen-year-old tennis star named Stacie Bates.

CHAPTER TWENTY-SIX

It was Monday, Thanksgiving week, and Green, working late, was surprised as he prepared to close up the empty t-shirt shop, to see Kay walk in carrying a gym bag and an orange and yellow arrangement of autumn flowers.

"Wow, what's this?" Green said. She looked, as always, amazing—casual tonight, with her hair in a ponytail through the adjustable band on a Saints ball cap, jeans, black Converse low-tops, and, most flatteringly, a sweatshirt that was one of Green's own designs, which she must've bought while he wasn't at work.

"Hi, handsome," she smiled, thrusting the bouquet at him. "For you."

"As an aspiring professional writer, I think I already said, 'Wow.' How about, 'Gadzooks!' or 'Zounds!'" Green said, taking the flowers and examining them. "The point is, thanks. I don't know that I've ever gotten flowers before."

"Maybe you could get used to it."

"Maybe I could. They're awesome. To what do I owe this gracious, gender-twisting exercise in chivalry?"

She hefted the gym bag onto the counter by the cash register and said, "I hope you don't have any plans before tomorrow morning."

Green raised his eyebrows, a ticklish feeling of delight and anticipation starting to swirl in his belly. "Jeez, you've got me curious. At this point, I'd follow you to the ends of the Earth. Even Shreveport."

"That *is* commitment." She laughed. "As it turns out, all you have to do is follow me to your apartment. We'll get you a change of clothes, get a bite to eat—then you can follow me to the glamorous Westin on Canal. I've got us a room with a view." At this point, she actually blushed as she pointed at him. "I hope you're ready to rock, big boy."

Green's heartbeat elevated pleasantly. *She was actually seducing him.* "You know what's even better? I *have* a change of clothes here. A lot of time I jog to or from work and shower in the back. Unless I need a tux or something."

Kay didn't answer. Instead, she pointed to a display of plastic Mardi Gras beads next to the cash register and said, in the time-honored Fat Tuesday request, "Throw me some beads, mister!" And without waiting for his response, she echoed the gesture of thousands of Carnival sorority girls before her by lifting her top and quickly baring her breasts for Green's stunned but happy appreciation.

This would be their third time to go out together, and Green had already been going through that dizzying period early in a relationship when all things shimmer with tantalizing promise. *Teenager Time*, he called it: already he found himself daydreaming about Kay, remembering things she said in late night phone conversations—he loved the *sound* of her voice, slightly husky and punctuated by laughter that reminded him of tiny bells tinkling. It puzzled him when he recalled ancient conversations with Crayton, who had broken it off with Kay because he thought she was a boring Tulane sorority girl. To Green, she was anything *but* boring.

She *entertained* him—made him laugh and think—and he found her to be clever and smart, with an intimidating knowledge of art and an almost belligerently feminist point of view. She wasn't interested in working her way into the family antique business. With her geology degree, she planned on landing a job with an oil company while she worked on her masters. She seemed to have things well and confidently thought out.

Dinner seemed part of Kay's seduction conspiracy. They sat by the open windows in Bella Luna on the river in the curiously warm breeze, and though barbecued quail in a ginger-orange glaze wasn't a typical staple of Green's diet, he was damned glad Kay had ordered for him. Afterward, they strolled down Decatur Street, arm in arm, pretending they were tourists, stopping for one drink at Tipitina's French Quarter, where Eddie Bo was ending a Happy Hour set. He played "Mister Popeye" and Kay dragged Green out to dance. He made an idiot of himself and loved every minute of it. By nine they entered the glowing lobby of the Westin, where a small crew of employees was already working on holiday decorations and half the front windows were laden with tinsel.

Inside their large room, all gold and red and featuring a king-sized bed, Kay removed several white candles from her bag, placed them for dramatic effect, then lit them.

"Good voodoo?" Green joked. They'd pulled back the floor-length curtains and were staring at the starglow vista of the Quarter and the lit steeple in Jackson Square.

"Well, the idea was atmosphere, but we'll settle for good voodoo, right?"

The subject of voodoo had inevitably come up during their burgeoning relationship, of course. Cray had cured her headaches through voodoo. The same night, Kay had told Green she had once seen a ghost. Green had told her about the Halloween party and the creepy gumbo and the suicide of the mortician. Talking with Kay was so easy that it all sort of spilled out without him intending for it to happen—and she was clearly on the same spiritual page. "Spookage happens," she'd said at one point, shrugging practically.

Now she echoed that acceptance. "Voodoo is voodoo," she said. "I respect that. Believe me." Then, casually as turning on a lamp, she reached over and unzipped Green's Levis and dropped to her knees. She spun her

Saints cap around backward, hip-hop style—that she did so instead of removing it had a skyrocket sensual effect on him—and smiled up at him. "Let's see what we've got here."

Much later, as they lay in one another's arms, taking a break, with the candles long burned down to hardening wax puddles, Kay clicked on the television to see if anything looked interesting. Instead, they grew interested, once more, in each other and the television was forgotten.

It was a good thing the volume was down though, because otherwise they would have heard the newscast about the sudden death of tennis star Stacie Bates, the sport's Teen Bad Girl, who just happened to be the second draftee on Crayton Breaux's corpse list.

CHAPTER TWENTY-SEVEN

Early the next morning, walking into the St. Ignatius courtyard, Green was surprised to see Crayton holding a manila envelope and leaning woodenly against the wall between their two doorways. "Lose your key?"

Cray started and smiled. "Hey, Green! I didn't see you," he said. "Trance Boy, here."

"Nothing wrong with trances. I'm sort of in one myself. C'mon in and I'll get us some coffee."

"Sounds good," Crayton said, following Green inside, where he stood looking at the Tennessee Williams poster. "Oh, I almost forgot," he said. "I brought back the excerpt from your novel. It's freakin' great!" He placed the envelope on the coffee table.

Green raised his eyebrows. "Thanks for reading it. You liked it?"

Cray dipped his head in a reverential bow. "Oh yeah. You can flat out fuckin' write, pal." He eyed Green, who ducked into the kitchen and pulled out a jar of instant coffee. "You'd said it was bizarre, but... Jeez, it's almost like Stephen King-y... And a character who kills himself with hornets? That's even cooler than doing yourself in with a a tro—a tro-whatsit."

Green laughed at Cray's stumbling allusion to Marcus and started heating water in the microwave. "I think it's 'trocar. '"

"Trocar. Right. "

"Hey, Cray, throw on some tunes, will you? I'll be done here in a second."

He heard Cray sigh. "Something tells me you haven't heard about Stacie Bates."

Green, pulling milk out of the refrigerator, glanced curiously at Cray, then the significance of the name hit him. He carefully put the carton on the counter. "Draft choice number two, right? Don't tell me—"

Cray let out a shaky laugh. "Yep. Draft choice number two is dead."

"Cray," Green said, and the back of his throat felt coated with cracker crumbs, "I guess you know this goes beyond weird." He wiped his mouth. "What happened?"

"Well, she had some rare form of cancer. We knew that, right?"

"We did? All I remember is that she's a—was—a real brat. Sort of like a Tonya Harding for the reality television generation."

"Well, I knew she had cancer," Cray said. "I mean, that's why I drafted her." He sounded slightly defensive.

Green shrugged. "Sounds like a shrewd choice to me." The shock was wearing off a bit—after all, the kid had been terminally ill. Green didn't exactly follow tennis. He carefully poured water into the two mugs. He slid one down the counter to Cray and placed milk and sugar between them.

"Thanks," Cray said, stirring the instant and sipping it black. "Anyway, the disease metastasized at some unbelievable rate, and she just...passed on."

Green murmured sympathetically and stirred sugar into his mug. "Well, if someone had to die, she sorta sucked, right?" He laughed. "I mean, not Hitler but..."

Cray raised his eyebrows and grinned. "I hadn't thought about it that way, but I suppose so." He thought a moment. "Has anyone else died lately?"

Green thought a minute. "I don't think so. I mean, it's way early. I'm surprised we have three."

Cray stood and wandered around the room. "Yeah, and I'm the only one who's got two corpses—both of whom were under forty and died in the exact order I picked them."

Green shrugged. "Yeah, it's weird." And it *was* weird. Green had to admit it. "But you just said Bates was terminally ill."

Cray took a deep breath. He seemed nervous. "Well, yeah, but still, what are the odds? I mean, I guarantee you J.C.'s gonna flip out and start screaming about voodoo and about me being a demon and shit."

Green glanced over at the answering machine by the stereo, where the message light was indeed blinking. "That probably *is* him. And it *is* weird. But look at the bright side. You've got two corpses and bonus points!"

Cray ran fingers through his stiff hair. "I guess," he said slowly, "but J.C.'s still going to claim I cast gris-gris spells and put hexes on people and who knows what kind of crap."

"Well, what about it?" Green looked at Cray, watching for his reaction. Given all the voodoo stuff that *had* happened, Green had been the one creeped out by it while the whole subject seemed to delight Crayton. Green didn't actually believe Cray was manipulating events—despite Papa's disturbing story at Prospero's funeral, he didn't believe that, even if unexplainable things happened in this world, they could be perpetrated by a garden variety civilian like Cray. At the same time, his pal *did* work in a voodoo shop.

Cray was actually gaping at Green, astonished. "What about *what?* Voodoo? You think I put *spells* on those people?! Jesus, Green!"

"You're certainly agitated enough. And it's not like you *couldn't* cast a few spells, or at least stick some pins in dolls or whatever it is you people do."

"'*You people*'? Christ, Green, I just work in a *tourist* voodoo store. Like you design t-shirts. I can't kill somebody with a voodoo doll!"

"I know you can't," Green said agreeably.

Crayton looked hopefully at Green. "You do?"

"Well, I hope not anyway." He continued to study Cray's face carefully. "I mean, you tell me: Are you fucking around with this stuff?"

"Absolutely not," Cray said firmly.

Green thought there was a false heartiness to his friend's conviction, but the guy was probably just shaken up. *And why not?* Still, he said, "You gotta admit, Cray, you've been getting a little further out, in terms of your clothes and the walking stick and the charms." He pointed at a necklace around Cray's throat: a red leather cord from which dangled the fang of a water moccasin and a tiny hawk feather.

"So what?" Cray said. "It's a *look*, you know? Like H-Man's always wearing suits, and Don's always got on sports jerseys."

"Okay," Green said reasonably, "if the voodoo deal's just a look, and you're not casting spells or consulting Ouija boards or tarot cards, then what's the problem? What are you so flipped out for? If I were you, I'd be *glad* the tennis player died. You're in first place by a mile. *I* haven't had one goddamned corpse."

"I suppose you're right." Crayton managed a smile. "I guess I oughta enjoy it while I can; Stacie's probably the last corpse I'll get for the whole year."

Green laughed. "There's that, I guess."

They talked for a few more minutes, comparing notes on the Kay and Eliza relationships, and Green admitted, without going into too much detail, that he and Kay had spent the last evening in the Westin.

Cray grinned happily. "That's awesome, brah. You and Kay are perfect for each other." He snapped his fingers. "That reminds me: Didn't someone mention getting together for drinks tomorrow night? Before everyone scatters for Thanksgiving?"

"Right. We're gonna meet at Markey's at seven-thirty. You guys in?"

Cray frowned. "Well, *I'll* be there at some point. I gotta take Eliza to the airport. Her plane leaves at eight. And I'm gonna take her to dinner at Dooky Chase first."

"Well, if we don't see y'all, tell her we said Happy Turkey and all that."

"Absolutely. You guys think you'll still be around? I can head to Markey's from the airport."

"Why not? It's a holiday after all—though my flight is at some ungodly hour Thanksgiving morning. But yeah, we'll be there."

"Cool. I'll see you then." Cray gave Green a thumbs-up, opened the door, and exited against a sky the color of weak lemonade. Green put on the Subdudes' *Annunciation* CD, sighed, then punched the blinking light on the answering machine. The only death league-related call was in fact from J.C., who was surprisingly mellow: "Mister Commissioner, there ain't no way that goddamn Crayton is practicing voodoo. Marie fuckin' Laveau couldn't pull off two in a row like that... Tell him I'll catch his ass though. I'm a Lou'sanna politican now, and there ain't *nothin'* more evil than that." Then his baritone cackle faded out, the machine beeped, and the next message came on.

It was someone named Chief Spencer, calling at the request of Papa Hipolyte, who'd had a massive heart attack and was in a hospital in Natchez, Mississippi.

CHAPTER TWENTY-EIGHT

Natchez, Mississippi

Papa was in a double room, in the bed closest to the door. On the other side of a partially drawn curtain, whispering, was a set of relatives huddled around a patient Green couldn't see. Green smelled antiseptic, mop water, and someone's Juicy Fruit.

Papa's eyes were closed. He seemed small and drawn; Green felt like he was looking at him through the wrong end of a pair of binoculars. Then the old man must've sensed Green's presence. He opened his eyes and blinked, grinning in surprise when he focused on Green. He beckoned, and Green felt immeasurably better when Papa said in a low but steady voice, "What brings you to Natchez, boy? We got better restaurants in New Orleans."

Green smiled. "Came to see this bad-ass piano player I heard about. Booker incarnate. You wouldn't know where I might find him, would you?"

"Ain't no piano folks around here, Greenie," Papa said. "Just hard-headed old men who don't listen to they own bodies or doctors."

Green took one of Papa's warm, papery hands in his own. "Go easy on yourself, amigo. Nobody wants to believe they're sick."

"Or mortal, Greenie," Papa said philosophically. "Or mortal."

"Nonsense," Green said with a bit of optimism he didn't really feel. "You're gonna live forever, brother."

"Well, a while anyways. Leastways, that's what the cardiologist says."

"Absolutely." The truth was, though, that while Green had no reason to believe otherwise, he was frightened for Papa. Chief Spencer, who turned out to be one of the musicians on the tour and had been the guy who'd found Papa after he collapsed, assured Green on the phone that Papa was stable, but reiterated that the old man had been asking for him. Green left at once in Cray's car, the keys of which his pal had instantly handed over on hearing the news. He'd even insisted Green take his Texaco card for emergency purposes.

Now, after Green had roared up I-55 in the Camaro, they talked about the tour; how much Papa had been enjoying it. They'd been all the way to South Carolina, Memphis, and the Florida Keys. Papa asked how things were back home. Green told him about Kay, and was delighted at the light of happiness that shown in the old man's eyes.

"See, I done told you," Papa laughed. "Good lookin' young buck like yourself, you always were gonna land a good'n. Now, I just gotta get off my ass and get back and meet this lucky young lady!"

The brief speech seemed to tire Papa, and he went into a brief coughing spell. Alarmed, Green started to get up from the chair he'd pulled over, but Papa waved him off. After a moment, the hacking abated. "I'm all right," he said. "Just need to throw that damn pipe away."

Green gazed fondly at Papa for a moment. "So. How long you stuck in this joint?"

Papa shrugged. "A few days, I guess. I was still hazy early this morning, but I know they said something about electrolytes and seeing how much actual damage been done to the heart."

Green said, "I'm sure they'll transfer you to New Orleans as soon as they can."

Papa laughed. "Goddamn, boy, you think I'm Donald Trump? I can't afford to transport my ass to New Orleans! I'll stay here till they say I'm well enough to leave, *then* I'll go home. But I ain't hiring no ambulance so I can sit in an exact copy of *this* place—just so's I can say I'm in New Orleans."

Green hadn't thought about money. He supposed one *would* have to pay to transfer from one hospital to the next.

"Speaking of money," Green said awkwardly, "I, uhm, have a bit of savings if it'd help. If you need anything or need to me to pay some bills until you get back."

Papa looked at Green for a moment. His eyes actually moistened. "You all right for a white kid," Papa murmured.

Green smiled. He knew Papa appreciated the offer. "Hey, I'm just trying to assuage the guilt of the centuries."

Papa nodded sagely. "Well, thank you, boy, but I'm fine. Always wondered if I'd get to use this Medicare and Social Security shit before the government fucked it up." He took a deep breath. "Or before I died."

"Nobody's dying here," Green said firmly. He stared at Papa till the old man met his gaze and nodded. "Is there anything else you need? Magazines? A soft drink?"

"Well, I wonder if I could ask a favor." He nodded at a cardboard box next to the bedside table. "Chief brought me a few things from the hotel. Nothing major. Some papers and clothes and such. Could you take 'em back and drop 'em at my place? It'd be one thing less to worry about."

Green, who had a key to Papa's, said, "Of course. I'd be glad to."

"Thanks." Papa paused and grinned. "You know what I really want? I want my pipe and a cold Miller and the piano at Lafitte's." Just as quickly, though, the smile faded. "Probably not gonna get any of that for a long time. Maybe never."

"Nonsense. You're pouting," Green said, and was relieved when Papa nodded, embarrassed. "You'll be back at the piano before you know it."

He was about to add that he'd read beer was actually *good* for recovering heart patients when an intrusive and inappropriate thought leapt into Green's mind.

Ask him about the Halloween gumbo.

The thought startled Green, not only in its inappropriateness, but also because it reminded him of how much voodoo stuff he'd wanted to ask Papa since he'd left—in particular about the gumbo and the chicken ceremony at the Halloween party and Cray's growing preoccupation with the material aspects of voodoo.

But Green couldn't—*wouldn't*—do that. There was no way he could bring up anything that might upset Papa. For the first time, it occurred to Green that he'd avoided thinking about certain things, the gumbo in particular, because he had an excuse *not* to think about it; he didn't have to because Papa could tell him *when he got back.*

He'd been using Papa's absence as an excuse to avoid dealing with the psychic hangover from Maman Arielle's gumbo—and that it was something that very much still bugged him. No pun intended. In that brief moment sitting in Papa's hospital room, he concluded that he himself would figure out what the deal was with the gumbo—even if it turned out to be nothing more than a truly odd but harmless bit of folklore...

And then Papa surprised him.

"Paramedics say I actually died for a moment yesterday morning," he said mildly.

Green stared at Papa. "My God." He was so shocked he couldn't think of anything to say.

Papa shrugged. "I guess it ain't all that uncommon. It's a strange thing to think on though. That you've been dead—even if it's only for a few seconds."

Green was fascinated, though didn't know how much he should pursue this line of conversation. Was talking about dying good for the patient? He thought for a moment, then figured it couldn't hurt to ask the one obvious question.

"Do you remember anything?" Everyone knew, of course, about the apocryphal light at the end of a tunnel, with the dead people immersed in a sense of warm well-being as they drifted toward the glow. Green wondered if Papa had experienced something like that.

"Not really," Papa said. He paused. "There was one thing though." Green noticed Papa was tugging at his fingers nervously.

"What?"

"I kinda remember Chief being there, pounding on my chest and performing some CPR shit and hollering." Papa's eyes squinted with concentration. "And then, suddenly, clear as a bell, a woman I knew long ago—somebody *dead*—was kneeling over me."

Green struggled to stay calm. "An old girlfriend? Your mother?"

Papa took a raspy deep breath and shook his head. "No, nobody good," he whispered, as though he were still amazed by what had happened. "You recall the voodoo queen I told you about? The one with the gator?"

"Yeah?" Green said fearfully. This was the last thing he expected to hear.

"It was her. Arielle."

Green stiffened. "Her name was *Arielle*?" He felt like he'd been doused in cold seawater.

Papa picked up a cup of water and sipped. "That's right. I never told you her name, did I?"

Then Green remembered. *His* Arielle—the fucking gumbo woman—was the daughter. He'd just been thinking about Maman Arielle, and now Papa was telling him that another Maman Arielle had appeared to him. Green's throat felt like it was full of paste.

Papa went on. "I swear to the Lord, it was like everything else just faded away and she was right there. It wasn't like an apparition, and it wasn't like she was alive either. But it wasn't zombie bullshit. I don't know *what* it was but...fuck, I could *smell* the patchouli oil she was wearing—" He shook his head and, Green thought, looked frightened. "Look, I told you. Voodoo is about spirits. Ancestors. They're always near in one sense or another. I mean—" He seemed like he was about to say something important, then swallowed and looked down at the bed sheets.

Green gave him a moment, then offered, "Maybe it was, like, a woman paramedic and you were...I dunno...confused."

Papa shook his head. "I thought about that. Then I asked Chief this morning. He says there wasn't a woman anywhere the whole time—and he rode in the ambulance with me to the hospital."

Green ran his hands back through his hair and wished desperately for a beer. Rationality told him Papa had experienced some adrenal or fear overdose and projected the woman—but then, as a guy who'd personally seen centipedes in soup, who was he to be telling someone what they'd seen or not seen?

"But why *her*?"

Papa licked his lips nervously. "I don't know why it was her... I mean, why not my mother or...?"

Green knew he had to stop this conversation; Papa was way too agitated. He also looked like maybe he *did* have a suspicion as to why Maman Arielle's spirit or ghost or whatever had appeared to him—and it was certainly not an angel if her dark rituals in life indicated anything about the beyond. "Strange things happen, Papa," Green said, trying to soothe. "To everybody."

"Damn right," the old man muttered. He paused, his breath ragged, and his eyes got large and distant with the recollection. Green glanced up at the heart monitor. The rate had definitely elevated, though it was regular.

"Papa, maybe—"

Papa cut him off. "No, listen. I got to say this," he said. He stared at Green and grabbed his hand in his own palms, which were now slick with chilled sweat.

"At first, I was sure she'd come to kill me, an' I could actually *feel* myself sinking down. But just before I passed out, her eyes meet mine and I feel this *surge* sweep through me. Like energy. And she says, 'Don't worry, old man, you're gonna be just fine.'"

Papa's grip on Green's hand was fierce as he leaned forward, staring with uncomprehending and tangible fear. "Now what the fuck does *that* mean?"

CHAPTER TWENTY-NINE

New Orleans, Louisiana

Crayton mumbled, "Eliza, can you answer that?"

The phone continued to ring and, as Cray crawled toward consciousness, he remembered Eliza probably wouldn't answer because, *oh yeah*, she had an early meeting and hadn't spent the night. His eyes creaked open and focused on the orange digital numerals from the alarm clock on the dresser across the bedroom. It was 4:19 a.m. The ringing continued, and Cray reached across the bed and patted around on the nightstand for the telephone. *Why hadn't the goddamned machine picked up?*

He grabbed the receiver and said, "Hello?" and tasted the stale funk of sleep on his tongue. There was a tinny, buzzy reception and a series of clicks. "Hello? Eliza? Who is this?"

No response, only a humming noise that sounded like a country road power line or the distant advance of summertime thunderclouds. Then, a voice.

"Crayton?" It was a male, not someone familiar, and sounded far away, as though speaking from a tunnel. "Crayton, I... I need my—" The voice faded in and out against the tidal hum.

"Who is this?" Cray was wide awake now. "Green? Is that you?"

The voice was back, competing now with a new sound, a high-pitched whine. "Crayton, please... Can you return my..." The next few words were garbled and Cray couldn't make out what the voice said.

"I can't hear you! Who the fuck is this?" Cray wasn't normally happy about prank calls or even wrong numbers—though whoever this was clearly knew his name—but something about this was eerie as hell. *Beyond the normal nuisance factor.* He realized he was actually nervous—yet he couldn't put the phone down.

"...knew you'd help... It's Marcus. Your old pal Marcus..." Then the phone went dead—not even a dial tone.

Cray finally clicked on the light and stared at the phone. "Who the fuck's Marcus?" he muttered, pressing on the phone's Talk button until at last he got a dial tone. *Well, at least* that *was back to—*A massive jolt of fear roared through him like surging water as Crayton realized that there was only one Marcus he could think of.

The fucking mortician.

Cray dropped the phone and whipped his head up, darting glances into the corners of the tiny bedroom as though imps might be hiding there. He realized he was panting in short gasps. Of course, there was no one there. Cray swallowed, tasting his fear, willing his heart rate to slow down while he tried to sweep out the tendrils of sleep from his system and think rationally about what could explain the call—

He laughed out loud when he realized what he was thinking.

What else could explain the call?

Who *else* would it be? Mama Arielle—with what was getting to be a routine stop on the mind-fuck highway. Fuck. It was a progression. Obviously—and it had all started with that first visit to the funeral home.

The grating sound of Marcus' voice bounced again through his brain and Crayton felt like he'd been jolted with a Taser. He fought to stay calm.

Okay. First things first. The old Ray Davies line came into his head. *Stay...in...control...*Cray willed himself to get out of bed and engage in normalcy. He would duck into the restroom and take a healthy piss, the sort you'd take even if dead embalmers weren't calling you on the phone. He flipped on the light and saw...

(Of course. No wonder you called, Marcus. The trocar you shoved into your own brain is angled in my sink...)

...a trocar extending over the rim because it was too long to fit. The bowl of the sink, the beige tile wall directly above the faucets, and the scratched vanity mirror were geysered with Rorschach patterns of dried brown blood. And the razored point of the tool, Cray was able to note before he sensibly leaned over the toilet and vomited, was flecked with bits of what could only be Marcus' flesh.

After puking prodigiously, Cray leaned back on his haunches, his feet icy on the cold tile of the bathroom floor, and wiped his chin with the back of his hand. *Well,* he thought, managing a shaky grin and thinking far more rationally than he'd have given himself credit for, *this gris-gris stuff will chew on your brain. No doubt about that...*

...A few hours later, Crayton sat behind the counter of the Voodoo Shoppe, distractedly pricing a shipment of High John the Conqueror root. It was sunny and cool outside, and the air smelled oddly clean for the Quarter. A brass band comprised of elementary school kids marched down the street, doing a credible "When It's Sleepy Time Down South," and it inspired Cray to slip Louis Armstrong and His Hot Seven into the store disc player.

But he couldn't enjoy it. Too much was happening. Earlier, after scouring blood off his bathroom walls—blood from a guy who'd been dead several days—he'd thought about knocking on Green's apartment door with the clear intention of explaining everything that had been happening. He damned sure wasn't going to confide in Eliza; she'd freak. But hell, he could tell Green, couldn't he? The guy was his best friend and had been there when Marcus eighty-sixed himself. He'd even tasted, ah, vermin gumbo.

Cray finished with the roots and started placing them back in the box for transport over to the herbal aisle. The thing was, up till now, Cray had enjoyed all the *Twilight Zone* stuff and didn't *want* to share it with Eliza or Green. He liked the implied secrecy of the whole thing—that it was being staged for him alone. And yes, fun stuff had been happening that couldn't otherwise be explained.

And the phone call this morning? Well, Maman Arielle had upped the ante—and no, Cray wasn't psychotic. He had a trocar and a dumpster full of slow-mo crows to prove he wasn't hallucinating stuff. So. Tell Green? Tell him *what?* That maybe the deaths of draft picks one and two weren't coincidences? That Crayton had a secret altar he'd constructed in the St. Ignatius garage where he'd actually placed improvised black magic spells on Sam Gallagher and Stacie Bates?

What if Green jumped to conclusions and accused him of something ludicrous, like murder?

Pinpoints of icy sweat surfaced on his palms, and suddenly the store felt dangerously short of air. Cray swallowed and his ears popped. *No*, he told himself, *it's definitely not murder. It's a shitty coincidence. Admittedly, I have no business jacking with stuff I don't understand, and it's wrong, but it ain't murder. And I'm through with it. I'll simply take down the altar like a day-after Christmas tree and be done with the whole fucking experiment.*

He came out from behind the counter with the Conqueror box and started stocking the empty bin between a display of chicken feet and a shelf of Power Oil bottles.

"How are you today?" From behind him, a woman's voice, musical and soothing, like slow waves on a warm sea, scared the hell out of him, and he knocked several roots onto the plank flooring. He hadn't heard anyone come in.

He spun and stared into the pleasantly smiling face of Maman Arielle.

"Jesus," Crayton breathed. He was aware, on some level, that *coincidence* no longer held any meaning for him at all.

Arielle seemed taller than Crayton remembered from her goofer dust visit to the shop and, improbably enough, younger. Today, she was dressed in an old-fashioned blue cotton dress with a swirling skirt that brushed the floor. It buttoned tightly up the middle from her waist to a low-cut neckline, and her massive breasts, the rich color of chocolate Easter bunnies, threatened to spill into the room.

Her blue-gold eyes, the color of a perfect autumn afternoon, held Crayton motionless. She looked at him with the affection of an aunt for a favorite nephew, but beneath her warm concern hovered a heavy aura like an electric charge. She exuded a heady scent of cooking spices, grapefruit, and bougainvillea that completely overwhelmed the ingrained and cloying patchouli incense smell of the Voodoo Shoppe.

"I'm sorry I startled you," she said. "You spilled the Conqueror."

"Uhm, no problem," Crayton stammered. It was difficult to tear away from her focus, but he finally did so, bending over to pick up the roots. He felt naked under her stare, so he said, "Feel free to look around."

"Thanks. I think I will." There was a hint of amusement to her tone, as though she knew her presence was making him acutely nervous. Cray straightened up and hastily crammed the rest of the roots in the proper bin, then scuttled to safety behind the counter where he could watch her.

She was moving casually through the rear of the shop with the delicate ease of a ballet dancer, humming some off-key show tune. Cray mopped his brow. He wished more customers would come into the shop; being alone with her filled him with a sense of vague dread.

Maman Arielle stepped behind a velvet rope and was standing before the pseudo-replica of Marie Laveau's altar in a tiny alcove at the very rear of the store. Cosima charged cretins five dollars to check it out.

Apparently, Maman Arielle thought it was funny, because she eased her way back to the front of the store, a huge smile on her face. She held out a five-dollar bill. "For the altar."

Cray rang up the money. She stood there, gazing at him with a pleasant smile on her face until he couldn't take it anymore. To break the tension, he asked, "Did you find everything you were looking for?"

"Actually, no," she said, shifting her stare and studying the shelves over Cray's head.

"Maybe I could help," Cray said, though in fact he wanted her to haul ass at top speed.

"Yes, I'm certain you can," she said, returning her burrowing eyes to Crayton's face. "I'd like my birds back. And the trocar." She pronounced the latter with a trilling accent on the first "r."

Cray couldn't believe he heard correctly. "Your *what?*"

She smiled at him pleasantly. "The birds you took out of Brother Arcenet's eye sockets. And the instrument Marcus used to kill himself. That was awful, no?"

A wash of white heat flushed over Cray and he gripped the counter, afraid he'd fall over. "I—"

She giggled like a cheerleader caught making a ribald joke. "Surely you knew I would come for them at some point?"

Cray simply couldn't compute what was happening. "I'm not sure I follow you, ma'am."

"Oh. Well then," Maman Arielle said with the exaggerated simplicity one would use explaining to a four-year-old why it was wrong to throw rocks at kittens. "The birds were part of a ritual, you see. And when you took them, you interrupted the ritual. And I presented you with the trocar and the flying birds as a sort of demonstration. Amazing, wasn't it? Marcus killed himself for *you*, after all—although I'm not sure he'd see it that way." She cackled.

It took Crayton every bit of self-discipline not to vault over the counter and out onto Dauphine Street, sprinting away like a drug-fueled Olympian. "I...I don't know what you're talking about," he stammered again. *Marcus killed himself for* me?

She sighed with infinite good nature. "Let me explain it this way," she said. "That altar"—she pointed over her shoulder to the rear of the store—"is ridiculous, right, *chér?*"

"Uh, sure," Cray said. He felt trapped. It was one thing to theorize the idea of Maman Arielle, New Orleans Voodoo Queen, as a shadowy concept. It was quite a-goddamned-nother for her to be *standing here* in front of him, *confirming it...*

And now she was babbling about the corny altar...

"It's ridiculous," she was saying, "but then, the building does not make the church, no?"

Cray stared at her, overwhelmed and not a little frightened. *How'd she know about the fucking birds?*

"Surely," she continued, smiling hugely, "God doesn't care whether we worship in the St. Louis Cathedral or in some tarpaper shack out in the bayou. Right?" She leaned over the counter. "You're sweating, *chér,*" she said, reaching out and gently wiping a droplet of sweat from his forehead. She slowly touched the finger to her tongue.

Cray didn't know what her agenda was, or how she'd orchestrated everything, but she damned sure hadn't stopped by to check out the big Thanksgiving Day incense sale.

"Why are you here?" he finally asked, his voice low and steady.

She looked innocent, puzzled. "Well, again, my birds. And we were talking about that altar back there. How *wrong* it is. It is nothing more than a cheap display that serves no power. On the other hand, in the service of power, with the proper conduit, is it actually possible for something like that to *be* wrong?"

"I don't know what you're talking about," Cray whispered, but it suddenly dawned on him that this seemed headed in a predetermined direction. He reeled at the thought that this woman knew *everything.* She'd given him the goofer dust—just before he'd started dating Kay. She was behind the birds, or at least had reacted when he blundered along and stole them from her precious fucking ritual. And what the hell did all this imply about the meaning behind that hideous gumbo?

Lost in an escalating panic, it took Crayton a moment to realize Maman Arielle was speaking to him. But when her words registered, he felt like someone had plunged a syringe of insect repellent into his brain.

"We're talking about *altars,* Crayton," she said, and when she used his name he actually moved one more step toward total hysteria. She leaned further and he was overwhelmed by a sudden and heady sense of eroticism suffusing her. "If you somehow tap into the power," she said, sounding all of a sudden like an engineering professor, "then anything can become a conduit. So you disrupted Marcus' ritual—*our* ritual—and now you have the birds. *Cher,* you placed them on *your* altar.

"And *it* worked, didn't it?"

CHAPTER THIRTY

Cray's answering machine came on. Again, Green left the time and a brief message reminding him, as previously arranged, that they were all assembled at Markey's for Thanksgiving Eve cocktails. He shrugged, exited the phone booth, and found Donny standing at the bar watching ESPN while he waited on a beer. Markey's was a longtime local's hangout. From the St. Ignatius Apartments, you simply angled a few blocks on Royal through the Marigny, into the Bywater and the corner at Louisa Street. It was a well-worn and comfortable bar—zero *turistas*, which was always good—with scuffed linoleum floors, tall round-top tables, pool tables, and a shuffleboard table. The ramshackle wood plank exterior was painted bright red and, it pleased J.C. to no end to note, a canvas banner, still hanging one wall, endorsed Uncle Wallace in his successful bid for congress.

"Can't find Cray?" Donny asked, accepting a Coors from the bartender and dropping bills on the counter.

"I don't know where he is. He should've been here by now."

They walked to the corner of the room by the shuffleboard table where Kay and Huey and J.C. and Darby were seated. The jukebox played Better Than Ezra's "WWOZ."

"Cray's not at the apartment or answering his cell phone," Green announced, sitting and draping his arm around Kay.

J.C. scratched his chin tiredly. "He'd best get his scarecrow ass in here if he wants to drink a toast with his J.C.-ness. I had a long day today and I've got an early day tomorrow." He took a healthy drink from his glass of Glenfiddich. "Darby and I are goin' to meet Uncle Wallace in Baton Rouge and drive him on in for the holiday."

"So, Darby, you're staying with J.C. for Thanksgiving?" Kay asked.

"Yeah," Darby said. "My family's in Rhode Island, and since I've got a shoot on Friday..." She shrugged and leaned over, grabbing her Perrier.

From what Green could figure, Darby's main job was as some sort of catalog model, though, given her decidedly bimboesque approach to fashion, Green could never quite pin down whom she might work for. He smiled, imagining the staid Bitoun family during the crystal-and-chandelier Thanksgiving feast as they attempted to reconcile their old-line Garden District image with Darby's deep cleavage line and aerodynamically enhanced hair.

J.C. said, "An' Green's going home to Houston, an' Kay's staying here." He looked at H-Man, who sat happily with a handful of popcorn in one hand

and a bottle of Abita in the other. "What about you, H-Man? You going to Lake Charles with Donny?"

"Might as well," Huey said. "All you bastards hauled ass last year and I ended up eating frozen eggrolls I microwaved at Lafitte's."

"Why didn't you come eat with us?" J.C. asked.

"You didn't ask," H-Man replied.

J.C. looked sheepish. "Surely it's not possible for a Bitoun to act so callous on such a day."

H-Man shrugged. "Egg rolls," was all he said.

"Change-the-subject time," Donny piped in. "We haven't discussed Stacie Bates yet. Is anybody here just a little curious about Crayton and his death picks? Am I the only one that thinks we're into bad karma here?" He wolfed down a handful of peanuts from a bowl on the table.

"Cray's as freaked as any of us," Green said wearily. "I saw him right after he found out about Stacie, and he was shook up." Kay gave his knee a supportive squeeze.

Donny held out his palms in a wait-a-minute gesture. "I don't just mean Cray, Green, though his deal, so far, is frankly impossible. But I've been thinking about the death league all day." He gestured at J.C. "He's got a corpse too."

J.C. and Green exchanged glances. "Isn't that the idea?"

"Well, yeah," Donny continued. "But it's actually happening. The entire concept is, I dunno, *unhealthy.*" He looked around and swallowed nervously. "Like we're *all* making it happen, just by being involved."

Huey barked in disbelief. J.C. selected the moment to light cigarettes for himself and Darby.

"Okay," Green said slowly, "let me see if I'm following you. What you're saying is that just by being involved in the death league, by *rooting* for people to die, so to speak, that collectively we're causing people to keel over dead. Right?"

Donny shook his head angrily. "I'm just saying it's not a great thing to do. It certainly *can't* be good karma. But to get back to Cray—"

Huey cut in. "Hold on a second," he said, signaling the bartender for another beer. "Here's what *I* think." He leaned forward as if to tell a great secret. "I think you're just pissed, Donny, because you're in last place." He looked apologetically at Green. "You and me and Green are, that is."

Donny started to respond, but Huey cut him off with a wave of his hand. "When Cray hatched this plan, you were the biggest supporter out of all of us. You were joking a mile a minute, yukking it up about 'corpses' and 'rot-cakes.' And now you're losing and you don't want to play anymore." He sat back and grinned, enjoying his analysis and Donny's discomfiture.

"Bullshit," Donny said. "I'll be the first to admit I thought it was a funny idea. Hell, I'm as cynical as anyone here. But the more I think about it, the more it seems like it's just not good karma."

"Okay, John Lennon," Huey said, taking a beer from the bartender. "But I know you pretty well, Don, and it seems to me that if *your* first- and second-round draft picks keeled over in order, you'd be strutting around like General Patton." He looked over at J.C., who was listening intently, puffing on his cigarette. "You too, for that matter, J.C."

J.C. raised his eyebrows and aimed a trail of smoke at the window. "I'm in it, I'm playin', and I admit it was a gas when one of my picks died." He drained his Scotch. "But unlike the rest of you, I *did* have doubts from the word go—and I said so." He crushed out his cigarette and stood up, holding out his arm for Darby.

"J.C., don't get pissed," Huey said. "We're just talking."

J.C. grinned amiably. "I ain't pissed; we've gotta go. But I'm telling y'all *this*." His smile faded and he looked at them earnestly. "I dig Crayton; think he's an entertaining dude. But there's something wrong with this voodoo stuff, and y'all can laugh your asses off at me if you want. If I ever find out, though, he's actually fucking around with it, trying to hurt people, I'll voodoo his young ass." J.C. shrugged. "Now. Y'all have a happy Thanksgiving." And so saying, he called to the bartender, told her to put everyone's drinks on his credit card tab, and ushered Darby out into the night.

They waited another half-hour. Donny remained adamant that something was out of kilter in Crayton's success. And that he hadn't shown up was definitely suspicious. But Green continued to defend him.

"Listen," he said, "we're all overlooking something here. Cray's prognostication doesn't seem that far-fetched when you remember that Stacie Bates had cancer. I wasn't aware of it at the time, but Cray was. He definitely did his homework. Hell, if *I'd* known she was sick, I'd damn sure have drafted her."

Huey, for the first time, looked troubled. "I didn't think anything about it when he drafted a sixteen-year-old kid. We *all* made some sick choices and besides, the Bates kid was a real jerk. But you're saying Crayton told you he knew she had cancer on *draft* day? On Halloween?"

Something about Huey's tone, and the looks he was getting from around the table, alarmed Green. "Well, I don't remember him saying *specifically* on draft day, but he told me this morning it was pretty common knowledge that she was already sick by the time we held the draft."

Donny slammed his beer down. "That's it! Fuck this! I'm gonna piss and go home. I don't need this bullshit." He stormed off to the restroom.

"What?!" Green was dumbfounded.

Kay took Green's hand, smiled gently, and said, "Okay, John McEnroe. I guess you're not much on tennis. Cray couldn't have known Stacie Bates had cancer on draft day. They didn't release her illness to the media till last week."

CHAPTER THIRTY-ONE

Throughout the gumbo z'herbes and fried chicken at Dooky Chase's, Crayton amused Eliza with a nonstop barrage of jokes and affectionate repartee—all to hide an odd, bittersweet sadness that had cloaked him since Maman Arielle's visit that afternoon.

He carefully observed Eliza's face and the way her eyes shone when she laughed; the way her tiny hands aimed her fork in the air when she made a conversational point; the way she tilted her head when fascinated by something he said.

Cray studied all these things with a desperate intensity, as though to preserve the moment forever in the photo gallery of his mind. Because he was somehow certain that, by the time Eliza came back from D.C., things wouldn't quite be the same. He wasn't precisely sure *why* he felt that way. But, en route to the airport, he felt a profound melancholy, as though he subconsciously knew something final had been set irrevocably in motion, and that somehow Eliza would not understand when it all actually played out.

When what *played out?*

Crayton had no idea. He took a deep breath and watched Eliza's plane sweep into the expanse of ink-blue night. He felt fractious over his odd feelings and determined to set his head straight by rendezvousing with the gang at Markey's.

Instead, though, without quite knowing he was even doing it, he skirted the Quarter, turned into the Fauborg Marigny, parked on Elysian Fields, and walked steadily back to Gris-Gris Gumbo. He stepped around the dinner line and went into the back bar. It was a small room—a waiting spot, really—with four stools at the bar and two round tables in the floor area. Crayton was the only customer back there. He shivered. Though it was a warm night, the bar was disconcertingly chilly.

The bartender finally came out from the kitchen, so Crayton ordered a bottle of Dixie and sipped on it. Only then did Cray address the question, *Why am I here?* Clearly, he was here of his own volition; when Maman Arielle had dropped by the Voodoo Shoppe, it wasn't like she'd casually suggested he drop by for a highball.

Cray took off his glasses and polished them with a cocktail napkin. There was a strange numbness about his every move, as though he'd received a mild general anesthetic, but the sensation was more puzzling than disturbing.

He took a sip of beer and propped his chin on his hands. Okay: he knew he'd left the airport with the conscious intent of going to Markey's—but then that wasn't *exactly* right. Part of him, the *thinking*, decision-making facet of his brain, told him he was going to Markey's. But another, more primal control force, rooted deeply in the cellar of his being, had taken over, and instead he'd come to Gris-Gris Gumbo...

A young couple dressed in evening finery strolled into the bar, loosely confident, and suddenly looked at each other as though the room was crawling with cockroaches. They backed out at astonishing speed.

Maman Arielle hadn't hypnotized him either; nothing quite so dramatic as that. In fact, after her bomb-dropping statements this afternoon about his altar, the trocar, and Joshua Arcenet's secret crows, she hadn't said much at all. She'd just smiled her lizard's smile, patted him on the cheek like he was a little kid, and left without the items she'd asked for.

When she'd disappeared on Dauphine and the store was empty save for the heavy musk of her presence, Cray experienced such a moment of fear that he thought his whole being would collapse in on itself, like an old building demolished by explosives detonated deep within its infrastructure.

In one horrible flash, Crayton realized that Maman Arielle possessed some force—the word she'd used was *power*—beyond anything he'd ever dreamed of, giving instant credibility to all the voodoo shtick he'd been fucking around with. Furthermore, she'd also exploded into cinders every comfortable religious conviction and sense of order he'd held as self-evident in his harmless, neat little world.

Cray took a deep swallow of beer and turned his thoughts inward. *And where do Sam Gallagher and Stacie Bates fit in? Those weren't just random bits of bad luck, were they? And you kinda lied to Green about the time frame on that one too. Because Stacie Bates didn't* have *cancer on Halloween. So where did it come from, that super-malignancy that spontaneously metastasized at a speed that staggered the entire staff at cancer-centric M.D. Anderson Hospital?*

It was at that instant that the reality of the situation reared up and smacked Cray between the eyes with the force of a two-by-four. And he realized with flashbulb clarity *why* he was sitting all alone in the back bar of Gris-Gris Gumbo: because somehow, when he'd plucked the baby crows from the eyes of Joshua Arcenet, he'd not only interrupted some ritual, but he'd somehow made himself privy to the magic—or whatever the hell you'd call what was going on. Somehow, he'd tapped into this...*power*. And in the past week, through a series of increasingly strange events, she'd decided *to let him know about it.*

He drained his beer; there was another one on the polished bar in front of him, though he didn't remember a bartender putting it there, or if in fact he'd even asked for it. No matter. Crayton felt an eerie, calm acceptance. The beer was there because it needed to be, just like there weren't any other customers because they didn't need to be here.

Yes, something was indeed going on. Cray had been drawn to Gris-Gris Gumbo and, in the end, it hadn't been necessary for Maman Arielle to invite him or hypnotize him or cast a spell to get him there.

Instead, she knew that, once he'd thought about it, he'd realize that Stacie Bates' cancer had started when he clipped her photo and blackened the eyes and lit his candles and muttered his half-assed and impromptu incantations—all under the sightless eyes of the dead crows. Just like Sam Gallagher acted on a whim to take a bike ride on a foggy coastal highway at the precise moment Crayton was hunched over in a cobwebbed and forgotten utility closet more than half a continent away.

Cray looked around at the empty tables, sipping beer and marveling how, in some improbable way, it had all come together. Suddenly, he felt terrific, the best he had in years. He took another thirsty pull on the icy Dixie, nodding to himself in the candle-lit, dappling shadows of the empty bar. Yes, he felt positively exhilarated and ready for whatever came next.

So he was hardly surprised when, a few minutes later, Maman Arielle came into the room through the swinging kitchen doors behind the bar. She was stunning. Her wild black hair looked like a lion's mane, and she wore a clinging, diaphanous white cotton gown under which her breasts rolled like strong waves. Crayton felt the air in the room crackle with a pagan energy, and when she smiled at him mellowly, her luminous eyes bore lazily into his brain.

Cray felt glacial anticipation course through him, and he couldn't take his eyes off her. She took his hand and led him from the bar to a corner table, where they sat down like secret lovers, and not until a silent bartender brought them two steaming mugs of a strangely spiced tea, then vanished into the back of the restaurant, did Maman Arielle finally speak.

Her voice was rich with the promise of the night, her accent lilted like ancient island song. "Tonight," she whispered, "you will meet the dead. "

CHAPTER THIRTY-TWO

Two hours later, in a small courtyard of aged red bricks in back of the restaurant—separate from the larger courtyard where the Halloween party had been held, and next to a small cottage Cray learned had once been a slave quarters where a family of seven had died of the Yellow Jack—the yellow fever epidemic that had killed over forty-thousand New Orleanians in the nineteenth century—Cray was initiated into *Les Culte des Morts*. And if, in previous days, the suggestion that the group actually required such a ceremony, much as, oh, the Cub Scouts are sworn in to do good deeds, might have struck Crayton as curious or even goofy, the actual procedure itself was awe-inspiring. There was no other way to put it.

There were perhaps twelve people in all: Cray, Maman Arielle, the Henri guy Crayton remembered from the Halloween party—he was, Cray learned, *La Place*, the second *bokor* behind Maman Arielle—at least four other men, and several women of varying ages. Except for Maman Arielle, all were dressed in loose white pants and diaphanous cotton jerseys. Somehow, Cray was similarly dressed, though he didn't actually remember changing clothes.

Because, by the time Maman Arielle introduced him in the small courtyard, pure reality was a bit of a gauzy concept. He dreamily assumed something was in the spiced tea he'd drank—something to heighten consciousness or perhaps bend perception to heighten the proceedings—and that was fine with him. Hell, maybe his perceptions *weren't* distorted. Maybe this was just the way it was going down...

He processed the imagery as though through water: *an incessant tattoo of drums—the same rhythm as when Marcus killed himself?—the sweat-box heat; a dark altar at one end of the courtyard, covered with feathers and beads and palmetto and sassafras roots, pictures of random corpses in open-coffin funerals, glasses of rum and pieces of fruit placed before a decaying human skull adorned with a black top hat and a cheery cigar; hypnotic swaying and dancing; the Impressionistic glow of gas lanterns and a hundred skittering candle flames; swirling clouds of incense; a black box before the altar containing Damballah, the holy serpent; the sour smell of body musk cut by the briny, rotted, cooking-blood aroma of gumbo bubbling in a black cauldron in the middle of the floor—a nganga, Maman Arielle calls it...*

He hasn't seen inside the cauldron, yet, but the feeling in his belly, like a sheepshank knot of cold grease, tells him this would be—would have to be—the recipe Green sampled.

Still, Cray is excited and astonished; whatever is going on here is real. He can taste power all around like a current-charged coin on his tongue. Maman Arielle, resplendent in flowing robes of red and white, calling out patois and, wielding a walking stick much like Crayton's, raises it to the sky and invokes the spirit of Baron Samedi to open the gate between the Visible and Invisible worlds. Cray feels as though sparks are randomly winking on and off just under his skin.

On one side, three men are playing wood-carved drums. Maman Arielle pours rum around the peristalses of the courtyard. Using a powder of ground bone—far heavier, Cray surmises, than mere ash or sand—she then draws a series of quick vévé symbols on a black sheet laid out on the ground. Throughout, bottles of rum and brandy are passed among them. Soon, as Maman works, the rest begin chanting in some garbled fashion; Cray recognizes English words, but the order is strange and makes no sense. He will later learn they're Catholic prayers for the dead, said backward. Some start to dance or convulse—and will do so throughout the ceremony—in a jerking, free-form spontaneity that Cray realizes, in a flash of wonder, indicates the supplicants are being ridden by the loas—*the spirits.*

Several offerings are made to Baron Samedi, first by Maman and then Henri, and more candles are lit. Then Cray is led into the center of the courtyard.

Maman Arielle gestures and Henri and another man emerge from the shadows, awkwardly carrying something, cloaked in a shroud, between them. Cray thinks it could be the body of a dog, perhaps, and his heartbeat shifts into high gear. They place the object prone at the foot of the altar and remove the shroud—and though he can distinguish no specific details, Cray can see well enough to know it's not a fucking dog. It's the corpse of a girl.

"Jesus, it's...a human," he breathes. Crayton's eyes widen and his stomach lurches, and beads of sour sweat form on his forehead and ooze like heavy oil down his cheeks. His hands shake. There is an instant when it seems to him that there is a cessation of his own internal gravity—and everything from the core values of his belief system to his actual knowledge of the rhythms and dimensions of existence have lost anchor and are tumbling weightlessly inside his brain.

Maman leads him to the body. As they draw nigh, Cray can smell a hint of decay, far different than the smoldering ruin in the...nganga (he has to think a minute to remember the odd word)... This scent is sharp, like a suddenly opened jar of moldy berry jam—and he determines mostly by the burial dress, some sort of plaid church school uniform, that the child is in fact a bit older than she at first appeared, though clearly she hasn't been dead long. She was maybe sixteen years old, with reddish hair in a feathered wedge style, Cray thinks ludicrously, that seems stylistically inappropriate for adolescence, as though her mother had been the pushy sort in a hurry for the kid to grow up and provide the opportunity for Mom to live vicariously through the child's glory. Well, *that* ain't happenin'...

He tries not to focus on her face, which is moon-pale and seems, in the pirouetting flames, to glisten with some moist sheen wrought of a post-exhumation change in temperature. In any case, the courtyard is too dim for Crayton to absorb any specific details as to her features—for which he is grateful. And though of course he wonders—who is this person and how did her cadaver end up here, a few hours before millions of homes across America will start roasting Thanksgiving turkeys?—he dares not ask Maman Arielle. One thing's clear: Henri or someone has executed a mission in which the body of a child was stolen from a grave.

Now Arielle is pressing something into his palm and whispering instructions, and he glances down in deep-freeze comprehension and sees a pair of tin snips in his hand. She pushes him toward the dead girl with gentle encouragement—and before he can think about what he's doing or whether he actually has the free will to choose not to do it, he fumblingly grasps the corpse's cool, slick right hand. Hesitating only a moment to peer at the shadowy face, as though idiotically to convey a request for forgiveness, Cray locates and grips the little finger.

He swallows and, opening the arms of the tin snips, gently tightens the blades till they close on the meat of the dead kid's finger...

With such effort that he gasps, Cray cracks through the bone and severs the digit—and though it plops to the ground and he cries out, he can't hear it for the roaring in his ears and the delighted, bird-like exultations of delight from the members of the cult standing in motionless periphery. Quickly, Cray kneels, finds the finger on the brick surface and offers it to Maman Arielle. In minaret hand gestures, muttering, she consecrates it and hands it back to Crayton. He tucks it into his pocket.

"This is your talisman, your protection," she says, smiling as though she handed him a four-leaf clover. "Now, one small sacrifice from you, mon cher." She nods and they move to the smoking cauldron. Henri materializes next to them. Steam rises in almost leisurely fashion, and the scent of putrescence is almost overwhelming. *Didn't Green say the smell was good?* Cray watches Arielle, trusting her despite a sense of dread. *Did he really think he'd go through this without offering something of himself?*

He realizes that, ludicrously, despite his manic state of fascination and near-terror, he is tapping his foot in time to the incessant pounding of the goddamn drums—*who are these Buddy Rich motherfuckers?*—and his eyes widen as he sees Henri holding a small silver knife.

"Hold out your palm, " Maman Arielle says. Cray jerkily extends his hand, face up, fighting the urge to bolt from the courtyard. Only then does he realize that his hand has stopped shaking—and a sense of calm creeps over him despite the fear, pinballing through the corridors of his brain, that perhaps his own little finger will be next...

"Good. You are relaxed." Maman smiles and tells him what is going to happen. Cray nods.

Henri actually winks and says, *"You won't feel nothin', brother."* He places one hand under Cray's outstretched palm for support, and with quick, feathery motions—so astonishingly performed Crayton is only vaguely aware of a slight stinging sensation—extracts a tiny, circular sliver of skin from Cray's palm, then drops it into the nganga. As if in afterthought, like it was expected of him, Cray gasps.

Maman Arielle tenderly takes his hand and turns it upside down over the cauldron, squeezing so that his blood drips into the gumbo. Cray can hear a crackling sizzle when the blood hits the surface. That's my blood, he thinks stupidly.

Then they're back standing next to the body of the dead kid. Henri hands Cray the knife and steps back. Crayton kneels on his haunches over the corpse—did someone tell him what he was supposed to do? They must have. Because he's doing it.

From somewhere an unbidden bit of mortuary science leaps through his brain.

They sew the mouth shut from the inside.

Cray bends his face over the dead girl's, studiously avoiding her closed eyes. He re-grips the knife in his right hand and with his left thumb and index finger parses her wormy lips as far apart as the industrial strength stitching will allow. With a quick, sure, delicate and perfectly aimed slashing motion, Cray cuts the thread. The pressure of his fingers forces her mouth open and a trace of trapped decomposition gas wisps into the night.

It smells, *he thinks, confused and giggling*, like Eliza's perfume. How does *that* work?

Out of nowhere, Henri kneels next to Cray, holding a dipper of the gumbo from the nganga. Carefully, so as not to spill any, he hands the dipper to Crayton. *"Pour some in her mouth,"* he says, his eyes warm behind the lenses of his glasses. *"Just a few drops. Her stomach's probably shrunk up, I'd think."* He laughs like Father Christmas.

Cray takes a deep breath and maneuvers the ladle, nibbling his upper lip in concentration. The stew dribbles into the corpse's mouth.

Henri nods, pleased at Crayton's calibrated effort. *"Now,* you *drink the rest of it."*

With only the slightest hesitation, and remembering Green's description of the Halloween gumbo as perhaps the best he'd ever tasted, Cray raises the edge of the ladle and tilts it. As he swallows, Cray can smell the disease in the soup. The sensation, though, is precisely as Green described—simply wonderful—but then something long and spiny catches in his throat. Cray reaches inside his mouth and extracts a soggy centipede and flings it away, shuddering in disgust, and...

...an image of Eliza flashes through his mind. He sees her laughing on a recent storm-splashed Thursday when she took him to Vaughan's in the Bywater to see Kermit Ruffins play. She's in love, Cray thinks happily—he's in love. It's fucking amazing. And they duck out of the soft rain under the bar's portico and she takes his hand...

...Maman takes his hand, staring at the dead girl. "Now, " she says like a magician in Jackson Square, "watch this."

Cray looks at the body—and weeps in disbelief.

The girl's eyes are fluttering—and then pop open. In the courtyard light, they glimmer with the sickly color of stale draft beer, and when she speaks her tiny voice has all the human quality of a heavy work boot squelching up from damp sand.

"Mama?" she says. "Daddy?"

CHAPTER THIRTY-THREE

Houston, Texas

Friday morning, Green was sitting in the kitchen of his parents' *Southern Living*-styled house, sipping coffee and flipping through the *Houston Chronicle's* weekend entertainment guide. His mom and sister had fallen into the Big Trap of the Christmas shoppers' calendar—bolting out the door early to get to the Galleria—and his father had actually gone to the office. His big brother Rod was playing tennis with old med school pals.

Green finished reading a review of a Mexican restaurant and, turning the page, spotted a small story touting an exhibit at the Rice University Spillman Art Museum. *Feeding the Drums: Art of the Voudoun.*

Green calmly smiled, as though some part of him had actually expected something like this; closure, perhaps, in cosmic retaliation for the note he'd found taped to his door yesterday morning when he and Kay were leaving for the airport. On a page torn from a legal pad, Crayton had apologized for not showing up at Markey's. He'd felt depressed about Eliza leaving, he wrote, knew he'd lied about Stacie Bates, and was sure Green was pissed. Finally, he *could* explain the Stacie Bates situation satisfactorily and had just acted on an impulse to be alone and get his thoughts together. It was cowardly, but seemed simpler at the time than facing them all at Markey's. He hoped Green understood, and was looking forward to seeing everyone after the weekend.

Green had reacted with more than a little skepticism. Indeed, his first impulse was to pound on Cray's door and scream a little sense into him. But Green realized, even then, that he was willing to give the guy a break, at least until they had time to talk—and Green had a plane to catch. Now, this unexpected opportunity for voodoo research seemed like an act of karmic debt.

An hour later, after parking his dad's spare Jeep in a mostly deserted campus parking lot, Green walked under a sally port and climbed the steps of the lovely Byzantine building that housed the Spillman Museum. The exhibit was in one wing off the main gallery. Green picked up a pamphlet off an unmanned information booth. There were about three people visiting the show.

Green decided to just wander around. The presentation was set up geographically, and as Green moved around the periphery, he saw work from Africa, Haiti, Cuba, Mexico, and, in a small alcove—bingo!—*New Orleans.* Obviously that was the place to start.

Inside the room was a series of photographs and paintings surrounding a glass exhibit booth in the center. Green studied the photographs first. They were black and white prints, taken from the days when licensed voodoo ceremonies took place on Sundays in the old Congo Square. The shots were grainy crowd studies, and the accompanying text didn't tell Green anything Papa hadn't already told him—though with a lot more cuss words.

He moved to the paintings. Among them was a familiar image of Marie Laveau under the moss-hung branches of a moonlit tree with a snake coiled around her neck.

The others comprised a series lurid in its day-glo depiction of a voodoo ceremony. Central to the action was a young blonde white woman being initiated into voodoo; the transformation in her face in the quartet of canvases, from rigid terror to lust, was comic book-like in its convenience.

Still, in the final two paintings, Green looked closely at a smoking cauldron set off to one side. In both works, the cauldron was simmering with a bubbling, yellow-brown broth. In the picture on the left, Green identified a human skull bobbing in the mixture, and in the other he could see a snake floating on the surface.

Maman Arielle's fucking gumbo! In actual paintings from fifty years ago! Green had found a fucking reference point for what he'd experienced in his absinthe undertow.

Maybe there *was* a history to this.

He thought back to his futile attempts to find out anything about the Halloween gumbo. He'd tried encyclopedias, the cheap voodoo books in Cray's store, even had Cray ask Cosima. Nothing. He'd even gone online. But what do you type in as keywords? *Vermin Gumbo? Soup Recipes Utilizing Insects and Human Body Parts?* He'd found nothing.

His best bet had always been Papa Hipolyte, with whom he'd spoken on the phone last night. Thank God the old man was rapidly recovering and might be home within a week. But who knew when *this* would be an appropriate topic for discussion? Depending on Papa's prognosis and how weakened his heart was, maybe never...

When he couldn't find anything else of value from the paintings, Green turned to the glass exhibit case. Aside from a few chicken claws, a voodoo doll, some herbal health remedies, a lump of John the Conqueror root, and a placard explaining the connection between Catholicism and voodoo, there wasn't much going on.

He walked back out into the main exhibit and saw a scholarly, older black guy dressed in brightly colored, traditional African clothing seated at the information desk.

Green walked over. "Excuse me, sir."

The man looked up and smiled. "Can I help you?" He had a cultured, British accent.

Green said, "Could I ask you a few questions about something in some paintings in the New Orleans section?"

"If I can help, I'll be happy to. Let's take a look." As the two walked over to the alcove, the man introduced himself as Dr. Harrison; he was a professor of anthropology at the university and had consulted on the exhibit.

Maybe today we get some answers, Green thought as they approached the paintings. He indicated the two cauldron pieces. "I was curious to know if there was any basis in reality in this gumbo, or whatever it is." He pointed at the skull and then the serpent cooking in the kettle.

Dr. Harrison put on a pair of gold-rimmed glasses and leaned over to study each of the paintings. "Well," he finally said, straightening up, "I don't want to sound like an academic, but I've got to give you an interpretive answer."

"*Anything* would help," Green laughed.

He glanced at the entire wall of paintings and frowned slightly. "Between us, they seem more like cover art from historical novels." Then he smiled. "But there *are* precedents for what the artist is depicting here."

Green nodded, hopeful.

Harrison said, "There are certain Afro-Caribbean dark religious sects whose rituals involve such a device. Santeria, Palo Mayombe, voodoo... " He pointed at the cauldron. "They're called *ngangas*." He spelled it for Green. "The *bokors*—priests who practice black magic—use *ngangas* as ongoing sacrificial vessels, stewing everything from insects and small animals to actual human body parts."

Green felt as though someone had dropped him into a well full of ice water. "What... Who are they sacrificing to?" If indeed Green looked horribly shocked, the professor didn't seem to notice.

"It depends on the nuances of the faith in question," he said. "In most cases, Baron Samedi or Baron Cimetiére—both names for the same lord of the dead. In any case, assuredly, they are sacrificing to some evil-spirit presence."

"What are they after? With these sacrifices?"

"Power. And that could mean any of a number of things—many not so great." He nodded at Green and smiled sorrowfully. "Does that help any?"

"Oh, absolutely," Green managed. "Thank you so much." He was overwhelmed with a montage of thoughts and images. *Maman Arielle is everything Papa said.* Then: *Did I ever doubt it?* Then: *Sure you did. Just like you doubt everything.* Then: *Exactly what the hell—specifically—is she doing with her* nganga?

Green had about two hundred follow-up questions for Professor Harrison, but he couldn't formulate any of them. Then the professor surprised him by saying, "May I ask why you're curious?"

Green adjusted his glasses. "Sure, sure," he said. "And thanks for the help, sir..." He thought a moment. "Well, I live in New Orleans and, uhm, voodoo has a fairly strong following there."

Dr. Harrison nodded and Green struggled for the right words. He damned sure wasn't going to admit he'd actually *tasted* from an actual *nganga*. "And I just thought I'd seen most of the stuff associated with voodoo in that context. I mean, there aren't any *real* ceremonies, or, if there are, *I* certainly don't know about 'em..." He grinned, knowing he sounded like a complete idiot. Professor Harrison watched with kind patience. Green ran his tongue over his upper lip and tried again. "I guess I just wondered if the artist knew something the rest of us don't. About New Orleans voodoo, I mean."

Dr. Harrison removed his glasses and folded them into a shirt pocket. "Well, I've never been to New Orleans. But I *can* tell you that the practice of voodoo is quite widespread as a serious faith. Like anything else, there are good practitioners and bad.

It wouldn't surprise me if black magic voodoo cults were practicing in New Orleans and utilizing *ngangas*." He looked again at the paintings. "Is that what you were after?"

"Absolutely, sir." Green hesitated, then blurted one last question. "*Is* there a specific dark voodoo sect in America that you know of? Organized?"

The professor blinked. "Well, yes, actually. There's probably more than one, but the one I know of for certain is *Les Culte des Morts*—the Cult of Death. Haitian in origin, I believe, though there was some question for a while whether they even survived the regime of Baby Doc. There was rumor some practitioners had migrated to America. I would think in most large cosmopolitan cities there are at least small sects—as you'd find with any occult or small religion. Miami, Los Angeles, New York...and certainly New Orleans."

He thought for a moment. "And, in your context, I wouldn't at all be surprised to learn they use a *nganga* as part of their rites. *Les Culte des Morts*, if I remember correctly, is an organization that utilizes the dead in ritual."

Green took a deep breath. "And this cult might've found its way to New Orleans?"

Dr. Harrison shrugged. "Well, New Orleans is certainly the nearest port offering a sympathetic societal structure." He peered at Green, not unkindly, and chose his words delicately. "Do you... Have you encountered something that leads you to ask these questions?"

Green smiled shakily. "Not really," he said slowly. He actually thought for an instant of pouring it all out for this pleasant stranger. But in the end he knew he couldn't do it. Finally, he just said, "Professor, in New Orleans, you see strange stuff every day—and that's just walking down the street."

CHAPTER THIRTY-FOUR

New Orleans, Louisiana

Here it was, pushing midnight, the evening after Thanksgiving, and Crayton was walking through the dead streets of the Faubourg Marigny like it was high noon at Jackson Square. Strangely though, Cray felt, well, *mellow* about the whole endeavor. He knew, with absolute certainty, that he was in zero danger—at least any danger from that portion of the Marigny's citizenry who actively practiced unlawful behavior. He *knew* it.

He supposed that had something to do with Maman Arielle's magic—she'd erected some protective gris-gris cloak about him, if you will—and he wasn't remotely concerned about personal safety. Wild, but true.

The pale orange moon, slouching like a filmy eye, offered far more illumination than the sporadic streetlights, most of which were broken anyway. It was cold too, with a wind that gnawed at you, and Cray accepted philosophically that, when he awoke in the morning, the tombs, graveyard statuary, and geometrically clipped strips of lawn in the River of Life would be pale with frost.

No problem. Cray, dressed comfortably for his grisly campout in black sweats, insulated underwear, a blue watch cap, and his red and yellow Eddie Bauer hunter's jacket, was oblivious to the chill. Maman Arielle predicted the weather and assured him it wouldn't bother him.

Yes: Maman Arielle told him he must spend the night in a crypt; that, having been ridden by Baron Samedi, the Ruler of the Cemetery, he must show respect. For, indeed, the amazing resurrection of the dead girl two nights ago hadn't been the climax of the evening. They'd drank more from the *nganga...*

Maman and Henri pouring ladles of the rank gumbo down their throats. All around him people are spinning and dancing to the jackhammer beat of the drums and tambourines, and he begins to dance, slowly at first, then spinning in frenzy like a maddened animal. Marcus is there—Arielle asks, Can Cray feel his presence?—and she explains that Cray is to be Marcus' successor—and then gumbo and blood are trailing down Cray's thin, bare chest. Somehow, he is naked. Maman stands before him, her hands stretched over her head holding a fat serpent—Damballah—and with her tender smile she implores him to listen as the moist stone walls around him come alive with the cries and moans of spirits long dead...

Cray opens his mouth and howls, and his eyes roll back in his head. He isn't aware of it until later, but Baron Samedi is riding him. He has segued into the world of the cemetery and joined the ranks of Le Culte des Morts...

Now, the ritual would continue. To be honest, he did feel a discordant swell of anxiety, but that was okay because he at least knew the deaths of Sam Gallagher and Stacie Bates had not been mere coincidence. And though he felt bad for them, he didn't entirely feel like a murderer either. Maman Arielle called it the Conduction of Fate, and said there were other factors involved enabling Cray's gris-gris to work. Besides, she'd convinced him there were worse things that could happen than to die. She said that, perhaps, he had done his victims a favor.

That reeked of rationalization. But he was so pleased to *know* that in fact his gris-gris had set it all in motion. He actually felt less guilt about the deaths than he felt a sort of religious ecstasy at his newfound knowledge. Still, he was jumpy. He reached into the pockets of his coat for reassurance: the small penlight, the insulated flask and its warming concoction of brandy and molasses, a Swiss army knife and a longer, exceedingly sharp bone knife, and of course, his talisman, the dead girl's finger. And she *was* dead— or dead *again*. After opening her eyes and whimpering for her parents she just sort of...*died* again. He'd asked if she was a zombie and Maman had laughed. "Too much Hollywood," she'd said. "I do not know of zombies." Apparently, the lesson further implied that the veil between the worlds of the living and dead was very thin indeed. If you knew what you were doing—and Cray was absolutely learning. Class, in fact, was in session.

He approached the River of Life Cemetery from the base of its L-shaped exterior, and he could just see the tops of many of the more extravagant tombs over the high mortar wall. Overhead, the chill wind stirred the dead fronds of a line of palm trees planted alongside the graveyard wall, and the sky was bright where a pale gray sea of clouds had overtaken the moon.

Just around the corner, as Maman Arielle had said there would be, was a narrow gate of piked wrought iron. Cray peered through it at the vast expanse of silent monuments. It was so quiet. He *knew* the graveyard would be quiet but, since he'd approached the cemetery, the city itself had grown silent. There were no cars on nearby Music Street, no airplanes passing overhead. Hell, there wasn't even any holiday weekend gunfire from the neighborhood convicts.

Crayton tentatively pushed on the gate. He frowned. It was unlocked as, somehow, he'd known it would be. He took a last glance over his shoulder—*the land of the living*—and walked into the cemetery.

The overcast sky bathed the crypts inside the cemetery in a milk-colored light. Cray was still for a moment, absorbing the surroundings, and the surreality of his situation pounded into his consciousness with each rasping breath. His heart kicked against his chest, and when he rubbed his sweaty palms together, he realized he was operating at the adrenaline-fueled level of high-grade anxiety.

He knew what he was supposed to do here, but Maman Arielle hadn't given him any instructions on where to go; she'd just said he'd know instinctively when he ran across something important. *Great.* Now he got to explore five hundred crypts looking for "the magic tomb." It wasn't enough, he thought bitterly, to simply pop into any old grave for a long winter's nap, plug into whatever cosmic power he was supposed to plug into, grab a few souvenirs, and get the hell out.

No, he had to go on a ghoul's Easter egg hunt, looking for a grave with power. *Power.* The word had definitely taken on a new meaning in the past few days. He reached into his jacket, extracted his flask, and took a healthy drink of his brandy/molasses mixture. Still, he thought, trying to bolster his confidence with positive thoughts, it *was* sorta peaceful here.

He took a few steps down the path, and a strong smell of moss, wild vines, and rotting flowers assailed his nostrils. His eyes were fully acclimated now, and Cray could easily see the basic layout of the River of Life. Along the left perimeter were the wall vaults, called "ovens" in New Orleans parlance. They stood about twelve feet high and were perhaps ten feet deep.

Crayton shuddered; he hoped the crypt he was supposed to sleep in wasn't in the ovens. They'd originally been designed during the yellow fever epidemic for indigent families and each vault contained the remains of several bodies. The strategy was, Cray recalled, that a year and a day after interment, a corpse could be swept to the back of the vault and a fresh one entombed—a practice which had spread to private vaults as well after cemetery space became premium.

He tore his gaze from the ovens and willed himself to look at the rest of the cemetery. There was a broad avenue which ran down the center of the L, which Cray realized was for hearses and funeral processions. Branching off that, though, were twisting paths where one could become completely disoriented.

Cray tried to think logically. Maman Arielle must've sent him to that particular gate for a reason; it would be close to the crypt she wanted him to find. Otherwise, he could get lost in the darkness and wander among the tombs until daylight.

Christ! Maybe that's exactly what she wanted! Maybe that was the whole idea, to trap him among the dead in a night without end, until he was found wandering and utterly mad by the graveyard sexton.

A massive jolt of fear bubbled in his throat and cascaded over him. He turned and trotted, whimpering, back up the path in the direction of the gate. Fuck *power*, his brain screamed wildly, *get the hell outta here.*

For only the second time since he wandered on autopilot into the bar at Gris-Gris Gumbo, Cray found himself thinking of Eliza and longing for the comfort of her arms. It was insane, really, to have gotten into this shit. He reached the gate and grabbed it to pull it open—and it was locked.

In spite of the chill, sweat ran into his eyes and Cray spun around to see if anyone was behind him, someone who had followed him in and locked the gate.

"Maman Arielle?" he called tentatively. "Henri?"

A breeze rustled a display of decaying flowers on a nearby grave, but the only human sound was the shuddering in Cray's own lungs as he gasped for air. He sat weakly on the path, feeling the cold gravel under his ass as the wind danced around his head. He was afraid he might start crying and reached into his pocket, mindlessly groping for the Swiss army knife. Maybe he could use it to jimmy the lock somehow. Instead, he closed around the severed finger. He jumped but, even as he did so, an image of Maman Arielle materialized in his mind and, as suddenly as the fear had welled up within him, a new calm radiated outward from his chest, pushing warmth to his extremities. Just like that. And he knew she wouldn't betray him.

He drank again and struggled to his feet and walked sure-footedly, through a series of twists and turns on the graveyard paths, in a direct course. Eventually, without having even one clue as to how or why he knew where to go, he stood in front of what appeared to be a recent burial site. He was in front of a modest, walk-in marble tomb, and the ground in front of the wooden door was blanketed with several arrangements of flowers. Gauging by the sickly sweet smell, some were fresh.

Cray pulled out his penlight and turned it on. Over the doorway, in *bas-relief* marble letters, was the name *PROSPERO GODCHAUX*. Underneath: *Thy Sweet Music Soundeth Still.*

Another gust of wind sighed, and a solitary leaf landed on his sleeve. He shivered and took another drink as he stared. *Well,* he thought, *the next part was clear enough, if not exactly easy. But it had to be done.*

The Hand of Glory.

Yes. A dark talisman that, in the possession of those who know—*Les Culte des Morts,* for example—unleashed an awesome and terrible power. The Hand of Glory: the severed left hand of an executed murderer.

Cray giggled nervously. This was one king-hell mindfuck. He turned and looked out at the vast expanse of graves that stood out bone-white and dull silver against the stark shadows.

It was all creepy and beautiful, but Cray knew he was stalling. He took a slow, deep, decisive breath and, with a resigned shrug of his shoulders, set his flask on the ground next to a clump of withered flowers—and set about breaking into the tomb of Prospero Godchaux.

CHAPTER THIRTY-FIVE

Houston, Texas

Friday night and Green was the only one still awake at his parents' house. He was in a recliner in the den, talking on the phone to Kay. The room was dark save for sleepy embers in the fireplace, but any hope of a romantic conversation was dashed when she told him about a phone call she'd just received from Eliza.

"Eliza called *you*?" he asked. "From D.C.?"

"Yeah. She can't track down Crayton and she's worried. Apparently, he never showed up at his parents'."

Green felt the stress that, lately, had accompanied any news or mention of Cray. "What do you mean he never showed up?"

"I don't know, Green, " Kay said. "Apparently, Cray was supposed to call Eliza Thanksgiving Day after he got to New Iberia. And he did call, but he was in New Orleans. He said he'd decided not to go home; he wasn't feeling well. Now he's not answering his phone."

Green reflected. "Well, his note said he was depressed. But that was because he'd lied about Stacie Bates. He also said he could explain it too, and—"

"And that he didn't want to face all of us and instead went to the Maple Leaf to have a few beers. I *know* what his note said, Darlin'. I'm the one who pulled it off your front door yesterday morning."

"Oh, right... But if Crayton called Eliza and told her he wasn't going to his parents', then maybe he got sick *later*, after you'd already driven me to the airport."

Kay thought for a moment. "Sure, but if he's ill, why isn't he answering his phone? Either he's too sick—in which case someone needs to check on him—or he's not sick. I dunno, Green. Eliza thinks he's up to something."

"*Up to something?* What does *that* mean?" Green shifted in the chair.

"She said Cray sounded very strange on the phone. He'd *been* strange at dinner the night he took her to the airport, and he seemed worried and detached."

Green sighed. "Well, he has a reason to be acting strange. He might be able to explain Stacie Bates, but I don't know how. I talked to my Rod, my brother, about her."

"Ah, Doctor Rod," Kay said. "The Hopkins family physician. And...?"

"He told me that, yeah, there *were* rumors going around the hospital when Stacie Bates died, maybe because it was such an unusual condition, maybe because Stacie Bates was a celebrity and a world-class asshole—not to speak ill of the dead. Anyway, apparently Stacie had acute lymphocytic leukemia."

"And that means...?" Kay asked.

"It means it was one motherfucker of a cancer—and a quick one. And get this: she wasn't diagnosed until *two weeks* before she died."

"Jesus. Then there's no way Crayton could've known on Halloween."

"Nope. It'll be interesting to see how he does explain it, since he says he can."

A thought hit Green. "What if Crayton really *did* come down with a twenty-four-hour virus or something? He couldn't make his parents' for Thanksgiving. Then, sometime today, he starts to feel better and either decides to go on to New Iberia or just hang around the Quarter and relax. It's not like he couldn't find something to do."

"Yeah, I *guess* that could explain everything. But personally, I think the whole thing that's bugging Eliza was just the tone of his voice when he *did* call. She said it was like talking to an actor Crayton had hired. Or like he was calling from another planet."

"Who can say? Maybe they're just having some problems that we don't know about, and Eliza just needed a friendly female voice to talk to." Green still had some bizarre faith that Cray was fine and everything could be normally explained. "I guarantee you, tonight or in the morning, Cray's gonna surface at his parents' or after a night at the Blacksmith Shop, and everything'll be hunky dory. And on Sunday we'll all be back in the ol' neighborhood and life will roll on like a river."

"I hope so." Kay paused. "I wish you'd come back. This whole thing is freaky."

"Not to worry, baby. I miss ya big. But I'm back in two days. 'Silver wings,' as Merle Haggard says."

"Only you would respond to a woman's plaintive cries for tenderness with a Merle Haggard reference. But, since you brought it up, I miss you too..."

"Merle Haggard is the blue-collar poet of love. And if you've checked my bank statement lately, I'm about as blue collar as it gets. Merle has another one, 'Working Man's Blues.'"

"I get the recurring motif, hon. And I'd love to sit here and discuss Merle's chord progressions, or whatever you call 'em, but I suppose I'd better call Eliza back."

"If she asks you about voodoo and the death league, just tell her you don't know anything new." Green thought about his experience at the museum. "*But.*"

"But what?"

Green told her what he'd found out about the Cult of Death and the *nganga*. Kay was creeped out, particularly by an official context and name—*nganga*—for the sinister cauldron Green had told her about from Halloween, but she didn't seem particularly shocked that a dark voodoo death cult could actually exist in New Orleans.

"Frankly, " she said, after they discussed it for a few minutes, "I'm sort of surprised something like this hasn't surfaced before now. " She also thought—and Green agreed—that it was best not to alarm Eliza further since Green's info had little to do with Cray. They *hoped.*

Kay said, "I'm gonna tell her just what you said—not to worry. *Someone* in this town is serious about voodoo, but I still don't think it's Crayton. Even *he* may *think* he is, but... I just think it's a good thing y'all didn't let that Maman Arielle woman in your death league. I don't think I want to know how *she* would have fixed my headaches."

"Goddamn, *that's* a fact." Green started to laugh—till a thought hit him: *What if Crayton* knew *Maman Arielle? Christ, what if she* hangs out *in the Voodoo Shoppe? He said on Halloween that he recognized her from her occasional visits to the store...*

Kay was speaking. "Anyway, if we haven't heard from Crayton by, say, noon tomorrow, I'll call you, and maybe J.C. will go with me to knock on his door. Just to make sure he isn't crumpled on the floor with a monstrous fever."

"That'll work. And let me know. " The Cray/Arielle connection still haunted Green, but he was quickly brought back to focus when Kay signed off by saying, "I love you, Green," just before hanging up.

It was the first time she'd said it.

CHAPTER THIRTY-SIX

New Orleans, Louisiana

At that exact moment, in the River of Life Cemetery, Crayton emerged from the fetid maw of Prospero Godchaux's grave and lifted the pianist's severed hand up to the sky like he was holding up an offering to a giant.

The Hand of Glory.

Prospero had been buried wearing his famous ring, and in the oddly luminous glow of the cemetery, the gaudy jewelry cast a pale gleam. Though he had the penlight, Cray had done the bulk of his work in darkness and now, for reasons that escaped him, he had no interest in studying his treasure in any greater detail than was afforded by the creepy night.

In fact, he only realized he'd been holding the damned thing in his outstretched arm when his shoulder began to ache and something wet—*embalming fluid?*—trickled lightly down his wrist. It occurred to Cray that he'd just been standing there for maybe ten minutes, gazing curiously at Prospero's once-magical fingers. Cray giggled nervously; on a certain level he realized he'd fallen off a definite moral tightrope. The thing was, he *loved* it.

Tucking the cold, death-cured hand into a coat pocket, he licked his chapped lips nervously. *The Hand of Glory; Cray* loved *the drama and promise of the phrase, though he wasn't quite sure what it would do for him... Not yet, anyway...*

Then, for no reason at all that he could think of, he began to trudge back into the deepest recesses of the cemetery, toward the gate where he'd come in. It seemed to Crayton that a mild, persistent buzz had crept into the night. He'd first noticed it in Prospero's crypt, the kind of hum you hear when you're near heavy-duty power lines, but maybe a bit more...*insectile.* Like cicadas maybe, but then again, more vibration than actual sound.

Nearing the quadrant by the locked gate, he spied the dark shapes of two statues nestled almost totally in shadow. Cray crept over to them—angels, he could see now, and both a good head taller than he was—looking protectively down on a large crypt which had sunken slightly into the ground. Like many graves in New Orleans, the crypt had a dark marble tablet across the front. The tablet served a dual purpose: the name of the interred family and pertinent information could be carved on the front, and it was also the portal through which, when necessary, another body could be placed inside. On either side was a marble ledge for floral arrangements.

Suddenly, intuitively, he pulled out the flashlight and aimed the beam at the face of one of the angels. Cray gasped. The face was remarkably life-like, its features reflecting an almost inhuman cruelty.

Cray staggered back against the wall of the tomb. The energized hum in the night seemed more urgent now, as though it had taken on a *rhythm*. It was nothing you could actually *hear*, but Crayton definitely felt it.

He passed the light over the face of the other angel, knowing in advance what he would see: an expression of profound horror. He was standing between the two statues Green had told him about—the ones Papa Hipolyte had described as the stone personifications of Cruelty and Despair.

In the stark, still, cold world of the dead, the stone angels were mesmerizing in their wretched perfection. Who would carve such things, and why were they positioned on either side of this particular tomb?

What was worse, Crayton now knew that this was the crypt Maman Arielle wanted him to find. He shone the light on the vault. Peering closely, he could see dozens of little red Xs chalked on the bricks, and in front of the grave, covering the floral shelves, were the remains of burnt incense sticks and votive candles. *Voodoo.* One of the ledges was presumably the site of Papa Hipolyte's supposed gator resurrection—a story that Cray had once regarded as apocryphal at best, and now with the utmost belief that it was true.

Yeah, Cray thought, whoever was interred here had been heavily into the gris-gris. Well, what the hell did he expect? Admonishments to read John 3:16?

Resigned but emotionally and physically drained, he sat on his haunches and aimed the light at the marble door, trying to make out the name on the vault. The tablet was very old and frosted with moss, and erosion had cracked and water-stained the inscription. Plus, it was in French.

With a yawn that surprised him in its genuine weariness, Crayton stood up. Shaking his head in compliance with the evening's descending lunacy, and using the screwdriver attachment from his Swiss army knife, he began working at the tiny screws holding the tablet to the crypt.

When it was finally open Cray was panting like a post-race greyhound. He leaned against one of the side walls of the grave, taking icy draughts of the November air and punctuating them with sips from his flask. The rhythmic hum that seemed to emanate from the night throbbed within him like the pain from a foul tooth—almost as though the cemetery itself knew he was stalling again, as he had outside Prospero's tomb. And he was.

Maman Arielle had told him there were *bokors* who spent one night a month with the dead, to keep in close touch with Baron Samedi. She said they *liked* it. He shivered and thought of the interior of Prospero's crypt: the odor and the insects and—oh yeah—a moist rat that had taken its leisurely fucking time vacating the vault when Cray had entered... Willfully, he cut off the image and ducked into the crypt.

The smell wasn't as *newly* decayed as Prospero's, which had knocked him over with its summer road-kill putrescence. This was rank too, but it was more of a damp, sour stench than any animal rot. If he had to describe it, Cray was reminded of moldy bone and rain-rotted hay.

And speaking of rain, there was significant seepage in the vault. When Cray aimed his flashlight around the interior, large skeins of white fungus obscured the bricks along the left wall and back corner of the tomb. For proper atmosphere, there were also several spider webs throughout the grave, though spiders didn't really bother Crayton. Besides, the only one he actually saw was small and not particularly intimidating.

He waited until last to train his light on the faded yellow pine coffin that sat on a small cement foundation. It, too, was traced with mold, and its cheap wooden veneer had rotted through in several places. Through one jagged hole, in the flashlight's shaky initial passage over the scene, Crayton thought he spotted a powder-blue glimmer of a tattered funeral dress, and through *that* a grayish-white wink of skeleton.

He exhaled and forced himself to hold the light as steadily as he could, horribly transfixed by his compounded obscenities. For some reason— probably because he was going to *sleep* here—he was looking around in far greater detail than he had at Prospero Godchaux's grave. There, he'd seen only what he'd needed to see; after breaking the lock off and propping open the lid of the casket, he'd put on gloves and, willfully avoiding any scrutiny of the corpse's face, had simply sawed off its hand as quickly as possible...

Now, in the second vault, Cray pushed forward another few feet until he could observe the entire top of the coffin. It had fallen in at several points, owing to a combination of humidity, water damage, and poor quality, and... Cray gasped. At one end, he could make out a pale expanse of cheekbone dusted with blue mold, an eye socket, and a crinkled and dry mane of wild hair. A silver earring lay on the rotted burial pillow beneath the skull.

But it wasn't until the light spangled off the shiny black exo-skeleton of a huge beetle as it crawled out of the eye socket that, for the first time in the entire mad night, Cray screamed.

He backed out of the crypt hastily, knocking his head on the brick as though in a Three Stooges pratfall, and stood in the sharp wind, staring at nothing and sipping comfortingly from his brandy/molasses concoction. Once more, his confidence and sense of morality—or whatever—had boomeranged.

Cray whimpered, reached into his pocket, and pulled out the Hand of Glory. He hesitated only a moment before throwing the damned thing with all his strength across the graveyard. Power or not—Maman Arielle or not—

Crayton had decided with that one freakin' beetle to abort the whole episode.

Who the fuck cared about power and *Le Culte des Morts*? Eliza would be back Sunday, and if Maman Arielle couldn't handle his defection, well, he'd have to take his chances. He knew she had power, but it wasn't like *he* hadn't killed anybody either. He'd been doing fine *before* she barged in on his act, and he and Eliza could simply bow out and head for parts unknown. What would Maman Arielle have to be pissed off about anyway? According to Green, Papa Hipolyte once practiced voodoo and had gotten out of it intact. He was in the hospital, sure, but he was also in his seventies and had suffered a perfectly natural, voodoo-free heart attack.

It was then that Cray hammered another long swallow—and realized for the first time that the flask was completely full. It was like he hadn't even opened it.

Cray peered at the flask in disbelief. He tilted the container back and gulped down several test-swallows of liquid, then examined the contents with his penlight. Still full.

And in the end that was all it took. At that instant, simply, Cray abandoned all thoughts of defection. True, there had been more bizarre things that'd happened tonight, but for some reason, it was the bottomless flask that caused Cray, without so much as another thought, to wrap his coat around himself snugly and work his way back into the crypt.

It was, he decided with calm logic, time for bed.

For a while he sat uncomfortably against the right wall near the vault opening, his knees drawn up against him, aiming the feeble glow of the flashlight around the perimeter like a patrolling sentry, taking studious care not to look at the casket. Eventually, though, he was too tired to care anymore and turned the light off.

Though a soft glow of night oozed through the tomb opening, its value as a light source was negligible. It was, Cray decided, actually better in the darkness anyway. *What you can't see can still hurt you, but at least you won't know it's coming...*

He closed his eyes and tried to think innocuous thoughts over the subtle rhythm of the drums—because that's what the incessant humming of the evening had become. There was an actual, identifiable beat now, as though a brass band was marching through the Marigny and all he could hear from several blocks away was the second-line rhythm of the drums.

He shifted, stretching one leg as far as it would go, determined to focus on the reassuring image of Eliza's face, when suddenly—

Crayton jolted awake in the tar-black interior of the grave. No longer did any outside light filter into the tomb, and he had no idea how long he'd been asleep. It didn't really matter because *something was in the crypt with him*. He could hear breathing.

But before he could flail out in a wildly instinctive gesture, a fresh scent filled the vault and enveloped him in a soft cloud of familiarity that drowned out the grim odor of death: musk, citrus fruits, patchouli, and the heady aroma of crawfish boil.

Maman Arielle. Cray couldn't see her—couldn't see an inch in front of his face—but he *knew* it was her. She giggled like a teenager in the darkness, and Cray had never known such relief. Though he'd been asleep, it had been a shallow, restless sleep, as though the sheer effusive aura of the tomb had forced itself into his unconscious.

Her voice was like music as she said, "Did you think I would make you face the night alone?" Then there was the rustling of cloth, and despite the absolute absence of light in the crypt and the frigid temperature, Cray knew she'd removed whatever she'd had on and was naked.

Before he could speak, a tender, warm finger traced the hollow of his cheekbone and pressed his lips shut. "Sssh," she whispered. "Do not speak. I want to show you something—even as you cannot see."

And with that Maman Arielle kissed him like he'd never been kissed. It felt like a cyclone blew through his brain, and her tongue, tasting of cinnamon and burgundy, twirled languidly against the roof of his mouth and teased his lips and gums.

Cray fell back against the damp mortar floor of the crypt and moaned in quiet sublimity as Maman Arielle hovered over him. Her hands, soft as velvet, quickly removed his clothes, and she fluttered kisses like butterflies down his chest and belly until she took him in her mouth...

At some point, Cray whimpered as he felt an insect brush across his hand. But Maman Arielle silenced his fear with a feathered caress of his forehead while she placed a heavy nipple in his mouth, and he suckled like a child.

For what seemed like days, Cray spun like a satellite in the vast universe of Maman Arielle's orchestrations, and he howled for air when, time after time, she coaxed him into new avenues of sensation.

Finally, she sat on her haunches astride him and lowered herself over his parched lips, and the wet tangle between her legs tasted of tangerines and a clean sea and sparkled on his eager tongue. He became dizzy at the sheer pleasure of it all, running his tongue around in a frenzied circle in her moist darkness until...

Something was horribly wrong. Cray tried to bolt upright in pure terror. The sweet, salty taste between Maman Arielle's thighs turned dry and foul, and the stifling scent of the grave ran over him like blood, and Cray struggled ineffectually against the dead weight collapsed against him. He tried to scream—and mercifully, instead, he fainted, toppling backward into the forgiving arms of the night...

Crayton was suffocating. He gasped for air, swimming upward through layers of darkness, trying to breathe through lungs that seemed painted with cold dirt. Then, suddenly, he was awake, pushing in terror against the crumpled form draped over his face.

The smell of death made him gag, and it wasn't until his eyes grew accustomed to the dark gray glow of dawn trickling in through the front opening of the crypt that he realized the casket had toppled off its foundation and lay on its side—cracked and empty. Next to it, ripped to shreds, was the powder-blue burial gown.

And Crayton, in a crush of incomprehensible horror, pushed out at the parchment legs wrapped around his neck and pulled far enough away from the ragdoll form to realize that the woman with whom he was intertwined had been dead for quite a while.

CHAPTER THIRTY-SEVEN

The last thing Green expected to see when he marched off his flight late Sunday afternoon was a welcome-home committee comprised of Kay, Eliza—and Crayton. But there they were, smiling hugely, each brandishing bottles of Dixie beer glittering with ice crystals. Kay was seductively waving a fourth in his direction.

Green laughed, gave Kay a quick kiss and grabbed the beer, then looked at Cray. "You had us worried, son."

"I know. Sorry. Just a little miscommunication," Cray said, shrugging sheepishly and reaching out to take one of Green's canvas travel bags. They headed up the concourse, pausing while Eliza and Kay went into the restroom. After a moment's silence, Cray took a deep breath. "Well, Green-o, some interesting things have happened. Thought I'd tell you about it over dinner."

"Dinner?"

"Yep," Cray said casually. "I thought I'd take us to the Palace Café...unless you've got other plans."

Green laughed shortly. "No, but what'd you do? Get lucky at Harrah's?"

"I got an early holiday bonus from Cosima," Cray said. "The girls are all for it."

"The Palace Café, huh? Sounds damned generous. Unless the Brennan family started handing out buy-one, get-one-free coupons."

"Not that I've heard," Cray laughed. "But I figure I owe you."

"Owe *me*?"

"Yeah. For one thing, let me just say I'm sorry I lied about the Stacie Bates thing. It was...the wrong thing to do."

Green raised his eyebrows noncommittally.

Cray sighed and glanced nervously inside a gift shop. "I didn't know she had cancer. I just had a feeling about it."

Green took a deep breath. "So you can't tell your best pal you had a feeling?"

"Green, this whole death league was probably a horrible idea—at least from the perspective that I've picked two correctly and I quote/unquote dabble in voodoo."

"Haven't we been over this?"

"Yeah. Yeah, we have. But I can't help but be paranoid. I *didn't* know of any medical condition for Stacie Bates. Like I said, it was just a feeling. So if it freaks *me* out, I can easily understand what someone as conservative as Donny might think."

"Donny? I thought you were worried about J.C.?"

"Kay told me about Donny flipping out at Markey's."

"Okay," Green said evenly, "let's just say you had a feeling. Christ, Cray, people have premonitions every day. So what? All I ask is that you tell me the truth. If you're a psychic or burning voodoo roots or, hell, if you personally traveled to San Diego and pushed the triathlete off a cliff—all I ask is that you tell me, and I'll be there for you. I mean, I just can't see that you're murdering anybody."

Once they arrived at the Palace Café, it was pretty much what Green expected from some place he'd never be able to afford. Part of the Brennan family's fleet of superb New Orleans restaurants, it was a massive, open room with exposed brick and pipes, perhaps fifty feet high, featuring two dining levels and a painted mural incorporating great figures, past and present, from the city's musical history. The scent of grilling fish seemed in concert with a leisurely hum of dinner conversation.

After they'd gotten their first round of cocktails and ordered, Green said, "Cray, I gotta ask: Where were you if you didn't go visit your parents over the weekend?"

Cray smiled apologetically at Kay and Eliza, who had apparently heard the story already. "Well, to be quite honest, the reason I didn't go on Thanksgiving Day was that I had a hangover. I saw Fred LeBlanc and John Thomas Griffith at Carrollton Station—I think I put that in the note I left you—and I just got splattered. Hell, I was still drunk when I woke up Thursday morning. So I passed out, and by the time I got up it was too late to go home. Then, Friday morning, Cosima called and said she had a cold and would I be able to cover her shifts that afternoon and night, and I said sure."

He looked down at the table for a moment, as though putting his thoughts in order, then went on to explain that he'd tried to reach Eliza but had lost her parents' unlisted phone number. And then he told Green how, on Saturday morning, he'd run into J.C.—who was in his own drunken stupor on Bourbon Street.

Green looked at Eliza and Kay. "You guys have heard all this?"

Crayton spoke. "Well, they know I was boozing it up with J.C. Saturday. I told them on the way to pick you up. But that's why I couldn't go see my folks on Saturday. J.C. needed me."

"J.C. *what?*"

Cray laughed and held his palms up in a *whaddya gonna do?* gesture. "He'd just broken up with Darby."

"He broke up with Darby?! I thought he actually *liked* her and might keep her around. "

Cray leaned forward. "Well, let me preface this by asking you guys this: What exactly is it that Darby does? For a living, I mean. What's her job? Does anybody know?"

Green, Kay, and Eliza looked at one another and tried to remember what sketchy details they knew about the girl.

"She's a model of some kind, right?" Kay offered.

Green knitted his brow. "Yeah. Catalogue shoots, maybe?"

Eliza snorted and took a hefty sip of chardonnay. "If you'd asked me, I'da said she was a stripper."

Green and Kay started to laugh until Crayton aimed his finger like a pistol and quietly said, "Bingo. Or at least it's in the ballpark."

"A *stripper?*" Kay and Green didn't exactly achieve Queen-style harmony on their unison screech.

Cray smiled tiredly. "Well, not *exactly* a stripper. Worse, I guess."

Then, after the waiter delivered entrees, including Green's andouille-crusted redfish, which literally made him weak with its greatness, Cray described running into a staggering J.C. at the unlikely time of nine on Saturday morning.

"I was walking up Bourbon and all of a sudden J.C. comes reeling around the corner looking like he hasn't slept in about two years. He's carrying a hurricane-size go-cup full of draft beer, and he smelled like Johnny White's Bar on New Year's morning."

Cray took a bite of panéed rabbit that oozed Gruyere cheese. "I thought, 'Well, you don't see J.C. pulling all-nighters very often,' so I wandered up and said, joking around, 'J.C., my man, are we drinking breakfast again?'

"And he looks at me and it's then I can see he's *crying.* So I immediately think, 'Christ, his mother died or Uncle Wallace or somebody.' And I said, 'J.C., are you okay?'

"He moans and says, 'Cray-boy, I can't fuckin' believe it. That fucking whore!'

"And I said, 'What is it, J.C.? What's wrong?'

"So he gets this brave smile on his face—even though there are literally tears running down his cheeks—and it's like he remembers his Southern Gentleman persona or something, so he makes a big production out of going over to one of those street-front beer vendors to buy me a beer. Which is about the last thing I want, but he's obviously upset and not pulling this binge 'cause it's his idea of wacky holiday entertainment."

Green felt Kay reach under the table to squeeze his hand.

"So I take the beer," Cray said. "And he holds up his cup as if to make a toast, and I hold up mine, and we smash our paper cups together and beer goes sloshing all over Bourbon Street.

"'To innocence lost,' J.C. says, and I take a sip and he inhales about half his cup.

"I say, 'Thanks, J.C., but why don't you tell me what's wrong.'

"And he says, "Fuck that, brah, I'll *show* you what's wrong.'

"He leads me down the block and into one of those porno shops. And we walk over to the magazine rack—I ain't talkin' *The Economist* and *National Review* here, I'm talking hardcore, okay?—and J.C. digs around for a minute and pulls out this shrink-wrapped magazine and shoves it in my hand.

"'Whaddya think a *that*, Cray-boy?' he says.

"And I look at the magazine—I'll never forget the title, as long as I live—and it's called *Spooge Gobblers*. And who should be on the cover performing, uhm, rather spirited fellatio on an anonymous and rather sizable male organ, but Darby? "

Cray told them that, after initially discovering *Spooge Gobblers*, J.C. had confronted Darby, shoved the magazine in her face, and said he didn't want to see her ass on the streets of the Quarter again.

"Jesus, J.C.'s always had a reason to break up with someone, but this is certainly different," Green said, watching Kay peel a prawn the size of a tennis shoe. "Do Donny and Huey know?"

"Nope. For one thing, I don't even know if they're back from Donny's parents' house. For another, I promised J.C. I'd tell you first."

Green said, "Which brings me to the next point. Where *is* J.C.?"

Cray said, "He and the congressman-elect caught a noon flight to D.C. He'll be back on Tuesday, but he said he'd call you tomorrow."

Green nodded, trying to absorb the strange twist Darby had thrown into J.C.'s life.

Eliza looked around the table. "Well, from what y'all have told me about J.C.'s dating habits, doesn't it seem ironic that this would happen to him? I mean, doesn't he normally dictate how everything works out? So now he's suddenly offended by Darby's secret life?"

Kay smiled ironically. "Point well taken. Even so, and not to sound flippant about it, but J.C.'ll bounce back. He always does, not that he's dated porn stars before. But what about Darby? Her whole deal just creeps me out. Like, who is she? Is Darby even her real name? Where does she really come from? What diseases does she have?"

Eliza shivered. She speared a chunk of salad tomato and twirled it aimlessly. "I mean, *I* even feel violated. There's no telling what J.C. thinks."

Green looked at Cray, staring out the window into the twilight. Christmas decorations on Canal Street, already in place and glowing cheerfully, added an out-of-tempo luster to their discussion. Green was glad Cray had met him at the airport and come clean about the death league, but it was all slightly odd nonetheless. On the other hand, the story about J.C. was pretty amazing—and obviously wasn't the sort of thing Cray would make up. He spoke. "So, Crayton, you kinda hung with J.C. Saturday night then, right?"

Cray chuckled a little. "*Last* night, you mean? Yeah, pretty much. I thought he was already pretty far gone, and that I could handle having a few cocktails with him, for his misery's sake." He shook his head. "But, man, was I wrong. We drank all day—and if it hadn't been under such weird circumstances, I would've said we had a great time.

"Finally, though, around dusk, I could tell he was reeling, so I got him back to his apartment and into his bedroom, and he passed out. I found a blanket in a closet and crashed on his couch."

Kay spoke up. "How was J.C. today?"

Crayton shrugged. "A little embarrassed, maybe. Grateful that I'd stuck with him. Definitely hungover. Sad. All of the above."

The waiter brought a check and Crayton handed him a credit card.

"Are you sure we can't chip in here?" Green asked.

"Absolutely not. I want to do this."

"Well, thanks," Green said. "And let me say that, not only do I feel bad about J.C., but I feel bad for thinking you were sneaking around engineering stunts of voodoo."

Cray said, "Hey, after Stacie Bates, I wouldn't blame you if you *did* think that. But trust me: it was a strange, crazy weekend, but absolutely void of any mojo activity." Then he grinned and glanced up at the musician mural on the wall. Green followed Cray's line of sight and saw the figure of the late, great pianist Prospero Godchaux.

CHAPTER THIRTY-EIGHT

Crayton woke up Monday morning feeling deliciously normal. He fixed Eliza bacon and toast and got her off to work, then puttered around getting ready for his own day. Yes, all things considered, it was an extraordinary weekend. And the paradox of it all, Cray thought as he tucked his black cat bone into his jeans, was the sense of friendship he'd felt sloshing around the Quarter with J.C. on Saturday. As miserable as the circumstances were that had resulted in their daylong binge together, Saturday was the first occasion when it seemed to Cray that J.C. actually considered him a genuine pal.

Then last night: taking Green, Eliza, and Kay to the Palace Café—that was a pleasure too, and provided a nice opportunity for Cray to apologize to Green about Stacie Bates. True, Crayton's voodoo rituals *vis a vis* the death league were going to have to remain a secret. But everyone was entitled to a little privacy, and if Cray had a few skeletons in the closet—or at least *parts* of them—well, so be it.

Firing up the Camaro, Cray slowly spun up Elysian Fields. He had a few shopping errands to run—assigned by Maman Arielle. Humming along with Fats Domino on WWOZ, Cray reflected on how the events of the Thanksgiving weekend had fallen into place like pieces of different jigsaw puzzles that somehow fit together anyway. If felt good. The sense of *belonging*, he guessed you'd call this immersion into *Le Culte des Morts*, was refreshing.

He'd feared the price tag for his involvement would probably have been his normal lifestyle and circle of friends. But instead of lunatic detachment or hoodoo zealotry, this was like being, well, a closet *Buddhist* or something: you've seen the light—or *darkness*—but, for a variety of reasons, known and unknown, you keep it to yourself. People wouldn't understand.

The thing he was most gratified about was that he came out of the crypt with a fresher sense of friendship and love for Eliza and his pals than he'd felt going in. Sure, with respect to Eliza, he'd felt guilt over his odd infidelity in the tomb, but it wasn't the sort of sexual indiscretion that would happen again. *Jesus, he hoped not.* The thought made him queasy, but he reminded himself to view the experience as a novitiate's rite of voodoo passage—a religious ordination, he supposed—and he absolutely believed he would remain faithful to Eliza henceforth.

Cray drove past Florida Avenue to an area of industrial warehouses. As for lying to all his pals, well, yeah, there'd been some deception required to pull the whole weekend off. But this wasn't garden-variety duplicity; this was something you could only understand if you'd been there. *Little* black *lies*, you might call them. And since Crayton was the only one of his friends who'd tapped into this, he'd have to employ discretion in the conduction of dual lives.

Crayton spied what he was looking for and pulled into a parking area fronting a series of metal Quonset hut industrial warehouses, mostly machine shops and repair joints. He left the car idling and leaned into the backseat. Cray needed a bit of room, so he swept all the Lucky Dog wrappers and beer bottles onto the floorboard—and noticed a manila mailing envelope. Scrawled on the outside in magic marker was, PAPA HIPOLYTE, PROMO PHOTOS.

What the hell? Then Crayton remembered Green said he'd brought back some of Papa's belongings from the hospital and dropped them by the old guy's cottage. This must've fallen out. The flap was secured only by a clasp, and Cray, not certain if it was something important, opened the envelope and peeked inside. Sure enough, it was just a stack of eight-by-ten black and white glossies showing Papa, grinning, a straw porkpie hat perched back on his head, and seated behind a white grand piano. It appeared to have been taken several years ago; there was a Jax beer can sitting on the piano, and Cray couldn't remember when *that* brewery went out of business.

He finished sweeping off the back seat and stuck the envelope between the gearshift console and the CD player. Now there was room. He started to get out of the car but paused, thinking back to Saturday morning, when he'd awakened with his head between the thighs of a dead woman.

When he'd realized what had happened, and crawled whimpering out of the crypt, his first rational thought was to grab a taxi and check directly into the Charity Hospital mental ward. And he *would* have, if he'd had the strength.

Instead, he'd huddled on the cold path for a while, just happy to be out of the grave and away from the...the... *Her.* His brain was mercifully numb, and he simply crouched there in a fetal position for who knew how long.

Eventually, watching the pink and orange shades of dawn creep through the tattered gray clouds streaming overhead, Cray's sense of revulsion gradually metamorphosed into a sense of survival and, eventually, a strange exultation.

Of, yes: *power.*

Then, as details of his immediate surroundings swam into view in the new light, something caught his attention from one of the marble candle shelves on the front of the tomb. There, perched daintily, palm up, was Prospero Godchaux's hand.

Dreamily, Cray smiled. *Ah, excellent,* he thought. *Now I won't have to go looking for it.* Cray accepted the hand's placement as easily as he would've a weather report calling for a slight breeze.

And that persistent hum in the night—the preternatural *pulse-beat* that had so intensified as events unfolded and Crayton's sense of reality had twisted and flapped like a flag in a cyclone—had internalized. It was *within* Crayton now, as though he had his own secret generator. It seemed comfortably eternal.

He'd gathered the Hand of Glory and tucked it back in a coat pocket. The sun arched over the wall, and a southerly wind sprang up and began its erosional work on the caked frost blanketing the graveyard. Crayton stood up, dusted himself off, and prepared to walk back to his apartment to clean up and prepare for—*what?*

Well, the *day*, he guessed. *Life.* He laughed; he was pretty sure there wasn't some follow-up class conducted by Maman Arielle wherein he and like-minded voodoo recruits compared notes on their mystic experiences with the dead.

No. He was the only neophyte, and though he was certain he'd see Maman Arielle soon enough, he was instinctively aware he'd need time to digest whatever had happened—whatever it was he'd done and learned—in the River of Life Cemetery. The one thing he was sure of was Maman Arielle had been right: he'd never look at the world the same way again. He felt lucky to have somehow crossed a shrouded bridge between the future and the past, life and death, the body and the mind...

Three guys from an engine shop walked out into the parking lot arguing about where they should eat lunch. They glanced curiously at Crayton, sitting in a smiling trance in the Camaro.Cray was wondering what was going on in Gris-Gris Gumbo right now. Hell, business as usual, he supposed. He liked the idea of Maman Arielle, do-rag wrapped around her forehead, standing in the heart of the steaming kitchen, studiously whisking roux in a cast-iron skillet. The image comforted him.

Much as she had soothed him the night before the cemetery, when she'd wrapped her arm around him like a junior-high basketball coach and told him all he'd need to accomplish in the cemetery. Three things: the Hand of Glory, sleeping in the grave, and one essential item he'd need for his altar...

...Cray recalled one final bit of business that morning in the River of Life. He remembered it clearly: as though he were doing nothing more than picking up the morning paper, he entered the crypt one last time. He took a deep breath and looked at the fallen coffin and the grotesquely splayed body in the deep shadows. In the morning gloom, the burial vault had lost whatever pagan energy had crackled there in the night.

Then, quickly, he edged to the rear of the tomb, stood on his tiptoes, and reached *over* a mossy cement partition—the wall beyond which were stacked skeletons deposited there over the years as newer bodies were interred.

He flicked on his penlight just long enough to find what he needed—and narrowed his focus to ignore heaps of bone, scraps of burial cloth, or scores of insects lazily going about their day.

Luck was with him. Only a few inches away was a skull. Before he could think about it, he reached and, with a small *snap*, pulled it free from the neck bone. Then, with a final sense of revulsion, Cray backpedaled into the astringent morning.

He'd taken a last look around the graveyard and, tucking the skull inside his coat like a pineapple thief, exited the unlocked gate and walked home...

Remembering it now, Cray laughed, poured out the remains of his Mountain Dew, and walked across the pitted asphalt parking lot and through the door of the Louisiana Wholesale Casket Warehouse. Inside was a small office, and behind a green steel desk, punching on the keys of a computer, was a middle-aged man who looked vaguely like Jimmy Carter. He looked up from his computer screen and offered Cray a grin with startlingly white teeth.

"Morning," he said. "How can I help you?"

Cray smiled. "I called earlier. Someone told me y'all sell directly to the public."

Jimmy nodded. "That's right. Whatcha need?"

Crayton took a deep breath. "Well, I'd like to see some, ah, caskets for infants. The smallest you have."

"Not a problem." President Carter stood up. "I think we can fix you up." He seemed totally uninterested as to why Cray might want a baby casket.

"C'mon back," Jimmy said, opening the door to the warehouse area. It was half as big as a football field, and Cray marveled at the aisles and aisles of metal shelving, stacked to a thirty-foot ceiling with caskets wrapped in clear plastic.

"Now, do you want a kid's casket—by which I'm talkin' a small child—or are we talkin' an *infant*? 'Cause they're two different things..."

Crayton listened as Jimmy went into his explanation, digging the guy's act, and smiled happily. Yeah, he thought, scoping out a powder-blue velvet coffin no bigger than a Popeye's Chicken family box, thinking about the power the casket would hold when properly consecrated according to the ritual prescribed by Maman Arielle.

He pointed. "I like that one."

On the way back to the apartment, with the Iguanas on the radio and the air scented with a hint of rain, giggling at the idea that there was a coffin in his back seat, Cray stopped at a gardening supply and antique dealer Maman Arielle had told him about. There, he purchased a large cast iron cauldron. The sumbitch must have weighed eighty pounds and barely fit in the trunk. It wasn't cheap, either.

But nothing else would do. It wasn't the sort of thing you saw much of anymore, not in this day and age. Cray wasn't sure he'd ever seen one.

Green had, though. Halloween night—and he'd even eaten out of it.

CHAPTER THIRTY-NINE

"Cray told you about Darby, I guess." J.C.'s voice, over the phone from Washington D.C., sounded composed, but Green could sense tension.

"Yeah, he told me. Christ, I'm sorry, J.C.," Green said. He'd only been home from work a half-hour or so and was still wearing his Pirate's Alley golf shirt. Seated at his tiny desk, he waved frantically at Kay and Eliza, over on the couch, to make sure they knew who he was talking to.

Kay gave him the okay sign, and the girls went back to poring over the issue of *Spooge Gobblers* they'd brought in a few minutes before. It was bizarre: Kay and Eliza sipping from cups of hot chocolate while they *oohed* and *ahhed* over a glossy fuck-book.

"I shoulda known somethin' was weird," J.C. said. "Bitch always had righteous cash, always goin' to work at odd hours—and yet she couldn't give me a phone number where I could reach her."

Green had never heard J.C. this upset. It was a potent brew of anger and embarrassment. He tried to soothe him. "Hey, you can't blame yourself if she was a little secretive. "

"She must have *zero* self-respect. Think about it..." J.C. was indeed on a roll, and Green was happy to let him ramble. In the meantime, Green glanced through the mail: phone bill, the new *Poets & Writers*...and an envelope from the Tennessee Williams Festival. Green took a deep breath, trying to calm himself and listen to J.C.

"...so I don't know where the fuckin' whore is now, but I think she's smart enough to know J.C. ain't bluffin'. If I *see* her again in the Quarter, I'll have the First District boys bust her ass righteously." J.C. was winding down.

"I suspect you won't have to," Green said. "People like that are always on the move anyway." Green didn't know what *that* meant, but it seemed like the sort of thing J.C. wanted to hear. As he spoke, he tore into the Festival envelope.

J.C. said, "I'll be back tomorrow. We'd best rendezvous, if you've got the time. Maybe get Donny and Huey and ol' Crayton. That damned voodoo nut came through *big* time for ol' J.C. Saturday."

"I heard." Green unfolded the heavy-stock stationery. *Dear Mr. Hopkins: This is to inform you that* The Pagan Malt Shop, *your submission in the 23rd Tennessee Williams Festival First Novelist Competition, has been selected as a finalist...* Green felt excitement well up from his stomach, and a grin broke across his face.

J.C. was talking about Crayton. "Yeah, maybe you were right about him after all. Is he there, by chance?"

"No, he's doing a late shift at the Voodoo Shoppe."

"Right. Anyway, we'll need some boy's night out action, whaddya think?"

"Okay, J.C. And stay strong, bro. New Orleans has the most beautiful women in the world."

"You got that right. " J.C.'s voice was a rasp, and Green could imagine him leering in a D.C. hotel room. "We got the Jazz Fest and the French Quarter Fest, and it's about time to inaugurate the first annual J.C. Bitoun Fuck Fest!"

Laughing, Green hung up and faced the couch. "You guys have terrific timing," he growled good-naturedly.

"Well, how'd we know J.C. would call?" Kay said.

"And what are you doing with that magazine anyway?"

Eliza grinned and held up a shot of Darby hoisting her medically enhanced breasts like sandbags. "Now you can't tell us, Green, that you haven't wondered if these things were real. At some point, you would've wandered into some Bourbon Street porn shop to take a look."

"Uhm, you're probably right."

The girls flipped a few more pages and Eliza called out, "Ohmygod!"

Kay gasped. "Come over here, honey! Darby's taking it in the *rear*!" The girls shrieked with laughter.

Green was amused but embarrassed too. "Y'all are something else." He wanted to tell Kay about his manuscript, but privately. Maybe he was overreacting, but it *was* kind of a big deal. Somehow, broaching the subject while all of them looked at pictures of Darby with, well, various objects stuffed up her ass seemed sort of incongruous.

Kay and Eliza broke into laughter once more, then Kay shook her head in disbelief and tossed the magazine onto the coffee table. "Okay," she said. "I guess we've seen about every inch of Darby it's possible to see." Eliza cracked up again, and Kay asked, "How's J.C.?"

"He's pretty shaken. I can tell by how tough he's acting."

Eliza said, "Oh, poor thing. Now I feel like a heel." She pointed at the magazine.

Green said, "Don't worry about it; J.C. never has to know. He'll be fine. J.C.'s a survivor." He smiled. "Besides, we *did* need to know whether they were real or not."

The girls grinned and Kay joked, "Man, her plastic surgeon must work at NASA!"

Green had to laugh. "Anybody want a beer? It's been a long day." He wandered into the kitchen. "Kay? Eliza?"

Kay said she'd have one, but Eliza thought about it and declined. "Not now," she said, "but thanks. I'm gonna head home and wash some clothes. See what Crayton's up to when he gets off work."

Green came back with two Dixies and handed one to Kay—and noticed Eliza was crying. "Eliza, what's wrong?"

Kay looked over and said, "Oh, god, honey, what happened?"

Eliza dabbed at her tears and managed to choke a laugh. "I'm sorry. I... It's just that, in the past few weeks, Cray's been so *weird*."

Green and Kay exchanged a glance, and Green said gently, "Cray *is* weird, Eliza. That's why we love him."

"I can't believe I'm doing this," she muttered, wiping her eyes.

Kay said, "Relax, honey, and tell us what's bothering you."

"I thought I could wait till I got to the apartment," Eliza said apologetically. "I could feel this coming on for days now."

"Is it something you want to talk about?" Green asked. He had no idea what to do; this had come out of nowhere. "Should I leave? Maybe you'd feel better talking to Kay."

Eliza shook her head. "You're his best friend, Green. Surely you see what's happening." She looked up at Green questioningly.

He frowned "Well, he's been a little out-there, lately, sure..."

Eliza took a deep breath. "That's one way to put it. Cray *is* eccentric. I mean, that *is* what's so interesting about him. But I *hate* the whole voodoo thing... Voodoo, the death league. None of it's funny anymore—and I don't believe him when he says he's doing it just to be entertaining."

Kay looked at Green questioningly. He asked Eliza, "Is he doing anything beyond the usual? I mean, I know about the kooky amulets, the candles and the incense, the clothing... I mean, is he conducting, like, *rituals* or anything?"

Eliza said, "Who knows? Nothing like sticking pins in dolls, if that's what you mean. It's like he jokes about it, but yet he's *not* joking. Does that make any sense?"

Green said, "Yeah, I can see that. It's subtle, but it's there."

Eliza nodded sadly, staring at the floor. "Yeah, it's there..." She paused, then shook her head, stood up, and sighed. "Again, I apologize. I thought I could make it home before the deluge hit."

"Nonsense," Kay said, giving her a hug. "And don't worry, darlin'. I'm sure Crayton's fine. We'll figure it out."

Eliza offered Kay a tentative smile, then looked at Green. "Thank you both."

"I don't know that we did anything, but it was our pleasure," Green said, standing to walk Eliza to the door. He helped her on with her jacket and opened the door for her. "You sure you're okay? You want us to call you a cab?"

Eliza said, "I'll be fine. I'll walk up Royal and the air'll do me good."

Green hesitated, wondering whether he should say anything else. "I wouldn't worry too much about Crayton, Eliza. He may be fascinated by voodoo while he's learning about it, and because of these strange death league coincidences." He thought for an instant, trying to be reassuring without revealing his own doubts—whatever they were. "I've talked with Cray about that. It troubles *him* too. So I think it's something he'll get out of his system. After all, he's got you to distract him."

Eliza leaned over and gave Green a quick kiss on the cheek. "Yeah, and think of all I learned today from *Wad Gobblers*. If I can't distract him now..."

Then she closed the door and was gone, and Green and Kay sat down on the couch and wrapped their arms around one another for a minute.

"Jeez," Green finally said. "Poor girl."

"I know," Kay said.

Green sat up and grinned. "Hey, not to change the subject, but I got some news." He picked up the letter from the Williams Festival. "*Malt Shop* made the finals!"

Kay squealed. "Green, ohmigod! That's *wonderful!* " She gave him a deep kiss. Then she held him at arms' length, grinning and searching his eyes. "Baby, I'm so proud!" She reached out and stroked his throat. "We are gonna celebrate. Let's go out!"

Green smiled, touched at her genuine enthusiasm. "Thanks, Kay. But let's stay in, okay? I don't wanna jinx anything."

Kay shrugged and kissed his nose. "Sure, darlin'. Whatever you think."

"Cool. I'll open a bottle of wine." A thought hit him. "But first I guess I'd better call over to Donny and Huey's. J.C. asked me to bring them up to date on his situation." He glanced at his watch. "And I'd like to call the hospital and see how Papa's doing. I wanna make sure he's coming home this week."

"Excellent. He's doing well?" Kay took Green's arms and led him in an impromptu slow dance.

Green held up crossed fingers as he shuffled awkwardly to Kay's lead. "That's what he said when we talked Saturday. Who knows with cardiac stuff."

Kay nodded. She broke off the dance. "Well, I'll go ahead and start on dinner. And afterward..." She picked up the magazine off the table and flipped randomly to a page and held it up. They were staring at a picture of Darby and a bulked-up guy with a Mohawk, entwined in a position that did not seem humanly possible. "Afterward," Kay continued, "we can work on this. You can work it into your *next* award-winning novel."

Green laughed, turning slightly red. "I still can't believe you guys bought that."

Kay wriggled her eyebrows like Groucho. "Seemed like a good idea at the time," she said, heading into the kitchen. After a few minutes, Green could hear her chopping vegetables.

"Kay?" he called.

"Mm-hmm?"

"What's your take on Cray?"

She stuck her head in the kitchen doorway and looked thoughtful. "I guess," she said, choosing her words carefully. "I guess I'd be a liar if I didn't think something was definitely different about him. It's almost like Darby, when you think about it. Sometimes I wonder if *he* doesn't have a secret life of some kind. At least in his head."

Green sighed and stood up. "I was afraid you'd say something like that."

CHAPTER FORTY

The next morning, after Kay left, Green grabbed the *Times-Picayune* and headed into the kitchen for a banana. He'd decided to try and learn as much about *Le Culte des Morts* as he could, and not just to put closure to the Halloween episode. That issue, after all, was *also* interconnected with Crayton. And as long as HE continued to throw down voodoo shtick, it would be hard to forget about it—even if they were working two different angles, the Cray/Voodoo Shoppe kind and the Maman Arielle kind.

What if it's the same thing?

He sighed. It was the second time he'd thought of that connection. But he was determined to put it out of his mind, taking a bite of the fruit and pulling out the metro section. On page two, though, a brief grabbed his eye.

Police Still Baffled in Cemetery Desecrations—Killer's Corpse Mutilated. Green felt a queasy shock. He dropped the banana in the trash and skimmed the article. It was a follow-up piece to something that must've run the day before, and simply reiterated that a cemetery sexton reported at least two burial plots had been ransacked over the Thanksgiving weekend, and that bodies at both tombs had been "disturbed."

Only one of the corpses was identified: Prospero Godchaux. "Fuck me running," Green murmured. There was a police statement saying they were looking into the incidents but suspected they were mischief. They also refused to comment on what, specifically, had been done to the bodies, but an unnamed source—the sexton?—confirmed that Godchaux's body was mutilated.

Green was disturbed, not so much by the actual incidents—frankly, in New Orleans, somebody did something weird in a cemetery on an almost lunar basis; a gutted dog had been recently discovered hanging in St. Roch's Cemetery—but because it hit home a little too closely. He'd bet a Sherlock Holmes deerstalker that the unidentified grave in the story was the one with those odd fucking angels on either side of the tomb.

Without even realizing he was doing so, Green grabbed a sweater and headed out into the chilly sunlight. He glanced over at Cray's silent apartment before setting off to the Hotel St. Pierre where he could grab a taxi.

A quarter-hour later he was standing in front of a small building of putty-colored bricks serving as the groundskeeper's shed for the River of Life Cemetery. It abutted the graveyard from the west wall, with a visitor's door on the street and a wide garage area for maintenance purposes opening into the cemetery from the rear. Green thought about asking the cab driver to wait, then realized he had no idea, exactly, of how to go about what, exactly, he wanted to do or hoped to find out.

Green had no idea. He could probably call another cab from inside or, if worse came to worst, walk back. He started to open the door, then thought better of it. Instead, he hurried around the corner to a public gate about fifty yards down a quiet residential street that bordered the long wall of the cemetery. Inside, the marble gravestones seemed to shimmer in the brittle sunbeams. This was a different perspective than when he'd been at Godchaux's funeral, and it took him a moment to get his bearings.

He'd wondered if there would be security, given the weekend chicanery, but he didn't see any uniforms. All he saw was an old woman in a blue dress, kneeling beside a modest grave. She was straightening a tiny American flag on a wooden dowel.

Overhead, geese flew by, and wind blew a wrapper from a Milky Way bar across Green's shoes. Late autumn leaves slouched in piles against the tombs.

After looking around, he thought he knew where to go. The skyline of crypts precluded him from actually seeing the creepy angels but, if he was correct, he did spy the chapel with the rusted bell tower Papa had shown him. The angels, then, should be in the opposite corner.

Green crisscrossed the paths, trying for as direct a route as possible. Then he saw them. "Gotcha," he murmured, glancing around with embarrassment that he would say something so corny. Still, he felt like he had to say something. You didn't have to be Peter fucking Straub to know strange things happened in this place—you could *feel* it, and as sure as he was breathing Green knew the sensation wasn't just his imagination.

Glancing back over in the direction of the maintenance shed to make sure no one was watching, Green reached down and plucked a reasonably fresh floral arrangement off a headstone, then strode casually toward the angels. He stopped about three graves away, pretending to study the nondescript resting place of one Emil Potter. If in fact the tomb with the angels was one of the desecrated graves—and Green had no reason other than his own hunch that it was so—he didn't want to be caught scrutinizing the damned thing. He reached in his pocket and put on his sunglasses, secret agent-style, and knelt before Potter's grave, arranging the flowers with care. Only then did he hazard a look over at the Cruelty and Despair angels.

They were every bit as disturbing as he remembered, though some bird had apparently crapped on Despair's head. Green had to laugh; it broke the tension a bit. He edged a few feet closer and studied the crypt beneath the angels. Hmm. From what he could determine, if indeed this was one of the crypts the prowlers had tampered with, Green could see no signs of it.

What the hell did he do now? What had he accomplished? For that matter, what the hell was he doing here in the first place?

Then an actual, usable thought struck him. Checking once more to make sure no one was watching, Green strode over to the crypt, hoping to look purposeful, and bent over the weathered nameplate. If he remembered correctly from his earlier visit, most of the letters had been obscured by erosion. But he'd also been too freaked out by Papa's story to actually think about reading anything. Now, he wondered if he could identify enough letters to infer an actual name.

He stuck his nose right up to the marble tablet—so much for his James Bondian discretion—and picked out what could have been an E, R, or P...there was a clearly defined X; that was good...and maybe an L or I. Or it could be a T... The rest were indecipherable.

Green straightened up and laughed again. Shit, if he kept kicking ass like this, he'd be promoted to police commissioner any day now. An oak leaf floated by, and Green snatched it out of the air, ripping it in half and tossing the pieces back into the breeze. Then he turned back toward the entrance. Might as well return the flowers.

"Sorry, Emil," he said, grabbing the arrangement. "It was only temporary." And that's when Green's next idea hit.

A bell tinkled when he opened the door to the cemetery office and Green found himself in a small front room furnished with a cheap desk and a coat rack. On the desk were a calendar, a lamp, and a telephone. A bookshelf behind the desk contained several industrial looking volumes that, Green assumed, contained grids of the cemetery plots. Through the rear door he could see shelves of gardening implements and a clod-spattered push mower. The place smelled heavily of gasoline and wet earth.

A large white man with curly gray hair and black-frame glasses, wearing engineer's striped overalls over a New Orleans Saints sweatshirt, walked out of the back wiping his hands on a grease-stained towel.

"Can I help you?" he said tiredly. Green suspected the guy had already had a long week of nuts calling since the news had hit the paper.

"Hi," Green said. "I just found out I have a distant relative buried here. If I give you his name, could you tell me where his grave is?"

The man's lips curled in full frown, but he sounded amiable enough. "Sure. What's the name you're looking for?"

"Potter. Emil Potter," Green said, spelling both names helpfully.

"Okay, hold on a minute." The man set his rag on the desk and pulled a folder out of the top desk drawer. He flipped through it, the tip of his tongue peeking through his teeth, then knelt heavily next to the bookshelf and tilted his head back to focus like one encroaching on the farsightedness of middle age. After a moment, he pulled out a volume, pushed himself to a standing position, and laid the book on the desk.

"Let's see..." He started turning through the pages till he found the one he wanted. "Emil Potter is in L-9, over in the southeast corner." He pointed vaguely toward the back. "I can aim you in the right direction—"

"Oh, I'll bet I can figure it out. Could I see that?" Green asked.

"Sure," the man said. "I guess that'd help, wouldn't it?" He spun the open book around and used a thick thumb to tap the area where Emil Potter was buried. "And we're over here," he added, drawing an imaginary line across the page. "Can't miss it."

"Right," Green said, studying the page intently. "Let me just gander at this for a sec." There were indeed the typewritten names of the deceased corresponding with the plots. Green quickly acclimated himself to the schematic and pinpointed the location of the angels tomb.

Freixenet et al, it said. The name meant nothing to Green, though he spotted a number of "*et als*" sprinkled throughout the page.

"What do all these *et als* mean?" he asked.

"Just that several people were interred in that particular spot. A lot of these graves date back to the yellow fever epidemic, when whole families were wiped out. And some of these crypts house entire *neighborhoods*, if folks were poor enough."

So the angel grave could have anybody in it, Freixenet or not.

"Anyhow," the man said, "you can't miss it. I'd show you myself but it's been a busy morning." He sighed. "You wouldn't believe."

Green grinned understandingly, then decided to try a slightly different tact. "Oh, I would. I read the *Picayune*. You have my sympathy."

The man nodded gratefully. "You know what happened then. This city..." He shook his head. "Fuckin' freak show, if you'll pardon my French."

"Absolutely," Green said. He was thinking the River of Life was one of New Orleans' smaller cemeteries, which meant this guy had to be the only sexton—and was probably the source for the information about the Godchaux mutilation. "What happened to drinking beer on Saturday night, y'know? Now you got nuts running around in graveyards."

The sexton laughed. "Hell, I know. But this town's always been full of wackos."

Green leaned forward conspiratorially. "The paper didn't say what happened to that Godchaux guy, but my girlfriend's cousin used to be a cop. He said it wouldn't surprise him if a policeman actually did it—Godchaux being a cop killer—and given the big deal funeral."

"Yeah, that *was* a big nigger show," the sexton said, picking up the rag and working on his hands again. "Like he was a hero. But, between you and me, I don't think it was a cop."

"No?" Green grew wide-eyed in surprise.

"Nope." He looked pleased that he possessed secret information and lowered his voice. "I came in around noon on Saturday, just to check stuff out, y'know, and I'm the one who discovered this shit."

"Wow." Green tried to sound impressed; the guy was getting on a roll.

"Yeah. And whoever done it left the nigger musician's casket open. They cut his *hand* off!" The sexton was giddy with information. Green couldn't have shut him up with a blowtorch. "Cops were thinking it was some sort of devil or voodoo shit—"

Green started visibly, hoping the sexton didn't notice, but the guy was too enthralled by his own breach of secrecy to care. He was saying, "Then someone pointed out the Godchaux dude had been buried with some famous ring on his finger. Some showbiz nigger shit."

Green wanted to wince at the grinding bigotry, but at least the clown was dishing out information. "Those folks'll dazzle you," Green commented with *faux* wonder.

The man nodded like Green was Descartes. "Anyway, it was probably just some crackhead music fan, figured he could sell the ring and score *mucho* dope-o." He crossed his arms.

Green decided to push further. "The paper mentioned two incidents..."

The sexton nodded wisely. "Well, yeah. But the cops asked me to keep that'n hush-hush." He winked at Green. "I tell you what though. Your uncle Eddie—"

"Emil," Green interjected smoothly. "My great-uncle, Emil Potter." Green didn't think he'd mentioned exactly what branch of the family Emil represented, but that was okay. The sexton was too busy rockin' the house to worry about such minutiae.

"Right. Emil," the man said. "Well, your great uncle ain't too far from where it happened."

"Really?" Green marveled. "Was it a famous musician too? Maybe *that's* the connection."

"Naw, we don't think so. Probably just a random deal," the guy said importantly. *We*, Green thought. *Everyone's a detective.*

"Hmm," Green said. "That's odd then."

"Yeah, who knows? It was one of them tombs where several folks have been buried over the years. Coulda been anybody. It's one of them *et al* graves you were talking about."

"Right," Green said, shaking his head, indicating the curious qualities of the world. "Well, I can't thank you enough for your help."

"Anytime, bud."

Green smiled once more. "Good luck."

"Gonna kick ass and take names," the sexton assured him, closing the book and setting it on top of the shelf.

Green wandered outside and edged around the cemetery wall. He could see a convenience store sign towering a few blocks over where he could call a cab. Detective Green felt some satisfaction, though he wished again he owned a cell phone. Still, he'd made progress. Someone had cut off Prospero Godchaux's hand, and at least some of the people in the angel grave were named Freixenet—whatever that meant.

When Green ambled into the litter-strewn parking lot of the store, he used a pay phone to call a cab then went inside for a Mountain Dew. He leaned against the building, sipping his drink and thinking, until a taxi pulled into the lot. Green had the driver drop him off in the Central Business District by City Hall.

Green had another tangent he wanted to pursue.

CHAPTER FORTY-ONE

Natchez, Mississippi

As Green Hopkins was orchestrating his amateur PI routine in the River of Life Cemetery, Papa Hipolyte, wearing a monitor of some kind and hooked-up to a mobile IV unit, shuffled down the corridor of Natchez Community Hospital and into the interior courtyard, hoping the mellow sun might kiss away the oppressive smells of illness.

Just to be outdoors was dessert-like in its sweetness. It was maybe sixty-five degrees, and the salt breeze from the Gulf, across the highway, was as healing as any of those pills they made him swallow when they insisted on waking his ass at three a.m. Overhead, a gull mocked infirmity with a series of shrill *cree-crees*. Papa grinned; he'd wondered if he'd ever hear a bird again.

Yep, as far as the trappings of medical architecture were concerned, Papa had to admit, these folks outdid themselves. Maybe it wasn't the Hanging Gardens of Babylon, but you could almost believe you were in the Commander's Palace courtyard.

There was a freshly painted white gazebo, its trelliswork clustered with vines and yellow blooms. Inside was a table and chairs, and three patients in robes sat playing bridge under the supervision of a nurse who cheered their game like she was courtside at an LSU basketball game.

Wooden benches dotted the courtyard, bordered by neatly clipped shrubbery. True, the three-story hospital walls on all sides were confining in their institutional gloom, but all in all this was a fine place to be.

He took a seat on one of the benches and turned his face to the sky, damned appreciative to be among the living. A heart attack—hell, *dying*—was major mind-fuck time, and one emerged from *that* with some battling emotions.

Papa reached into his robe and pulled out a paperback mystery Green had brought him. But he just set it on the bench. It was nicer to relax in the breeze and let his mind wander.

Only now, a week after he'd keeled over making gumbo, did Papa think he might've reached some form of closure with regards to that all-important Mental Attitude the doctors kept yammering about.

It had little to do with religion; the house padre had been by a few times, and Father Timothy from St. Lydwine had driven up from New Orleans as soon as he heard the news. Papa was as comfortable with his beliefs as he'd ever been. True, he was still perplexed by the vision he'd had at the moment of the cardiac arrest—Maman Arielle, clucking with tender concern that he'd be all right—but he had to admit that, since he'd awakened in the hospital, the horrible gris-gris dreams that had plagued him for years had completely vanished. In fact, since the attack, he'd slept well for the first time in thirty years... Maybe it was because he'd talked with Green about it, gotten it out in the open.

In the end, Papa supposed it was a will-to-live thing. A lot of patients, faced with their own mortality—and dying on the ratty carpet of a cheap hotel is about as mortal as it gets—turn inward and live out their days captives of their own fear. Fear was a self-perpetuating gig, and not at all good for anyone seriously interested in longevity.

Papa was cool with that. He *thought* so, anyway. Papa had reached a weird sort of peace with the idea of death. Based on what the doctors said, this cardiac shit would kill him eventually—and whatever time he had left seemed a bonus. If God pulled his plug tomorrow, well, he wouldn't bitch.

Besides, he *did* feel good. It was like he'd told Green on the phone last night. "Feelin' feisty, boy. You run down to Lafitte's and tell 'em to dust off my piano stool. I'm fixin' to come back and make some music."

"Not a problem. The dust is cleared and the bar is waiting. They got lines stretching down to Esplanade waiting for you to get back! It's like the Neville Brothers were playing there!"

Papa had laughed. Lines all the way through the lower Quarter. That'd be the day!

Now, he tilted his face to the sun and closed his eyes and let the music play in his head. There was always music there—his own personal jukebox. He settled back and enjoyed the sounds. James Booker doing "Junco Partner."

Ain't life grand?

CHAPTER FORTY-TWO

New Orleans, Louisiana

Inside City Hall, Green negotiated through a weekday crowd of civic workers and folks snagged by the in-triplicate net of day-to-day life. Pinballing from one office to another, he finally ended up in the room where city tax files were stored. A sullen, middle-aged woman with animal breath led him through dusty corridors of floor-to-ceiling shelves crammed with huge binders. There was no plan or method to what he was doing—and he had no idea what he hoped to learn. He *ought* to be working on his manuscript. But checking this stuff out left him feeling less helpless about everything.

At the end of one row was a cardboard sign casually marked E - H. "Down there," the woman recited. "In alphabetical order. You wanna copy something, there's machines in the front. Costs a quarter. We don't make change."

"Gee, thanks," Green said.

She padded off and he wandered down the aisle. Amazingly, Green found the volume he was looking for almost immediately and carried it to a table at the end of the aisle. Sitting down, the Hardy Boy-style detective's exhilaration he'd been feeling began to vanish and all he felt was tired.

The pages were computer printouts, early dot-matrix stuff on primitive gray-and-white striped, perforated paper that indicated that the city of New Orleans was operating with outdated equipment. *What else is new?* Green leafed though pages and ran his finger down columns of type. He stopped his cynical philosophizing when he spotted what he was looking for.

GRIS-GRIS GUMBO, 442 Frenchmen Street. Permittee: Henri Vidrane. PROPERTY ADJOINS DWELLING AT MARAIS STREET. ASSESSED VALUE: $270,000.

Green processed this. Maman Arielle didn't own Gris-Gris Gumbo and the house on the other side of the courtyard—or at least her name wasn't on it. Someone named Henri Vidrane—

Wasn't the host at the Halloween party named Henri? He jotted down the information, though he wasn't sure what he'd do with it or why he'd even looked it up. Still, he knew stuff he hadn't known when he woke up. Whether there were any connections or he could ever put everything together, or whether it meant anything if and when he did, well...

Green closed the volume and thoughtfully replaced it, then made his way out of the stacks. The clerk was inspecting a donut and ignored him. In the corridor, he noticed a BIRTH AND DEATH CERTIFICATES sign with an arrow pointing down another hallway.

Instinctively, Green headed in that direction and shortly found himself looking through a bound volume similar to the tax rolls. It took him a few minutes to find what he wanted, and he was surprised to note there weren't all that many Freixenets in Orleans and Jefferson parishes. He wasn't sure what he was looking for here, either, but when the fourth document he came across was the birth and death information for one Arielle Anise Friexenet, Green gasped.

Someone named Arielle *was buried in the Friexenet tomb—the grave with the angels Papa had told him about!* And Arielle from the Gris-Gris Gumbo just happened to be the daughter of a voodoo queen Papa had referred to the day of Prospero's jazz funeral. They *had* to be mother and daughter!

Green looked back down at the dates and saw that the mother Arielle had been born in 1922 and had died forty-three years later. Well, that sounded right.

Logically, then, there had to be birth records for the daughter too, right? *The gumbo chef?* He thumbed through the A's, but there was only one Arielle. Green supposed "Arielle" could be a middle name or nickname—but then she could also be listed under her father's name—whomever that might've been. Green thought about looking through all the Friexenets but glanced at his watch, remembering he had to be at work in the not-too-distant future. Not only that, but he supposed maybe she hadn't been born in Orleans or Jefferson parish. So the birth records would be somewhere else.

He sighed and closed the book.

Maman fuckin' Arielle Anise Friexenet. Unbelievable. Green figured he had enough time to swing by the Acme Oyster House. A few dozen on the shell would go down nicely right about now, and he could ponder whether he was solving mysteries or creating them.

CHAPTER FORTY-THREE

J.C. himself invited Eliza and Kay to come along to his Boys Night Out commemorating the sordid discovery of Darby's secret career. He called them personally—not knowing they'd already studied the evidence—delicately broaching to each of them his girlfriend's substantial and numerous infidelities, and telling them it would do him good to be around women of character and honor.

Now, gathered around a huge table in the tiny back room at the Port of Call at the lower edge of the Quarter, Cray thought it a fine and generous idea to have the women present. He was happy for anything that would promote general harmony and good vibes.

Lately, around his friends—or *not* around them, as with last Wednesday night when he no-showed at Markey's Bar—he felt like a man trying to tightrope across a thread of dental floss. His attempt to patch things up at the Palace Café had worked, at least that night. But Eliza was still acting withdrawn when they were alone, and tonight Green was a bit distant too.

A lot had happened since the gang had last rendezvoused—*besides* the discovery of Darby's secret life—and Cray, his radar on full blast, thought the aura at the table seemed convivial. He was next to Green, with Donny and the H-Man anchoring either end of the booth. J.C. was in the center, flanked by Kay and Eliza. J.C. wasn't exactly his old self, but he did seem to have recovered a bit of personal dignity and was clearly pleased his friends would turn out for the occasion.

They bantered about late-breaking news. Huey had scored a lecturer gig at UNO and would begin teaching philosophy in the spring semester. There were toasts to that news, as well as to the word that Green's play was a finalist entry and would be excerpted at a reading during the Tennessee Williams Literary Festival in March. And Kay was leaving for a weekend geology field trip somewhere out in the swamps; Cray wondered if this was maybe why Green was a bit quiet.

Just after the waitress took orders, J.C. chimed on his Abita bottle with a fork and got everyone's attention. With jovial (and possibly false) bravado, J.C. brought up the subject of Darby, her career, and subsequent exile.

"Far as I know," J.C. said, his drawl adjusted to the *I'm A Martyr* setting, "she done gone back to New England to explain to her folks why she's doin' po'nography for a livin'. Or, who knows? Maybe she's in L.A. Now *that's* a town that can presumably appreciate more completely her artistic sensibilities."

Cray was gratified that J.C. treated him as a new confidante. He winked at Cray as he regaled the table with a hazy recollection of the two of them staring Saturday morning in slack-jawed amazement at *Spooge Gobblers*, then navigating erratically from bar to bar across the liquid expanse of the Quarter, tempering their collective disbelief in cheap draft beer and expensive single-malt scotch.

The anecdotes—and Cray's timely and witty interjections—also helped to smooth over his absence at Markey's. Only Green seemed less than enthusiastic during the course of the evening, though he seemed thoughtful rather than bummed out.

Still, it bothered Cray. Subsequently, as the whole table watched Huey impersonate his new department head, Crayton's mind wandered. He had to admit he wasn't pulling off his double life very well—cause for major concern. By now, whether he liked it or not, and he vacillated almost hourly between exultation and despair, he was inextricably entangled in *Le Culte des Morts*. But he wanted his other life too—*this life*, he thought, looking at his friends.

The fact was, for the first time ever, Cray was popular. He had *secrets* and got phone calls and had *power* and pals to do stuff with and an awesome *girlfriend*—and he *liked* it. *All* of it... But, filling out his mental scorecard tonight here at the Port of Call, Cray had to admit that the two people he cared most about in the world, Eliza and Green, weren't handling it very well.

Crayton chewed his hamburger and it could have been cardboard for all he tasted, and he laughed in the right places, but gradually he sank into his own brain. He couldn't put his finger on Green's demeanor toward him. Green was clearly annoyed by the voodoo shit on a much bigger overall level.

But Eliza was a different story. Throughout dinner Cray watched Eliza wistfully. She and Kay were laughing and cracking jokes with J.C., feeding him bites of baked potato—and she looked like she was having *fun*. Cray tried to fight off the icicle stabs of jealousy.

If Crayton was losing Eliza, and deep down he suspected he was, voodoo was absolutely the cause. It was obvious in the way she kissed him now—with hurried reluctance, as though he were a favorite but antiquated uncle with breath like turning pears—or in her fidgeting impatience whenever they were alone together. Cray wiped his mouth with a napkin and vowed to have a talk with Maman Arielle. There *had* to be a way to make this all work...

Then Donny leapt out of the booth like a musketeer. "Hold on!" he cried, pointing up at the television in the corner. He reached and cranked the volume on a local talking head giving a promo on what New Orleans could expect on the ten o'clock news.

"That's Cat-Daddy Phelps!" Donny exclaimed as a photo of an old black man filled the screen.

"What?" "Who?" The table was a puzzled flurry of confusion at Donny's behavior, and he quickly quieted them down in time to hear the female newscaster announce that Cat-Daddy Phelps, a local clarinetist, had been found dead of apparently natural causes in his Ninth Ward home.

"Yesss!" Donny said with the fiery determination of a high school football coach, "O-*kay!*" Then he pumped his fist and spun to face the table. He looked at Green.

"Remember when I replaced Dick Van Dyke with Cat-Daddy Phelps?" he asked, thumbing back at the television. "Well, Phelps is outta here." Donny smiled proudly.

Green's look of confusion cleared. "Oh," he said, as though reminded of an impending visit by an IRS agent. "The death league."

Cray broke in, finally understanding. "Wait a minute," he said to Donny. "You dropped Dick Van Dyke from your roster? And replaced him with Cat-Daddy Phelps? The Preservation Hall clarinet guy? When did you do that?"

Green glared at Donny, then asked Crayton, "Don't you read the roster updates I give you?"

Cray shrugged. "Well, not every day. I mean, this isn't like rotisserie baseball, where something happens every hour. We've had—what?—four deaths? And besides"—Cray dipped his head in *faux* modesty as he instantly decided to throw in a little bravado for purposes of appearing normal—"up till now I'm pretty much the only guy with dead bodies piling up."

"Well, not anymore, pal!" Donny crowed.

Kay and Eliza, who'd been following this exchange with something less than understanding, finally got their attention. "What the *hell* are you lunatics talking about?" Kay asked. "Is it the death league?"

"I thought everyone was pissed off about that," Eliza said. Green slid out of the booth and stood, staring at Donny. "You are unbelievable," he said mildly.

Donny looked guilty. "What'd I do?"

Green said, "First J.C. and now you." He waved his arm in a sweep as though indicating the whole world was guilty. "You guys get all pissed off and upset at Crayton when *his* people die, calling him witch doctor and voodoo priest and wanting to cancel the league, but as soon as one of your *own* guys dies, hey, this is the greatest idea of all time."

Donny nodded calmly, all agreement. "Of course, Green. It's called competition. I'm a shitty loser." He spun his Saints ball cap around so the bill was now facing backward. "Nobody really believes that voodoo stuff. Right, Cray?" He reached over and aimed a palm for a high-five. Crayton, still bewildered by the rapid turn of events, complied with moderate enthusiasm.

"Who in God's name is Cat-Daddy Phillips?" J.C. finally spoke.

Donny glanced at J.C. "Phelps," he corrected quietly. "Cat-Daddy *Phelps*." He directed his comments at Kay, Eliza, and J.C. "Cat-Daddy actually played with Louis Armstrong."

They shrugged and Donny cried, "The D-Man is in the corpse-hunt!"

Green fell back in his seat and took a drink of beer. He shook his head and looked at Kay with that sort of invisible significance that couples have, as if in complete disbelief. "Right," he said quietly, "nobody here was worried about voodoo at all."

Donny laughed. "Oh, the voodoo stuff was a little irritating, sure," he said, winking at Cray to show he'd never really been irritated. "See, the whole complaint all along was that people were dying in order. I mean, that's *still* weird, but hey, the whole world's weird, right?"

Green smiled bitterly. "You people are driving me insane." He looked at J.C. "And Donny's little attitude adjustment here doesn't bother you?"

J.C. shrugged. "I'm cool with it. I been cool with it all along."

Cray, watching, had to admit he felt like this was a good development, though Eliza sat with a less-than-happy expression at this turn of the conversation. But maybe it'd take some of the pressure off. After all, he'd pulled back a bit on the whole voodoo shtick, opting for more normal clothes, less jewelry, and pulling out his birthday cane only for special occasions rather than as a daily accoutrement.

"Fine," Green was saying mildly. "Then all I've got to say is, if Crayton's next four picks die in order, *in the next twelve hours*, I'd better not hear a word from *any* of you about voodoo." He winked at Cray, but then held his glance for an extra beat as if to say, *Your next four picks better* not *die in order. Not* any *of them.*

Cray decided it was best to shrug sheepishly as Donny cried, "It'll never happen. From here on out, only *my* people die!"

A look of sudden comprehension flashed across Green's face. "Say, Don," he said slowly, "about Cat-Daddy Phelps."

"Yeah?"

"You traded him out for Dick Van Dyke, right?"

"Right."

Green scratched his head. "Wasn't Dick Van Dyke *your* first-round pick?"

An amazed expression flashed across Donny's face. "Yeah. Yeah, now that you mention it, I guess he was. And I guess that makes Phelps my number one pick. Kinda."

Huey flashed a mock stern expression. "Hmm, so now *your* picks are dying in order. You're not casting any gris-gris, are you?"

CHAPTER FORTY-FOUR

Eliza's unhappiness was underscored after she and Cray returned to his apartment and started getting ready for bed. Her reticence grew with each stage of his nighttime ritual: lighting the votive candles and burning sticks of incense, and particularly when he put John Campbell on the stereo and the late bluesman started singing about hellhounds and angels of sorrow.

"Why are we listening to that spooky music?" Eliza said, coming out of the restroom after washing her face.

Cray, reading the sports page in a cane-backed chair in the corner of the bedroom, hoping somehow the mood would return to normal, looked startled. "I thought you liked blues."

"I do," Eliza said. "But why John Campbell? Why does everything in your life have to be related to voodoo?" She stood by the bed in her red-striped nightshirt, staring with troubled eyes.

There wasn't any point in lying about Campbell's voodoo affiliation; his CD photos were rife with animal bones, claw pendants, black cats, and gris-gris charms, and liner notes thanked High John the Conqueror in twelve-point type.

"Voodoo or not," he said finally, "I like him because his music is authentic. He's the real thing."

Eliza snorted. "He *was* the real thing. He died in his early forties, of mysterious causes. That's hardly a recommendation for this infatuation you have, Cray. His songs are about dancing in graveyards or tiny coffins or secret gardens at midnight. He's probably the only other white person besides yourself I can think of that got so caught up in the trappings of voodoo—and it worked out real well for him, didn't it?" Sarcasm notwithstanding, Cray was grateful she at least crawled into bed and pulled the covers up.

In spite of her agitation, Cray was impressed. "How do you know so much about John Campbell?" Maybe she was more intrigued by voodoo than she let on.

"As you said," Eliza replied, her voice cool, "I like blues. I saw him in D.C., opening for Buddy Guy. Campbell had about six thousand candles lit on stage, and incense burning everywhere. Just like this apartment." She pointed around the room at the votives, Cray's flannel charm bag sitting next to his wallet, a chunk of High John the Conqueror root, the stick of incense smoking hazily in a coffee can. She managed a half-smile. "The only thing you don't have that Campbell did is a human skull."

Cray started and hoped she didn't notice, thinking of course of his recent acquisitions from the River of Life Cemetery now sitting on his dark altar in the St. Ignatius garage, next to—yes—a tiny coffin.

Their eyes met. "I hate it, Cray," she said softly. "I don't care how much you say you're joking, or how far you're really into it, it's not good for you. Or us."

Cray started to speak, then thought the better of it. Any defense now only sounded like so much weak bullshit. He'd tried explaining to Green at various points and it hadn't worked too well. He'd best hold off on any more extemporaneous rationalizations, at least until he could confer with Maman Arielle.

Eliza watched him a moment longer, troubled. "I'm very fond of you, Crayton," she said, "but I just don't know about all this. I..." She worked her throat, shaking her head sadly, then switched off the reading light and turned against the wall. "We have to talk, Crayton. Soon," she said.

Cray's tongue felt lined with thistles. "We will, kiddo. Trust me." He struggled to think of something else to say, but what was there? She was right. The cloud of voodoo hung over the room like the goddamned incense he was burning—in supplication to voodoo. *But it's* power, he wanted to say. And it wasn't like it was all dark either. He'd put a good gris-gris on Papa Hipolyte; he'd even asked Maman Arielle about it. They'd been seated in a small park between Frenchmen and Elysian Fields during a windblown twilight. School kids darted around a paint-starved seesaw, shrieking in pre-supper glee. Across the street, slackers in Lenin caps and camouflage were clustered around the front of an activist bookstore, awaiting an appearance by a militant poet.

"Do we ever do good?" Cray had asked.

Maman Arielle laughed gently. In the blood-red sunset, her eyes shone like stained glass in a church people were afraid to enter. "Good?" she asked in mock surprise. "Why, child, we are doing good —just not within the accepted standards of society. We doin' good for us."

Cray smiled, nervous and uncertain. "But what about helping someone just for the sake of it?"

Maman, playfully: "Oh, I dunno, lagniappe. What did you have in mind?"

Cray thought for a moment, unsure if it had been wise to even bring the subject up. "There's this old man—a friend of my pal Green's—and he's got a really bad heart condition."

Maman thought for a moment, tracing her pointed fingernail across the back of Crayton's hand. "Do you know this man?"

Crayton said, "I've met him. He plays piano around; he's a street artist too. Green calls him Papa Hipolyte. He's been a real father figure to my friend..."

It seemed to Cray there was an instant of recognition as Maman Arielle's brow furrowed, but it might've been her frowning into the last sunray. She paused, then laughed. "What could it hurt?" she asked good-naturedly... Then she told him what to do.

Cray watched Eliza sleep. He went into the living room and shut down the stereo, then came back and sat in the chair, wrestling with his emotions by the jumping shadows of candlelight.

When it seemed Eliza had shifted into deep sleep, he removed his clothes, brushed his teeth, and crawled in bed, snuggling up against her. She instinctively shifted so they could spoon properly.

"Cray?" she asked, her voice muffled against a pillow. He had awakened her.

"Yes, baby?"

"Make everything all right. Okay?"

"Everything's gonna be fine, kiddo," he said, feeling empty because he'd somehow managed to screw this up. He held her, feeling her mellow warmth and breathing the scent of magnolias in her hair through the cloying incense that suffocated the room. He wanted to make love to her, then confess everything about voodoo.

Eliza rolled over and faced him, and in the candle's Impressionistic glow her face was beautiful and melancholy in its desperation and longing. She kissed him, tasting of mint toothpaste. "Make love to me, Cray," she whispered.

He was instantly erect and eager, and closed his eyes and buried his face in the nape of her neck. At that moment, though, the sudden lightning-flash memory of the dry, foul taste between a corpse's thighs surged into the back of his throat like vomit, and he went soft at the precise moment the bedside candle sputtered and blinked out.

Cray fought panic and struggled to regain the moment, kissing Eliza's breasts and moaning her name. But even after she dipped between his legs and took him in her mouth, it didn't work. As somehow, frighteningly, he had known it wouldn't.

He renewed his efforts, but after a few minutes, he fell back helplessly on the bed, fighting tears that pooled in his eyes. "I'm sorry," he whispered. "I'm so sorry."

Eliza took a deep breath and he knew she was thinking it was stress from all the voodoo crap. But all she did was kiss him lightly and wipe his tears away.

"It'll be okay, baby," she said. "It's all right." She stroked his hair, telling him everything was fine, and eventually snuggled back up against him in their original spoon position. Cray felt molded of Styrofoam, unable to move or fathom what he should say.

Presently, Eliza's breathing pattern altered and relaxed, and he knew she'd fallen asleep. Cray gently disentangled himself from her slumbering form and rolled onto his back with his hands folded behind his head, staring up at the dark ceiling.

After a while, without Cray so much as moving, the candle beside the bed hissed faintly, and suddenly, the wick popped back into flame. And in the living room, so softly that only he could hear it, the stereo clicked on. John Campbell's voice was a rasp, breathy and urgent, singing in his wounded baritone.

The song was "Wolf among the Lambs," the last cut off *Howlin' Mercy*—which was interesting because the disc they'd been listening to before bed was *True Believer*. Just after the second chorus, right where Campbell's guitar solo normally started, the song shifted dynamics and dropped into a mournful instrumental section Crayton had never heard—*because it wasn't on the record in the first place.*

And when Campbell spoke into the room's dim light, it was like he was whispering to Crayton from three inches away. In fact, though Cray had clenched his eyes shut at the sound of the voice, he could feel the dead man's breath on his ear and smell moldy pockets of old whiskey and harsh nicotine. *"And all took responsibility for their wickedness,"* the voice said, *"as well as their power."*

Cray's eyes shot open at the proximity of the words—and in the lazy glow of the undead candle, beheld the wispy but corporeal image of Marcus dressed in a dark burial suit already bluish with mold.

The corpse's eyes glittered like orange sparkle, and he tilted his head back—cheeks waxy and glistening in the early stages of decomposition—to giggle softly. Cray could see the dented demarcation where the undertaker—*another* undertaker—had utilized embalmer's wax to fill in the hole torn in Marcus' throat by the trocar.

Even after all he'd seen and experienced in the past few weeks, Cray instinctively started to scream—but Marcus placed a cool, greasy palm over his mouth and shook his head.

"You don't want to wake Eliza, " he whispered in a slow, hesitating voice with the quality of sandpaper. "She sleeps like the dead..."

CHAPTER FORTY-FIVE

Green was helping Papa out of Crayton's Camaro when a piece of paper fluttered from under the front seat and out onto the street. Green knelt and plucked the paper, stuffing it in his rear pocket. It was a receipt of some kind.

They'd had a pleasant, hopeful drive from Natchez, Papa all free and easy, loosed on the world with medications, detailed instructions for proper nutrition and exercise, and pamphlets for how to live to an even older age with and through the magic of a positive attitude.

They'd dropped by St. Lydwine Church, where Green helped him through the narrow alleyway and waited patiently out front while Papa went inside to thank Father Tim for his prayers. Within five minutes Papa emerged, smiling, and Green took his arm to get him down the flagstone steps. At the bottom, Papa paused and glanced at the church. "Man, it's good to get back here."

"No doubt, Papa. I'm happy for you."

Papa clapped Green on the back, then looked up at the silent bell tower and pointed.

"Just once, I'd love to hear them bells chime," he said. "Just one time, Greenie. Man, that'd be like God sittin' in with Booker, wouldn't it? The way I got it figured, that's the kinda stuff that happens in heaven..."

The image delighted Green. "I'll bet it is, Papa. I'll bet it is at that."

Back at the cottage, Papa stood by the car, appraising the sun-teased day and savoring the brisk wind from the river. A small gray bird darted overhead like a spear. Tears glistened in Papa's eyes.

"Goddamn, boy," he said shakily, putting his hand on Green's shoulder, more out of affection than support. "Truth is, I didn't know whether I'd see my little home again."

Green placed his hand on top of Papa's, squeezed it gently. "Well, I knew you would."

Papa wiped his eyes and took a deep breath. "Let's check it out."

Papa lived in a small garden cottage behind a two-story Creole townhouse, just off Barracks at Chartres. Green ushered Papa through the wooden gate in a high brick wall and down a moist brick path bordered by foliage separating the house from the cottage: magnolia bushes, elephant ears, and knee-high saw grass.

The path opened into a small courtyard, bordered on three sides by the unkempt foliage and on the fourth by the cottage, painted pale gold. The courtyard was thick with windblown leaves. Though Papa's bedroom window overlooked the courtyard, the only door to the cottage was in the back, where they mounted three steps to a small screened-in gallery as Papa fished in his trousers for keys. He got the door open and they stepped inside the musty, pleasantly worn living room.

It was an older person's clubhouse: a vinyl recliner, covered with a knitted comforter, facing a small television set on a shelf unit full of records and old books. There was a large cuckoo clock on the wall next to a sunlit window facing the townhouse, and a clean ashtray and a pipe rack sat on an end table next to the recliner. In one corner was a wooden rocking chair. Against the far wall was an upright piano.

The cottage was familiarly scented with fruity tobacco, coffee, bay rum, and lemon furniture polish. A small kitchen was off one side of the room; a hallway opposite led to the bathroom and bedroom in back. It was all plank floors and bright white painted walls and lucite-framed photos of jazz and blues musicians.

Papa took it all in, grinning. "Goddamn," he said excitedly. "Every man's a king, and every home's a castle."

Green laughed. "Welcome back, Papa."

Papa nodded. "Damned good to be here."

Green watched him absorb the sights and sounds of his past, knowing Papa was thinking a million private thoughts. He said, "I left the box from the hospital in your bedroom. And I'll go get your luggage."

It wasn't until Green pulled the suitcase out of the back seat that he remembered the receipt he'd stuffed in his pocket. He pulled it out, smoothed it, and glanced at it. He blinked and looked again. *What the hell is this?*

It was a receipt from the Louisiana Wholesale Casket Warehouse. Someone had purchased a "Littlest Angel" infant's coffin. The cheerful handwriting further noted that the coffin was powder-blue and had cost over three hundred dollars.

Blood roared in Green's head and he suddenly felt jittery, like the time in college he'd snorted some crystal meth to study for an exam and had ended up driving all night to Galveston. *Why* would Crayton buy a baby's casket? The answer was so easy and clear-cut, Green answered himself immediately: *Fucking voodoo...*

Beyond that though, Green didn't know how or why Cray would need such a thing—and he didn't even want to entertain the most sinister implications. After all, what do you do with a coffin?

You put someone dead in it.

Green tried to think of the most rational, least disturbing answer. If one considered the strange rituals of voodoo, the serpentine interaction between the living and the spirit world, and if you remembered the obsessive attention voodoo folks paid to various symbolic trinkets of death, well,

Green just hoped there was some goddamned explanation for the whole thing.

Besides a corpse.

Green briefly rested his forehead against the cool metal of the car roof. He wished he could talk to Kay, but even as Green had been seeking out answers, she was neck-deep in preparation for her geology field trip. It was *the* Big Deal Project of her senior year, and since Thanksgiving they'd barely had time to sit down together, much less discuss the ever-confusing voodoo stuff Green continued to dig up through his Sherlock-styled magnifying glass.

Like this baby casket. Apparently, Cray was going to keep pursuing this no matter what—and no matter what the cost might be in terms of friendship or, in the case of Eliza, love.

Back inside, Green put the luggage in the bedroom and got Papa some orange juice, started a load of laundry, arrayed medicines on a night table by the bed, and took inventory of essentials he could pick up at the Matassa family grocery on Dauphine. Throughout, Papa jabbered excitedly about the simple pleasures of being home. He put on a celebratory record by Sidney Bechet, opened a window to let in some air, and finally sat down in his recliner and sighed.

"I'm already wore out," he said, but his tone was happy.

Papa's spirits delighted Green, though the coffin receipt was driving him crazy. Here he was, five feet from a living, breathing source rich in lore and history, but he was afraid if he broached the troubling subject of voodoo, he'd agitate Papa unnecessarily.

For that reason, Green hadn't brought up the desecration at Prospero Godchaux's tomb. Hell, looking back, Green hadn't told Papa about his Halloween party freak out or Marcus' suicide, much less Maman Arielle's *nganga* or that there was no record of her owning a house or restaurant in the Faubourg Marigny. And who the hell was the Freixenet family? There were plenty of questions he'd love to ask.

But, lost as he was, Green knew this wasn't the time. He'd leave Papa out of it and find his answers some other way. He wouldn't risk Papa's health.

Out of nowhere, Papa said, "How's Crayton?" He gestured out the car window and laughed. "Nice of him to let us use his ambulance."

"He's a good guy. A bit strange, but good." He smiled, hoping his concern wasn't poking through his veneer like an errant tree branch.

Papa nodded. "He still at the Voodoo Shoppe?"

"Yeah. Yeah, he is." Then, before he could stop himself, Green blurted, "Papa, speaking of voodoo, what purpose would a baby casket serve? In ritual or whatever. Does that mean anything to you?"

Papa cocked his head like a spaniel, as though he hadn't heard correctly. "A *baby* coffin? What the hell you talkin' about?" Papa frowned, though the morbidity of the subject didn't seem to have upset him particularly. He did peer at Green with suspicion. "You always got the damnedest questions about the gris-gris. What is it with you, boy? You studying to be a bokor?"

Green tried to smile. "A *who*?"

"A bo-core." Papa pronounced it. "A dark sorcerer. You workin' on a voodoo degree?"

Green looked at Papa directly. "I am certainly not." He sighed. "On the other hand, I don't know *what* Cray's doing, if you wanna know the truth."

"*He's* got a baby coffin?"

"Well, I don't know. I found a receipt for one in his car."

Papa pondered the information, drumming his fingers on the arm of his chair. Green could hear the ticking of the cuckoo clock over Bechet's clarinet trills. A rush of breeze blew through the curtains and ruffled an old stack of *Times-Picayunes* in one corner.

"Well," Papa finally said. "A baby coffin means one thing." He absently took a pipe from the rack, fingered it lovingly, muttering, "What the hell am I doing?" before setting it reluctantly back in its slot. Green waited. Papa looked at him. "Baby coffin means one thing," he repeated. "Means someone's building an altar."

Green moaned, popping his knuckles. "That fucking nut," he breathed.

"But that ain't necessarily *bad*," Papa said.

Green looked at him curiously. "An altar? With a *casket*? Isn't that pretty creepy? A *baby* casket?"

Papa held up a hand, palm out, warning Green not to get carried away. "Voodoo is *about* death—or at least the communion between the dead an' the living. Just 'cause it's a baby's casket don't mean it's necessarily about *babies*. It's a symbol."

Ah, symbolic trinkets after all. Green thought this was better than the dark alternatives he'd been contemplating. But if Cray was building his own altar, that wasn't so hot. He said so to Papa.

Papa leaned back and the recliner shifted into full relaxation mode. "I'd say our boy is definitely moving beyond innocent curiosity. But hell, probably thirty percent of the folks in this city—the black folks, anyway—got some form of altar in their homes, hidden in a closet or a garage or something. Even the church-goin' folks."

"With *caskets*?"

Papa sighed and closed his eyes. Green could tell he was tiring. "Caskets, skulls, headstones...*somethin'* to symbolize the dead. Don't necessarily mean black magic."

Green had a million questions, but Papa needed rest. "Papa, you want me to help you to bed so you can nap?"

Papa opened his eyes and smiled. "Tell you what, Greenie. Right where I'm at feels pretty damn good. I may just snooze here for a while." He opened his eyes wide for a moment, and for the first time Green saw a bit of doubt. "Speakin' of gris-gris, I ain't had bad dreams or any trouble since I was layin' on that hotel floor and had that vision—or whatever it was—with Maman Arielle telling me everything was gonna be just fine." He gripped Green's hand. "I still ain't figured that out, but since then, I've had this...*feeling*... Well, we'll talk about that some other time." He shook his head and smiled, but there was confusion in his face.

Green shrugged. "If you feel safe, I wouldn't question it." What else could he say? He and Papa both knew what the gris-gris woman represented—and it wasn't good. So how do you explain that she'd appeared at the moment of Papa's death—to *reassure* him? After all, Papa had *died.*

Who knew what had gone on in his brain during that eerie period before the EMTs had jump-started his heart, or why it had been Maman Arielle he thought he saw. God knew *Green* had certainly dreamed of her several times since the night of her Halloween gumbo; *nightmares* might more accurately describe those visions.

Apparently, though, Papa was through worrying about it for now. He squeezed Green's hand once more and released it. "Bless you, boy. Don't let any folks tell you you ain't salt of the earth."

Green grinned, focusing again on the real world. "My pleasure, Papa. Good to have you back. The city wasn't right with you not around." He reached for a light blanket folded on the rocking chair and placed it on the arm of Papa's chair. "There. In case you get cold."

"Thanks, Greenie." Papa's eyes were already heavy-lidded and he was almost asleep.

"You've had your medicine," Green went on hurriedly, thinking for the millionth time that he needed to join the modern age and buy a cell phone. "And I'll stop by the grocery before I come back. I've got some errands, but you can always leave a message on my machine; I'll check it while I'm out."

"Right."

"And you've got the number on auto-dial, number three, and the phone's right here on the table." Green felt like somebody's mother. Papa chuckled softly and patted Green's hand again.

"You've got me taken care of, Greenie. Now go tend to your own life and I'll be fine." Papa smiled. "And bring that fine girlfriend you got, if you get a chance. I'd sure like to meet her."

"She wants to meet you too, Papa." He took another quick look around to make sure he wasn't forgetting something. "'Bye, Papa." The old man waved, smiling with his eyes closed. Green locked the door, trying to organize the afternoon. He had to drop Cray's car off in the St. Ignatius garage and take the keys by the Voodoo Shoppe because there'd be zero parking on Dauphine.

As for whether he'd bring up the baby coffin—and a fucking *altar*—well, Green couldn't say yet. It seemed like every time he and Crayton talked, there was some sort of argument about voodoo. Besides, Cray had just done him another huge favor. Maybe Green should let it rest. In the meantime, he had a few things he *could* check out, just for his own peace of mind.

CHAPTER FORTY-SIX

Pulling into the St. Ignatius parking lot, Green was dismayed to see an old Ford of unknown origin angled awkwardly just through the entryway. It looked like someone's car had crapped out and they'd pushed it into the St. Ignatius property just to get it off the street.

Green maneuvered around the vehicle. The "garage" was nothing more than a walled-in yard paved with gravel. Just inside the gate was the covered two-car space—now inaccessible. In the far corner, under a weather-beaten roof supported from the rear with two-by-four columns, was a forgotten shed that used to house maintenance equipment long ago.

Green angled the Camaro as close as he could to the tool shack, figuring he'd give the other St. Ignatius driver room to get into the lot. It was tight against the shed area and, in order not to scratch the door against one of the wooden supports, Green had to flatten out and ooze through as though squeezed from a toothpaste tube.

He detected an odd scent emanating from the shed; a crazy mix of incense and roadkill. He sniffed again and shook his head curiously before wriggling out; strange, sure, but no single combination of even the most peculiar smells attracted much attention in the French Quarter. Probably some animal had crawled back there to die.

Green locked the car, squinting through the sunlight into the shadowed gloom of the old shed, and noted a pile of abandoned timber and wooden dowels haphazardly stacked at the back wall of the garage. Something tugged in the catacombs of his brain as his eyes swept over the scene—something triggered, perhaps, by the strange scent—and a momentary flash erupted in Green's memory. But before he could zero in on what it was, it vanished.

He shrugged it off and headed out at a slow jog toward the Voodoo Shoppe, thinking about the casket receipt. Suddenly, it occurred to Green that it might be nice to have a few moments alone with Cosima. It was lunchtime; with luck, Cray might have wandered off for a bite.

Sure enough, when he stepped into the shop, Cosima was behind the cash register, her Cousin It hair hanging below the shoulders of a red and yellow muumuu. Curls of incense smoke billowed in the displaced air of the opening door, and Cosima smiled when she recognized Green. Native American flute music piped over the speakers.

"Hi, Green! Long time no see! How are you?"

"Great, Cosima. Have a nice Thanksgiving?"

She shrugged. "Not bad. Yourself?"

Green smiled. "Lots of turkey and relatives—though a few were interchangeable." Cosima beamed. Green jangled the keys. "Cray in? He let me borrow his car and I wanted to return these."

"You just missed him. He was headed over to Country Flame for *ropa vieja* if you want to catch him. Or you can leave them here if you're in a hurry."

"I'll just leave 'em with you, thanks." Green picked up a voodoo doll off a display by the counter and casually said, "Cray said you'd been a bit under the weather. You feeling better?"

"Cray said that?" Cosima looked slightly puzzled. "Well, I did have a cold, but that was before Thanksgiving, and in any case it wasn't anything worth mentioning."

Green grinned in Boy Scout good cheer. "Well, we were at dinner Sunday and he was talking about work and said you'd been ill. Just thought I'd ask. You look well."

"That's kind of you, Green," she said, looking at him warmly. "The cold was rather annoying, but nothing my herbs couldn't handle." She pointed at a holistic medicine shelf.

Green said, "Absolutely. Echinacea's good stuff." He manipulated the arms of the voodoo doll in his hand, working a little Broadway style choreography. "Plus, it's good Cray was in town over the holiday so you could take time off." Green glanced up from the doll.

"Oh my," she laughed, "I wasn't *that* sick. Certainly not enough to ask one of my employees to come in. I always try to work the slow holidays like Thanksgiving!"

Green swallowed tightly, thinking about Cray's casual allusion to filling in for Cosima that Friday. *Because she was sick.* That was why he couldn't go to his parents' in New Iberia...

Green set the doll back in its display case and lightly saluted at Cosima. "Well," he said. "Glad to hear you're doing better."

"You're a nice young man. Just like Crayton."

"He's a good guy," Green said, forcing a thin smile. Then a thought hit him out of the nether regions of his brain. It was a long shot, to be sure, particularly given Cosima's precarious grasp of reality, but Green had nothing to lose.

"Hey, Cosima," he said, "did you see in the papers about the grave desecrations over in the River of Life Cemetery?"

Cosima nodded in grandiose solemnity. "Oh my, yes. Prospero Godchaux. Terrible stuff. Very dark. Very dark." She fingered a long strand of hair and twirled it like a lasso.

Green leaned forward conspiratorially. He figured, since Cosima thought aliens had murdered Martin Luther King, she might be into a little free-range gossip. "A friend of mine knows a cop who says that whoever did it chopped off one of Prospero's hands."

"Oh. My. God! It *fits*! A convicted murderer!" Cosima crowed in such triumphant fashion that Green actually stepped back. He had no idea what she was thinking, but her lunatic eyes shone like daubs of fresh paint. Her voice dropped to a dramatic whisper. "The Hand of Glory," she said.

"The *what*?"

"The Hand of Glory," Cosima repeated. "It was the left hand, wasn't it?"

Green had to think a minute. "Well, maybe," he said slowly, trying to recall what the sexton had said. He didn't remember if the guy had mentioned which hand, but it was the one with the famous ring on it. *Was it the left or right?* "I guess it *coulda* been the left hand."

"Of course," Cosima said, visualizing. "There's been all manner of cemetery vandalism in the last year or so. Police and the newspapers pass it off as gang stuff, but I'm telling you it's voodoo or Satanists."

"What exactly *is* a Hand of Glory?"

Cosima raised her eyebrows significantly. "The severed left of hand of an executed murderer," she intoned as though reciting text from an encyclopedia, "is said to possess sinister powers, and is a sought-after talisman for those enmeshed in the dark arts."

Green swallowed. "Unbelievable," he said. As corny as she was, Cosima had a way of making you feel pretty spooky—and this about the Hand of Glory was interesting stuff. Green wondered if he'd underestimated her; she was probably the voodoo connection he'd needed all along. He felt like Travis McGee was whispering over his shoulder. *Crime College Tip #1: Never overlook an obvious source because of prejudicial preconceptions.*

"One more question," Green said. "What does the demon worshipper—or whatever—do with a Hand of Glory?"

This caused Cosima to laugh. "Why, now that you mention it, I don't know! I don't *have* one!" She laughed harder and tears formed in her eyes as she enjoyed her quip. "But it supposedly has great power. Maybe I'd go to Mars!"

Green nodded cautiously. *Of course you would.* The Hand of Glory info was useful, but it was also entirely possible that Cosima was completely insane. He thanked her for her time and backed out into the street like a robber exiting a bank.

So Cray *didn't* cover for Cosima over Thanksgiving, which meant that...*he's a lying sack of ass!* Green slammed a clenched fist into his open palm—hard enough to sting substantially.

"Goddamn it," he muttered, "what the *fuck* is going on?" He walked aimlessly toward Canal Street, where he would grab the streetcar to meet Kay, trying to sort out his thoughts. What was Cray *not* lying about? The whole meet and greet at the airport, then the sumptuous meal—it all seemed too easy. It was as though he and Kay and Eliza were being manipulated by some slickly orchestrated campaign of Crayton's to damned well ensure that the whole Markey's/Stacie Bates situation was smoothed over.

Well, he thought, *at least the story about J.C. and Darby was true.* The girl *was* a porn actress, and J.C.'s babe troubles were real.

What if Cray was seeing another *girl, one besides Eliza?* Green groaned at the information overload, but that was a considerably less sinister possibility that would explain all the sneaking around. Yet the idea seemed almost more preposterous than the voodoo stuff. Cray was rapturous over Eliza.

On the other hand, he'd seemed rapturous over Kay too. Maybe he was just one of those guys who's obsessed with a girl till he actually *gets* her—then the magic wears off.

And maybe Crayton *did* go to the LeBlanc/Griffith show Friday night and got hammered and picked up some bar pig on a one-nighter deal. It wasn't Green's cup of tea—and it didn't seem like Crayton's—but, anymore, Green didn't know what to think.

So if he wasn't in New Iberia, could Cray have visited the cemetery?

Green shuddered as the streetcar made the big turn at St. Charles, fingering his coins. He might have been slow about some of this shit, but surely Cray wasn't digging up graves. *Was he?* Which could it be: Did Crayton have a voodoo altar with a freshly harvested Hand of Glory taking center stage? Or was he just fucking over his girlfriend and lying to everyone he considered a friend?

Or both?

CHAPTER FORTY-SEVEN

"You're telling me you think there's a connection between Cray and this Hand of Glory thing?" Kay's tone was troubled, though there was certainly a healthy dollop of skepticism too. She held a fork with the remnants of a shrimp salad-stuffed avocado in one hand, suspended halfway to her mouth.

"All I know is Cray's up to something," Green said mildly, "and that he's not a friend of the Truth as we know it." They were in Ye Olde College Inn, not far from Kay's sorority house, inhaling lunch before she had to pull out on the geology field trip. Outside the sky was completely gray, and overhead a fan struggled against the heavy humidity.

Kay said, "Hey, I've got a question."

"What's that?" Green took a final bite of his oyster loaf and groaned with pleasure. At the bar, two Southern Bell linesmen loudly called out for more beer.

"This altar of Cray's..."

"Yeah?"

"Where is it? I mean, if he's got an altar, we're pretty sure it's not in his apartment. You or, for certain, Eliza would've seen it. Right?"

"Yeah, I was kinda wondering about that." Green glanced at the check and tossed some bills on the table.

Kay shrugged. "So, where is it? In the trunk of his car?"

"No, it's not in his trunk," Green chuckled. "I just got Papa's luggage outta there." Then he paused as once more a thought flashed into the passing lane of his brain and blew by him. Something he'd sensed parking Cray's car. *Fuck.* He chewed his upper lip, then let it go. When he least expected it, it'd come to him. He *hoped...*

Thirty minutes later, Green was sitting on Kay's neatly made twin bed, on a purple, gold, and green Mardi Gras quilt, watching her stuff toiletries into zip-lock sandwich bags, when the phone rang.

"Hey, Eliza," Kay said. She listened a minute. "Yep, the bus rolls any minute now." Kay cradled the phone between her ear and shoulder and continued to pack while she talked. "As a matter of fact, he's here now. I can't get rid of him." She winked at Green. "Hold on a minute." She held the phone out. "It's Eliza." Green raised his eyebrows and Kay whispered, "She seems upset."

"Eliza," Green said, "what's up?"

"Green, I don't know what to do anymore." She sounded like she might cry.

Green was instantly filled with dread. "What's wrong? Is it Cray?"

"It's the goddamned voodoo stuff. He knows it bothers me—that it's affecting our relationship—and he just gets worse."

Outside, raindrops began to fall in twirling winds. "What did he do now?" Green asked, and a grotesque image of Cray kneeling in supplication before an altar supporting a baby coffin, festooned with carnival beads and a severed human hand, flashed in his brain.

But Eliza's words, spilling out in a rapid current of bottled-up frustration, actually lessened his nightmarish conjecture. "I don't know," she said, "it's just the whole scenario. It's become all-consuming. 'Light this candle 'cause it's Tuesday.' 'Oh, I nicked myself shaving; let's put a cobweb and grape leaf poultice on it.' Incense, powders, charms...those goddamned Conqueror roots all over the place. It's morbid. And, no offense, he's obsessed with that part in your novel about the suicide with the hornets..."

Green started to comment, but Eliza was on a roll. "And he gets angry. This morning he couldn't find his walking stick—that horrid snake-headed thing—and he accused *me* of hiding it!"

Kay was watching Green and he shrugged and made a *Who knows?* face, saying slowly, "I guess he buys into some of it, in a sort of spiritual church sense." Green was beginning to believe it went beyond that but, at the moment, he didn't want to alarm Eliza any more than necessary. Like: "And, oh yeah, Cray might be a grave robber."

But she was still upset. "Oh, God," she moaned.

Green hastened to assure her, though he felt a little guilty about that strategy since he didn't know *what* Cray was. "In New Orleans, spiritual churches are everywhere. It's like voodoo for modern times, very little witchcraft and a lot of holistic medicine and Catholicism." Then, as casually as he could, he asked, "Does Cray have an altar in the apartment?"

There was a sharp intake of breath. "An *altar?* Hell, the whole *apartment's* an altar, if you ask me. But what do you mean? Like a church altar?"

Green considered how far he should push this. Clearly, if Cray had an altar in his bedroom with a baby casket on it, they wouldn't be having this conversation. She'd probably be in another state. He decided to back off that topic. "No, nothing like that," Green said. "Just, you know, kind of a shrine. Like a lot of that folk art stuff."

Eliza sounded doubtful. "I don't know. I mean, nothing in the bedroom or anything other than what I've already described. And you know what the rest of the place looks like. Relatively normal. CDs, books, that Maravich guy's poster on the wall...that sort of thing."

"Right," Green said. "It's nothing important, Eliza—particularly if he doesn't have one." *Not in plain sight, anyway...*

"So, he's not like a Satanist or anything?" Eliza laughed shakily. "God, I must sound absurd. But...he's not the same guy."

Green hesitated. "No, Eliza, he's not. But I do know that he worships *you*, and it would tear him up if you left. Maybe you just need to be honest with him and tell him what you've told me." *Even though Green wasn't being exactly forthright himself.*

"I've tried. The fool just tells me it'll be okay—and turns right around and lights a yellow candle rubbed with magic love oil or whatever. To *make* it okay. It's like I say, 'Voodoo bothers me,' and he goes, 'I know how to fix *that*. I'll whip up a little voodoo so it doesn't bother you!'" She sighed. "Thanks, Green. You've been a big help. I know Kay's gotta get on the road. Tell her I said to be safe."

Green felt lame. "But I didn't do anything."

"Yeah you did." Eliza sounded resolved. "Maybe I just need to be more forceful. I'm gonna head over to Cray's after work and we're going to talk it out. No bullshitting around—I want to know what his involvement actually means and we'll take it from there. Maybe honesty *is* the way to go with this."

"Maybe so, Eliza. It couldn't hurt. Good luck, and let me know what happens."

CHAPTER FORTY-EIGHT

Over in the Marigny, Crayton was seated in Gris-Gris Gumbo, waiting on the lunch rush to dissipate so he could have a few words with Maman Arielle. He'd only seen her once, briefly, since his night in the River of Life Cemetery and, though there was a ceremony scheduled this Saturday, Cray had a few questions that couldn't wait.

When he'd returned to the Voodoo Shoppe after lunch, Cosima gave him the keys Green had dropped off, chirping about how sweet Green was and wasn't it funny that they'd had a conversation about those graveyard desecrations over Thanksgiving weekend. "He was asking about voodoo things and I told him all about the Hand of Glory," she'd gushed proudly. Did Cray know what a Hand of Glory was? she wondered.

Yeah, said Cray grimly, turning glacial, he'd heard something about it once or twice—and he damned well invented a convenient stomach ache about a half-hour later so he could haul ass over to Gris-Gris Gumbo before he flipped out. *What the fuck was Green doing?* Cray loaned the guy his car whenever he needed it, bought him nice dinners...

But every time Cray turned around, there was Green, sneaking around behind his back with another question or giving him shit about voodoo. Christ, it seemed like Green was jumping his ass about every fucking thing he did. Not only that, but why hadn't *Cray* thought of asking Cosima about the Hand of Glory? That could've saved who knew how much time and...*what?*

For a fleeting second, Cray wondered if maybe none of this would've happened if he'd known about the properties of the Hand of Glory all along. But he shook those mental incursions from his head and forced himself to be resolute. In the great cosmic context of things, he was where he was for a reason.

Gris-Gris Gumbo was crowded; the sky was a deep purple-gray, streets clotted with heavy rain, and customers seemed reluctant to leave. Maman Arielle was bustling around like a matronly steam engine, all-business in her white do-rag and red-checked gingham dress. Still, she was clearly happy to see Cray.

"Crayton," she'd whispered fondly as she seated him in a semi-private booth on the upper level horseshoeing the restaurant where he could watch the wintry downpour. Even though he told her he'd just eaten, she brought him a cup of seafood gumbo, a pitcher of ice-drizzled Dixie, and a tray of boiled crawfish. Cray picked at the savory crustaceans, but he was too worried to eat. Instead, he drank beer and stared emptily out the fogging window where, in the neon echo of a beer sign, raindrops hung fatly on the glass like pink freshwater pearls.

At last, Maman Arielle slid into the booth across from him, plucking a sizable mudbug off his tray. If she noticed he'd scarcely touched his food, she didn't mention it. In a particularly adept motion, she twisted the crawfish sharply, sucked the fat from the head, and gnawed the sweet tail meat.

"So, *lagniappe*," she said softly, "what's troubling you? Is it the night in the *cemetiere*?"

Cray shook his head. "No, that's okay. I understand that. It's fine." And the thing was, the sleeping-in-the-grave deal and severing Prospero's hand *was* fine. But since then, other things bothered him—like Green creeping around—and, in particular, like last night. Sex—or *not*—with Eliza. The sudden appearance of Marcus in his bedroom...

"I know why you sent me to the River of Life," he said finally. "It wasn't just to learn the ritual, but also to commune with the spirit world. To sense the connection between the living and the dead. Right?"

Maman smiled and nodded encouragingly. It was precisely for this reason that he wasn't going to mention Marcus appearing in his bedroom. The apparition had frightened him at first but in the end he realized that it was something he'd best get used to. The dead *lurked*. Perhaps Marcus had appeared simply to keep Cray focused.

Cray continued. "I know I'm not supposed to understand everything yet, or even what it is I'm supposed to do with this power you keep talking about... Like, what do I do with the Hand of Glory now that I have it?"

"Be patient, child," Maman Arielle murmured, putting on a pair of gold-rimmed spectacles. She sometimes looked so young and erotic, and other times appeared wise and almost grandmotherly.

"Oh, I'm patient," he said. "I'm happy to learn. It's just that I haven't figured out how to reconcile this among my friends, particularly my girlfriend, Eliza, and my best pal, Green."

Maman clucked sympathetically, dipping a cracker in his gumbo. "Hmm. They think you are acting strange? They disapprove?"

Cray nodded miserably. "All of the above."

"Sure," Maman said.

"Obviously, it's intensified a bit," Cray said, taking another swallow of beer. "So I just kinda act like it's a hobby." He chewed his thumbnail and regarded Maman Arielle nervously. "But it's certainly not a harmless hobby to Eliza, and Green is snooping around like he's a fucking detective or something."

"Well, you *are* different now, *cher*," Maman Arielle pointed out gently. "Let's talk about Eliza first. You aren't the same man Eliza fell in love with when she first met you. She may not be able to handle it."

"But I don't want to lose her. She's the only girl I've ever had—that I cared about, anyway." Cray felt absurdly close to tears.

Maman Arielle smiled faintly. "You can always keep her through magic."

Cray laughed without humor and poured more beer. "Would that really work? Not that I'd do it."

"Would it work?" Maman Arielle shrugged. "Who can say?" She grinned slyly. "There *are* precedents."

Cray watched her, contemplating, then shook his head no. "I don't want to manipulate something like that."

Maman nodded pleasantly. "That's something *you* decide, *lagniappe.* But voodoo or not, we all change, Crayton. And sometimes the sad truth is that our friends and lovers don't change with us. Or we don't change when they do. And...Green?"

"It's not so much that he's in my face, though he has bothered me about it some. It's more I get the sense that he's always just a few steps behind me. While I was at lunch today, he was in the Voodoo Shoppe asking Cosima about stuff. Somehow, he ended up talking with my boss about the Hand of Glory and the grave-robbings in the River of Life!" Cray was sweating and agitated, though he had the good sense to glance around and make sure he lowered his voice. Fortunately, the booths on either side had already emptied out. "If nothing else, those were felonies I committed in that graveyard!"

Maman took one of Crayton's hands in her own and soothed him like a puppy. "Calm down, *cher,* calm down. No one will ever know about your work in the *cemetiere.* It's part of the magic."

"Okay." Cray took a deep breath and nodded thanks. "Okay."

She went on. "I t'ink your friends are scared of that which they don't understand. Because they've been introduced to voodoo through you. They see someone close to them become infatuated with something new and strange—something they've probably ridiculed all their lives—and it disturbs them. And this Green: well, your silly death league has made him suspicious."

She smiled and ate another crawfish. Cray winced as a crack of thunder shuddered the window of the booth. The rain hammered Frenchmen Street at a viciously acute angle. Cray said, "So what do I do? About Eliza *and* Green?"

"You say you don't wish to manipulate those you love. You'll have to deal with Eliza as your brain and heart tell you." Her voice took on a warning tone. "But remember, this is not a Halloween party now. This is not Mardi Gras, where we take off our masks tomorrow and carry on in the plain and simple world. There are things required of you now, times when you will have to account for your whereabouts and activities—like this Saturday night. It's nearly time for the new moon."

Cray re-filled his beer mug. It was a bit early to be getting smashed, but though his talk with Maman Arielle was soothing him a bit, solutions weren't as clear-cut as he'd hoped. "I can work it out with Eliza," he said finally. "I've *got* to. She means everything... But should I worry about Green? I mean, the guy *is* my best friend. And even if he is sneaking around a bit, he's only doing it 'cause he's worried about me."

Maman shrugged, glancing through the open window into the kitchen area to check the work progress. Then she stared straight into Cray's eyes. "The obvious answer is simply to stop acting in a way that arouses his suspicions. Now it's time to stop this stupid death league. It's hard, *lagniappe*, but the power is stronger than any drug. You tapped into it accidentally, it's true, but you have it nonetheless. You must learn that the urge to manipulate it in everyday affairs is tempting—and foolish. Like this death tournament. You've learned what you need from it. It serves no more purpose."

Suddenly, a wave of sorrow washed over Cray like cold river water. "Yeah," he said sadly. "There's that." Cray's voice dropped to an urgent whisper. "People are actually *dying*. I mean, that's the main reason Green's so suspicious." A solitary tear welled up behind his glasses and rolled down his cheek. "But it's like I *can't* stop..."

Two lunchtime stragglers edged by the booth and Cray and Maman Arielle waited until they'd passed.

"This is not simple, *cher*," she said softly, before Cray could finish his thoughts. "It's about energies—darkness and light—and tapping into other worlds. Nothing is clear-cut. Those people who died in your death league? Perhaps their lives were consumed with dark energies to begin with. Perhaps you were performing a service. Perhaps you are nothing more than a conduit to a more ancient power."

She reached out and wiped the single teardrop off his face, and her touch was like a hot feather. Instantly, a sense of security spread throughout his body. "So it's not murder?" he asked hopefully. "I can't just kill anyone I want, right?"

Maman Arielle inclined her head forward a bit, and a curious, faraway light like the glow of a firefly shone behind her blue-gold eyes. "Not yet, anyway," she said softly. Then she did a curious thing. She pulled a crawfish from the pile and set it in the middle of the table. Muttering softly under her breath, she rubbed her finger lightly over the creature's lobsterish form.

Cray frowned. It appeared for a moment like the crawfish's feelers began to twitch. Then, to Cray's absolute horror, its legs began to move, stretching slowly and experimentally.

"Jesus Christ," Cray breathed. "That...that's *dead*."

Sluggishly, the mudbug began to crawl feebly toward the bowl of gumbo. In an instant, Maman Arielle plucked it off the table and twisted its head off, disposing of the two halves neatly in the pile of discarded shells.

Without mentioning the incident at all, or acknowledging Cray's slack-jawed astonishment, she tilted her head at Cray and asked, conversationally, "Did you do what I told you? Did you get the coffin for your altar?"

"Yes," he whispered.

"Have you consecrated it with oil? Utilized it in ritual?"

Cray nodded. "Yeah. In the death league. Like you told me." *The crawfish. What the hell...?*

"An' what happened?"

Cray swallowed. "The guy died."

"Yes, he did," she agreed. "I read about it in the *Picayune*." She chuckled. "Don't fret, Crayton. This is what it's all about. The bridge between life and death." She gestured toward the pile of crawfish shells. "You see, it's a bridge more easily traveled than you think. One of the things you'll learn about the acquisition of power is what a luxury conscience is.

"That sounds harsh, I know. Conscience deals with only a surface reality of *this* temporal world, no? There's a reason you've been blessed, after all."

Cray suddenly smiled and lifted his beer mug. His hand shook slightly, and his emotions were shifting like one of those moronic lava lamps. "And I suppose I'll learn *why* I've been blessed. In good time."

Maman Arielle said, "Yes, as the corny movies say. All in good time. Whatever happens, happens for a reason. Remember that."

Crayton nodded. "Absolutely." His face took on a queer, stubborn cast, and his grin seemed frozen, like the work of a funeral home cosmetician. "But I'm not giving up Eliza."

Maman Arille smiled back curiously. "Well, perhaps you won't have to." She squeezed out of the booth and stood up. "Enough for now, Crayton," she said softly. "I've got a kitchen to run."

Cray drained his beer. "Thanks, Maman Arielle. For everything," he said, rising also. Then he remembered something. "Oh, Maman?"

She looked at him expectantly. Cray glanced around to make sure no one was within hearing range.

"About the skull I took from the crypt?"

"Yes?"

Cray looked embarrassed. "Er, it's kinda scuzzy."

Maman Arielle looked puzzled. "*Scuzzy?*"

"Well," Cray said, trying to explain. "It's got, like, *gunk* on it and stuff." He frowned. "Plus, it smells. Not a lot, but it's kinda rank. I'm afraid someone'll smell it and start fishing around."

She started laughing. "Oh, Crayton, am I going to have to put you to work in my own kitchen and teach you *ever'ting*?" She leaned forward to whisper in his ear, and olfactory wisps of filé, citrus, and stewed mustard greens emanated from her warmly. "Put the skull in the cauldron full of water and boil it clean. It's the first step toward having the *nganga*. But burn some incense; the smell will not be pretty."

Cray nodded. "Got it. Oh—and the Hand of Glory." He shrugged. "What do I do with it? I mean, it's just sitting there."

Maman nodded. This time she put her mouth directly into his ear and told him what she wanted him to do. He nodded; it seemed odd, but whatever she wanted was fine with him. He kissed her lightly on the cheek and left her standing by the booth, chuckling. Over his shoulder, he heard her murmur, "Lord, *gunk.*"

CHAPTER FORTY-NINE

Perhaps if Cray hadn't stopped at the French Market Grocery for a twelve-pack of Abita Turbo Dogs on the way home, it would all have turned out differently. But there was no reason not to feed the pleasant buzz he'd kindled at Gris-Gris Gumbo. After all, he'd just watched an old woman bring a dead crawfish back to life with a lot less effort than it took to boil the little fucker in the first place.

So Cray had no problem slamming a quick beer in the short, drizzly walk back to the apartment. Then he opened another one, stuck the rest in the refrigerator, and grabbed a toolbox and a folded paper grocery sack. There was one more thing he needed, and he had to search through a jumble of newspapers by his CD stacks, but he eventually found what he was looking for.

Cray ducked back outside and jogged to the parking lot. If anybody had been watching, he'd have looked like Joe Maintenance Guy, but the wet streets were deserted. Preoccupied, Cray went into the lot, frowned momentarily at the odd parking job Green had done with the Camaro, then crept behind the dilapidated tool shed to his altar.

There was unquestionably an odor—like dirt and old bones and sour cat food—and Cray hurriedly lit several sticks of incense. It occurred to him, for the first time, that someone in the parking lot might well wonder why the old shed smelled of incense just as much as they would a decomposing skull.

For an instant, Cray panicked. *Had Green smelled anything when he parked the car? And why was it at such a curious angle?* But Crayton calmed himself; the smell wasn't *that* bad—it was the French Quarter, for chrissakes. By definition it was gonna stink...

Cray decided the whole thing was a conundrum to be worried about later. Right now, he had to get the skull back into his apartment and into boiling water. He pulled the flashlight out of the toolbox and shone it around the altar. It had definitely changed in structure and substance since his bumbling and amateurish attempts before he met Maman Arielle and spent the night in the cemetery.

There were flowers now, at either end of the top shelf, taken from a fresh grave. His black candles were anointed with Spirit Oil—an ingredient he'd dismissed only a few weeks ago as a completely horseshit tourist con.

In the center of the top shelf, between the pictures of Saints Thomas, Barbara, and Patrick, and the Indian chief Blackhawk, was the skull he'd taken from the tomb. A few small patches of scaly flesh festered like scabs on the yellow-gray bone, and long tufts of bristly black hair stuck out like obscene ponytails from under the purple top hat Cray had perched jauntily atop the head.

As into the whole thing as he was—and even now Crayton could feel the compelling buzz of strength at his core, vibrating like a summertime bee—Cray removed the top hat and regarded the skull queasily. The eye sockets were finely laced with skeins of blue-green mold and seemed to stare, black and empty, into the dappling shadows of the tool shed, and its caramel-colored teeth were iced in a creepy grin.

Cray held open the grocery store sack at the edge of the shelf and, with a quick nudge—the way you might flick at a worm you found crawling over the edge of your pillow—he knocked the skull into the sack. That done, he took a deep breath and glanced down at the base of the altar.

It was there that he'd placed the baby's casket. When Maman Arielle told him he needed a small casket for his altar, he was afraid he'd have to take it from a cemetery too—and the prospect of *that* would've just seemed too much. Fortunately, the store-bought version was fine.

In any case, no kids would go in the earth in *this* one—though its purpose was possibly even more morbid. Tall black candles perched at either end of the powder-blue box, and laid out across the closed lid was a series of items: a crude cross fashioned of chicken bones, the fur of a black cat wrapped in red silk and stuck with black hatpins, and in the middle, sprinkled with powdered wormwood and graveyard dirt, was an 8 x 10 black and white promo of jazz clarinetist Cat-Daddy Phelps.

Cray had clipped out Phelps' eyes in the photo and stuck a thorn from a dead rosebush through the chest area. Plus, since Phelps had lived in a small shotgun shack over in the Bywater, Cray had taken the precaution of visiting the man's backyard late one night, burying therein a rotted trout. He'd stuffed a piece of paper with CAT-DADDY PHELPS written on it inside the fish, along with some dandelion petals and salt, then stitched the fish up with black thread.

So actually, Crayton hadn't been too surprised when Donny's jaw had dropped at the television news flash in the Port of Call and he'd rejoiced in the miraculous news of Phelps' death. Cray was pretty sure it hadn't been a miracle at all—though it *was* kinda significant how it had changed Donny and Green's perspective on the Vieux Carre Fantasy Death Society to think Donny's number one pick could kick off just as easily as Crayton's had.

Cray finished his beer. He had one more chore to attend to, and turned his attention to the far left side of the altar and Prospero Godchaux's severed hand, the gaudy ring glittering in otherworldly fashion even in the dark shadows of the closet. Cray had drained it, wrapped in gauze—fashioned from the corpse's burial shroud—and placed it in an earthenware bowl, drying it in salt and filé. Now, he followed Maman Arielle's instructions to the letter, then clicked off the flashlight.

He felt tired and a bit dizzy. The truth was, he'd had mucho brewage since Gris-Gris Gumbo, and he hadn't slept a helluva lot last night after his non-performance with Eliza and the visit from guest star Marcus. It was time, he decided, to put the skull on the stove to simmer and grab a brief nap.

Only after he'd locked the door to the altar and turned to slide out the back crevice did he notice the pile of wood in the corner—and there was his snakehead walking stick, the one he'd been missing for a few days and had accused Eliza of taking.

Jeez, he thought, picking it up and feeling its familiar heft, *guess it wasn't Eliza after all. Guess I set it down unlocking the altar and forgot about it.*

Since it was generally dark when he was out here, it was easy enough to see how it could happen. He'd have to apologize to Eliza, of course, but it was damned good to have the cane back...

Back inside the apartment, Cray gingerly put the skull into the new cauldron—which looked ridiculously large on the apartment stove—and waited for the water to heat while he finished off yet another Abita. If he couldn't sleep on his own, he reasoned, he'd lube the concept with beer. The water hit a rolling boil and Cray adjusted the heat to ensure a steady simmer.

In his beer fog, he forgot to light the incense Maman Arielle had told him about. The reek of the decayed flesh and muscle particles slowly emanating through the apartment as the skull cooked clean was far worse than anything Crayton had smelled in a tomb. But in the depths of his slumber, although he winced and moaned at the odor, Cray didn't wake up.

In fact, Cray was sleeping so soundly that he also didn't hear the persistent knocking at the door when Eliza came by after work, as she'd told Green she was going to do, in an attempt to try to salvage their relationship. He didn't even stir when she used the key he'd given her to open the door and come on in. It was only after she'd retched at the horrible smell swirling about the apartment like an obscene fog, and stumbled into the kitchen and found the skull, its wisps of hair floating lazily in the bubbling water, that Eliza screamed and Crayton woke up.

CHAPTER FIFTY

Standing in the hushed nave of the empty St. Lydwine Church in the quiet hours just before afternoon mass, Papa Hipolyte gazed around him in puzzled amazement. As much as he took solace in the whispering ritual of the mass and in the spiritually supine order of confession, it was in these moments of solitude, with the gray afternoon twilight fractured through the scarlet and blue stained glass, and dozens of votive candles flickering in the shadowed silence, that Papa felt closest to the Church.

He'd wandered over here not so much out of spiritual necessity—though it always felt good to be back in one's home church—but because he'd felt a creeping, suffocating sense of fear in his own little cottage. After Green had left, Papa took his time strolling through the house, lingering in each room, soaking up the pleasant sight and scent associations of worn, familiar things.

At first, it'd been a joy, but slowly he'd begun to feel listless. He'd walked the perimeter of his garden, now brown and dozing in the dawn of winter, pondering idly on what he might plant in the spring, then went back inside and felt the energy flow through his fingers as he worked through some simple block chords at the piano.

But while there was always magic in music, Papa couldn't concentrate. It was then that he'd decided to wander over to St. Lydwine. He'd scrawled a hasty note to Green and set out at a leisurely pace through the cool, cloud-thickening afternoon. Papa took an umbrella—it was clearly gonna storm like a sumbitch later on—but he liked rain and wasn't afraid of getting a little wet. Inside the church, Papa had lit a candle for the souls of those who'd gone before him. Then, much as he'd re-explored his own house, he maneuvered around the circumference and nooks and crannies of St. Lydwine, Star of Our Suffering.

He could hear muted bustling in the rooms beyond as the fathers prepared for afternoon mass, and a few isolated parishioners came and went. Papa took comfort in all this, but his brain was working. He was like a squirrel tugging at an acorn lodged in frozen ground.

Papa knew the source of his consternation was the appearance—at the moment of his own death—of the vision of Maman Arielle, telling him all would be well. But it wasn't that he couldn't figure out why he'd had the vision of Maman Arielle. It was that, in consideration of the doctors' unanimous agreement that he had a cardiac "situation"—those fuckers could diddle the words, couldn't they?—it occurred to Papa that his center of focus was off.

He turned and went into the dark room where Father Chet was buried. There was such a sense of permanence in this church, a sense of fear overcome and a timeless quality of peace that lay well beyond the anxious constraints of a human lifetime. Now, staring at the remains of Father Chet through the glass, in a quiet so profound that one could almost hear the wax of the candles burning, a paradoxical thought came to Papa.

He was frightened because, for the first time in his adult life, he *wasn't* really frightened anymore—at least in that larger, enveloping sense that had been with him, seemingly, forever. Papa realized with a sense of detached awe, almost like it was happening to someone else, that, if he'd handle one piece of business, right here in this church, right now, his one remaining fear would be that...*he wasn't afraid anymore...*

A few minutes later, he entered one of the gloomy confessionals and knelt down on the carpeted bench.

"Forgive me, Father, for I have sinned," Papa said, curiously buoyant that this long-held secret was about to set him free. "It's been six weeks since my last confession."

Through the shadowed screen opening, a priest blessed him.

Then, after a moment of reflection that spun him back thirty years in the dizzying fashion of a kaleidoscope, Papa said, "Father, a long time ago, I killed someone..."

PART THREE

CHAPTER FIFTY-ONE

Green slept late Saturday morning. Around noon, someone pounded on the door, startling him so that he dropped the clean towel he was folding. It was Cray. He looked like he'd marinated all night in gin. His hair was plastered to his head, his Saints sweatshirt looked wrinkled and stale, and he carried a quart bottle of Dixie beer. In his other hand was his walking stick, which he raised in greeting like a shepherd.

"Well, Green," Cray said, struggling to sound sober, "Eliza broke up with me." He peered like a drunken owl through the filmy lenses of his glasses. "She's gone."

"Christ, c'mon in," Green said, alarmed at Cray's appearance and statement. "You smell like Mardi Gras. All of it." He pulled Cray into the apartment, took his walking stick and leaned it against the wall, then seated Cray on the couch. "Now what's this about Eliza breaking up with you?"

Cray sniffed deeply, like he had a runny nose, and took a sip of his quart. He grimaced at the taste. "Just like I said, man. She split."

Green pulled a chair over. "Slow down, amigo, we'll figure this out. Now tell me what happened."

"My question exactly," Cray mumbled, staring vacantly at the floor. "What happened?"

"Let's get you some coffee, first off."

"I don't *want* any coffee," Cray said petulantly. It was the voice of inebriated obstinacy, and Green, a veteran of bars across New Orleans, had heard it a million times. So he poured himself a cup and sat back down across from Crayton.

"Where's Eliza now? Do we know?"

"Green, I can't believe it," Cray said, ignoring the questions. He was as blasted as Green had ever seen him.

Green spoke patiently, as though to a child. "Did you guys argue?"

Cray lurched to his feet. His bloodshot eyes narrowed. "It was the voodoo, Green. Of course it was." He looked at Green with embarrassed dignity. "She couldn't handle the voodoo."

Green felt a cold scalpel of fear trace down his back. "What'd you do, Cray?" he asked softly.

Cray laughed, weaving slightly. "Just normal stuff. I didn't *kill* anybody, if *that's* what you're worried about. If that's what you *all* think. It was just...normal stuff."

"What normal stuff, Cray?"

Cray hesitated, and Green could see the gears clanking slowly in his pal's muddled brain. "Just simple gris-gris, like I tol' you all along. *Innocent* stuff." He looked around the room like he'd never seen it before, then moved suddenly toward the door. "I gotta get some fresh air."

Green positioned himself between Crayton and the door. Cray's transparent explanation led Green to believe that, whatever he'd done, it probably wasn't "innocent."

"When did this happen, Cray?"

Crayton seemed to ponder the question. "I guess that would've been, oh, Thursday evening. About twilight. She came over, got pissed off, and that was that."

Green calculated. He'd probably been at Papa's when this happened. "What were you doing when Eliza got to your apartment?"

Cray snorted. "I was *sleeping*, Green." Then he dodged around Green and opened the door. "I gotta have some air," he said again, and went outside. Green swore, grabbed a denim jacket and a New Orleans Zephyrs cap off the counter, and hurried after Cray, who had already pinballed into the street. Green jogged after him, figuring it wasn't a bad idea to walk Cray around a bit.

"Crayton! Wait up!" he called. Cray turned and smiled sadly, a disheveled scarecrow weaving slightly in the middle of Governor Nichols Street. Green pulled even with his friend and clapped him lightly on the shoulder. "Let's take a walk down by the river. We'll discuss the mysteries of heartbreak and see what we can figure out."

But while the sharp wind off the river might well have had a reviving effect on Crayton, the open bars that lined the streets were too convenient. It was, Green had to admit, one of the problems you faced trying to sober someone up in the Quarter. Where the hell do you go to get away from the temptation? Cray kept sipping go-cups of beers and mumbling that Eliza didn't understand. He should have known all along he was too ugly for someone like Eliza.

"Just tell me about the gris-gris," Green would say. "If we can show Eliza it's all innocent, we can work this out."

"Moot point, Greenie," Cray would burp philosophically. "The damage is done. It's gone beyond that now." Not only was Cray *not* sobering up, he was rapidly approaching a state of total incoherence.

They spun back down Decatur, and Green was about to give up and try to guide Crayton back to the St. Ignatius. That way, he figured, he could pour him into bed and maybe scope out Cray's apartment for an altar. Maybe it was in the laundry closet or something. But even if Cray wasn't saying, *something* voodoo-related had sure as hell caused Eliza to flip completely. Or Green could simply get Cray to bed, then try to find Eliza and get her side of the story.

Just as North Peters split off from Decatur, Cray bellowed and bolted across the street, narrowly avoiding a horse-drawn carriage carrying two newlyweds. The nuptials stared in disbelief at the skeletal, catsup-haired loon cawing like a crow gone mad.

Green raced after Crayton, who was standing on the *banquette* in front of Margaritaville, visibly shaking and pointing a bony white finger just inside the open-air French doors of the club.

"You! *You!*" Cray cried. "Oh, you sonofabitch! I shoulda fucking known!"

Breathless, Green joined him on the curb. He shook his head painfully at what he saw. Sitting by the window, on the same side of the booth, were Eliza and J.C. On the plank table before them was a bottle of Tattinger *Blanc de Blancs* champagne.

Eliza stared at Cray in horror and guilt. J.C. was trying to maintain his aristocrat's demeanor, but an element of fear twisted his expression into a quivering sneer.

"You! You!" Cray continued, like a novelty alarm clock that wouldn't turn off. He was livid with rage and betrayal, and all traces of inebriation had atomized in a jet-burst of adrenaline.

"Cray, it's not what it looks like," Eliza stammered, though Green couldn't honestly imagine a scenario where it could be anything *but* what it looked like. It looked bad.

J.C. swept back the wave of blond hair across his forehead, and seemed to struggle for his composure. He stuck his hand, palm out, through the window in a calming gesture.

"Cray-boy," he said, "take it easy. This here is nothin' more than—"

Cray, his eyes blazing and refracted through tears, seized J.C.'s hand in his own. The strange gesture was almost tender. He caressed J.C.'s palm as though he was a blind man exploring another human hand for the first time.

They all stared at Cray. His eyes were focused on the damp *banquette* under his feet. Suddenly, J.C. moaned in revulsion and tried to draw back his hand, but it was as though it was locked in a vice. J.C. was clearly straining, his face blanched in fear, and Green was afraid Crayton was utilizing some gris-gris-powered strength to perhaps shatter J.C.'s hand. Instead, though, Cray's lycanthropic fingernails merely moved delicately over the contours of J.C.'s palm with no visible signs that he was using force to hold J.C. against his will.

Finally, snapping out of his trance, Crayton turned loose of the hand, and J.C. pulled back as though from the jaws of a gator. He started at Cray in mute terror. Green and Eliza, motionless, watched uncomprehendingly.

Cray looked woozy, like he didn't know who he was or how he'd gotten there. Then he shook his head, trying to clear it perhaps, and focused, at last, on Eliza. His face crumpled in heartbreak. Then he turned and sprinted off down Decatur, stumbling on the uneven bricks as he ran.

Green started to call after him, then turned to confront J.C. and Eliza—but stopped in confusion. Eliza had stood up and edged unconsciously a few feet away from the table. She held a clenched fist to her mouth, queasy with fear, and stared at J.C.

His brows were knitted in consternation, his face pale and sickly, and he whimpered as he worked his throat like a dog trying to dislodge a bone. Suddenly, with a raw, strangling sound, J.C. coughed harshly. Eliza screamed and Green himself staggered back, weak with disbelief.

A large black spider had crawled out of J.C.'s mouth.

CHAPTER FIFTY-TWO

It wasn't until they managed to get Eliza back to J.C.'s apartment, where they stuffed a few Libriums down her throat and she finally went to sleep, that Green could take stock of the situation.

J.C. was functional, if somewhat trance-like, and Green found a bottle of Jack Daniel's behind the polished walnut bar and poured them both hefty shots. Then he ushered J.C. out onto the balcony and sat him down. Strolling past the Café Pontalba toward the river, with a retinue of second-lining tourists, a brass band was playing "Rudolph the Red-Nosed Reindeer." City workers were putting the final touches on holiday decorations before the "Lighting of Jackson Square" kicked off the city's month-long holiday celebration.

Green took a deep breath. "I'll get to the details of what the piss you were doing with Eliza in a minute, but first, do you realize what just happened?"

J.C. managed a sickly laugh. "You're goddamned right I know what happened, brah! It was my goddamned mout' that thing crawled out of!"

"And we both agree that it wasn't some strange coincidence, like the spider was somehow bottled-up inside the champagne bottle, right?"

J.C. snorted. "Christ no! Somehow, ol' Cray really has tapped into the voodoo, son." The whiskey had apparently calmed him a bit, and he seemed almost impressed by Crayton's feat. "I mean, I know he's fucked around with it, but I never believed it. Not like this."

"So exactly what *were* the two of you doing drinking champagne, on the same side of the booth, in one of the most visible tourist traps in the Quarter?"

J.C. sighed heavily. "I *know* how it looked, Green," he began. Then he told about getting a hysterical call from Eliza on Thursday. She'd just left Crayton's, where she'd walked in and found him cooking a human skull.

"A *human* skull?" Green digested that tidbit. "Are we sure it was real? It might've been some souvenir deal," but he knew he didn't sound very convinced.

J.C. snorted. "Why would he be boiling a souvenir? And trust me, from the smell she described, it was real all right."

"Jesus, where did he get a human skull? What'd he do, murder—" Green froze as the thought hit him. *The desecrations at the River of Life Cemetery.*

"What?" J.C. stared at him, holding a newly poured shot of Jack halfway to his mouth.

"Well, nothing," Green said slowly, trying to remember if the sexton had described anything missing besides Prospero Godchaux's hand. "Just something I wanna think about..."

J.C. shrugged. "Well, hell, maybe he *did* murder somebody. That was Eliza's first thought anyway, that she was dating Jeffrey Dahmer or something. But apparently Cray told her it was some kind of ritual thing he was going through, that it was only a skull he'd taken from some cemetery."

Yep, it *had* to have been Cray in the River of Life. And if he took a skull from—presumably—the Freixenet crypt, then he also sawed off Prospero Godchaux's hand. Which meant that, not only was his friend a true freak, he had in his possession a Hand of Glory—whatever the fuck *that* actually translated to. After all this time, it wasn't rage or even fear that actually washed over Green like lava, but a strange sense of sorrow. "I think," he said slowly, "this has gone a lot further than any of us thought."

J.C. nodded, looking up wonderingly at the quilted sky. "You ain't tellin' me nothin'," he said mildly. "I just had a spider the size of a golf ball crawl outta my mouth." He shuddered involuntarily and spit on the balcony floor. When he spoke again, his voice was shaky. "Whaddya think that means, Green? Am I cursed?"

"I don't know what it means," Green said, wondering whether he should tell J.C. about the Hand of Glory before deciding not to send his pal into further panic. "But I'm going to find out." He stood up. "In the meantime, we gotta get Eliza out of here. Any ideas?"

J.C. said, "I've already thought about that. I don't know what the hell's goin' on around here, but I ain't taking any chances, and she is *totally* flipped out. Do we agree on that?"

Green nodded.

J.C. said, "So I thought I'd put her on a plane to D.C. after I let her sleep for a few hours. Get her back to her folks' house and away from the son of Marie Laveaux for a while. She can call in sick for a day or two till we figure this stuff out."

Green said, "You may be right. In any case, it can't hurt for her to get out of town for a few days." He thought for a second. "Okay, I'm gonna head out and check some things. You gonna be all right?"

J.C. shrugged. "How the hell do I know? For all I know, I'm cursed." He laughed, but it contained the fragile tone of hysteria. "Don't worry. I'm definitely covered—at least so far as the real world is concerned." He pulled back his jacket so Green could see the butt of a pistol sticking out of his pants.

Green shook his head. "Jesus, get rid of that thing. Don't freak out on me, J.C. Something weird happened, that's for goddamned sure, but I don't know what good a gun's going to do. I also don't know a lot about voodoo, but I do know enough that any victims of gris-gris spells always died not because the curses worked, but because the victims *believed* they would work. The fear factor."

"Right," J.C. said. He exhaled and stuck a cigarette in his mouth. "I ain't gonna go *gunnin'* after no one. I jus' keep it for protection." He shook his head again. "I fuckin' can't get that *taste* outta my mouth, the way them fuzzy-ass legs come ticklin' up my throat..."

Green slapped him lightly on the cheek. "Don't think about it, J.C. Take care of Eliza. Get her out of town, and we'll figure this thing out. Call Huey and Don, get them over here. I'll be back when I can."

J.C. looked at him gratefully. "You goin' after Cray?"

Green scratched his forehead with his thumb. "Frankly, I'd have no idea where to look. No, I think I'm just gonna do a bit of research first. And, J.C.?"

"Yeah?"

"So what *were* you doing with Eliza in the first place? She just called you, out of the blue, after finding the skull?"

J.C. hesitated, as though he were about to fabricate something, then thought better of it. "Apparently, she and Cray argued. She told him he'd pushed the voodoo shit too far, and that she didn't wanna see him anymore." He shrugged. "And she called me."

"Why you?"

"Hell, I don't know, Green. She said she didn't call you 'cause you're right next door to Cray, and she didn't wanna be anywhere near him."

Green ticked off the elements of the scenario: "And let me guess. You told her to come over because she was extremely upset, and you comforted her, and one thing led to another, and because you're J.C. with a totally uncontrollable dick, she spent the night in the safety of your arms. And so on, *ad nauseam.*"

J.C. swallowed and put his head down, embarrassed. "I guess that's pretty much it."

"Christ, J.C., you are one true pal."

J.C. looked up, his eyes pleading. "Look, Green, I know I'm an asshole, but this nutso's puttin' the gris-gris on me. Can we get rid of the voodoo and *then* worry about what a jerk I am? Who knows what'll come crawlin' outta my mouth next?"

Green glanced back down at Chartres Street—and started. Walking slowly past the cathedral, watching a juggler in front of the Cabildo, was Papa Hipolyte. Green jumped up. "Just get Eliza out of here and track down Donny and H," he said. "I'll be back as soon as I can."

CHAPTER FIFTY-THREE

"Okay, voodoo. It's time, I think. We been dancing around this too long," Papa said. Green thought the old man looked tired but there was a...a sort of serenity about him that wasn't as reassuring as it should be. Whatever that meant.

They were seated near the door at the bar in Johnny White's on Bourbon. A crowd of regulars was clustered at the far end, mesmerized by a big screen television airing the Mississippi State/Ole Miss game. A bony female bartender of indeterminate age had taken their order and returned with an Abita for Green and a Dixie for Papa. Green nodded at the bottles. "Uhm, I don't know how you are with drinking. I mean, with your heart and all."

Papa winked. "I ain't gonna get into the whiskey, if that's what you worried about. But a few beers? Hell, the doctors say it's *good* for me." He shook his head in appreciation. "If I'da known *that*, I'da had a heart attack maybe twenty years ago!"

"Okay," Green said, getting back to it. He took a deep breath. "I'm just going to tell you everything. It could take a while, so stop me if you've heard any of this before, or if you don't feel like getting into it."

Papa nodded and gestured to go ahead.

Green chewed his lip, trying to organize the thoughts fluttering around like dark moths, and finally said, "I figured a lot of the weird stuff started with a club we made up called the Vieux Carre Fantasy Death Society. But I think it probably goes back further. Do you remember when Crayton made that delivery to a funeral home? You tried to warn me, even then, but I blew it off. In retrospect, things got real strange real quick after that..."

Forty minutes and two beers later, Green finished by recounting the scene that morning with J.C. and Eliza and the spider. The old man had listened carefully, interjecting a few questions along the way. He'd shook his head at the description of the Halloween party and the *nganga*, and flat-out grimaced over the cemetery and in particular, Prospero Godchaux and the Hand of Glory.

Green started to say something, but Papa cut him off by holding up his hand. "Thing is, Greenie," he sighed, "it's black magic stuff. *Le Culte des Morts.*"

Green slumped. "I'd...I'd hoped, somehow, that maybe Cray wasn't involved."

Papa sat for a moment, lost in thought. Now his skin looked tired, like onionskin paper someone had spilled coffee on. Finally, he said, "You know the word *necromancy?*"

"Sorta. I mean, I can figure it out. Some kind of magic having to do with the dead, right?"

Papa nodded and took a swallow of beer. "Now I got a story to tell *you,* boy." He looked at Green for a moment, as though peering inside him for something he didn't really expect to find, then said, "First off though, I'm gonna say something about your pal Crayton." He scratched under the brim of his hat.

"Unless I'm wrong, your boy's got *power.* I don't mean power like you get elected mayor. I mean magic. How he got it is anybody's guess, though that day he went to the funeral home and found the corpse with the eyes missing, that's probably how it started. He walked into the middle of a ritual, y'see, and whether he knew it or not interjected himself into the whole thing.

"The other thing is, Cray had to be susceptible in the first place—like some folks got intuition and some don't. Could be you'd have walked into the same ritual and nothing woulda happened. Follow?"

Green nodded. "How would Cray get into the actual cult though? Does a representative contact him or what?"

Papa used his index finger to trace random *vévé* symbols in the moisture on the bar. "Voodoo is about the worship of and communication with ancestors—communicating with the dead. Lotsa graveyard symbols and funeral icons. And some just...follow a darker path. They believe that true earthly power—and eternal life—come through black sorcery, through blasphemous interaction with the dead. *Not* zombie shit. That's Hollywood— or at least Haiti. If Cray somehow had this power, this quality of *simpatico—* and stumbled into a situation where they could become aware of it—they'd find him."

That Cray could somehow be mixed up in this scenario seemed almost ludicrous, at least until Green summoned the image of a human skull simmering on Cray's stove. "What do you mean by 'power'?"

Papa thought for a second, staring into the dirtstreaked mirror behind the bar. "You ask most priests if there was something supernatural or even otherworldly about their decisions to enter the priesthood, and most of 'em—if they're honest—have had *some* experience the rest of us will never have. Something that convinced 'em of a higher power."

He wet his throat with a quick sip of beer. "Same in voodoo. There *are* forces out there—and I don't wanna sound like a dotty ol' man—that folks tap into. And it's true in voodoo just like anything else. You can't really learn how to *get* power, but if you *have* it, it can be nurtured by a sorcerer."

Outside, the mid-afternoon December light was beginning to weaken a bit. LSU was playing in the Superdome tonight, and the Quarter was already rocking with the lunatic fringe from Baton Rouge. Green said, "And Crayton has this power?"

Papa raised his eyebrows questioningly. "*I* can't make a spider come outta somebody's mouth. Can you?"

Green felt sheepish. "Well, no."

Papa laughed sharply. "Now, first off, this boiling the skull thing you told me about. Cray took a skull from a grave and had to clean it up. Consecrate his own *nganga*—which you apparently learned about Halloween. Along with the coffin, that's for his altar."

"Jesus."

"The worst, though, is the Hand of Glory."

"I was afraid of that." Green took a sip of beer. The entire conversation was taking on a chatty, surreal tone of acceptance.

Papa said, "If Cray took Prospero Godchaux's left hand, he's got big power, boy, universally. Across the board, bad guys have sought the Hand of Glory for centuries."

Green's voice was petulant. "Where did he pick this shit up? I've looked around and I haven't found anything remotely instructional in this context. Did Crayton even know he had this...this *power*?"

Papa sighed. "He probably started to suspect it, just from changes in his life. He's a *conductor* of power at this stage, kinda like a lightning rod, and at a certain point stuff started happening that made him suspicious of himself."

Papa paused, trying to explain it delicately. "Them death league people that passed away—Cray probably didn't consciously plan anything, any more than he probably expect the spider to crawl out of J.C.'s mouth. He *might've* though. He might have just *thought* them dead. Probably not, but who knows?

"Eventually, nothing weird would exactly *surprise* ol' Cray either. But if he's just now getting around to getting a casket and a skull, he's fairly early on in, I dunno, what you might call an apprenticeship. But now...someone *is* leading him down the path, so to speak. Plus, the sheer seduction of the power's enough. You gotta be really strong to resist it. I'm sure he's having second thoughts about a lot of this stuff, but the power gets to you. It's like dope, boy. *Good* dope. Plus, the Prospero thing was timely. You can't just *order* the corpse of a convicted murderer like you would a po'boy."

Green's head spun. Not only was his friend lying to him, but there was the small matter that Green was walking around in a world where voodoo really existed. Where normal guys were hooked up in death cults. He shivered. What was next? Werewolves on Toulouse Street?

Papa waved at the bartender, and after she set down two new beers and a bowl of peanuts, Papa swallowed a handful, wiped his mouth with the back of his arm, then held out his hand in front of Green. It was shaking. Green was alarmed by how faded the old man suddenly looked in the glow of the neon beer signs.

"I figure it's time to move on to the big subject now," Papa said with a weak grin.

Green's apprehension suddenly twisted; he'd thought they'd already *hit* the big subject.

"Lord, I thought I was through being scared about this," Papa mumbled quietly, shaking his head in wonder. "And now..."

Green had no idea what Papa was talking about. "Papa, you okay? Maybe we should stop all this—"

"No, no," Papa interrupted firmly. "You need to know what's happening here. Thing is, when I talk about someone showin' the ropes, so to speak, well, you ain't got to look very far to find out who it is."

"It's Maman Arielle, isn't it?"

Papa laughed harshly. He tossed more peanuts in his mouth.

Green closed his eyes as the ever-expanding nightmare seemed to compete for space in the tiny barroom with its miasma of cigarette smoke. *Fucking Crayton.* "That reminds me," he said wearily. "I can find no birth records for this Arielle—the daughter—in either Orleans or Jefferson parishes. You wouldn't know enough about them to know where she was born, would you?"

Papa raised his eyebrows. "You've seen the right birth records," he said, not commenting on Green's detective work. "There ain't no daughter. This Maman Arielle is my sister."

"Your...*sister*? The one at Gris-Gris Gumbo?! But...*how*? You told me..." Green shook his head slowly. He felt like someone trying to do his taxes while surfacing from a dentist's anesthesia.

Papa put his hands on the edge of the sticky bar, grasping it firmly in an attempt to keep them from shaking. His voice was raspy with tension. "It gets worse."

Green stared at Papa, certain he was about to have a stroke. "Papa—"

"I'm okay." He opened his eyes and said, matter-of-factly, "This Arielle—my sister, the one that runs Gris-Gris Gumbo—she's been dead thirty years."

"What the *fuck* are you talking about?!" Green had to re-run the statement through his brain, positive he'd misunderstood the lunacy that Papa had just uttered. For an instant that left him ashamed, he wanted to slap Papa. "What do you mean she's dead? *Dead?* She's been dead *thirty years*? What the hell does *that* mean?" He had to rein his voice in, checking the television end of the bar to make sure everyone was entranced by Ole Miss' final two-minute drive. Even so, the bartender glanced down at them.

Papa looked at her desperately, pointing at a bottle of Jameson, then swirled his finger around their half-full beer bottles to indicate another round. Green sat tiredly, trying to assimilate that not only was the whole voodoo scam real and that the guy who was maybe his closest friend was at best a grave robber—but also that the whole thing was being orchestrated by a *ghost*.

"How...*how* can Arielle be dead?" Green finally asked after the bartender had brought their drinks. "This woman—your *sister*—is running a gumbo shop. I went to one of her goddamn parties. She washed *dishes*, for Chrissakes!" He realized he sounded like a spoiled punk, but he couldn't help it. "What do you *mean* no zombies?"

Papa tossed back his whiskey. He stared at the dingy, smoke-treated ceiling. "No zombies. And she's absolutely dead." He glanced around the bar wearily, as though he might never see it again and wasn't sure whether he wanted to remember it. "She's a spirit. A *ghost*. Her power ebbs and flows based on the energies—and fear—of the living. The necromantic rites...they're...whatcha call it? Self-perpetuating."

He closed his eyes momentarily, then leaned toward Green, who could smell liquor on him as though it was somehow a neurochemical byproduct of exhaustion and stress. Tears flickered in the corner of Papa's eyes like funeral candles. "I kept this secret forever, then went to St. Lydwine's and confessed earlier this week. Now this is the second time I'm telling it, and I guess it'll be the last..."

He wiped his mouth and stared at Green a moment. "You asked how I know Arielle dead?" He actually smiled at Green, though there was absolutely no humor there. It was like the pitiable smile of an alcoholic friend telling you how he fell off the wagon, who was hoping somehow you'd *support* his decision. His voice dropped to a whisper. "I know 'cause I killed her."

CHAPTER FIFTY-FOUR

For the first time since he'd met Maman Arielle, Crayton felt the full surge of power blow through his system. It was a curious mix of energy and lazy warmth, not unlike, Cray suspected, the speedballs John Belushi had ultimately and fatally found more attractive than cheeseburgers *Well, too bad, Johnny B,* Cray thought, *I don't need chemicals for this rush.*

After running away from Margaritaville, Cray had sprinted all the way to Armstrong Park across Rampart Street from the Quarter, the site of the old Congo Square, where slaves had once congregated on Sundays to dance the Calinda and Bamboula while white folks stared in fear and amusement at the darkies' zany voodoo antics. Now, few tourists roamed the perimeter of the park; it was late afternoon and after sunset the park would become dangerous.

Cray slowed to a walk, panting ridiculously. *Not exactly Sam Gallagher in the ol' conditioning department,* he thought. He passed the enormous bronze statue of Louis Armstrong, holding his magical horn and staring in perpetuity toward the Quarter. Speakers placed throughout the commons softly ladled New Orleans music into the air from hometown station WWOZ, located in a building at the rear of the park. Guitar Slim sounded resigned as he sang "The Things That I Used to Do." *Slim's got that right.*

The breeze felt brisk against his sweating form. Cray followed the path back onto Rampart Street and wandered along the wall of St. Louis Cemetery #1, where, on Halloween Day—just over a month ago!—he'd stuck some ridiculous gris-gris bag at the base of Marie Laveau's tomb in a silly attempt to psyche out his death league competitors.

He sidestepped a passed-out wino near a wooden bench and gazed absently at the tops of the tombs and crypts, feeling no trace of the alcohol he'd consumed almost nonstop since Eliza found the skull. As soon as her screams had awakened him from his beery nap and he'd grasped the reality of the situation, he'd known their relationship was over. It was heartbreaking, but there was no way to repair the damage. He knew it.

And if that wasn't enough, he also knew word about the stovetop skull would get back to Green and the others. Well, they'd either stay his friends or they wouldn't. Somehow, he figured he'd eventually be able to smooth it over with them, or at least Green—who was really the only one he gave a rat's ass about anyway.

J.C. was absolutely no longer part of the equation.

Never in a million years had Cray expected J.C. to move that fast. He'd known all along about the guy's quicksilver dick, of course, but this was unbelievable. Even if they hadn't become good pals of late—and that hurt too; Cray had never *had* friends until he moved to New Orleans, and had lately come to think of J.C. as a righteous guy—the sheer speed with which he'd zoomed in on Eliza was...well, without *decency*.

As for what to do now, he had a few maneuverings he wanted to take care of at the altar before full dark, then he thought it best to get away from the St. Ignatius for the night. Though he wasn't exactly sure what he'd been doing when he'd grabbed J.C.'s hand—it had all been instinctual, as though some ancestral finger had been guiding Cray's actions—he knew *something* had happened after he'd run off. He'd actually felt a curious internal force draining *into* J.C.

It was like Maman Arielle had been whispering over his shoulder. He knew some...*warning* had gone down, and whatever it was, it was going to be a serious mind-fuck.

A splash of twilight sun pierced through and dimpled the odd layers of gray clouds in dark bursts of orange and gold, and, without being truly aware what he was doing, he veered across Rampart to Our Lady of Guadalupe Catholic Church. Established in 1826, it was known as the Old Mortuary Chapel because it had been constructed as a burial chapel for victims of the city's horrible yellow fever epidemic.

Abutting the church proper, on the downriver side, was the grotto at Our Lady of Guadalupe, a wonderfully eerie spot and one of Crayton's favorite places in the city—or it *had* been before he ran into Maman Arielle and her spiritual bent. As the name suggested, the grotto was fashioned to resemble a natural rock outcropping housing a cave—like something built by Disney folks for a theme park ride, perhaps—and the visitor descended into the subterranean structure through a wrought iron gate.

Inside, the deeply shadowed space was tiny, perhaps the size of an average, if narrow, bedroom. The low, rounded ceiling was only slightly taller than Crayton, and the *bas-relief* walls and roof were inlaid by dozens of tiles containing parishioners' messages of gratitude and hope to Our Lady—a pacific and concerned statue of whom perched in a hollow atop a *faux* rock ledge near the top and rear of the room.

Other than a small window behind the statue, floor-to-ceiling shelves tucked against the walls housed the only source of illumination: hundreds of lit prayer and vigil candles in glass containers of blue, red, white, yellow, and green that fluttered and glowed in carnival incandescence. Directly under the statue, dozens more candles were clustered on the cinnamon-colored tile in flame-dotted petition. Cray had actually seen Aaron Neville in here once, lighting a candle.

Despite the brisk temperature, Cray could feel a comforting and palpable heat from the lit candles. There was a churchy scent of melted wax to counter the damp, gritty city smells of late fall, and though he could hear a bus race by outside, there was a hushed quality inside the grotto. At the bottom step, Cray had a moment of detached curiosity about whether, in his present state of—what, *lack* of grace?—he would experience some sort of massive, blasphemer's electro-shock reaction. If anything, though, he felt that sense of power and well-being. It didn't lessen the intensity of his righteous rage, but he was less jumpy and thought perhaps he would be able to focus on the tasks ahead with rational precision.

Only after he took a deep breath and peered around into the deepening twilight shadows did Crayton realize he was not alone. There appeared to be a figure—a young woman?—kneeling with her back to him in the right corner under the statue, hunched over and presumably lighting a prayer candle.

She did not seem to be aware of or bothered by the fact that he had entered, and Cray felt momentarily foolish, as though he'd interrupted a private moment. He didn't know whether to sneak back out or clear his throat and apologize. Or just go about his business, whatever that was. The grotto was, after all, open to the public for all the right reasons.

Before he could arrive at a conclusion, however, the figure rose with delicate grace from the floor and began to turn, and Cray could see that, indeed, she had been tending to a candle. Something about the tapir, though, drew his focus from the woman and he peered closer at it. For one thing, it wasn't in a glass container. For another, it was black and figural in construct, and it only took Crayton a moment to recognize its shape in spite of the gloom.

What the fuck?

Cray had seen these in other voodoo shops—*real* botanicas—and that he would find someone placing such a thing in *here*, in the grotto at Our Lady of Guadalupe, made no sense at all. *Talk about blasphemy.*

The candle was a carved figure of Baphomet—the Sabbatic Goat—a winged, horn-headed man whose origins as a ritualistic talisman for dark magic were cobwebbed in centuries of secrecy and debauchery. *But what was it doing here?*

All these thoughts spun through Crayton's brain in an instant, and only then did he shift his gaze to see who the hell had perpetrated such a thing because it required some massive nuts.

She met his stare and offered the hint of a smile and, as with her candle, Cray was struck by a sense of familiarity. She was young—maybe sixteen with a feathered wedge of hair—and, in the shuddering light, exceedingly pale. Her eyes glittered like mercury in swimming pool water. She was wearing a plaid wool skirt and a matching vest over a white blouse, like a Catholic girl's school uniform. She took a shuffling step toward him—and it hit Crayton with Taser intensity.

The hair. The school uniform...the eyes... It was absolutely her...

He staggered, reaching out for balance against the candle shelves. "No fucking way," he whispered. *Not even after everything he'd been through.*

She took another step, only a few feet away now, and he caught a hint of her odd decay, that saccharine tang like moldy marmalade. Her smile broadened, exposing for the first time her gleaming teeth, and even in the murk of the room he could see tiny, spaced snippets like white whiskers hanging from the underside of her upper lip.

They were the remnants of the thread the mortician had used to sew her mouth shut when she'd been embalmed, and which Cray had scissored through in Maman Arielle's courtyard a few nights ago. He couldn't help but wonder about the thread and laughed hysterically. Did they use *dental floss?* Maybe the next time Marcus dropped by, he could *fuckin' ask him! Ha!*

He took a deep breath. Cray felt dizzy and psychically ambushed—but absolutely not scared. Impressed, maybe—*awed* might be the better word for it—and later he would realize that "awe" was precisely what he was *supposed* to feel. After all, she'd died—*again*—back in the courtyard, only a few moments after Cray had orchestrated her resurrection through his blood sacrament from the *nganga*.

Now, though, he couldn't stop staring at those goddamned loose stitches.

Until, in that most girlish of gestures, she ran her hand through her hair, pushing the bangs off her forehead—though she did so in skittery fashion, like maybe the synapses that orchestrated the impulses from the brain and down her arms and into her fingers were sputtering.

And when she spoke, her delivery was plodding but steady and contained no palpable sense that lungs had forced air through a human diaphragm and voice box. Instead, stale words simply materialized and hung in the still grotto air like sticky pollen.

"I can't believe that J.C. guy," she said hoarsely. "After all you did for him. I can't believe he'd fuck Eliza."

CHAPTER FIFTY-FIVE

At the moment Papa admitted he'd killed Maman Arielle, it flashed through Green's system that he'd reached the proverbial point in nervous agitation where absolutely nothing surprised him anymore. Papa was starting to explain and Green was trying to focus and listen to the old man despite the great, frothing waterfall of astonishment still roaring through his ears.

"It was the voodoo," Papa was saying with a painful earnestness. "She'd started using it for evil. She'd gotten into *Le Cults de Morts*." He shrugged matter-of-factly. "I couldn't get her out of it, and it got to the point where I was afraid she'd drag *me* into it... So I...I drowned her in the Bayou St. John, on St. John's Eve." He laughed, choking back a sob, trying to regain composure.

Green wanted to reach out but was still frozen with sensory overdose. When he finally opened his mouth, his thoughts and reactions were so tangled he wasn't even sure what he would say until he heard his own voice gently protest, "But, Papa. She's *here*."

Papa extended his arm and placed a trembling hand on Green's shoulder. "Yeah," he said sorrowfully. "She has been, off an' on, for years."

"Off and on," Green repeated dully. "She started getting evil. You killed her. And she comes back."

Papa nodded, almost eagerly. "Right. See, she got into the death cult stuff real gradual. Like I said, this was, oh, maybe thirty-five years ago, back when I was in the voodoo." He looked into his lap. "The rituals started getting more and more involved with blood, with more and more she'd have some animal sacrifice. Arielle started casting black gris-gris on folks.

"I tried to head her off. 'Keep it pure—it's a *religion*, it ain't for evil,' I done told her—but she wouldn't listen... By then, she knew she had the power. She was *drunk* with it."

Papa paused and wiped his mouth. The bartender made a bored pass by their end of the bar, then returned to the football zealots at the other end. Green waited patiently, feeling a lunatic acceptance steal over him like sundown. *No wonder Maman Arielle's so weird*, he thought fuzzily. *She's fucking dead.*

"One night," Papa finally continued, "Arielle stole the body of that monsignor across from our family crypt..."

Green blinked, remembering Papa's first account of that story, way back during Prospero's funeral, and said, "Wait a minute—it was *Arielle* who stole the priest's body?"

Papa nodded, miserable.

"But weren't you already a member of St. Lydwine? I know you made up the story about the Irish Channel murderers, but..." The words sputtered out of Green's mouth as his brain OD'd on information and shock. "You told me about how Father Chet petitioned for the church and what a wonderful guy he was and how the chapel bells haven't rung since he was killed..."

Papa listened. "All that's just the history of the church. Everyone who's a member there knows the stories. I joined *after* Arielle stole the body. She drove me to the Catholic Church, so in some respects I guess I owe her."

"And it was the theft of Father Chet's body that was the final straw?"

"That's when I couldn't take it no more. The rituals...she'd started using corpses. Then she began using her power to injure and kill folks... It was self-perpetuating." He fell silent for a moment, thinking back on some dark instant in the past. "I tried to just let it go, but I couldn't. I *tried*. But she had the power, not me. Like your pal Crayton's got the power." He swallowed painfully.

"And one night I decided to put an end to it. St. John's Eve, the Bayou St. John. Everybody went home after the ceremony, an' Arielle tell me she's going back to the cemetery to sleep with the corpse of a monsignor. She told me his body was already laid out there, waiting.

"'Leave me be, baby brother,' she said to me. 'I gots magic to do.' Before I even knew what I was doing, I knocked her out with a big cypress log I found on the bank, then I held her under the water till she was dead." He turned his eyes to Green and locked on him calmly. "And I figured that's the end of that."

Then a look of helpless desperation etched his lined face, and his voice dropped to a harsh whisper. "But I was wrong."

Green thought for a moment. "Are you sure she was dead? Maybe—"

"She dead, Green. I checked her pulse for five minutes or more, then threw her back in and watched a bull gator pull her down." Papa was stone-faced in his certainty. "I went back to the crypt that night, after I killed her. I was gonna return the monsignor's body to his grave—and that's when I saw the stone angels on either side of the tomb had changed. Cruelty and Despair. But they were normal graveyard statues *before* I drowned Arielle—and that's when I knew I'd fucked up."

The football game ended at that point, and a general upheaval occurred as several men scurried to settle their tabs and began to head out of the small bar into the late afternoon. Someone fed the jukebox and an old Radiators song came on. Green turned to Papa. "I know you, Papa, I believe in you, I trust you." He swallowed deeply, then added, "I love you." He could see a brief moment of pride and affection sparkle in Papa's eyes.

"But, Papa, the only answer is that she wasn't dead. For God's sake, what other explanation is there?"

Papa nodded, listening rationally. "Okay, say I was wrong. Say I only *thought* I killed her. Then how do you explain a seventy-five-year-old woman who looks like she a twenty-year-old model some days or a forty-year-old school teacher some days?" He shook his head belligerently. "But she damned sure don't look like she's seventy-five *any* days." He turned away and grabbed some peanuts. "Moot point anyway," he said with quiet stubbornness. "She was dead."

Green decided to let the whole corporeal spirit thing rest a minute and pursue something else he'd been thinking about. "So, your full name is Duane Hipolyte Freixenet?"

Papa started. "How'd you know that?"

Green smiled faintly. "I just put it all together." He told Papa he'd seen "Duane Hipolyte" on his hospital chart, and that he'd come across the Freixenet name in the cemetery grids. "I'm assuming it was a family name," Green said. "Did you drop it after...after Arielle died?"

Papa said, simply, "Yeah. I'm a Freixenet. Hipolyte originally my middle name, called after my maternal grandfather's last name. Like you say, after...after Arielle dead, I just shortened it. Trying to make a break, I guess."

A thought hit Green. "How come I didn't see your name on the birth records?"

"I was born in St. John the Baptist Parish. Mama went into labor while she was visiting relatives."

Green nodded. That made sense. If Papa sensed Green was even slightly doubtful about the whole revelation, he didn't show it. And the thing was, Green *could* believe it. After all that had happened, he could so easily just...step across that line of skepticism with ease. Maybe he already had.

Green went on. "The tax rolls show Gris-Gris Gumbo and the adjoining house are registered to Henri Vidrane. I'm assuming he's actually alive and some sort of apprentice sorcerer."

Oddly enough, the old man looked *less* tired than even a half hour before, as though this second confession and subsequent conversation had somehow unburdened him. Papa lifted his beer, then set it back down without drinking from it. "Yeah, there's always one of those Henri folks around," he said. "They're kinda like her earthly"—he struggled for the proper term—"well, like one of those personal assistants that corporate executives got doing all the mundane shit for 'em. What's the word? A, uh, familiar, right?"

Green nodded. "Or a *bokor* in waiting." He actually grinned at Papa, who seemed impressed. "So eventually, then, he'll be his own wizard or whatever."

"You *have* been studying up on this."

"Yeah, well, *you* told me that, back before any of this got started..." Green looked idly down the bar, where the bartender was ending her shift and counting the tip jar bounty. The new bartender, a young guy with a wispy mustache and a greasy, lacquered straw cowboy hat, stood impatiently by the cash register, working a toothpick in his mouth. "But you're right. You were in the hospital. Things were getting weird. I had to try to figure it out. Guess I didn't figure out enough."

Papa said, "Sounds like you're doing all right to me."

Green leaned toward Papa. "Help me figure *this* out then. If Maman Arielle's dead and has come back"—and he nodded to show Papa he was ready to accept that—"then why is a dead woman leading a death cult? What good are the rituals performed on and with the dead if you *are* dead? And more importantly, *how* is this happening?"

Papa gave Green a look of defeated helplessness. "Because she *ain't* dead."

Green looked confused, and he had to caution himself to keep his voice down. The new bartender had set up his cash register and would be heading over soon to check their drinks. "But you said you killed her! That's what we've been going over for thirty minutes!"

"I *did*. I did kill her. But somehow—and I don't know how—she's *back*. That's what I'm telling you. She ain't like a zombie, but even as a spirit, over time, she gets stronger and stronger. We're talkin' years, sometimes, when the energy ebbs and flows. But...she's fuckin' strong right now, Greenie. Your boy Cray done guaranteed that."

Green chewed his lower lip. "You're right. She *is* here and, if you say so, I guess she's been around for years. Maybe hibernating or something in between folks like Cray. But if you killed her thirty-five years ago, and she's back running this *Culte des Morts*, then how come she's let *you* live all this time?"

A new song had come on the jukebox, and over and over. Paul McCartney was singing, *Let it be, let it be / Speaking words of wisdom / Let it be...* Something flashed through Green's mind at hearing Paul's mantra, but he was more concerned with Papa.

The old man shivered and seemed to shrink into himself. The brief energy he'd shown dissipated. He shrugged, ashamed, then quietly said, "I have no idea. Maybe because, I suppose, she figures I'm a lot more miserable alive than I would be dead. All this time, I'm scared every goddamned day." He hung his head like a beaten boxer. "She *likes* it that way."

When I find myself in times of trouble, Mother Mary comes to me... Green sat upright and blinked. "Papa?"

"Yeah?"

"When you had your heart attack? In the hotel room?"

Papa looked at him curiously. "Yeah?"

"You said it was Maman Arielle that appeared and soothed you, right?"

"Yep, it was her all right."

"But that's got to mean something, don't you think?"

"Yeah, it means something, I guess. I told you. It's been puzzlin' me since it happened."

"Well," Green said finally, "what do you think it means?"

Papa looked back at Green calmly. "I don't know what it means. Woman was probably waiting to welcome me to hell!" He laughed shortly. "Thing is, though...I don't know if I actually worry about it anymore." He shrugged. "I used to be frightened constantly. When's she gonna pop up? When's she gonna finally get tired fucking with me and just go ahead and kill me?"

He shrugged. "But now... I'm just not that worried about it. I don't know *what* I am. But since I had the heart attack and listened to the doctors, and made a confession"— he looked at Green—"made *two* confessions now I ain't *terrified*, I guess. And *that's* different."

There *was* something peaceful about his entire demeanor that seemed out of whack with everything they'd talked about. And it seemed as though the whole tone of the conversation had shifted significantly when Green had brought up the vision of Maman Arielle. Slowly, an idea began to suggest itself in his head.

"Well," Green said, consciously altering the focus of their talk, "as far as Arielle actually walking around the planet, we know voodoo people are actually 'ridden' by spirits or *loas*—and there are plenty of documented occurrences where scientists and photographers have actually recorded it as it happens."

Papa nodded. "Right. Not to mention that I've seen it myself, dozens of times."

"So—somehow—her *loa* has moved to the next step." Green paused, trying to think of the right way to describe it. "It moved beyond the temporary occupation of a random human body, like it happens during ceremonies. Somehow, her spirit is permanently manifested corporeally—if that's a word—in her own body. She gets power from her acolyte—from Cray. And you... I dunno, you're adjunct energy. Another battery or something."

Papa thought a moment about what Green was saying. "Sure. Makes as much sense as anything." He took a deep breath and softly added, "Greenie, I know you're trying to make logical about all this. But I don't know if that's possible." He looked straight into Green's eyes. "Right now, all this ain't helping the situation with Cray and J.C. and Eliza."

Green started and looked at his watch. Papa was right, and they'd been sitting here almost two hours.

"You're right," Green said worriedly.

"Now listen," Papa said earnestly. "You've got to get to Crayton's altar. That's the source of his power. Whatever shit he's pulling down, it all originates there. The spider thing was a sort of instinctual warning. I ain't even certain Cray knew he did it. But it *was* a warning—and he ain't finished. You've got to get to the altar."

Green said, "Christ, that could be anywhere. I mean, it's certainly not in his apartment."

Papa shrugged. "Probably not. You never know though. Voodoo folks are damned creative when it comes to stuff like that. Knew a guy who had an altar in an old freezer on a back gallery."

Green thought about Cray's apartment but, again, dismissed it. He and Eliza had too much free rein there. Plus, the layout of the units at the St. Ignatius simply didn't allow for a lot of spatial creativity.

"One thing though," Papa went on. "It's gotta be close. Remember that. He can't go tooling off halfway across Orleans Parish every time he wants or needs something."

Green nodded. That made sense. *So where the piss is it?* "You're saying I need to get my ass in gear."

The old man closed his eyes tightly for an instant, as though experiencing a spasm of pain, then sighed. "We've gotta save Crayton—if that's possible—and we've damned sure gotta make sure this gris-gris with J.C. and the girl don't go no further."

Green had one more thought. "Papa, if Cray somehow came to his senses, would Maman just let him walk away? Or would she turn on him?"

Papa laughed, but there was no humor in it. "This ain't the junior high football team, Greenie. I don't think Cray just turns in his cleats when he feels like it."

Green nodded. "Somehow, I didn't think so."

CHAPTER FIFTY-SIX

Cutting across Jackson Square, Green looked enviously at a group of mirth-making tourists seated at Cafe Pontalba, then accessed the private stairway to J.C.'s apartment. Every light in the place was on, and J.C., Donny, and H-Man were gathered around the dining room table, which was clustered with beer bottles and cardboard food containers of Chinese food.

They looked up as one, chopsticks suspended, as Green tossed his denim jacket on the couch and pulled a bottle of water out of the refrigerator.

"What'd you find out?" J.C. said tensely.

"In a minute," Green said, pulling up a chair and stealing a skewer of chicken and peppers off a serving tray. He took a bite, looked around the apartment, and asked, "Did you get Eliza out of here?"

"Not yet," J.C. said.

Green raised his eyebrows.

"She's really knocked out," J.C. said. "I guess we medicated her more than we thought."

Green looked alarmed. "She's not ODing or anything?"

"Naw, she's been up once or twice," J.C. said. "She's just exhausted. She'll cry for a minute, then start this weird laughter. We about half figured she'd had a breakdown, then she gets calm and reassures us—and goes back to sleep."

Donny spoke. "We'll all stay here tonight and she's gone first thing tomorrow morning."

J.C. smiled briefly. "It may work out better this way, Green. She's catchin' a ride to D.C. with Uncle Wallace on his private jet. He's got some big deal committee meeting tomorrow and his plane is leaving at eight a.m."

Green nodded. "That *is* excellent." He looked at Huey and Donny. "So I guess you guys are up to date on the spider?"

Huey nodded. "Goddamnedest thing I ever heard." He glanced at J.C., then back at Green. "No offense, J.C.," he said, "but, Green, there's no chance it was some kind of set-up?"

Green yawned; he couldn't help it. "Penn and Teller couldn't have pulled this off. And if I hadn't believed it when I saw it happen, I'd believe it now, after talking to Papa Hipolyte." He took a drink of water and rinsed it around the inside of his mouth. "So I guess it's time to confirm that Crayton's in this juju shit far more than any of us believed. Maybe if I'd listened to y'all about the death league from the word go, we wouldn't be where we are now."

Huey shrugged. "We all went along. And where exactly *are* we? Spiders notwithstanding."

Green took another quick bite from the skewer. Even in the bar with Papa, he'd known instinctively that the part about Maman Arielle being dead was something he'd keep to himself. "Okay, this isn't just Papa's word on this stuff; I've been looking into it as well—"

"We trust both of you," J.C. interjected tersely, leaning forward. "Just get to it."

"Right then. Here's how it's all come to pass." Green took a deep breath and started talking. "Y'all remember me telling you about the weird shit in the River of Life Cemetery, when I went to Prospero Godchaux's funeral with Papa? Well..."

Green went through the whole thing, adding the latest information he'd discovered or learned from Papa. Genealogically, he was content to explain Maman Arielle as Papa's much younger sister. As for Crayton's involvement with *Le Culte des Morts*, Green said they had no proof, but that it was possible. He concluded by relating Papa's belief that the spider was a warning—and that it was possible Cray didn't even know it had happened.

"Goddamn," J.C. breathed, looking extremely nervous. "A *warning*? What does that mean?"

Green shrugged tiredly. "We don't know, J.C. That's why I've got to find Cray and defuse this. Now." He also thought it best not to mention that he was looking for an altar, figuring hysteria was as big an enemy as Cray.

Christ, did he really consider Crayton an enemy?

Huey said, "So you guys think Cray's actually tapped into some sort of voodoo power source?" He didn't sound doubtful, exactly, but as though it was tough to absorb.

"Yeah, I believe it," Green said simply.

Huey slammed his palm on the table, then stood up and walked aimlessly around the living room. "Am I really hearing all this? I'm—"

"Believe what you want," Green said, cutting him off. "But I don't have time to discuss whether John Locke would find this empirically verifiable. I'm going to find Cray."

"And do what?" Donny demanded. "I think we should all stay together."

Green shook his head. "Cray isn't going to hurt me. For all we know, he isn't going to hurt anybody. Maybe he's just sad about Eliza. Maybe he couldn't hurt anybody if he *wanted* to. Papa says there's no way we can know, at this point, to what extent Cray controls or can harness his power."

"What about Papa's sister—this Arielle—the restaurant woman?" Huey asked. "She's the one twisting his head, right?"

"I guess so." Green swallowed nervously. "Papa's going to see what he can do from his end."

"Well," J.C. said hopefully, "maybe this will all work out. I mean, I'll happily apologize if you think that's a good idea."

Green had no doubt J.C. was sincere, but it was also obvious he hoped there was a better solution than that. "It'll work out," Green finally said. He stood up and stretched. "So, you guys are gonna make sure Eliza gets on that plane to D.C., right? If Cray was going to punish her for her tryst with Brad Pitt, here"—he nodded at J.C.—"Papa says *she* would have gotten the spider. So we'll assume she's safe for the time being. But Papa still thinks it's a good idea that she's out of sight for a while. Not necessarily for voodoo reasons; just so Cray doesn't pull any real-life, unrequited lover bullshit."

Green looked once more around the table. "You guys take care. You can call me at the apartment, and leave a message if I don't answer. I'll probably be there waiting on Cray to come home—if he isn't there already."

CHAPTER FIFTY-SEVEN

After knocking on Crayton's door—lights off, nobody home—Green unlocked his own apartment and settled exhaustedly on the couch. He was overwhelmed by the whole day, and in particular the idea that Maman Arielle was dead—and then *not* dead—when a thought crept up on him like a quiet animal.

Maman Arielle's life force is that Papa fears what she might do to him.

It was pretty simple really, and made complete sense—or at least it wasn't any more preposterous than anything else that had happened lately.

The more Green thought about it, the more it became plausible.

She's fueled both by Cray as a familiar and also by her brother's terror of what she might do to him.

It was the ultimate manipulative vengeance.

Green shook his head at the simplicity of it all.

Well, why not?

Dark voodoo was based on fear, right? Victims of spells perpetuated the curse through their fear that the hex will actually work. Maman Arielle had found a way back to the living through the spirit world—and Green still had a hard time believing he could logically walk *that* construct like an oatmeal cookie recipe—and she maintained finite shape and function through the terror and guilt Papa felt since he'd killed her.

Therefore, it was essential to her that Papa stay alive, because without the power source she drew from her sibling's naked fear, maybe the rituals and acolytes aren't enough to sustain her.

Or maybe she just likes fucking with the guy who killed her.

He laughed as exhaustion and the sheer lunacy of what he was thinking saturated his brain. But: if he was gonna play in this ballpark, so to speak, he had to admit the concept, goofy as it was in the rational world, made sense. He decided to call Papa. The phone rang four times and the answering machine picked up. Well, maybe he *was* already asleep.

"Papa, this is Green," he said. "Sorry to call so late, but I've got an idea about...what we were talking about at Johnny White's. About Maman Arielle... Uhm, call me. I'm at home."

When the phone finally rang though, it was morning, and J.C. was calling to say they'd gotten Eliza safely aboard Uncle Wallace's private jet. Green squinted at his watch through the shrouded early sunlight. Christ, he'd *fallen asleep* on the couch and it was almost nine! He'd been asleep all night! He'd accomplished *nothing*.

"So she's safe," J.C. said. "Anything up on your end? We hadn't heard from you." He sounded utterly drained, and the sheer weight of stress seeped through the phone lines in his voice.

Green sat up and rubbed sleep out of his eyes. "Not that I know of," he said. He realized he'd never heard back from Papa and that, if Cray had come or gone in the night, he hadn't heard him. "I've knocked on Cray's door and left phone messages, but I don't know where he is. You okay?"

J.C. took a deep breath. "So far, so good," he said.

"Excellent," Green said. He felt he'd let J.C. down, but didn't know what the hell else he could have done. In the back of his mind, he even wondered if somehow Cray had put him in some deep sleep zone. Groggily, he forced himself to pay attention. "How was Eliza?"

"Freaked but holding on. She was damn happy to get on the plane, I'll tell you that. She may *never* come back to New Orleans."

"Well, I can't blame her," Green sighed. "Now listen, J.C. I'll find Crayton. Everything will be okay. I know it."

"Yeah, well, I appreciate the help," J.C. said, trying to sound optimistic. "He'll turn up eventually and maybe this will all blow over. I'll do whatever I can." He paused for a moment and a note of desperation crept into his voice. "If I could just talk to him. Explain the way I am. It wasn't personal, brah, you know that..."

"We'll work it out," Green said, allowing J.C. his few moments of regret. "Did Huey and Don go home? Can you get some sleep?"

"I dropped 'em off coming back from the airport. We were up most of the night tryin' to play cards—scared like fucking Cub Scouts telling campfire ghost stories. I kept expectin', at any moment... Well, I don't know *what* I expected. But it wasn't good."

"Unplug the phone and try to rest a few hours. I'm going to grab a quick shower and track Crayton down. He's supposed to work today, if that means anything."

"I'll leave the phone plugged in," J.C. said. "But I'm gonna swallow about half of one of them Libriums and see if I can't nap without dreaming of spiders."

"Sleep tight, hoss. I'll call you when I find out something."

It was when he reached over to hang up the phone that Green noticed Cray's Papa Legba walking stick leaning against the hat rack in the corner. He remembered Cray waving the cane around when he'd wandered in yesterday morning, and he must've left it there when they hit the streets.

And just like that, it all fell together.

Green knew where the altar was.

"Sonofabitch," he said softly. He remembered returning Crayton's Camaro after bringing Papa home from the hospital. Something had bothered him about the pile of wood at the back of the parking lot—and now he knew it was because one of those shadowed forms had been Cray's juju cane. It just hadn't clicked in Green's head what it was. Cray was always leaving the fucker somewhere, and that day it'd been outside the shed.

It fit. There had also been the odd smell: incense and maybe a whiff of rum and...*rotting meat.*

"Oh fuck," Green moaned. *Don't let him have one of those fucking* ngangas.

He forced himself to think calmly. Thinking back over his research, he remembered that even the "good" voodoo altars sported occasional offerings of food and rum and cigars. Green reached for the phone and dialed Papa again. They'd discussed the urgent necessity of finding Cray's altar—*but nobody told Green what the piss to do with it if he found it.*

No answer again. This time, he was more worried. But he decided to check out the altar first. Then, depending on whether Cray had any virgins tied to the altar or a simmering *nganga* pot—Green would try calling Papa once more before he headed over to check on him.

And sooner or later, Green supposed, he'd run into Cray.

CHAPTER FIFTY-EIGHT

Green grabbed a flashlight and a crowbar and walked outside into the cool morning. He knocked on Crayton's door, thinking more about what he'd find on the altar than what he'd do if Cray was actually there—and was scarcely aware that no one had answered and he'd already walked around the corner and into the parking area.

Green stood outside the front of the shed for a maybe half a minute, marveling in the magical quiet that overtook the post-dawn lower Quarter, squinting in the sunlight and sniffing the air like a wary deer. It was only when he wriggled around the back corner of the shed, saw the padlocked sliding door and was able to actually detect a gamy melange of sinister odors, that it registered with Green that this was all very real and that Cray actually did have an altar.

He froze in a moment of fear-driven claustrophobia until he actually felt a low undercurrent of rhythmic pagan energy. Hell, he could almost *hear* it. He thought back to the drums in the embalming room the day Marcus had killed himself.

Oddly enough, the sensation jump-started him into action rather than feeding a more typical compulsion—such as hauling ass. It was probably because he was so worried about Papa and J.C.—and, for that matter, Crayton—and also because he was frankly fucking *sick* of worrying about the whole situation.

He gave Cray's padlock a cursory examination and almost laughed. It was of sufficiently high quality, but the door paneling itself was so cheap and old it was almost like shirt cardboard. Green couldn't imagine what sort of security Cray thought he had.

Fitting the tip of the crowbar between the shed frame and the edge of the sliding door, he pulled sharply in one quick motion. In the narrow confines, there wasn't room for much leverage, and the crowbar pinged immediately against the cement wall behind him, but not before the door cracked. Green couldn't draw his fist back far enough to muster any substantial power, but a quick series of well aimed rabbit punches ripped gaping holes in the paneling, and he was then able to kick a sizable opening in a few seconds.

Only then did he duck inside the shed and allow himself to turn his attention to the altar itself. As his eyes adjusted to the dusky gloom, the disturbing chemistry of smells became much more obvious: patchouli and rotting flowers, strong rum, mold and dead candle wax, and, coating everything, a foul and overly sweet mist of turned meat.

Green set the crowbar down. He unconsciously rubbed his nose and he began to breathe through his mouth as he attempted to catalog the obscene panorama before him. The first impression was an overwhelming collage of indistinct images dominated by a tiny, blue velvet casket in the foreground of a waist-high workbench draped with a black lace cloth, jutting out from the back wall. The lid was closed, and on top, wearing a purple top hat, was a human skull whose features seemed to regard Green with quiet amusement. On an almost subconscious level, Green realized this was probably the skull Crayton had been boiling when Eliza walked in. Flanking the skull were the spent nubs of black votive candles that had melted wax onto the surface of the coffin.

The skull's jawbone anchored a photograph. In an instant quick as a strobe flash, it registered to Green that the picture was of Cat-Daddy Phelps—the recently deceased clarinetist from Donny's death list—and that Cray had blackened the musician's eyes and stuck a penknife through the heart.

"Jesus Christ," Green murmured, his throat suddenly crisp as burnt toast. "Fuckin' *Crayton* killed him." The duplicitous genius of the maneuver was immediately clear: to make Donny back off his anti-voodoo campaign and to misdirect the rest of them in the midst of mounting suspicion. Green took a measured breath and swirled his head around the shed's interior, trying to absorb everything at once.

Behind the casket were three narrow wooden shelves, festooned with colored beads, several black and red candles, strewn chicken bones and heaps of coins, and perhaps a half-dozen framed likenesses of saints. An open bottle of rum was on the top shelf, next to a large, half-smoked cigar sitting in a glass ashtray.

On the middle shelf was the source of the meat smell. The headless body of a black cat lay in a sodden, post-rigor lump of limp, greasy fur, the neck opening mercifully angled away from Green. An opaque liquid had formed beneath the animal's mass and dripped slowly onto the main surface of the altar behind the casket.

Green's hands began to shake and he felt lightheaded and queasy. He glanced on the floor under the shelving—and there, in a cardboard box direct from the factory, was an "ornamental garden cauldron," complete with colorful image of a happy woman kneeling amidst plants, tending to bright red flowers in the black pot.

Green suspected that Cray had another purpose in mind, not quite so *Better Homes and Gardens-y*. As in, his own means to a *nganga*. The box was just sitting there, like something to be wrapped and placed under a Christmas tree, at the ready when Cray found the time to start making his own scorpion gumbo. Green shook his head sorrowfully—and to the right spied two tiny, desiccated objects that could've been delicate origami figures constructed of brown and gray tissue paper—until he realized they were the nearly mummified corpses of baby birds.

The crows from the funeral home.

They had to be. Green's sick feeling intensified as he realized Cray had been lying all along. Around the crows, crudely fashioned of ash, was a semi-circle of *vévé* symbols. Dead funeral sprays took up every other available bit of space on that side of the altar. Green blinked in overwhelmed stupefaction, and only then did he look to the left and zero in on an image of Papa Hipolyte.

"No," he whispered. Not on top of everything else. "*No...* Crayton, you motherfucker." *Why? Why, Papa?* He knitted his brow in an attempt to understand what sort of gris-gris Cray was attempting to perpetrate. An 8 x 12 publicity still of Papa was crudely gripped in the waxen brown fingers of a severed hand—and on the middle finger, shining dully in the closeted gloom, was a gaudy ring.

Prospero Godchaux's hand. The Hand of Glory!

The grotesque display was ringed with melted white candles—*white?*—and individually placed, freshly cut chrysanthemums. Green immediately reached out to pluck the photo from the hand—then caught himself. He had no idea what he was doing. What if his removal of the photograph actually quickened whatever gris-gris Crayton had put in motion?

But before he could think any more about what the hell he should do, the sound of Cray's mellow, disc jockey voice caressed him from over his shoulder.

"Sorry, folks, but visiting hours are over."

Green spun with the adrenaline-boosted shame of a teenager caught with his father's *Playboys*. Just as quickly, rage flooded over him like lava.

Cray was standing in the narrow chasm between the shed and the wall, smiling an odd, mean smile in the shadows. He reached up and rubbed his chin thoughtfully.

Green pointed a shaking finger, his voice quivering with fury. "Fuck you and your voodoo bullshit, Crayton, but you fix this curse on Papa or so help me I'll fucking kill you." He reached behind him and felt around until the crowbar fit into his hand.

"I'm fine, thanks," Cray said with chilling sarcasm, "even though my girlfriend's been shacking up with J.C. Bitoun. Thanks for asking, buddy."

Green had never been anywhere near this angry in his life. Still, he managed a halfway rational tone. "I'm sorry about that, Crayton, but you fix this gris-gris on Papa right fucking now!" Green's eyes bugged out as a burst of emotions hit him like a wall of water. "You...you've *killed* people here," he muttered. Tears welled up in his eyes at the reality of his friend's activities, then he shook his head and pointed at the Hand of Glory. "Fix it, *now*, and then we'll talk about Eliza and J.C."

Crayton took a deep breath. "It's, uhm, not a death curse."

"I've been pretty stupid through this whole thing, *pal*"—Green spat the last word with such viciousness that a brief glimmer of hurt showed in Crayton's eyes—"but I'm not a total idiot. That's Papa's picture in the Hand of Glory!" He shook his head in disbelief. "I can't believe you crawled into a crypt to get that."

Cray took another deep breath and closed his eyes momentarily. "I can't believe I've done a lot of things, Green," he said quietly. "You'd...you'd never understand." He gestured into the shed. "But I assure you that Papa is absolutely safe. That's precisely why his photo is there—to protect him."

Green lowered the crowbar a bit and he looked at Cray with skepticism. "To *protect* him? What the hell are you talking about?"

Cray tried a small grin. "I *like* Papa. I know what he means to you. You probably think this is all crap, but believe me, Green, there's more going on than you ever thought about." He said it with a queer mixture of pride and regret.

Green waved at the altar. "Oh, I believe it. I don't know how you got so fucked up in all of it—or maybe I do—but I damned sure believe it."

Cray hesitated, like he was going to try to explain the whole process, but instead just said, "So I told Maman Arielle I wanted to help a sick friend of mine, and she told me about a protective gris-gris using the Hand of Glory. That it would keep him safe."

"Maman Arielle," Green said, closing his eyes tiredly. "You really are mixed up with her." He sighed. "And she told you this would protect Papa?"

He nodded eagerly, like the old Cray, and Green knew he was telling the truth.

It makes sense, Green thought. *She's gotta keep Papa alive at all costs—at least until Crayton has enough power to sustain her.* Green saw where the heart problems were causing Arielle to walk a bizarre tightrope between keeping Papa alive on the one hand, but also sufficiently frightened of her that she could siphon power from his anxieties. *No wonder she'd appeared to him when he had the heart attack.* An actual bubble of relief popped up within Green. *He's gonna be okay—for a while anyway.*

He asked quietly, "What are you gonna do with all this?"

Cray gave a short bark of humorless laughter. "Well, what do you think, Green? I mean, I've pretty much screwed stuff up, wouldn't you say? Eliza's gone, and I can't imagine that you wanna hang around me much after all this." He looked around his altar, and a quick mixture of emotions crossed his face—chiefly a great sadness.

Green swallowed. "I don't know, Cray, this would be hard to get over." He glanced at the headless cat and winced. "But not as much as the fact that you've lied to me all along."

Cray nodded with sudden acceptance and rubbed his face with both hands like he'd been up too long. Finally, he said, "I never meant for it to get this far along, Green. It's...it's like a drug."

Green said, "It must be, I guess. I'm sorry for that. But what are you going to do about it? I don't suppose you just hand in your resignation to Maman Arielle."

Cray looked at him admiringly. "You figured it all out then."

"Yeah, Cray, with the help of Papa." He looked again at the dead cat on the shelf and then pointed at the picture of Cat-Daddy Phelps. "*Le Culte des Mort.* Jeez, Cray, I can't tell you how creepy this all makes me feel. I mean, are you *you*? Who the hell *are* you?" He actually took a step backward as the full implication of all the deaths and killing cats and mutilating corpses tumbled in on him again. "I can't even comprehend the criminality...the sheer viciousness of all this. I'm sure it'll all hit me at some point. But I can tell you I feel betrayed. And as far as friendship goes, that's the worst."

Cray, stung, snorted laughter. "Well, maybe. But I never set out to hurt you guys. You *are* my friend, Green. And speaking of friendship, what about the concept of betrayal in the context of our fuckin' buddy J.C.—whom *I* thought of as a friend, particularly after babysitting his ass when the Darby deal went south? What about Eliza? I guess you're surrounded by a whole squadron of folks who could put Betrayal on their resumes."

Then the flash of eerily convivial conversation was over. Green said, "Whatever, Cray. All I know is nothing better happen to J.C. or Eliza, buddy, or your little voodoo club is going up like fireworks. Now I'd better go; I'm assuming you're going to tear all this shit down." He moved forward, angling toward the brick wall in a maneuver designed to force Crayton into the altar shed so Green could get by and out into the parking lot.

Cray was livid, flashes of pain and rage alternating on his face, though he stepped aside to let Green by. "So that's it then, huh? What? Do we ignore each other on the street too, or is it okay if I say hello when I see you?"

Green stopped and turned around. He pointed at Cray in *faux* surprise, as though he was just walking along and happened to spot him. "Hey, Cray!" he said buoyantly. "How's tricks? Voodoo tricks, I mean. Killed anybody cool this week?" He looked a moment as a strange smile froze on Crayton's face, then turned and edged around the corner of the shed and out into the sunlight.

Cray slithered out of the shed and hurried after him. "Hold it, dude! Forgot to tell you something!"

Green was already halfway across the parking lot but, against his better judgment, he turned back around. "What?"

Cray trotted after him, holding a scrap of paper in his hand. "Here's a roster move you'll want to show the league."

Green's initial impulse was to actually hit Crayton—no crowbar—just punch him right in the middle of the parking lot, and to hell with the possibility that Cray might do a vengeful voodoo war dance or whatever. Instead, he just said, "Keep it, Cray, it's over," and started walking.

Cray caught up, though he seemed to have the good sense to stay at arm's length, and held out the paper. "No, really. Here. A little maneuver for the Vieux Carré Fantasy Death Society," he said, smirking. "From your league leader."

Green stopped and with great effort controlled himself. In fact, he saluted. "You're right, you *are* the league leader—what a surprise! Don't worry though, the pot's all yours. I don't think any of us would want the money anyway."

"I don't care about the money, Green. I just wanna play. Particularly at this juncture." He smiled hugely.

"I told you about J.C. and Eliza, Cray," Green said, staring intently into Crayton's eyes. "Leave 'em alone. I mean it."

Now Cray was holding both arms out in a con man's gesture of innocence. "Nobody said anything about J.C. or Honeybunch," he said in a singsong voice, holding the paper out teasingly. "And I might just keep playing anyway, Green. All by my lonesome. Go, team, go! Never give up! Never say die! Wait—did I just say that?" Then, laughing, Cray bowed deeply in a grotesque, Vaudevillian gesture.

Green moved around Cray and started up the street, struggling for nonchalance in spite of the quickening fear he felt at Cray's possible retaliations. The more Green thought about Crayton's power, the more he realized it was probably dangerous to make an enemy out of the guy.

And whose name was *on the paper anyway?*

"I'm dropping Jennifer Love-Hewitt," Cray called at Green's retreating form.

Green refused to look back.

"And let's replace her with, oh, I dunno… How about the honorable congressman-elect, Wallace Bitoun!"

Green stopped at once and turned to face Cray in dawning horror. Crayton chuckled at Green's reaction.

"Cray, listen to me: Did you put a gris-gris on Wallace Bitoun?" He strode back toward Cray, fear and concern etched on his face.

Cray, oblivious to Green's changed demeanor, fluttered the paper tauntingly and, in his best phony-politician voice, said, "I nominate good ol' Uncle Wallace, the people's favorite! The Son of Louisiana! Our man in D.C.! The—"

Green reached Cray and grabbed him by both shoulders, shaking him violently. "*LISTEN TO ME, YOU IDIOT!*"

Cray finally shut up and stared at Green, his eyes enormous behind his glasses.

Green moved about two inches from Cray and said, "Listen to me! Right at this moment, Uncle Wallace is on his private jet to Washington D.C., and Eliza's on the plane with him! Now—yes or no—did you put a spell on Wallace Bitoun?"

Cray blanched and the paper fell like a leaf to the grimy sidewalk. "Eliza?" he asked stupidly. "Eliza's on an airplane with *Wallace Bitoun?*"

"That's what I'm telling you, Crayton," Green said, gripping Cray's shoulders so tight he winced in agony. "She caught a ride home with him. So if you put a curse on Uncle Wallace, and the goddamned plane goes down, pal, I don't have to tell you who goes down with it!"

Tears instantly formed in Crayton's eyes. At that moment, he looked nine years old—and Green felt an inkling of sympathy, not only for Crayton but also for their friendship and everyone damaged by Cray's reckless descent into voodoo. He whispered, "What did you do, Cray?"

Cray looked blankly into Green's eyes as though he hadn't heard him. "Help me, Green. Help me. I don't know how...I don't know how to fix it."

CHAPTER FIFTY-NINE

"In spite of Maman Arielle and the whole voodoo ritual stuff, most of this I've just made up all along." Cray and Green were standing back inside the tiny shed, squeezed together shoulder to shoulder over the altar as they might have, even two weeks before, crammed under the hood of Cray's Camaro, changing sparkplugs and just goofing around. Now, though, Crayton was speaking with a hurried earnestness as he swept the skull and candles off the top of the casket.

"Aw, no," Green said as Cray opened the lid. Inside was a *Times-Picayune* photo of Wallace Bitoun, taken the evening of his election, holding his clenched hands overhead in triumph. Cray had inserted a single rosebush thorn through Bitoun's chest. Next to it was a BITOUN FOR CONGRESS button—"handed to me personally by Uncle Wallace and with one of his hairs I plucked from his jacket," Cray explained—and both were encircled with a ring of dirt.

Green muttered, "I suppose this is graveyard dirt."

Cray nodded, business-like. "Yeah. It seemed like a good idea at the time." He glanced at Green with hope. "I mean, it's the first time I've tried it this way. For all I know, it won't work."

"You did this last night?"

"Yeah." Cray's tone took on an urgent air of desperation. "You've got to understand, Green. I mean, I know I blew it with Eliza, but did J.C. have to descend on her so fast? She's...vulnerable... I mean, the guy's like a shark!"

"I know, dude, I know." Green studied Cray, who looked as though he'd taken an elevator down to hell and took a moment to look around—then somehow got to come back to the real world and was trying to digest what he'd just seen. Green was tired. "I feel for you, man, but that doesn't change all this." In a sudden angry burst, Green twirled and, with his arm, swept the entire contents of the top shelf crashing against the shed wall. "God *damn* you, Crayton! Look what you've fucking done!"

Cray winced and tugged on Green's arm pleadingly. "I *know*, Green. But what do I do about Eliza?"

Green's eyes blazed. "And *Uncle Wallace*, Crayton! As long as you're being Mr. Sympathetic, why don't you remember he's another innocent victim, goddamnit!"

"Right," Cray amended quickly. "And Uncle Wallace."

Green wiped his mouth, his eyes etched in worry. "I don't know, Cray. This is your bullshit. What *are* you gonna do? The goddamn plane's been in the air at least half an hour, maybe more. You're running out of time."

A thought hit Crayton. "Hey, maybe it won't happen that way," he said brightly.

Green shoved him then—hard—and Cray bounced against the ledge, shaking the Hand of Glory and Papa Hipolyte's picture. Green reached over hastily, in case the display fell—and froze in a sickening flash of comprehension.

Cray righted himself. "I'm sorry, Green, I'm just so worried about Eliza—" He stopped as he caught Green's frightened expression.

"What, Green? What is it?"

"Tell me I'm wrong here, Crayton. Tell me I'm wrong." Green was staring at the Hand of Glory and shaking his head warily.

"About what? *What is it?*" Cray's glasses were askew, and he tugged on them as he looked frantically at the altar, trying to determine what was freaking Green out.

Green nodded at Prospero Godchaux's hand and spoke with quiet urgency. "Crayton. The Hand of Glory. By definition it's the severed left hand of an executed murderer, correct?"

Cray nodded eagerly, not understanding. "Yeah. I mean, that's what Maman Arielle told me when...when she sent me to the cemetery that night."

Green closed his eyes in pain and shock and started to move. "I've gotta get to Papa Hipolyte. I've got to go."

He started to duck past Cray, who reached out and grabbed him, a look of wild uncertainty creasing his face. "Green, what the hell is wrong?"

"This isn't the Hand of Glory, Crayton. It's Prospero's *right* hand, Cray. You *cut off the wrong fucking hand.*"

Cray stared at the severed hand in mute shock, fingering his own left thumb as though trying to verify that what Green said could possibly be true.

"Oh my god," he breathed.

"Cray. Listen. Papa's *not* protected after all. And you've got to figure out the curse on Uncle Wallace. We're out of time. Call Maman Arielle if you have to—just... Whatever you need to do, do it."

"No! No...that won't work. I can't go to her with this," Cray said. He looked around fearfully.

"Why the hell not?" Green demanded impatiently. "She's the voodoo queen, pal—your *mentor.*"

Cray suddenly looked terrified. "If we go to her with this, it'll only get worse. As it is, she probably knows we're here right now."

Green kicked at the wall angrily and said, "Figure it out, Cray! It takes about two hours to fly from New Orleans to Washington D.C. Do you want to take the chance there won't be a plane crash? If it hasn't crashed already?"

He skittered through the passage and back and built to a full sprint by the time he hit Dauphine. He thought of calling Papa, but what was he going to say? It was better to just get over there and make sure the old man was all right. Green wasn't worried about Maman Arielle doing any damage—after all, she had every reason to want Papa alive—but he *was* terribly afraid what Papa might do if somehow he'd reached the same conclusion that Green had: that his very existence perpetuated Maman Arielle's presence.

Green ran past the innocuous alleyway leading to St. Lydwine's Church, offering up a quick prayer his friend hadn't drawn any hasty conclusions—that maybe he was inside the chapel right now, taking his regular Sunday morning mass. He also wished, not for the first time, that he'd joined modern society and invested in a cell phone.

Green tore around the corner at Chartres, ducked through the wooden gate and down the water-puddled flagstone path, and came upon Papa's cottage from the rear. In spite of his desperation, Green slowed to a cautious walk. The courtyard was thick with the fragrance of out-of-season wildflowers and wet vines. The windows were open, and Green listened for the telltale signs of the stereo. Green knew him well enough to know that, if Papa was awake and home, WWOZ would be blaring out of the speakers.

It was quiet, save for the distant sound of a truck's shifting gears on Decatur. Sweating heavily and suffused with a sense of dread, Green walked around to the front of the cottage and up the three gallery steps. Green was peering through the shadows, trying to see signs of life through the windows, and didn't actually glance at the door till he'd crossed the gallery.

There was an envelope fastened to the doorframe with a tack. In Papa's distinctive loopy handwriting, it was addressed to GREEN HOPKINS, MON AMI. Green pulled the envelope free and felt his spirits sink. Up in the right-hand corner, Papa had written, "Sat. 11 p.m."

Green's feeling of premonition spiraled down into a suffocating sense of loss and certainty. He sat down on the top step to read Papa's note, not wanting to look inside the cottage yet, and unaware that the first tear had already pooled in his right eye and was trailing down his cheek.

"Papa, you're amazing," he said softly, proud of the old man. "You figured it out."

CHAPTER SIXTY

Nine hours earlier

The thing Papa noticed first—more than the shimmering city spread out before him in the brittle night as though some giant had sprinkled a Milky Way of spangly jewels across south Louisiana—was the astringent waves of brisk, cold wind ebbing and flowing over him in great uneven bursts. The effect was exhilarating, and Papa whooped like an eight-year-old.

Papa couldn't remember a recent time when the surge of life had so completely rushed through every pore of his body, like each drop of blood was charged with electricity. *Must be like what them junkies feel*, he thought, ironically grateful at this point that he'd somehow managed to avoid *that* shit over the years. He flashed back to the good men and ladies he'd known who'd been ruined by the dope or the booze, and sighed with the protracted sense of loss. Dead years and dead friends—all now spider-webbed in his mind like a Halloween funhouse.

Out on the dark expanse of river, a brightly lit paddle-wheel boat slid through the currents. Papa could make out tiny revelers clustered on the decks and hear the faint notes of a Dixieland band. Man, he could see *forever* from here! The ethereally glowing steeple of the St. Louis Cathedral, the dark hulk of the Superdome, the skyscrapers in the CBD, the stretches of Mid-City and Uptown and the Garden District and out to the racetrack, where the normal glow of houses and buildings had blossomed into firework colors with the seasonal addition of Christmas lights...

Behind and slightly above him, cars raced by, their tires *click-clicking* as they went over stress breaks in the bridge in time to the bounced-up tempo of his old, scarred heart. His arthritic hands and wrists were sore and tight from holding onto the guard rail behind him, and his tennis shoes were slick on the tiny iron ledge beneath his feet.

Man, just one more time, he'd like to hear Booker play "Papa Was a Rascal" or "Angel Eyes"; watch that crazy bastard with his star eyepatch and his big smile sittin' at the piano in the Maple Leaf Bar with that left hand scurryin' like a baby squirrel, doin' things no normal person could do...

Papa took a deep breath. It was time to stop fucking around.

Lord, the world was full of mysteries and, looking back, it was hard to believe he'd spent three decades cringing in terror over things a *ghost* might do to him—not realizing it was that very fear that gave her energy... She was preparing Crayton now—her new power source. But maybe he could still short circuit that plan.

Papa was cold now. The lunatic exuberance of his decision was dissipating. The crazy thing was, crouched up here high in the night at the apex of the huge arc of the Greater New Orleans Bridge like some crazy bird, tumbling back into the past on his own cyclonic wind of memory, Papa had decided on this course of action *before* he figured out that he was Arielle's life force.

The heart attack had been a slap in the face from Fate, saying, *Dig it, old man, what the* hell *are you thinkin' about, wanderin' along at 75 years old? You think you're gonna live forever?*

Death was inevitable, but now, with his cardiac situation, too much of the mystery had been removed. Instances of joy at being alive were genuine and intense, but very brief and quickly replaced by melancholy—another sort of fear independent of his terror at Arielle.

With that, Papa sealed off his regrets like you'd lick and close an envelope. He gave one more thought to Green Hopkins. He hoped the kid would understand—*knew* he would. Most of all, Papa hoped this would free up Crayton and rid their beloved city of Maman Arielle—like he thought he'd done over three decades ago.

Off in the distance, he could hear the jaunty tinkling of piano keys. It was James Booker, of course: his irresistible version of "On the Sunny Side of the Street." Booker—crazed and tragic, lecherous and beautiful and, always, infinitely sad—letting golden joy drip out of his fingertips from some wellspring hidden deep inside his scarred body. Because, in the end, *that's* where the happiness was, not out here in the world. You used the world to decorate your happiness like a cake—and if you weren't happy to begin with, no amount of sugary sprinkles was gonna make it any better.

Papa unhooked his rusty fingers from the railing and stood there for an instant, balancing like an arthritic tightrope artist, Booker's piano clusters now roaring cheerfully in his mind, the heady, dank scent from the sturdy river below, his city laid out before him like a waking, stretching ballet dancer under the soft Southern night—and stepped out into the sweep of wind and the distilled ecstasy of the music.

Funny, Papa thought, there was no sensation of falling—none at all. He just seemed to rise into the sky.

CHAPTER SIXTY-ONE

Left alone with his altar, Crayton was freaked to the point of incapacity. For one thing, he couldn't believe he'd cut off the wrong hand.

How the hell did I do that?

But when he leaned over to study the damned thing like it was a med school specimen—and experienced the first shudder of revulsion since the night he'd actually broken into Prospero's tomb—he saw Green was right. Somehow, in the dark, probably in some technical form of shock, wriggling around in a dark crypt and reaching within the black confines of a casket—not knowing what would crawl up his arm at any moment—he'd just grabbed the wrong hand. Fuck. Anyone coulda done the same thing.

Cray rocked back in astonishment and fear. He didn't actually know what Maman Arielle would do, or even the ultimate significance of the Hand of Glory, but this probably wasn't going to go over well at all. After all, she was clearly monitoring his situation—how and why else did the dead babe show up in the grotto to pour a bit of psychological fuel on his rage against J.C.?

He couldn't get her voice out of his head—*I can't believe that guy J.C., I can't believe he'd fuck Eliza*—and then she reached out her cold hand, the one missing the consecrated finger that was now nestled protectively in Cray's jeans pocket, to momentarily lay her palm against his cheek in a fashion of sisterly comfort. It was absolutely corporeal and she'd been absolutely dead—and *then* she'd just...*dissipated* into the air like black spray paint aimed into a dark room. Just *gone*. And Cray had *loved it*. He literally whooped in the tiny chapel like someone giddy at a rodeo. He thought it—

Goddamn! He started—*What the hell was he screwing around for?*—and spun around to try to figure out the best way to undo the Wallace Bitoun gris-gris. The problem was, he had no fucking idea. Cray felt panic bubble up in his throat and he jerked spasmodically like a puppet, reaching out and grabbing the newspaper clipping—and then set it down on the altar beside the casket, unable to act in any definitive way. What if he'd fucked something up just by moving the victory photo?

Cray felt like screaming.

He forced himself to think. His only choice was to finish his attempt to abort the spell, and hope for the best.

Or better yet, just destroy the whole fucking altar. Why not?

Cray didn't consciously ponder the decision or the sudden changes working within him; Eliza's safety was paramount, and Green's reaction to the vast implications of the altar had blown a hole of reality in Cray's heart in ways he'd never remotely envisioned.

Without question, the Power of *Le Culte des Morts* was addictive. But Cray suddenly realized it had also ruined everything he held valuable. He studied the altar. Physically, it seemed just as he had left it moments ago, but something was *different* too. The shed seemed to glow with a pale luminescence, and Cray could feel the sluggish hum of a force that suddenly seemed alien to him. He hesitated, frightened now that the power here was no longer his, and an insectile buzzing seemed to throb around him.

Suddenly, the close air came alive with the foul smell he remembered from the crypt at the River of Life Cemetery. Crayton knew for certain, then, that Maman Arielle was at work, and she knew he'd betrayed her.

Great time to turn into a Hardy Boy, Cray thought, picking up the newspaper photo of Wallace Bitoun. *I love you, Eliza,* he thought, grimacing, knowing the irony of offering up what passed as a prayer for her safety. He took a brief gulp of air and ripped the newsprint in half, tearing the meat of his thumb on the protruding thorn. A bead of blood popped to the surface; unconsciously, he wiped it on his pants as the walls of the shed began to shake faintly as though in a small earthquake. He wadded the paper and tossed the two halves on the floor.

Cray forced himself to think. He knew from Maman Arielle that the life forces of his altar were the consecrated skull and casket. Without giving himself the time to reflect on all that he might lose, he picked up the skull and slammed it against the concrete foundation with a force that amazed him. It shattered on impact, and thousands of blue sparks sizzled and filled the tiny room with the rancid smell of burning flesh.

In dumb amazement, he adjusted his sweaty glasses. The buzzing in the tiny space was louder now. He glanced up and saw that the photos of the saints were turning black in their melting plastic frames and that the various animal bones rattled and tumbled off the shelves.

Cray had strung brightly colored feathers around the ceiling perimeter; now they burst into orange, turquoise, and purple flames. One sparking feather dropped onto the body of the cat, and immediately the rancid smell of burning fur and scorched dead skin filled Cray's nose and mouth. Two glass Saint Death candles rolled off the shelf and exploded at Crayton's feet.

He was terrified, somehow aware that the altar *hated* him now. Cray felt a searing heat on the outside of one thigh and instinctively reached in his pocket for the severed finger talisman. He yelped as the finger burned his hand and he dropped it on the floor, where it curled in on itself, black and gray and smoking.

Cray whimpered and turned to slide out the door, but his eyes fell on the coffin. He groaned, knowing he couldn't leave without trying somehow to destroy the ritual significance and power of the casket.

Through the sparks and smoke of the quivering shed, he slid the coffin toward him. He winced as his wounded thumb caught on a splintered edge of the box and a new rivulet of blood welled up. He ignored it though, noting a sheaf of papers peeking out from underneath the box.

"Jesus!" He lifted the bottom of the casket and saw an excerpt he'd Xeroxed from *The Pagan Malt Shop*, Green's novel. The pages were bound with a rubber band and wrapped in the bloody handkerchief he'd loaned Green at Café du Monde. *Hadn't he removed these?* The thought made Cray feel momentarily ashamed. He'd originally planned to put a little good gris-gris on the manuscript to help Green's chances at the Tennessee Williams Festival. But then Green started bugging him about voodoo and Cray had got annoyed and yanked the excerpt. And yet, here they were. Cray would have thought he was losing his mind—but it was probably too late for that assessment. Hey, look: Green *had* made the finals. Maybe Cray helped and maybe Green was just a bad ass. At this point, anything positive was good.

Cray started coughing. The feathers had burned out, but smoke was thick in the closed quarters. The ethereal buzzing seemed loud as a Superdome crowd, and Cray was so rattled he couldn't concentrate. An angry buzzing began to sound from within the casket itself. Cray stared at the handkerchief where he'd intermingled his own blood with Green's, then looked at the casket. Hadn't he left it open when he'd removed the Wallace Bitoun photo?Cray shook his head with a growing premonition. But there was no possibility, at this point, that he could just turn around and leave. After all, there was still the Bitoun campaign button inside the ring of graveyard dirt, and he'd best deconstruct it. Thinking again of Eliza, he felt for the fasteners underneath the lid of the coffin and wrenched upward.

Instantly, everything in the shed stilled and the buzzing stopped—and Cray went motionless in the suffocating realization that he'd fucked up probably for the last time.

Inside the coffin were hundreds of hornets, so many that the white satin lining was completely obliterated by the insects. For an ominous moment they just sat there, a few crawling over one another sluggishly.

In the split second afforded him, it occurred to Crayton that Maman Arielle had probably cooked up this particular gris-gris treat with a wry nod to the excerpted section from Green's book—where the guy committed suicide by raising hornets specifically for that purpose.

Cray supposed, as the insects erupted and swarmed him with countless pinpoints of searing pain, that in his own way, he'd done precisely the same thing.

CHAPTER SIXTY-TWO

After he read Papa's note, Green sat on the porch for a minute, smiling as he wept. Hell yeah, Papa had figured it out—crucial hours ahead of Green.

Trust me, Greenie, this isn't as cowardly as it looks. For sure, I don't wanna sit around and wait on my poor old heart to explode, but even if I'd never had cardiac problems, this would be a good thing to do... It has to do with Arielle, and now you know what I'm talking about...

Green read on—*ah, Jesus, he jumped off the bridge*—and then folded the note and put it in his pocket. Then, because in spite of his grief there were other things to think about, Green wiped his tears and stood up. Using his own key, he let himself into Papa's cottage.

There was already a slight difference to the very scent of the place, as though the cottage itself had made some chemical adjustment to Papa's absence. Green could still smell wisps of tobacco and bay rum, but the frail hints of liniment and arthritis creams were virtually gone.

Green, on autopilot, would have enjoyed just lingering a bit—maybe seated himself at the piano bench and looked through Papa's photographs—but instead he grabbed the phone. He should've called J.C. back at the St. Ignatius when he first found out about the curse on Uncle Wallace, but the chance he could save Papa blew Green's emotional circuits and overrode everything else.

Green glanced at his watch. Surely the jet was in D.C. by now—if it hadn't crashed—and he had to let J.C. know Uncle Wallace was the latest beneficiary of Crayton's never-ending gris-gris adventure.

Dialing the old-fashioned rotary phone, Green hoped maybe it wasn't too late to at least get word to Uncle Wallace to be careful—but of *what*? What could J.C. say? *Hi, Uncle Wallace, I'm calling to tell you to watch your step. It seems a friend of mine put a voodoo curse on you. And here's the thing: he's really good at it...*

The fucking line was busy and J.C. didn't have call waiting.

Green slammed his fist on the desk in frustration. And what was Cray doing? Was he indeed trying to abort the spell, or had he in fact decided the existing gris-gris was a hunky-dory concept—that life in *Le Culte des Morts* was fine?

Green dialed and got another busy signal. He hung up and stared at the floor. He felt light-headed and fractious, as though whatever decision would be wrong. Glancing around the inside of the cottage once more, he decided to head back to the St. Ignatius. He could check on Cray, and use his own phone to call J.C. Hell, maybe J.C. had left him a message.

Five minutes later, as he jogged up to the gate at the apartment complex, his first thought was to head to the garage and see if Cray was still there, doing God knew what, but he opted for his apartment instead. He got J.C. on the first ring.

"Yeah?" J.C. sounded tense.

Green tried to speak calmly, but there was too much to say and the words came out in an irrational torrent. "It's me, Green, and listen, Cray's still playing the death league and he insists he traded for Uncle Wallace—"

"Green," J.C. interrupted, but Green couldn't shut up.

"He put a curse on your uncle, J.C., and it's been Cray all along. Sam Gallagher was a curse, and the tennis kid, and Donny's guy, Cat-Daddy Phelps—*that* was Cray too. And he can't take it off. And Papa's dead too, J.C. Christ, he jumped off the New Orleans Bridge, and you've gotta warn Uncle Wallace before...before—" Green worked his mouth desperately, but the power of his emotions overwhelmed him.

There was a moment of eerie silence and Green wondered if J.C. understood anything he'd said. Then he heard J.C. took a deep breath. "You tellin' me Cray put a juju on Uncle Wallace?"

"Yeah. I guess it was his way of mind-fucking you."

J.C. actually laughed, but it was shaky, and Green could discern a kernel of fear there. "Well, Green, that's interesting, because I just got some bad news."

Green groaned. J.C. was going to tell him the goddamned jet had gone down. "What is it?"

"Uncle Wallace had a stroke on the plane."

For an instant, the tiny living room twirled around Green like a carnival ride. He stumbled over and sat down on the couch, taking a deep breath as J.C. went on.

"They emergency landed in Spartanburg and got him to a hospital, but he's in surgery and it ain't looking good."

"Oh man, J.C.," Green whispered. "I'm sorry."

J.C. was surprisingly calm. "Eliza's okay, physically, but she's having a rough time. They told me they carried her off the jet and she was ramblin' on about voodoo, but they say she'll be all right." He cleared his throat. "You tellin' me Papa killed himself? Was that Crayton too?"

"No, it was... Well, it's complicated, but...he had heart problems. I'll explain it later."

J.C. asked—too casually?—"So where's my friend Crayton?"

"I don't know. The last I saw him, he was trying to take the curse off your uncle—or at least I *think* that's what he was doing. But he didn't know how." It occurred to Green that J.C. might actually come gunning for Cray, so he said, "Listen, J.C., this shit's gone far enough. It was Cray all along, but it wasn't either—"

"Now that makes a lot of sense—"

"Listen, J.C., it was Maman Arielle behind it. She's got power over him—"

"A zombie, huh?" J.C. said mildly. "Well, that don't matter. I'm gonna kick his voodoo ass when I find him, you know that, don't you, Green?"

"J.C., he's not a zombie. There *aren't* zombies—at least not the way you think. He's like what they call a familiar in folklore."

J.C. was ominously silent and Green tried again. "Think of Cray as a sort of battery that provides energy—"

"A battery, y'say? Like that Energizer bunny?" J.C. barked tired laughter. "Ol' Cray's a bunny."

"J.C., he's way fucked up over this and what he's done. He's being used and enough people have died or been screwed up here. Cray was...it was just... I don't know... Somehow he got caught up and it got away from him. Then you and Eliza happened and he flipped out. But it all goes back to Maman Arielle, J.C. *She's* the one—" Green stopped suddenly.

What about Maman Arielle? Where was *she* in all this, now that Papa had sacrificed himself to staunch her power flow?

"Yeah, I see it now," J.C. was saying. "How many people did you say Bunny's killed?"

"J.C., I've gotta go," Green said hurriedly. "I think something may have happened here. Check on your uncle. Call me back or I'll call you." He hung up. Maybe Maman Arielle was...*gone...* Maybe, somehow, between Papa and Cray and himself, maybe that's why Uncle Wallace hadn't fallen over dead on the plane. Maybe he would survive the surgery and come out okay...

The phone rang.

Fuck.

It was probably J.C., wanting to threaten Cray again, or maybe with news about Uncle Wallace.

It was Crayton, though—and he sounded horrible, like he was breathing over a respirator.

"Green," he wheezed, "can you come over? I'm scared, Green. I can't breathe, Green, and it's...it's bleeding." It was as though his entire throat was swollen. *Ibe thcared, Greed. I cad breathe, Greed, and idth...idth bleeding.*

"Cray, where are you? Have you been shot? Where are you bleeding?"

"I'm home, Green," he rasped, sounding momentarily indignant, as though of course he'd be home.

"Cray, what happened? Are you alone?"

"Green, could you come over? Maman Arielle knows." Green felt icy with apprehension. Cray wasn't making much sense and sounded like he was talking with a dozen caramels in his mouth. Cray mumbled again. "I...I tried to make everything okay, but I think she got me, Green."

Green felt a new blur of fear spread throughout his beleaguered nervous system. He couldn't figure out if Cray's call was some kind of set-up or if the guy was really hurt, but Green couldn't afford to stall. "Cray, help me out, buddy. Is someone with you? Have you been shot? Have you called 911?"

Cray laughed like there was sand in his lungs, and weakly he said, "I'm alone, Green. It's just me and the blood..."

CHAPTER SIXTY-THREE

Green pushed cautiously on Cray's apartment door and stepped inside. The shades were drawn and only a naked bulb hanging in the kitchen cast a weak glow over the deeply shadowed living room. Green peered guardedly around the apartment. It looked like a bomb had gone off. Gris-gris roots and candles, masks and incense holders had been knocked off shelves and the wall and were strewn over the floor. Green nudged a smashed chicken claw out of the way with his toe; it appeared to have been stomped on. Finally, he tore his gaze from the wreckage and looked over at the couch against the wall.

Cray—or what Green *assumed* was Cray—was sitting on his haunches on the sofa like a begging hound. He was rocking to and fro slightly, his harsh breath whistling.

His head was bloated beyond recognition—his face splattered with grotesque red blotches and the arms of his glasses stretched to the breaking point over the cartoon proportions of his skull—and his entire body had the balloon exaggeration of a drowning victim.

"My God, Cray, what happened?"

Cray's voice was worse than it was over the phone. "Got...got into a little hornets' nest," he managed. "In the voodoo shed." He tried to smile, but the effect was hideous. "Straight outta your book, buddy. How's that for irony?" He shook his head painfully. "I think I broke the power, though. I think everything's okay."

Green couldn't believe what he was looking at. "Cray, have you called an ambulance?"

"I think this will end it, Green. The power is gone... I think maybe Maman Arielle too, but I don't know how..." Cray's throat was so constricted he was having trouble talking, much less breathing.

"What hornets? Are you allergic?" Green asked ridiculously. He looked around for the phone. The guy was dying before his eyes.

Cray laughed painfully. "They were in the casket. I shoulda figured it out. Your manuscript was underneath. I was bleeding..." He was babbling now, and Green was searching frantically through the ruin of the living room, trying to find a telephone. "I crushed the casket, though," Cray mumbled. "That fucking skull too." He waved his porcine arms around the room vaguely. "I think...I think maybe Uncle Wallace will be fine now. Have you heard? Is Eliza... Is she okay, Green? Is Papa okay?"

"Yeah, Cray," Green lied. "They're all excellent. Cray, listen to me, man. We've gotta get you some help. *Where's the goddamn phone?*" Just as he said it, he spied the portable under a couch cushion on the floor and dove for it.

The line was dead.

"What the fuck?! You just called me!"

Cray tried to smile. He looked like a rotting Jack-o'-lantern. Green could barely decipher what he was saying. "Idth Maman Arielle," he said, his voice slow and thickening. "Idth too lade." He reached out an enormous hand and tried to calm his friend. "I guess she's sdill god sub power."

She's still got some power? *But Papa was gone! Cray was clearly dying. Shouldn't* she *be gone? Or at least...dissipating?* Green backed away, moaning, trying to focus on the temporal. "No, no, Cray, we gotta get you to a doctor. Where are your car keys?"

Cray shook his head slowly and slid into a fetal position on the couch. His breathing was cruelly labored. "Green, look," he said painfully, as though remembering something important. It sounded like *Greed, loog.* Cray pointed a finger like a boudin link at the wall behind Green's head. "I tode you. Idth bleeding."

Tearing his stare away from Cray, Green turned slowly and looked up to see the framed poster of Pete Maravich—the only decorative item in the room that Cray hadn't destroyed. "Jesus," Green said, and what was left of his spirit deflated like a punctured rubber life raft. He knew at that instant that Crayton was right: Maman Arielle—whether her power was dying or not—had kicked Cray's traitorous ass permanently.

The photographic likeness of the basketball star was bleeding from the eyes and mouth. Green stared, and it struck him that, even after everything that had happened, he still wanted to believe this was fake—some madcap Industrial Light & Magic showcase Cray had somehow staged.

The trickling blood, gleaming wetly in the dim light, had pooled slightly at the bottom of the picture frame, and the overflow had started to crawl down the grimy wall like a line-graph depiction of a falling stock.

Green turned back to his friend. Cray's mouth was open like a fish's now, and he was gulping helplessly for air. Green knelt by the couch and took Cray's monstrous hand in his own.

"Green," Cray panted,"I'b sorry. I'b...sorry." Cray closed his eyes briefly. "Thags for being my friend." He blinked painfully—his eyes mere slits against the swelling—and looked at Green with tears squeezing down his fat cheeks. His fight for oxygen grew more intense—desperate, gritty moans—as the sheer volume of poison shut down his system. Green was too frightened to leave his side.

"It's all right, buddy," Green whispered. "It's gonna work out okay."

"Tell Eliza..." Cray started. He gasped, his mouth expanding and contracting in great O's. "Tell Eliza..."

And with a shudder and final exhalation, Cray's head slumped against the couch and the terrible tension in his obscene body finally relaxed.

More than that though, the tension in the entire *room* was gone. Green didn't know how to explain it, but the whole power source *buzz* that had seemingly trembled throughout the lower Quarter—Arielle's *presence*, he supposed you could call it—was gone too. Or so he fervently hoped.

Green swallowed, thinking of Cray's final wish to be remembered to Eliza. "I'll tell her," Green said softly. "Don't worry, pal. I'll tell her." He blinked like a fighter who'd just somehow survived an unbelievable blow and hadn't yet realized he should fall over.

Eventually, Green let go of Cray's hand and stood up. He felt absolutely numb and had no idea of what to do. Any exhilaration that Arielle was gone—and, somehow, he was sure of it—was watered down by the immediacy of personal tragedy. Finally, he supposed he should go next door and make some phone calls.

And how do I explain all this?

He turned to go out the front door and a shadow paused outside the entrance foyer.

Grand, Green thought wearily. It would no doubt be J.C., come to cowboy Crayton because Uncle Wallace hadn't made it. "Looks like Maman Arielle saved you the trouble," Green whispered as he walked outside to head off J.C. and tell him the news.

But it was Kay. She'd come back to Green like some stunning, merciful angel, still dressed in her TULANE GEOLOGY DEPARTMENT sweatshirt. "Hi, darlin'," she smiled. "I knocked on your—" Kay went pale as she took in Green's utter despair. "What's wrong, Green?"

"Cray's dead," Green said vacantly. "Papa's dead too." He sighed, scanning the vacant pool area before falling into her outstretched arms. He smelled hints of oranges and swampgrass in her windblown hair.

"Oh Jesus," she moaned. "Are you sure? Both of them? What happened?"

"I'm sure," Green said. He pulled back and eyed her steadily. "Kay, I'm not crazy. It was that fucking voodoo." He shook his head, then the words started pouring out. "Papa committed suicide last night, but it was like a sacrifice. It's... And then, just a few minutes ago, Maman Arielle killed Cray—at least, I think she did—but—" He struggled with the words, trying to sound in control. "Cray tried to get out of it. It was so fucking powerful..."

"Papa? Suicide? Where's Cray? Is Maman Arielle here?" Kay looked overwhelmed and frightened, but also determined. She draped her arm around Green's shoulder and pulled him into the sunlight.

"She's not here," Green said, laughing suddenly. "She may not be anywhere." Then he stopped abruptly and a solitary tear trailed down his cheek. "Cray's inside," he said, nodding over his shoulder. "On the couch."

"Okay then, listen to me, baby," Kay said soothingly, and Green knew she was trying to make any sense possible out of his meandering. She bit her lower lip and stared at him as a doctor would. "Are *you* okay? How's Eliza?"

"I'm fine," he said, struggling to get it together and help her out. "Eliza's fine too. She's on her way home. To D.C." He took a deep breath. "It's a long, long story, Kay, and I'll explain it. But first, I want you to know that I think everything will be okay now."

He took her hand and led her into Cray's apartment, pointing through the shadows at the unrecognizable figure on the couch. "He's dead," he repeated.

"My God," Kay breathed. "What happened to him?"

"Hornets," Green said, and a sliver of lunatic laughter barked into the air. "Something to do with my book, somehow." He shrugged and closed his eyes, rambling. "Maman Arielle was behind this all along. Cray just got in over his head. In the end, he tried to fix it..." He opened his mouth to go on but couldn't say anything else.

Kay went to the couch and checked for Cray's pulse. Green had to hand it to her, she had some guts.

Kay straightened up and swallowed, then gave Green a reassuring kiss on the forehead. "We'll handle this," she said simply. "Have you called an ambulance?"

Green shook his head. "Not yet. He just died a minute ago, and his phone's out. I was on my way to use mine."

"Okay," she said, thinking a moment. "Let's call, then you can give me an abbreviated version while we wait. If it's voodoo, they're gonna think we're nuts. So I'd better know what happened too." She held out her hand and Green took it, loving her cool head and immediate and unequivocal acceptance of the situation. Then she gave him a quick hug and whispered in his ear, "I'm sorry, baby. I...I know you loved them." She wiped a tear of her own out of the corner of one eye and pulled a cell phone out of her side pocket.

Green blinked and nodded. "Yeah. Yeah, I guess I did." He started to say more but pain welled up in his throat and he couldn't speak. Kay kissed him lightly on the forehead.

"I know, baby, I know," she soothed, then guided him gently toward the door. But Green paused for an instant and looked back at Cray, wanting to trust the burgeoning feeling that his friend had been right: that maybe, with his and Papa's sacrifices, it really *was* over.

Then Green glanced up at the Maravich poster one last time. He gasped, fighting back the morning's final tide of lunacy.

The flow of blood from the picture had stopped, but Pistol Pete's eyes were still glistening. Green looked closer. The poster was *weeping.*

The blood had turned to tears.

EPILOGUE

New Year's Day, 1999. New Orleans, Louisiana

Green Hopkins was up early, wearing his one nice pair of dark slacks, a white dress shirt, and a tie depicting dozens of tiny bottles of Tabasco sauce. As the sole heir to Papa Hipolyte's modest estate, he'd appropriated the tie from the old man's rather impressive collection.

Kay was still sleeping, so Green kissed her lightly on the cheek and walked out into a cotton-aired, cloud-marbled morning, headed to St. Lydwine Church. The streets were absolutely silent; it would be hours before the New Year's Eve celebrants in America's most famous party city began to stir and reach for aspirin bottles and Bloody Mary mix.

Timing it so he missed the morning mass and would have the tiny church more or less to himself, Green opened the heavy wooden door and stepped into the hushed sanctuary. He paused a minute, glancing in the side vestibule where the body of Father Chet Darbonne was interred and, soothed by the sturdy flickering of prayer candles, made his way into the main body of the church. He stood at the top of the aisle, waiting for his eyes to adjust to the dim light, then selected a deserted pew toward the back, sliding across the cool wooden surface. A priest busied himself on the altar, tending to some post-ceremonial duty, and, down front, an older woman dressed in mourning black rose painfully from a prayer bench and made her way arthritically up the aisle.

Green took it all in peacefully, just sitting there for a few minutes, not thinking of anything really. He watched as a tall, fat guy wandered into the church and entered a confessional. Green sighed, wondering what he himself would say if he decided to just pop into a confession booth and let fly. But he wasn't ready for any such theological commitment; the mysteries of religion and magic hadn't become any clearer since Papa and Cray had died. *Au contraire.*

In the meantime, Green was faced with the very real and gratifying knowledge that he'd inherited Papa's little cottage—and wasn't really surprised to learn it was worth quite a bit of money. French Quarter real estate was at a premium—not that Green had any intention of selling the place.

He shook his head at the enormity of it all. Every day, Green thought, the future came tumbling in on him like an ill-structured house of cards. Already, he could see substantial change. Uncle Wallace was recovering, but it would be slow, and Green knew J.C. would probably end up in D.C. on a more or less permanent basis. He'd see less and less of Huey and Donny too. The death league had concluded with the force of a train wreck and drained a lot of spirit from their protracted and collective friendships—a crashing, foul-tasting, and perhaps symbolic coda to the whole idea of perpetual youth. Perhaps oddly, Eliza had indicated she might come back to NOLA at some point. Despite everything, she said, the city had its own undeniable power—and Green certainly knew that to be true.

Green supposed they would all get together for occasional beers at the Blacksmith Shop or see some jazz at the Funky Butt, particularly if J.C. was in town, and they'd have some laughs. It wasn't like they wouldn't be friends anymore. This was just what happened when you grew up, though hopefully most folks segued into Life's Next Chapters in somewhat less dramatic fashion.

Last night, at a quiet and early supper at Arnaud's, Green had raised his glass to Kay and toasted, "Voodoo breakin' up that old gang of mine," and Kay had smiled sadly back as they drank to Cray and Papa H and, yeah, the future.

Thank God for Kay, Green thought, saluting in acknowledgment toward the crucifixion over the altar. If anything, these last weeks had brought them even closer together. Love worked.

Amen to that. Green nodded at the altar once more. Then, wiping his brow with a palm that was suddenly moist with sweat, he took out his wallet and extracted a folded piece of paper. It was a letter he'd found in his mailbox two days after Crayton died. It was addressed in Cray's handwriting and was postmarked that previous Friday—which meant it had been written two days before the final acts of bad craziness descended.

Frankly, the note was kinda spooky, and sometimes Green told himself he was hanging onto it because it was the only tangible evidence he had that Crayton had even existed. But the real reason, he knew, had nothing to do with physicality—and certainly not with the disconcerting death league premonition therein.

No, Green kept the note, despite its eerie quality, because of what it said about their friendship. And that's why Green suspected he would continue to keep it, probably for as long as he lived.

On a piece of yellow ruled paper torn from a legal pad, Cray had printed:*Hey Green! Regarding the Vieux Carré Fantasy Death Society: I just want you to know I now regard this as one of my all-time bad ideas. Even so, and though it'll probably piss you off, I've got one last roster change, my man. Kindly drop my fourth pick, McCauley Culkin, and replace him with*
ME...

I think you'll understand by the time you read this. Thanks for everything, amigo! You've been the best friend I could ever have hoped for. Take care of Kay. That's a forever gig. Your brother,

Cray

Green read through the note twice, feeling the sadness well up in him again, and the tears ducts began to crank into overtime. But he fought them back, swallowing painfully a few times, and folded the note and tucked it back in his billfold. When he was sure he was composed, he got up and moved slowly to the back of the church. He paused in the vestibule and went over to a small statue of the Virgin Mary, where he lit a prayer candle for the soul of Papa Hipolyte—and this time a few tears actually made it to the surface. He let them roll freely, enjoying the wet trail down the side of his face.

And finally, because he'd promised Kay he'd take her to the jazz brunch over at Café Brazil, and he wanted to beat the hungover crowds who would be already jostling to kick the ass out of New Year's resolutions barely ten hours old, he walked out of the church and down the steps into a soft river breeze.

He was halfway across the small courtyard in front of the church when the sound hit him. Above and behind him, church bells had begun to ring. Green spun around and glanced up at the top of St. Lydwine, trying to believe his ears and eyes.

Sure enough, the bells that had been inexplicably frozen since the murder of Father Chet were chiming in the new morning air.

For an instant, Green panicked, wondering if he'd snapped and was hallucinating. But then the door of the church flew open and two priests rushed out, crossing themselves and talking excitedly about miracles as they stared up toward the steeple.

Green smiled and looked beyond the steeple into the towering sky, taking a deep, easy breath and enjoying the crystal sounds of the bells. He thought of the excited words of Papa Hipolyte on a hopeful autumn morning that already seemed a thousand years ago.

In fact, he could almost hear his voice.

Just once, Greenie, I'd love to hear them bells chime. Just one time. Man, that'd be like God sittin' in with Booker, wouldn't it? The way I got it figured, that's the kinda stuff that happens in heaven...

ACKNOWLEDGMENTS

I've always regarded New Orleans as my spiritual home even if, despite numerous efforts to relocate there permanently, Fortuna has decided otherwise. Still, though I've spent a lot of time down there and I think I know the city pretty well, I remain an outsider. And yet ... it's precisely that in-between status that made this novel possible.

Several years ago, I was poking around in one of the French Quarter's many tourist-happy voodoo shops, thinking it'd be entertaining to work in one of them and perpetuate eerie and misleading stereotypes for the thrills of visiting folks from Des Moines or Utah or wherever. Out of nowhere, I was turned into a rabbit!

Kidding! What did happen is that I got an idea for a story. What if I *did* work there, a twenty-something slacker living in the perpetual carnival of the Quarter? What if, while fooling around with the amulets and charms and, yes, sundry gris-gris, I *did* tap into some sort of seductive and dark power?

Well, I know ME. I'd be screwed. That seemed an interesting concept to explore.

Gris Gris Gumbo has traveled an arduous road to publication, and I'm very happy and appreciative that Scarlett Algee and JournalStone decided to give us a chance. Thanks, as well, to Sean Leonard for his kestrel's eye when reading the manuscript.

The amazing Ace Atkins saw potential in this early on and offered encouragement and suggestions. Thank you, brother. Ernie Myers, your insights are spot-on despite the absence of a giant hawk. Maria Reagan, I remain astonished by and grateful for your creative vision. My sis, Mic Koster, is a fellow traveler in the Land of the Macabre and, as a nurse, answered many medical questions for the purposes of this book as well as my chronic hypochondria. Zak Kretchmer provided unerring legal advice and has learned the value of fine music, well played.

James Lee Burke is a wonderful writer and, if it's possible, an even better person.

Stephen King, you write good. Or something like that.

There was no shortage of music providing appropriate atmosphere as I wrote: James Booker and Professor Longhair and in particular Dr. John and his *Gris-Gris* album. And the greatest, most haunting song about New Orleans ever written by someone not from there is "Toulouse Street" by Patrick Simmons of the Doobie Brothers.

Big thanks to Jan Ramsey and Joseph Irrera at *Offbeat*, the finest music magazine in the world. And Ian McNulty is a genuine force for Goodness and Light at the *New Orleans Advocate/Times-Picayune*.

Most importantly: My lovely wife Eileen is a remarkable editor and writer and is always an inspiration, a punchline algorithm unto herself, and an eerily patient person who fixes or repairs everything I break. Love ya BIG! Ours is also a life enriched by rescue dogs. Remembering with gratitude Puppy Brown, Moosie, and Gumbo—and currently celebrating the four-pawed gris-gris of Virgil and Mabel.

Finally, this one is dedicated to the memories of those most recently lost: My sainted Mom, Thelma Koster, and trusted pals Dave Schulz, Ron Uyeshima, and Steve Colwick.

ABOUT THE AUTHOR

Rick Koster, a former rock musician, is a longtime arts writer for *The Day* newspaper in New London, Connecticut. His previous books include the nonfiction histories *Texas Music* and *Louisiana Music* and the comic crime novel *Poppin' a Cold One*. All were bestsellers, if by "bestsellers" you mean "grotesquely unsuccessful." Rick and his wife Eileen Jenkins live with their rescue dogs Virgil and Mabel by the ocean—just far enough from the water that they can't see it.

CPSIA information can be obtained
at www.ICGtesting.com
Printed in the USA
JSHW020801160623
43335JS00002B/146